Trevor Ripley was born and still lives in Rotherham, a place he loves dearly. His life revolves around his beautiful family: his wife Catherine (of 30 years), their two daughters and their playful dachshund.

Trevor's inspiration comes mainly from his surroundings: from friends and family or from his own life experiences and interests. He is very aware of both local and national issues and uses this knowledge to add an element of education to his work.

Trevor mainly writes for young adults and children and is passionate about getting children to engage their imagination, often attending schools to deliver a fun presentation on how to create exciting stories.

T P Ripley

Enjoy x

For her fab editing skills and her great patience, huge thanks to my wonderful wife Catherine – you're the best x.

For the many hours spent making up bedtime stories and inadvertently helping to develop my storytelling skills, thanks also must go to my daughters Kazia and Aniela. I'm so proud of you both and love you loads.

I can't leave out my little dog Kala, who fills my days with laughter and (don't tell the girls), I love the most.

Trevor Ripley

THOSE HIDDEN MONSTERS

AUSTIN MACAULEY PUBLISHERS™

LONDON ∗ CAMBRIDGE ∗ NEW YORK ∗ SHARJAH

A CIP catalogue record for this title is available from the British Library.

ISBN 9781035824519 (Paperback)
ISBN 9781035824526 (ePub e-book)

www.austinmacauley.com

First Published 2024
Austin Macauley Publishers Ltd®
1 Canada Square
Canary Wharf
London
E14 5AA

I would like to acknowledge *The Last of the Mohicans* by James Fenimore Cooper, for the profound inspiration it offered.

Table of Contents

Chapter 1
Broken Hearts

It was meant to be a warm day today, with a promise of sunshine. I was looking forward to a glorious day. I always loved the sun; it made me feel happy. I liked that freedom that comes with not having to wear too many layers of clothing. I always loved wearing shorts and short sleeves. I can imagine it now. Playing with my friends on the street or on the field; the game did not matter; it could be anything. Whatever, it was okay as long as the sun was shining.

That didn't happen today. No sign of the sun. That's promises for you. Instead the skies were the darkest grey; black in places, just like coal; and the rain, how it came down, it just kept on falling. I'd never seen it rain so hard. Relentless it was, and cold, it felt solid somehow—it hurt. Nothing was spared. This rain was all inclusive, leaving nothing dry. What it didn't land on, it sought out, seeping into cracks like little worms and soaking into cloth. Our clothing was already heavy with it, we were drenched and it showed no signs of stopping. We were all so cold, shivering, and no matter how close we clung on to each other, we simply could not stop ourselves shaking. It was indeed a miserable day; not just outside, but also inside—of all of us!

Yes, a truly miserable day and yet Mama said spring had arrived—I didn't believe her. Spring is a happy time, a sunny time bringing warmth, none of that was evident today, only April showers, in abundance. And what a sorry sight we were; there was nothing cheery about us either, a small band of bewildered children, all helpless and motionless—like statues in a line, and we were in fact all grey to look at, the weather had somehow changed the colour of our clothes to match it. We also felt it—grey, if you can actually feel a colour, that is.

Some of us were close to tears and we were all unable to hide our fears. None of us were really sure what was going on and we were all desperate for answers to why this thing had to happen. This thing! This going away thing—how I wished IT would go away. We needed answers. We craved them. They said it was for our safety, for our own good. None of us were asked, and none of us wanted to leave—couldn't we stay—just a short while longer.

Klaus, my brave younger brother, stood shaking. He was wearing his school shorts since Mama thought the weather was going to be nice. At least, his cap kept his hair dry and tidy, but his little nose was all red and I could tell he was holding back the tears. His bottom lip trembled so. He commented on how sad we all looked. I corrected him—we were devastated! You see, we had never been apart before, except when we were at school, of course. But even then, our mamas were present, first dropping us off before chatting with each other outside the iron gates for what seemed like hours. Even in the rain they did this, but you know, when I recollect, most of the time it was sunny—funny hey!

At school, there were signs of Mama everywhere; in our lunch boxes, the way she removed the crust from the bread and how she shaped our sandwiches— triangular, we loved them like that. We could smell her on our clothes; the way her sweet perfume lingered. And we were reminded of her when we looked into our satchel; everything we needed for the day would be neatly packed; our pencils, our books, spare handkerchiefs. How thoughtful she was, she forgot nothing.

Mama never let us down. Though we had left her side for the day, all too soon she would be back at the school gate with the other mamas and we'd run into her arms. What a very happy time it was then, everything was just perfect. Sunny days—nice days!

This was very different of course. They kept saying what a great time we would have; it would be a fine adventure with our friends. We wouldn't be afraid when we reached our destination, we would be too excited and we would have so much fun. How did they know that? All the kids from school would be there, there was no question of staying behind. We would have such a good time that we would forget all about our parents and all the boring grown-ups and all the boring things grown-ups do. We'd soon forget how unhappy we were at leaving them behind.

But there would be no mamas chatting, no triangle shaped sandwiches and no hugs to greet us at the end of the day. Mama said it again, that it would be an adventure; we would enjoy it—like a holiday. We would have each other for company, what could be better? And we would become more independent which would help us grow up and prepare us for adulthood. Yes, this would be a great adventure, something that we would talk about for the rest of our lives, we must enjoy it. We weren't convinced.

There were eleven of us, eleven children in an exclusive secret party. We all stood apart. The boys smart in their shirts and pants, and all the girls pretty in their best dresses. It was nice that we didn't have to wear our uniforms, our Hitler Youth uniforms that is. The shorts and white shirts, all stiff from all the starch were not good for this kind of weather at all—what a relief. Each of us had a suitcase full of everyday clothes and some new knitwear which would be needed for the cold mountain air. Of course, we had to take our Hitler Youth outfit with us, just in case, which left little room for nice dresses. Some of the girls had asked for a second suitcase which had been forbidden. One girl, Heidi had actually put on two dresses, one over the other just so she could take it with her. Good idea, I remember thinking I'd wished I had thought of that, especially as it was so cold already.

Ummm! A holiday, an adventure they said. But I had my doubts you know— I don't mind telling you, I had a bad feeling about it all and I didn't like it. It was a strange feeling—a foreboding that I just couldn't shake, no matter how I tried to reassure myself. It was a sense of doom! Yes, that's what it was and it made me feel frightfully nervous. It wasn't so stupid really; after all it was war time. I remember an anxious feeling made its way from my tummy to my head, I was all queasy inside. Something was going to happen I simply knew it. But I didn't know how to tell Mama. She would say I was being silly—that's all.

We huddled tightly under the corrugated shelter of the old railway platform along with the other kids, all clinging tightly to our mama's hands. Like the rest of the village, the station was very small and neat, except for an unusually long platform that didn't seem to belong here. The station house was usually very pretty with flowers spilling out of window boxes and tubs all painted in pastel colours. Despite the rain, the flowers were lovely, every colour was here and so many different kinds. I would often come here just to admire them; the purple daisies were my particular favourite, though today I didn't feel like looking at them.

I glanced at the clock. It was a nice clock, calming somehow. The hands seemed to be moving faster than normal today and I remember wishing they would slow down. The train would arrive any minute and that would be a minute too soon; how I wished it would not turn up at all. Very soon we would be separated! For how long we didn't know. How could we know? War is a terrible thing, full of uncertainties. Yes, we were all very unhappy. Even the big boys, even Boris Smidt!

Boris was a Hitler Youth leader. He was tall and strong and he could be more than a little bossy, even horrid at times, especially with the little kids. I usually had to intervene when he was being nasty, when his mean streak took over. You see, he was never nasty to me. He liked me you see, from when we first met. Since then, he did whatever I asked of him, most of the time anyway; this is why the little kids ran to me for protection.

Boris was my age, fifteen, and he was very tall; have I already said that? And yes, I have to admit, he was very handsome. His hair was, of course, blonde and thick and always seemed neat and tidy. His eyes: sky blue. When he smiled, they seemed to sparkle; there was no denying he was a handsome boy. He wasn't perfect though—no way.

You would call him a bully, I suppose. But he had a nicer side—if he liked you of course. He was incredibly smart in his uniform and all the older girls fancied him. I have to admit, I liked him a lot, well perhaps a little too much. People were beginning to notice. Why even my little brother Klaus would often tease me saying I wanted to marry him. I didn't think so; after all, he was just a silly boy. Boris did come to visit quite a lot though, to be honest. Wherever I went, he seemed to be there with his awkward smile—yes, definitely a silly boy.

I could tell Boris was upset; I knew him too well. For all his, what do you call it—bravado, he wasn't tough right now. I found myself liking him more for it. But he would never willingly show his emotions, I knew that for sure, he was a tough nut to crack was Boris. Oh, poor boy, it must be hard for him always hiding his true feelings, always trying to be a grown man. I smiled at him. He sort of returned the smile and I could see he was trying to hide it from the others, but I had seen enough to be satisfied.

I watched as Boris turned and glared at a younger boy. Otto Klein wasn't holding anything back; he was crying his eyes out and simply not caring who was watching him. Boris didn't approve of course and showed it. Poor Otto was much younger than him, if I recall he'd only just had his tenth birthday, and here he was, after such a happy occasion, holding tight to his mama and sobbing so. From a distance, Otto was a miniature version of Boris, even though they weren't related. All the boys had blonde hair, though there were variations in shades—that's Aryans for you I suppose. Otto certainly didn't want to leave his mama and from his sly glances towards Boris, he didn't relish having to spend time with the bigger boy either. He would be okay though; I would see to that.

Both Boris' and Otto's papas were army officers just like my papa, and they were all great friends. In fact, all of the kids on the platform that day were children of officers; senior officers, not regular guards or even sergeants. All the other children from the village had already left. Well, not all of them, only those that were considered to be Aryan; there were still a few others in the village who had been left behind. Despite this, the school had closed and the teachers had accompanied the children on the earlier train; we would be joining them later today.

We were important you see, or so, we thought. Sometimes when I look back I wished we hadn't been so important; just ordinary like the kids we left behind. Perhaps then we wouldn't have had to leave. Instead we would be carrying on with our normal lives; happy I suppose, but completely ignorant of what is happening around us. You know something, being ignorant of what goes on in the world is not a good thing. Right now, I couldn't think of anything worse!

Indeed, until then, I had never witnessed a more miserable day. And to make it even more miserable, Frau Leshnik had arrived. She was going to take charge of us during our holidays. She would teach us and care for us—if you could call it care. What a wicked old woman she was. How I hated her.

Frau Leshnik was the head of our school. It was only a very little school, perhaps no more than seventy students give or take a few. We all knew each other and played together. It was a very nice school, except for Frau Leshnik that is. With her wrinkled face and those black spot things on her chin and cheeks, she must have been a hundred years old and looked just like a witch. She was as wicked as one that's for sure. She was a very small woman, and her bent spine made her even smaller. She used a cane to help her walk a little more upright. It was a weird thing, more like a twisted branch of a tree, with no bark and a knob on the top. It was a mix of dark and light brown and it was highly polished. The awful woman took every opportunity to beat us with it.

The Frau wore her blonde hair (well I say blonde, it was mostly grey these days) tied up in a tight bun and she wore the most awful dresses that her son brought back from his many visits to foreign lands, they seemed to hang off her bent back like drapes.

More horrid than her face was the many rules she forced on us on a daily basis. She had so many, it was impossible not to break them: silence in class, the yard is the place for noise; silence in the yard when Frau Leshnik is about. No running in the corridors, no running in the yard, make sure you are smartly dressed at all times, eat up all your food—you are lucky to have it, speak only when spoken to, speak clearly, speak up, shut up, work hard, respect your elders, respect your senior officers, respect all Aryans, and on and on the list of rules went. How pleased we were to go home at the end of the day just to get away from Frau Leshnik and her damn rules.

Even at home we weren't free from the old bat. I shouldn't call her that name, but I've heard Papa say it, so I do. She often came to our house for tea, usually inviting herself. For such a short woman, she always seemed to make her presence known. Most of the time she was quite disrespectful to my mama and my papa, despite her own rules; she was the only one to get away with this. Whenever she left, Papa would start cursing, but Mama would just laugh.

Frau Leshnik never allowed anyone else chance to talk you see, and she was always telling tales. Mostly lies about what Klaus and I got up to at school, how we had broken her rules; or she would rant about her son's adventures. Her son, Herr Leshnik, I forget his first name, is a famous army commander fighting our enemies in the East. Some of the things he has done, I simply can't tell you; it would make you cry. He sounds like a horrible man—a monster! Though my papa always praised Herr Leshnik, I'm sure he didn't really approve of him and the things he got up to.

I remember the last visit Frau Leshnik graced us with. As usual it was unexpected and, as always, it was as we were about to sit down to dinner. Of course, we offered all the usual courtesy, as expected of true Aryans, but the Frau—well, she was simply rude! Mama greeted her politely and offered her hand. In reply, Frau Leshnik simply nodded curtly, almost disapprovingly before barging past Mama and placing herself at the head of our dinner table. The cheek of it! Papa was absolutely fuming. How he didn't throw the Frau out of the door was a mystery. I was proud of him then, for controlling his anger; that took great effort for him, whereas Mama remained calm as always, as if Frau Leshnik didn't bother her at all. She simply proceeded with the meal in a normal fashion as if nothing was untoward.

I remember as Frau Leshnik dominated the conversation at dinner, Mama caught my eye and offered a secret smile. I was instantly filled with love and pride; I remembered Mama's words, "No matter what Frau Leshnik thinks, we are better than her, Mona."

I have wandered from my story a little. My favourite teacher, Frau Fischer who teaches languages (French and English are my favourite, I am not fond of Russian), often warns me about this; it is called digressing, so let me go back to my tale.

At last, the moment we had all dreaded arrived. We could hear the train before we saw it. It sounded like some mighty monster approaching, the chugging was there as expected but it seemed to scream at us and this awful black smoke appeared above the trees to turn the fluffy grey clouds into swirling plumes of soot. Then finally, the great ugly thing emerged through the rain like some giant metal dinosaur. What a racket, what a smell—choking us all! I wondered why we needed such a machine to carry away eleven tiny children.

Within seconds, the station was filled with the steam and smoke which seemed to brush the rain away. The engine was a dull black with very few shiny parts. Close up, it was massive and powerful, easily pulling behind it a dozen wagons loaded with trucks and tanks and other weapons of war. Next came three grey carriages full of soldiers, all waving at us through the windows and finally, sandwiched between the soldiers and the guard wagon right at the back, was the carriage set aside just for us, It was not like the ones used for the soldiers, it was elegantly painted in maroon with gold trim, and I could see inside it had curtains at the windows and electric lights. Though our coach stuck out like a sore thumb, it was nice, reassuring in a strange way—perhaps this wasn't going to be all bad after all.

The brakes screeched and we had to hold our ears as it approached, but the huge wheels didn't want to stop, how I hoped it wouldn't. Hopes and dreams, they never come true as I was later to find out! The train eventually stopped of course—a carriage door right in front of our little family. This was it! There was no turning back now; how awful we all felt. At least, we could get out of the rain, thank heavens for small mercies and our mamas could return to our nice cosy homes. Home—how I missed it already!

I turned to Mama, tears in my eyes. She beckoned me closer, giving me a stern look at first, but she couldn't keep up the pretence. I could see the love in her eyes, fighting her Aryan pride. I pushed towards her, my sweeping arm pulling Klaus along with me; he was visibly shaking and sobbing as he struggled desperately not to cry, what a brave boy he was. As we fell into Mama's arms, she also began to tremble, glancing back and forth from Klaus to me, trying to soak us up, unable to let us go. We clung to her tightly, pushing ourselves into her, smelling her clothing and feeling her face against ours, it was so comforting.

At last, the tension was too much and Mama's legs buckled. She fell to her knees, pulling Klaus tightly to her, her arms wrapped around him, squeezing him ever so hard; I thought she might hurt him. I allowed tears to fall down my cheeks. Mama noticed, and I too, was pulled to her; all three of us hugging each other tightly. I would not let her go—ever!

"Come—come children, get on the train—NOW!" The emphasis Frau Leshnik applied to that 'NOW' was finalised by the sharp clapping of her hands. She slowly forced herself past all the little families who were desperately trying to let go; her face was like thunder, darker than the skies, poised to make her demands. "You will not be separated for very long. We are not monsters you know. We do not go around separating families without reason. I too have been parted from my only son; we all have to make sacrifices in war time. Soon this damned war will be over. Our beloved Fatherland will be victorious and we will all safely return home to our loving families. Now I order you to get on the train. I will not tolerate further delay."

Instantly, without thinking and like good Aryans, the parents and children began to part; a strange urgency to follow Frau Leshnik's orders. We reluctantly let go of each other, but unlike the others, Mama, Klaus and I didn't move. We simply stood there, motionless in the rain; just staring at each other and crying.

More clapping and two guards appeared—army soldiers. They instantly started to load the carriage with bags and children, making no distinction between the two. More crying followed, with some kicking and some screaming. Some mamas were on their knees, unable to watch whilst others stood tall and proud, their faces stern—hard as rock.

Otto Klein was already on the train, his face pushed hard against the glass. I could see him pleading to get back off until his mama, with her face in the air, allowing the rain to dilute her tears, turned and walked away proudly. Otto's ordeal was over, or so, I thought. I remember thinking how brave he and his mama were.

Mama pushed Klaus and me towards the carriage door. "Be brave, Mona, be brave for little Klausy. You are his mama now, until you return." Then, turning to Klaus, she repeated her kind words. "Be brave, Klaus; a brave little soldier. Remember in wartime, we all have to make sacrifices, just as Frau Leshnik said.

But we will be together again soon. You have your big sister to look after you. Have a great adventure. Come back and tell me all about it—you promise."

We didn't expect it, but Klaus answered her, "Yes, Mama, I promise. This will be a good adventure and Mona and I are going to have a wonderful time."

He looked up at me, his eyes red and his bottom lip trembling. I nodded my agreement—how proud I felt at that moment. Then taking hold of my little brother's hand, we took one pace towards the waiting guards. But before they could grab us and haul us aboard the train, we both threw ourselves at Mama who was angry and sad and happy all at once. We kissed and hugged and rubbed our faces into her body, breathing in her mama smell and feeling her warm love. It was a special moment; one that I would never forget for the rest of my life.

It had to end—didn't it? The guards pulled us apart and lifted Klaus and me into the carriage. Neither of us made a sound—perhaps we thought it would spoil the moment. We raced to the window where Otto had been, placed our cheeks to the tear smeared glass and simply stared.

Mama stood silently in the pouring rain, huddled with all the other mamas who couldn't bear to leave. She had time to wave just before the train suddenly shunted forward with a clang of wheels and metal parts. Tears wet my cheeks as I clasped Klaus tightly around his neck. We waved back at Mama, rubbing the tears against the glass with our fingers.

Mama and a few others began to follow the train along the platform, totally ignorant of the rain which had begun to fall harder. As the train picked up speed, so did they; running along the platform at the side of the carriage. All the children were waving and shouting goodbye as loud as they could. Then one by one the other mamas stopped following, but our mama reached the very end of the long platform before she came to a standstill, frantically waving, unable to follow any further. The last I saw of her was when her head fell into her hands. "Goodbye," I mouthed; the words would not come out, but Klaus did better and his voice was the last to quieten as the secret train picked up speed and the little, miserable, rain-soaked station dwindled in size and faded out of sight.

That was the beginning of my story. I mean—the real beginning. The start of a nightmare! But wait on, I am jumping ahead. Let me tell you a little bit about myself, and my family and about some people who were to become very dear to me.

Chapter 2
Mona

Now where are my manners? Let us start with hello first of all.

Hello! My name is Mona. I am fifteen years old, although I look older; you see I am very tall for my age. In better times, I liked playing the piano, dressing in fine clothes and making my hair all pretty; you know the kind of stuff that girls of my age do, after all we are all growing up; I am a young woman now really. You know something though, sometimes, secretly, I still liked to play with my dolls house, and dress my dolls up in their lovely frocks, it was something I was just not ready to let go, I suppose.

At home, I also enjoyed other things, in fact I liked quite a few activities; I was never a lazy girl. Horse riding was one of my favourites. Although we didn't own horses, Papa could borrow them from the army, a major perk of his rank, and the horses were such fine and splendid things, always well behaved. I had also recently started playing tennis—I was hopeless at it, but I was making progress, or so my coach, Herr Weber said. But I know he was just being nice.

Things I hated then included needlework and learning to speak Russian, needlework hurt my fingers and Russian is just a horrid language to learn; I do much better with English and French. Why do you have to do things you don't like doing? To be honest with you, now that I think about it, some of my favourite things, the things I liked to do most of all and the things I miss the most are actually playing boys' games; especially football with my little brother and the boys on my street. I was very strong you see and I could easily take the ball from most of them. How they hated to lose the ball to a mere girl.

My second name is Lange. There was a time when I was not allowed to tell you that. It was a secret you see; but I'm not so sure if it matters all that much now. Papa used to say there were many spies around to hear what they ought not to hear and to see what they ought not to see; and I believed his every word—then! He said there could even be spies in our house. Can you believe that?

Our house was so beautiful. It was huge and comfortable and, and homely. It was always clean and tidy and there was always something cooking in the kitchen. Oh, how Klausy and I loved the kitchen, it always smelt so great and the food was always delicious. We used to steal the best stuff, the biscuits and cakes—how naughty, but we couldn't resist.

Well eventually I am going to tell you my tale. It's a story that needs to be told. It must be told and the sooner the better! It is not a nice story I'm afraid; more of a horror, with a lot of sadness and suffering. Are horror stories sad, I don't really know—what do you think? I have strayed from my point; I have always done that—digressing again. Funny how some things remain the same isn't it, no matter what happens to you.

Let me begin. So…this story is about what happened to my brother Klaus and me, along with nine other children. Here goes then. At the beginning of my story, or should I say once upon a time…Oh no, that will not do at all. We must reserve those words for fairy stories only, and this is definitely not one of those.

So, let's start yet again. But where—how about when I was eleven years old? Yes, that's a good place to start. You see, it was about that age when I suddenly became aware of strange things going on around me, crazy things that I didn't really understand. There was a kind of tension in the air; the whole country was buzzing. Some people were excited by this feeling, others seemed afraid. Whatever was happening was having a strange effect on the entire population and I was sure it was spreading far beyond the borders of our land; our great Fatherland—Germany.

I became aware of politics at a very young age. I think I was six when I first asked Papa what the word meant. It was all the grown-ups talked about. Why, I believe I have never heard adults speak about anything but politics. I knew that the change in the air had to be something to do with politics. I was a child and I wasn't at all interested. Well not really, I suppose an awareness of what was going on around us sort of settled on us—without really trying; oh, it's so hard to explain. Later, when war broke out and our great country, our Fatherland, invaded the country next to it, called Poland, without realising it, politics was all we talked about—Poland, and war and how we were the greatest people ever to walk the earth. We simply forgot about lessons, what a blessing that was—where

Russian was concerned at least. We were Aryans and we would take what was rightfully ours and for some reason, this was the correct thing to do.

Let me set the scene a little. I am a German and a true Aryan. At that time, we Germans believed that true Aryans were the best type of people, dominant in every way. For example, Aryans are beautiful women and handsome men, they all have blonde hair and blue eyes (well most of them) and they are all extremely intelligent. Aryans have perfect health and are great sportsmen and women. They are strong and powerful people who are also marvellous leaders that everyone can turn to for help and advice. There is no need for concern when Aryans are around, they can be thoroughly relied upon to solve any problem fairly and offer full protection to weaker and more dependent people.

This is where it gets confusing. You see, not all Aryans are the same! There are different levels of Aryans, a sort of, how do you say it, a hierarchy. The best Aryans are the most successful people: the scientists, the inventors, the great leaders, the men who cannot be defeated in battle, who build great cities and who lead the way in all things. We call these people the Master Race.

My family belonged to the Master Race; we could not have been prouder. Papa used to call me his Aryan princess; my younger brother Klaus, his Aryan prince. Klaus is seven; he is a small skinny thing, but we always promised he would grow up tall and strong—how he liked that. My papa is called Ulrich. At that time, he was a powerful man, he still is I guess; an army officer, a colonel no less. Papa is a huge man, well over six feet tall and he's actually a little big around the waist, if you know what I mean, that's Mama's cooking for you I guess, plus Papa is partial to a glass of red wine, now and again, more again I would say. It didn't matter at all that he was a little overweight, we all loved him; he has a kind face, despite everything! Especially his eyes, they are the deepest blue, I loved to gaze at them, and when Papa smiles, he is so endearing.

My mama's name is Maria; she is a very beautiful woman, both on the outside and on the inside. She is such a lovely person, always agreeing with Papa, doting on my brother and myself; she never has a bad word for anyone. You know, when I think back, perhaps that was her biggest fault. Mama's hair is like pure silk, mostly wavy with curls at the end, without the curls I bet it would have reached her waist. Of course, her eyes were blue and I could not remember a time when her lips did not shine, like red glass—almost. Mama's nose is very small and sort of turned up at the end, which makes her a little distinct—well, I always thought so; I remember wishing my nose was the same.

We were all very happy in those days, you see. We were the lucky ones I guess. Papa said we were going to rule the whole world someday, thanks to our magnificent leaders. The process had begun, with our victorious invasion of Poland, it was only a matter of time before the rest of the world fell quaking at our feet.

This kind of talk increased our excitement of course, and we were caught up in the passion that was felt by all the people in Germany. Or maybe, you could say, the craziness of our people—the true Aryans. I couldn't for the life of me work out why us kind and gentle Aryans would want to see all the other people quaking at our feet. Papa said it is how things should be and that I was too young to understand. "Be content and be proud to be part of it my princess," is all he had to say.

Yes, we were a proud family, and so lucky. We all had lovely blonde hair; Mama put ringlets in mine. She wore hers up in a bun, at least she used to. I haven't seen her for a long while. Big blue eyes shone proudly from our beautiful faces. "True Aryans," our mama used to say, we were all so strong and healthy and prime examples of the human race, and both Klaus and I were prominent attendees of the Hitler Youth Group to boot.

Oh yes, Hitler Youth Group, I must tell you about that. This was a camp we attended often after school and at weekends. We took part in lots of activities at Hitler Youth Group; there were all sorts of sports and strength building exercises. We also learned martial arts and how to defend ourselves, though we weren't sure why. We were all good children and paid attention as we were taught about the world and our enemies living in it, though to be honest I found this part really boring, but I couldn't let on. You see I was soon to become a Hitler Youth leader which made Papa very proud of me. We used to promise Klaus he too would be a leader one day when he grew older. How wrong we were!

We both wanted to be like our great leader—Adolf Hitler; the leader of the Nazi Party and the Chancellor of all Germany and the Aryan people. Back then, I didn't really know what the Nazi Party was, but it sounded fun to us, and Papa said it was the only party that could lead our great nation to victory. We Aryans call Herr Hitler the Fuhrer and we have to salute every time we see him, or a picture of him, or even if we mention his name; after all, he wasn't an ordinary leader, but the leader of the Master Race. I always thought it was strange how he neither had blonde hair, more a dark brown and to be honest, I can't remember his eyes being blue, what I do know is, well, he didn't look all that strong and healthy!

I met him once in his little house in the Bavarian Alps. What a beautiful place that is. The world is full of beautiful places. I loved being in the mountains, they were so majestic, so mighty and clean and…and peaceful. How I wished I could return, and of course there are many other beautiful places to see, all over the world. I had intended to visit them one day.

Anyway, back to the story. I thought Herr Hitler would be scary, but he didn't really scare me. He looked quite funny with his little moustache. My arm ached with saluting though, which wasn't fair because Klaus was too young and so didn't have to do it.

You see, Papa was a good friend of Herr Hitler's. He had secret meetings with him all the time, and they made plans on how to defeat our enemies. True Aryans have many enemies according to Herr Hitler; from all over the world. My papa would often tell us how we Aryans were the superior race and were destined to rule the world, which is what Herr Hitler wanted to do most of all. All other races were the 'Untermenschen', the sub-humans. When I remember these words, these awful words, I become so sad. Oh Papa!

Papa is not only a personal friend of Herr Hitler's; he is also one of his most trusted generals. He is in command of the camps that look after our so-called enemies; so that they can't cause mischief and poison our minds. Well, this is what he used to say and to my regret I used to believe these things. Dreadful really! But I was very proud of him in those days. I thought he was protecting us from our enemies by keeping them locked away. We were both so very wrong.

I know this now, but there was once a time I thought Papa was always right. I would never have doubted him, not in a million years. Why would I, with him standing there, tall and handsome in his pristine uniform. Such a powerful man, how could he ever be wrong? I loved to hear him speak and tell his tales of how our great armies were reshaping the world and making it a better place for everyone. How I imagined a wonderful peaceful paradise, created and ruled by us Aryans of course, where everyone was happy and content and wanted for nothing.

As I got older I could not get enough. I wanted to hear the news; what was going on around the world, how were the true Aryans faring, I suppose I was addicted to, you guessed it—politics! My need for news became so bad that sometimes, when I should have been in bed, I'd sneak back downstairs and listen to Papa talking with Mama and our important friends about how things were progressing. He talked of how he was dealing with our enemies who obviously wanted to ruin everything that the Aryans had achieved. But not to worry, Papa promised that it wouldn't be long now before everything was under control. The war would be over all too soon and we could get down to the business of cleaning up the mess and creating order. Papa insisted that he had already started doing this, cleaning up the mess that is, and his friends would always agree with him and congratulate him on his successes.

Of course, it was wrong to creep downstairs and listen to Papa talking to his friends, but I couldn't help it. It was fun, and very interesting. Papa was right about one thing, I guess. He'd often say there were spies around listening to what they ought not to hear. I was one of them!

The first time I did it, I remember feeling very naughty, yet, very excited, it was like stealing cakes I guess. I was very quiet and listened carefully as my papa talked about some new enemies. These enemies were very clever men, Aryan, just like us, but they had strange ideas, they had their own party and didn't agree with Herr Hitler. Papa said he would deal with these fellows first; he would look after them well. He must have done a truly good job because he didn't mention them much after that.

But for us true Aryans there were many other enemies. Papa often talked about Communists who caused him lots of stress and bother. Anti-Nazi people were really bad, always causing trouble for him. Then there were the French and the Russians who we were fighting. The Polish people had been conquered but yet still annoyed Papa somehow. Papa especially hated the people in Britain who gave him nothing but headaches and he simply detested the Gypsies, whoever they were.

Worst of all, though, in Papa's opinion, were the Jews. He was not alone, all true Aryans seemed to hate them, though at that time I had no idea why and now that I am more aware what goes on in the world, I think it should be the Jews that hate the Aryans. My point is there were so many enemies. I laugh about it now, but I used to hope Papa's camps were big enough to look after them all. How silly I was to worry. There is always room for more in the camps, they never get overcrowded.

At that time, I had never seen any of our enemies, except for the Jews. Another confession! I harboured a little secret, even then; although I was so proud of my papa and thought he was always right, I used to think he must be a little mistaken about the Jews. You see, there was a wonderful girl living nearby, she was my best friend. Her name was Ola.

Ola was older than me; sixteen years old and fast approaching her seventeenth birthday. She couldn't wait for her birthday to arrive; it couldn't come soon enough and she could barely contain her excitement. She constantly talked about the presents she had asked for, how she would dress up in her lovely new dress and have a huge cake with seventeen candles; and of course, I was invited and must wear my favourite dress. We were great friends, the best of friends, despite the age gap.

Ola was always so kind, always finding time for me and she was the only one who could get me to do girl things. She'd brush and style my hair, allow me to try on her dresses; she had so many, all of them were so beautiful. She applied make-up to my face and we did all sorts of things like that. We would often tell each other secrets, about what we wanted to do when we grew up, which boys we liked; she often asked about Boris and I have to admit I always had something to say about him. Ola also believed I fancied him, I could see it in her eyes, her lovely brown eyes, they seemed to shine when she asked; it was as if she knew I was hiding my true feelings. I constantly denied it. She would simply smile and sometimes tut. Why, one time, she even accused me of loving him. I was shocked and denied it immediately, whilst Ola just giggled and continued to brush my hair. How we laughed together, I loved being with her, I bet you have a friend just like Ola.

The thing is you see; Ola was a Jew and so were her mama and papa and her whole family. They weren't our enemies at all! They were our friends, the nicest people I had ever met. You couldn't wish for better neighbours.

Mama and I used to walk to school with Ola and her mama, and Klaus used to play with Ola's little brother, Jan. Jan used to make me smile, he was six years old and always looked so scruffy, despite his mama's constant attempts to smarten him up. My papa used to have his suits made by Ola's papa and he said they were the best suits in the whole of Germany. So, I ask you, how could they be our enemies? It was just so confusing for me. I was approaching fourteen years of age at that time, I was eager to learn and though I wanted to accept everything that Papa was telling me, I was also battling with my own thoughts and ideas. The Jewish people may well have been our greatest enemies, but my best friend Ola was one of them and no matter how much Papa explained I could not bring myself to call Ola my enemy.

Then one morning as we walked to school, we called at Ola's house; her family lived above her papa's tailor shop. We were shocked to see the shop had all been smashed up, there was broken glass everywhere and all the suits gone. There was no sign of Ola and her family either. Had they packed up and left, without saying goodbye? Surely not! What about the birthday party! We had all been so excited about that. I looked for my best friend day after day but there was no sign of them. Ola and her family were nowhere to be found; I was heartbroken. Where was my best friend, had she been harmed, what about her family and her little brother Jan.

Mama remained calm as ever and promised they would return but I knew she was only trying to make me feel better. I couldn't tell you how sad I was when I finally gave up my search, and I was also a little annoyed at Ola for leaving without word; did they have to leave in such a hurry?

At the time, Papa said not to be concerned, it was for the best. Jews, he said, were like rodents; they spread diseases and get everywhere. I remember feeling a little angry at this and trying hard to listen without speaking my mind. I asked him if he meant head lice and measles and he replied, "Sort of." I remember thinking how funny this was because all the children in my school, even Aryan children, got head lice now and then. We usually got them from Jonny Weiss, and he was most certainly Aryan; he had to be, his papa was a major general or something like that, though his hair was blonde, it was filthy all the time, like all the other boys.

Then, a short time later, and a huge surprise to us all, Ola's shop was repaired. I thought she had come back but instead, a strange Aryan family from a different country had moved in. They didn't really look like Aryans; they neither had blue eyes nor blonde hair, and they spoke in a funny way too. Papa explained they were definitely Aryan; but from a lower level, so I guess they had to be. They had a young boy, his hair was almost black, but at least it was clean and combed to the left. He reminded me of Herr Hitler and I asked Papa if Herr Hitler belonged to the same level of Aryans as these. Papa just gave me a really annoyed look in reply and warned me never to say such a thing again. I had no idea what I had said that was so offensive, but I didn't always understand things then. Come to think of it, I still don't.

For instance, I don't know what has happened to us—I simply can't work it out. There was this little argument and now it has come to this? It's completely mad, and I can't for the life of me comprehend what is happening in the world around me. And I mean the whole world, not just our little Aryan part. Did I just say 'for the life of me'…oh wait! That was a slip of the tongue, 'for the life of me'…how funny. Never mind that now, I'm just rambling on, I have always done that. So, this is going to be a long story, I suggest you make yourselves comfortable.

Where was I—oh yes, I was talking about the world. There is so much sadness, so much suffering going on right now and no one seems to take any notice. You know what—it is all Herr Hitler's doing. Yes, he is the cause of it all. Well him and his close friends and perhaps other similar men in other countries; like my papa I guess, the men who are making all the decisions, who have put themselves in charge—these are the ones to blame.

I have to be honest with myself. It is time to face the facts and it is time to face the truth. But it's quite difficult, even now, what with all these lies and secrets. Already, I have told you that I thought Papa was wrong about Ola and the Jews. Well I am making quite a few confessions lately, perhaps it is time to come clean; I never really believed everything my papa said, in fact I doubted much of it. I have been thinking about this long and hard lately, it is all I have thought about. It makes me angry, but being angry helps keep the worry away.

Anyway, I am rambling on again. You see, I have come to a conclusion, a stark and shocking conclusion, that Papa was probably wrong MOST of the time. No, not most of the time, in fact, I now believe he was wrong ALL of the time—and I am so annoyed.

I am annoyed with Papa for, well, just being Papa I guess, for getting everything wrong, for listening to his friends and doing what they asked of him; and of course, I am annoyed with his friends for just the same things. They were all in this together. I am also annoyed with Mama for being so nice and agreeing with everything Papa and his friends said. Did she know what was going on—it makes me wonder. And I am definitely annoyed at Herr Hitler, he is a horrid man!

But mostly I am annoyed with myself. Why did I listen to my papa and his crazy notions? Why did I adore him so? I loved him so much you see. That is not an excuse…I know, but I worshipped him. This is why it is so hard to bear. My heart is truly broken. Oh Papa…oh Papa what have you done!

Excuse me. Forgive my tears…I will just compose myself. I wish I had a handkerchief, never mind, I'll use my sleeve…There that's better, I can go on now. It seems to me that whilst I was listening to Papa and believing his every word, I was also having silly notions of my own; silly notions that blinded me from the truth. Now my eyes are opened wide, I see everything. The truth has definitely returned to haunt me.

After all, Papa was wrong about Ola and her family, they are not like rodents, and he was wrong about the Jews spreading head lice and most of all he was wrong about the train; it did not take us away from danger—far from it!

So now you know who I am and you know of my family; you know who you are dealing with. You also have an idea where I am, though I am aware I have been vague, I don't want to spoil my story for you. We have a lot to talk about and we have to do it in the correct order. We are only at the beginning of the adventure—of the nightmare I am about to tell you. Can you bear to hear it? Where shall I start? Oh yes—here is a good place…It was a year before the train.

Chapter 3
Spies

"Maria, bring me my boots. Hurry up! Himmler will be here any minute."

"Don't worry, Ulrich. You will be ready and looking splendid as usual." Mama rushed in with the boots and knelt at Papa's feet. "Give me your left foot," she demanded and started to push the awkward boot on to Papa's rather large foot. "This is hard, do they actually fit, Ulrich?"

I laughed, "No, Mama, not like that." I recall I ran over to help her. She smiled at me. "Oh, Mama, these are the wrong boots, these are Papa's camp boots. Look, they have dust on them and these red scuff marks. What is this red stuff, Papa?"

"That's nothing, my little Princess, only dirt from the camp. Be careful not to touch it. They should have been cleaned by now." He glanced towards the door and shouted, "Samuel, come here now."

Samuel was one of our house servants; we had two of them, Samuel and Liza. They helped with all the house chores. We had such a large house and in those busy times we needed all the help we could get. There was always something going on; meals to prepare, silver to polish, clothes to wash, dusting, repairs, gardening, I could go on and on and that was just ordinary days. We also had many special days with major events occurring and important visits were often scheduled during the week which all had to be organised thoroughly. That's where Mama's secret talents came in handy—she was such an organised person and nothing seemed to cause her concern or worry; we could all rely on her, except when it came to helping Papa with his boots.

Samuel and Liza had been borrowed from one of Papa's camps and they were always kept extremely busy. They were our enemies of sorts, but Papa said it was okay, because they were only half Jew. The other half, the bigger half, was German—but definitely not Aryan.

Samuel would be in big trouble now; Papa might even threaten to send him back to camp. This would upset Samuel, I just knew it, and at any rate, I liked having Samuel around. He was such a nice person and so clever; I believe he used to be a science teacher at some famous university. But that was before the war. Now he had to make do with being a servant, how war changes things. I was terribly fond of him, but the little man always seemed nervous to me. Papa said Samuel suffered with his nerves—that's all; which is why he always shakes so much.

"Please, Papa," I begged, "don't be mad at Samuel. He has been busy helping me make a bird feeder. He must have forgotten to clean your boots, I'm sure it won't happen again."

Papa laughed. "You are a little angel. Samuel is lucky to have you around." He glanced at Samuel who had appeared at the lounge door. "Okay, I will go easy on him, this time! But remember my love, to be successful and gain respect, a man needs to be hard and ruthless. Most of the time anyway," he added with a smile. I smiled too but Samuel held his head down and came running into the room, all worried with shaking hands as he knelt to collect the dirty boots.

Samuel was a little thin man with very short hair; to be honest, he was looking quite ill. Papa had been very kind and provided both him and Liza with appropriate clothes suitable for their status. Papa refused to have the ugly camp prisoner clothes in our home; the stripes as he called them, they reminded him of his work and his many duties. Home was a place to relax, he'd often say, a sanctuary away from the difficult decisions he had to make whilst he was on duty.

Papa scowled at Samuel and demanded his dress boots. They were much fancier but less practical than his camp boots. Samuel scurried off to find the desired boots but he need not worry so, Liza appeared at the door with them in her hands. How relieved Samuel looked at that moment—what a silly man, I remember thinking. He took the boots and Liza vanished as suddenly as she had appeared. Soon Samuel was on his knees pushing the wonderful clean boots onto Papa's feet—he was more successful at this than Mama had been. At last, the dirty boots were exchanged for the black shiny ones.

I watched carefully, trying to learn from Papa; though he frowned at Samuel throughout, he did not shout at him. Instead, he turned and smiled at me and I smiled back. How I loved him then, to me he was kind and strong, handsome and smart; and we all felt safe in his presence.

At last, Papa stood up, proud and magnificent in his pristine uniform which was a greyish-blue colour. I never really liked that colour, to be honest and though it was smart I always found it rough to touch; very itchy. That didn't matter as it was decorated at the cuffs and collars with gold embroidery and his many medals for conduct and service to the Third Reich hung neatly from Papa's left breast pocket.

Papa stood and stretched himself to his full height, which at over six feet threatened to dislodge the chandelier. He brushed invisible fluff off his tunic and slipped his cap onto his head ensuring he tucked his lovely golden hair beneath it. Of course, his hair would stay in place, he had covered it in a sort of greasy substance which I hated to touch, it was a wonder his cap didn't slip off.

Finally, Papa glanced into a full-length mirror and gave himself a nod of approval. Then, as if remembering something, he turned his attention back to Samuel to remind him he had me to thank for his kind treatment and he would get what was coming to him later. Samuel obviously misunderstood as he began to shake again, but I smiled. Papa was offering a reward! Yes, my papa was a very kind man indeed.

Just then we heard the squeaky brakes of a car pull up with a slight skid on the gravel outside. We knew it was Uncle Heinrich of course. We had been expecting him and as usual, he was dead on time. Papa was cutting it fine though as Uncle Heinrich was a very important man indeed, even more important than Papa, he shouldn't be kept waiting. Uncle Heinrich was in charge of Herr Hitler's personal guard, the Schutz-Staffel or SS as we liked to call them. The SS was the largest and most powerful organisation in the Third Reich. The Third Reich! That is something that is always discussed at our house, though no one has ever explained what it truly means.

Papa shooed Samuel away and unable to hide his relief, the little man scurried away to complete his many other tasks. Meanwhile Papa guided me to the door quickly to greet my uncle. I watched from the door with Mama and Klaus; we stood in line at the top of the steps, from the biggest to smallest. Papa quickly skipped down the steps to meet Uncle Heinrich as the important general stepped out of his huge car, his arm already stretching to greet Papa. As usual, my uncle was not alone, at least six guards accompanied him and other important men climbed out of other vehicles that had parked further down the drive.

The guards stepped aside to allow Papa through, then he instantly grabbed hold of Uncle's right hand and shook it eagerly before hugging the important man with all his might. Uncle Heinrich was nearly lifted off the ground and the silly spectacles he wore nearly fell off his face. It did not matter. They were so happy to see each other. They had been friends since boyhood, closer than brothers. In actual fact, Uncle was not our uncle at all, but we made out he was and he didn't object, he liked it when we called him Uncle, it made him feel part of our family I guess. It had been so long since Uncle Heinrich had visited. He was such a busy man with no time for social visits; but despite the dress code and the guards, this was just such an occasion.

The two great men looked marvellous together. Two very powerful men indeed, both splendid in their uniforms, radiating authority and beaming with confidence; their medals of honour dangling from their chests, clattering together as they embraced.

Uncle Heinrich removed his cap and waved at us, a huge happy grin on his face. Klaus started to run towards him, but Mama called him back. He returned and was given a quick slap on the hand. Moodily, my little brother took his place at the end of the line. I held his hand and smiled at him. Reassured, he smiled back.

Then Uncle Heinrich approached, climbing the porch steps two at a time. Firstly, he greeted Mama with a kiss on her cheek. Next, he took my hand, firstly shaking it then playfully he kissed it and said. "Is this my little Mona, my how you have grown. What a fine, young and beautiful lady you have become. I always remember your face when I am feeling sad. It makes me smile."

"You always say that," I giggled as I curtsied.

Klaus gazed up at him, his eyes beaming; how he adored Uncle Heinrich. Uncle then turned to him and bent down on one knee. I thought he would dirty his smart pants, but he didn't seem to care. He held out his arms and instantly Klaus pounced on him and clasped his arms around Uncle's neck; Uncle's spectacles nearly fell off.

Mama protested, "Klaus be careful." But she didn't really mean it, I could tell because she was smiling. Both Uncle Heinrich and little Klaus giggled like lunatics and Papa joined in. Then Uncle picked Klaus up and held him in the air. "My God boy, you are getting heavy. What are you feeding him Ulrich?" He always said that too.

Papa laughed again. "That's enough now little Klausy, your uncle and I have official business to attend to." Though Papa's face was serious it didn't stop Klaus from protesting. He needn't have worried, Uncle said he would play with him later and this made my little brother happy again. Papa pushed the door open and ushered Uncle inside, but Uncle Heinrich refused, stating on such a fine sunny day they should be outside enjoying the sun. Papa agreed and we watched as the two great commanders nonchalantly strolled away down the garden towards the lake, followed at a distance by all the other soldiers.

I placed my arm around Klaus who had begun to sulk. "Change your face silly, I have a plan." Our garden was huge with many trees and bushes. It had grown a little wild lately since Papa had sent all the gardeners back to camp. They were not trustworthy he said, better to have a wild garden than wild men around the house.

Klaus and I preferred the natural look, it was more fun. We played for hours on end in the long grass, often war games, me against Klausy which was unfair I guess; only I often let him win. We built tree houses, which fell down all too easily and some of them were quite high up, which was risky I suppose, but we enjoyed them. Other times I would collect wildflowers; Klausy hated those times. He didn't think it appropriate for a boy to collect flowers and so he would sulk until at last I would have to beg Mama to arrange for his school friends to come around; after all, I couldn't spend all my free time entertaining my little brother.

Our garden had more than trees and grass. There were many ponds and even a lake which was quite large. Klausy loved pond dipping and sometimes, when he was off duty, Papa would take us fishing in the lake, ensuring Klausy always caught a fish. The garden was great fun, which was good because apart from school we rarely left the house, though often our friends would come to visit and the war games became more serious. We had small armies, often led by the bigger boys that ambushed each other at every opportunity.

There was also a flat lawn where we used to play football, and everyone played, both boys and girls. But our pitch too was now overgrown and so the wooded area became our favourite part of the garden, with its many logs to jump and twisted trees to climb or hang swings from.

Once, on the rare occasion that I was alone I built myself a wonderful tree house. It wasn't too high up and when I stood back to admire it, I realised it had a large window and so I made it into a shop. I busied myself searching for items to sell, pinecones and pebbles that took my fancy, you know the sort of thing. I was having the most wonderful time all by myself, and then I heard a voice, a boy's voice, here to ruin my carefree day.

"Hi Mona," the boy said and as I looked up I was surprised to see Boris. He was all clean and wearing his smartest clothes, his hair flattened back with that grease boys use; he was even wearing a tie fastened smartly around his neck, it was black and contrasted with his immaculate white shirt which was tightly fastened at both neck and cuffs. I could see he was not comfortable in his outfit. Boris liked his shorts and dirty vest.

"Boris! What a surprise. You look so smart. What are you doing here?" I wasn't nervous, Boris never made me feel nervous, just, well, you know, surprised that's all.

"Just passing through," he said shyly—I suppose. "We are on our way to a funeral; some of Papa's men have been killed recently."

"Oh." I had nothing more to offer and just shrugged. "Are you sad?"

"No. Not really. I did not know them. I would just rather not go."

He looked so miserable and I couldn't help smiling. Boris smiled back. "How long do you have before you leave?"

"Ten minutes, maybe a little longer."

"Good," I said. "You have time to visit my shop. I hope you have brought lots of money." Boris was clearly horrified and attempted to protest but I offered no escape. I rushed towards him and grabbed hold of his hand, pulling him as hard as I could towards my shop. I was so excited, not just for the shop but because, and don't laugh or say I told you so, but I was pleased to have Boris all to myself.

"Mona! Are you kidding? I will not play at shop."

"Shush Herr Smidt. Now tell me. What would you like to purchase today?"

Boris frowned and I unwittingly mimicked his face which made him smile. I had him hooked. "Okay, if you insist. But if you tell anyone of this." He could see his threats had no effect and so, frowning, he gave in and started to read from his pretend shopping list. Ten minutes later he was laden with cones and pebbles. He stood back, desperate to laugh but I forbade it with a stern look that said he must not spoil the game. Instead he asked, "How much Frau…"

"Bernhard." I said offering my mama's maiden name. "Fleur Bernhard."

"Fleur—a wonderful name," Boris said, "for a…"

"For a…what? Herr Smidt?" Boris had turned red and hung his head in embarrassment. He had got caught up in the game and had almost, very nearly, offered me a compliment. "You were saying," I urged with my most charming smile.

"You know, you are a mean girl, aren't you," Boris smiled. "Okay, then I suggest you listen very carefully. I will not repeat this, though I am sure, a meanie like you will insist I do. I was going to say Fleur is a wonderful name for such a pretty girl—like you."

His blushes were matched by my own. "Why, Herr Smidt. Such a daring compliment deserves a reward." I said and leaned into Boris, my eyes closed and my lips ready for the kiss. It did not happen! I opened my eyes to see Boris, frozen still and red as beetroot. I frowned. I knew he wanted to kiss me and he had just missed the greatest opportunity. It was rare that we were alone together and both of us in such good moods. "Boris!"

"Hush Fleur," Boris warned. "There are spies around here." No sooner had he given the warning, Boris jumped into some bushes and flushed out a spy.

"Klausy! How could you spy on us like that?"

"I am practicing my combat training," my little brother protested. "You said I should practice whenever I could. Can I play?"

"I suppose so." I said and my disappointment was known to Boris who quickly made his excuses to leave. "Goodbye, Herr Smidt," I called after him. "Remember, you have unfinished business with Fleur."

I knew he was both blushing and smiling as he walked away. So, I continued playing shop with my brother. It wasn't as much fun as playing with Boris—I can't explain why. Come to think of it, I can't explain why I told you this story—perhaps it will be useful later!

Anyhow, since that day I realised my pesky brother needed practice at spying and as our overgrown garden provided many secret hiding places, we began playing at spies quite a lot. Today would be no different—you guessed it—we would spy on Papa and Uncle.

So, on hands and knees we crawled and scampered through the long grass from one hideout to another, not worrying about our lovely clean clothes, we were only interested in getting as close to the great men as possible. It was hard going but lots of fun; too much fun to be honest, Klaus could barely contain himself. We were commandos you see, crawling through mine infested terrain, the enemy within earshot. Klaus kept giggling as we popped our heads up now and then to view the foe we were hunting down.

Klaus wasn't the quietest commando I had ever known, he coughed a lot, and sniffed and his breathing was quite exaggerated, neither could he keep his head down; that's excitement for you I guess. Many times, I reminded him that in real combat, the noise he made would have caused him to suffer a violent death. I had learned this at Hitler Youth; they taught us some strange things there, now that I think about it. Poor Klaus struggled to understand any of it, how I despaired that he would ever make a good soldier.

We had kept to the bushes and trees. There were also large dips here that we could hide in. It was hot work—indeed it was a hot day, the sky was clear blue and the sun shone bright. I think it dazzled the guards who had gathered with the other officers a distance away from Papa and Uncle, they were smoking cigarettes and joking and not watching for spies at all. It was easy to pass them undetected. From bush to bush, we dashed and this gave Klausy all the confidence he needed to make a great spy.

Soon we found ourselves near to the enemy, their voices drifting overhead. We were lying in tall grass; who'd have thought a lawn could grow so tall. It was full of insects, and though I didn't mind the spiders, the ants were another matter and the moths and flies threatened to give our position away. "Keep your head down, Klaus," I ordered, "or we'll be in big trouble." We kept still, hardly breathing, a task that caused such a strain to appear on my little brother's face; I nearly laughed out loud, especially when a bright green bug crawled across his forehead, his face was so funny. Then we heard voices again, we froze instantly. They were so near!

"They will start bombing us soon—mark my words." This was Uncle's voice. I glanced at Klaus and smiled. He was about to speak so I shushed him with warning eyes.

"How could the Russians join the allies? What is all that about Heinrich?"

"Stalin is a peculiar fellow. We can deal with him. We can deal with all our enemies."

"But on two fronts. Do we have the manpower with the Jewish problem to contend with? Have we bitten off more than we can chew?"

None of this made any sense to us. Klausy's face was a picture of excitement. I pushed his head into the grass and we allowed ourselves a giggle.

"Nonsense, Ulrich—don't say such things. There are treacherous people about, trust no one. If you are heard talking this way, you will be in for the chop."

Klaus and I looked at each other uneasily. The chop, what is that?

"The final solution is in progress. It is working excellently, better than expected. The camps are very productive, that side of things is going well. Britain is of concern. We should have destroyed their airfields. We are attacking the wrong targets, we are bombing civilians, and we are destroying towns and cities. I don't really agree with it, Heinrich."

"Don't worry so much. Ulrich. It will all work out soon enough. We are developing new weapons, working out better strategies. The Reich cannot fail. You know this."

We listened for a very long time. How Klaus managed to keep so quiet for so long amazed me, he did very well indeed. It seemed he would make a great spy after all. We heard many strange things and we learned such a lot. Oh, we would be in such trouble for listening—for spying!

Things were happening all over the world. Terrible things! The world was at war, and Germany was in the middle of it. We heard about other countries, about England, about the Japanese, about the Americans and French and Italians and many other people we had never heard of before. Many of them hated the Germans, especially the Aryans. Papa was right. We had so many enemies, and they were coming to hurt us.

And that is when we heard about the trains—the secret trains. These trains were very special and they were for Klaus, and me, and all of the children living around us. They would take us away, to a safe place. Well out of the reach of our enemies.

My heart sank. Consumed with sadness. Klaus looked puzzled; he hadn't really understood what he had heard; which was a blessing in disguise I suppose. I took hold of his hand and whispered, "Don't worry, it's alright. We'll be perfectly safe." But even as I said those words, I did not really believe them.

Chapter 4
First Class

Frau Leshnik soon took charge. "Here are the rules," she declared and the tiresome list went on for thirty minutes as we all sat in silence, in accordance with rule number one—absolute silence when Frau Leshnik is speaking. The old woman speaks in an irritating manner, slow and deep, she makes every word count and waits to make sure that every sentence she utters is heard and understood. Eventually she finished her list with a wave of her cane, an obvious threat to follow her stupid rules. There was no need, we remained silent, all of us thinking about our mamas.

The carriage was very comfortable; surely, with its plush seating and its fancy lamp shades it must be first class. There was quite a lot of space too, between two double seats that actually faced each other there was a large table. There must have been twelve of these in a row, and the same at the other side of the carriage. We had so much room for so few of us, it was crazy really.

I decided to explore—from the comfort of my seat. The walls were covered in polished wood, probably oak. Dotted around were a few old looking lights, again made from oak, with very fancy glass shades that flickered as the light shone through. The seats were trimmed with wood, that matched the tables and the walls, they were covered in a plush material which I suspected may be velvet; it was a very bright green. Yes, this was obviously a first-class carriage; I'll bet some very important people had used it before us.

Klausy and I gaped out of the window for a long time. I smiled at him as he scratched his head with quite some vigour, another attack of head lice thanks to Jonny Weiss no doubt. The rain kept falling hard for what seemed like ages, but it was probably no longer than an hour before eventually it fizzled out and the sun began to shine through the clouds that were now disappearing. I'm not sure how long we had been travelling by then—a couple of hours maybe. A huge rainbow appeared, the best I'd ever seen, and all the kids gawked at it in wonder. Smiles, too, began to appear and faces turned beautiful once again.

Outside, the countryside rolled past. It was lovely, with many fields, crowded woodlands, lonely farms and tiny villages and settlements scattered around the place. Every now and then a church seemed to pop up out of nowhere or an abandoned station came into view as the train rushed past. It was all so calm and idyllic, not touched by war—yet! I began to relax a little, though the unsettling feeling had not left me, I still felt something bad was going to happen, I had no idea why, but at least it had subsided—just a little.

I sat next to the window and Klaus sat next to the isle which ran down the centre of the carriage separating the tables that were fixed beneath the windows at each side. There were more tables than our small group needed which allowed all the children to spread out, some children had an entire table to themselves, they looked so lonely.

Klaus surprised me yet again with his request. "Do you have paper and pencils Mona?" I rummaged through my school satchel and gave him the desired items. "I'm going to draw that rainbow for Mama," he said smiling. "Do you think she will like it?"

"She will love it. We will send it to her the first chance we get." I was pleased. Klaus had cheered me up. Perhaps this trip wouldn't be so bad after all.

I began looking around the carriage. The other children had brightened up a little also and were beginning to chat to each other. All, that is, except little Magda Heyde who sat alone in a corner seat, rubbing her eyes and sobbing uncontrollably.

Magda appeared terrified, poor thing! She was only eight years old and all alone…That should not be, but what can you do. We were at war after all, and we all have to put up with a little hardship—don't we! But she didn't have to suffer all alone and so I pointed her out to Klaus and whispered in his ear. "Let's call her over; we could care for her." Klausy eagerly agreed with a smile and I beckoned the girl over with both hands. Magda noticed me and looked stunned. I smiled at her pretty face, she always reminded me of a doll, with her rosy cheeks and beautiful hair that curled inwards at her shoulders.

Instead of accepting our invitation, though, Magda half turned away, refusing to join us, perhaps she was a little shy maybe. Then Klaus offered her some paper and pencils—what a clever idea. She smiled at that. She was hooked and after a little more coaxing, the little girl occupied the seat opposite my little brother and me. Klaus instantly joined her and I smiled yet again. They made a cute pair sitting together, smiling at each other and comparing their drawings and soon enough they were getting on like a house on fire. That's a funny thing to say isn't it, 'like a house on fire'. It sounds like a bad thing, but it's actually a good thing you know. Perhaps it was appropriate for Klaus and his new friend who pretty soon started to test each other's strength to see who should be boss. I left them to it.

Regardless, we had definitely done a good thing, and I wanted to continue what I had started and so I searched around for my next conquest. In all, there were nine other kids travelling with Klaus and I. We were the last eleven to leave our village; I'm not sure why, but all the other kids had gone on ahead of us on an earlier train. Besides little Magda, there were three more girls travelling with us: Leni Koch, Gretl Neumann and Heidi Wolfe. Leni was the most adorable six-year-old girl, always pretty in her frocks and pigtails. Her family lived quite near to us. I was so fond of her but she was incredibly shy, frustratingly—you could never get near the girl. Leni's papa was a senior tank commander, what an amazing thing that must be, to drive a massive tank. Leni wore her hair quite straight; it was almost ginger in colour and she kept it in place with clips, one of which had fallen out; I watched as she wrestled to get it back in.

Gretl Neumann, like me, was also fifteen, but she had always been a little taller than me. Gretl was always fun to be with; she had a mischievous side to her and because of this, had become one of my best friends in school. Her parents were scientists working on some secret project to do with radios I think; Gretl could never keep a secret, her face always revealed she had something to hide and so we were forced to get it out of her. She was always smiling and she had the biggest and most gorgeous eyes and her eyelashes were to die for. Gretl was always up-to-date with the latest fashion; even her hair was cut short and very neatly styled.

Sitting next to Gretl was Heidi Wolf, they were good friends but Heidi didn't really like me all that much, I can't think why. Though Heidi is as tall, if not taller than me, she was a little younger, fourteen, I think. Heidi also had short hair but hers resembled a boys really. The thing about Heidi was her nose; it seemed to turn up sharply which gave her a sort of snooty look. Well, she was always snooty to me in any case.

There were five other boys: Boris the bullying Hitler Youth leader who you have already met and his best friend Ludolf Brenner. Ludolf was a little taller than Boris, and his hair seemed to stand up, adding another two inches to his height. But he was exceedingly thin—his legs were like poles and his arms seemed extra-long—I suppose he is lanky; no doubt he would fill out someday— If he is lucky that is? Both boys are the same age as me. Ludolf was also a Hitler Youth leader and together this pair could make big trouble. I had my work cut out. Their papas were officers stationed somewhere on the Eastern Front; not a nice place I'm told, exceedingly cold and the fighting is fierce.

The other three boys were: Otto, Gunter Roth and Victor Schulze. They were all ten years old and all quite nice for boys. Except for a few differences in height and weight, these three could pass for triplets; it was difficult to tell them apart. You know, come to think of it, we all appeared quite similar—quite boring really. The three young boys had settled at a table a little distance from Boris and Ludolf which showed me they were intelligent at least—for boys that is. Again, their papas were high ranking officers and I believe Gunter's mama also had an important job in Herr Hitler's personal staff.

That made eleven of us in total; eleven elite Aryan children who had been whisked off to a place of safety. Far away from the bombs that were expected to fall onto the little town we called home.

Of course we weren't alone—if only. No we had the evil Frau Leshnik to make sure we behaved and we also had the guards. There were two of them— Artur and Karl. They occupied the back seats of the carriage, smoking like chimneys. They were brothers, but you would never have guessed, they were nothing alike.

Artur was lanky, a little like Ludolf, but he had filled out a little. He stuttered when he was nervous, but he had kind eyes; though not true blue—more grey in colour. He was sort of handsome I guess. Karl was the shorter brother, but strong looking, and determined. He was also the oldest, perhaps twenty-two; Artur was younger, about nineteen.

Karl was not handsome. He had small dark eyes, like marbles, and they seemed to be sunk into his puffy cheeks; he also had quite a thick nose but only a short chin which gave him a peculiar look. His beard was wispy—barely a beard and such a funny colour, a mix of yellow and ginger.

Karl had a mean streak which also set the brothers apart; I didn't like him from the start. Both brothers had short, cropped hair, Artur's was dark and Karl's that funny yellow. They both wore a very plain uniform; there was nothing special about it, no shiny buttons nor lapels. I suppose the word to describe their uniforms is drab! Yes that's it, drab, and it was a grey colour held together with a black belt. Their uniforms were finished off with a little grey cap and a rifle, all standard issue. The pair sat quietly, rarely speaking to each other. Artur, like me, spent most of his time staring out of the window, whilst Karl simply glared at us.

Anyway, I digress! I can see it as if it was yesterday. Frau Leshnik was sitting quietly with her eyes closed at one end of the carriage and the guards were as far away from her as they could get. I remember wondering what the old bat was thinking.

She, too, puffed on a cigarette, choking us all; the whole carriage filling with vile smoke from both ends. I don't know why people smoke; it smells really bad. I had to open up all the windows. Surely smoking can't be good for you.

So what happened to start all our troubles? Let me think. That's it, Boris and Ludolf of course!

I noticed the crafty pair staring at the guards, they kept whispering and laughing, they were definitely planning something. I watched as Boris nudged Ludolf and the whole thing kicked off. Ludolf, like a good soldier, obeying orders, left his seat and casually approached the guards. Meanwhile, I switched seats and went to sit with Gretl, Heidi and Leni; they were nearer to the guards and I needed to know what was up.

"You two guards—give us cigarettes," Ludolf addressed the guards with authority and determination and also with a look of contempt and disgust on his usually handsome face.

So that's what those two were after—cigarettes! "Don't give them cigarettes, Artur," I whispered to myself, willing the guard to refuse the request. "This place stinks bad enough already, we can barely breathe."

I needn't have worried. Karl was clearly displeased with how he had been spoken to and there was no way, in a million years, he was going to hand over cigarettes now. He scowled at Ludolf and stepped towards him, his chest inflated to make himself bigger and his eyes nothing but slits. His attempt to intimidate Ludolf was almost comical as Ludolf stood almost a foot taller. Karl didn't seem to notice and with one finger, he prodded Ludolf in the middle of his chest. "Go away little boy before you get yourself into trouble. Frau Leshnik is watching you and she is eager to use her cane." Karl leaned close into Ludolf's face and sniggered.

The whole carriage fell silent. The boys listening excitedly and the girls, bewildered. Ludolf hesitated for a second before making his demands. "Leshnik is nothing to me. Do you know who I am? Give me cigarettes, I command you."

"You are not in a position to make demands or give commands little boy. For your information, I do not know who you are nor do I care who you are. What I do know is that you are a little spoilt brat. You are all little spoilt brats." As the guard's voice rose, the children watched, unable to take their eyes off the expected commotion. Frau Leshnik also pricked up her ears, I knew this, but still she kept her eyes closed.

Karl noticed the attention and he was encouraged. "You are sent into hiding whilst every other German kid has to stay at home to face the bombs. You are spoilt and cowardly." He sniggered again and took a deep long puff at his cigarette before blowing the awful smoke directly into Ludolf's face.

Ludolf gritted his teeth and scrunched up his eyes, he was clearly infuriated and surprised. Spittle sprayed from his mouth as he screamed his words. "How dare you talk to me like that—YOU scum!" Then instantly, he realised he was shouting, surely the Frau would be on them in an instant—but no, she remained asleep—pah!

Never, before, had Ludolf been spoken to in such a manner. The nerve of it! None of us could believe it either, from one so low in society. Ludolf was desperate to address this insult, and rightly so, but I couldn't help thinking he deserved it, at least a little. He had been knocked cleanly off his stride and he was also aware that we were all watching what he would do next—would he back down?

Karl was cautious and careful, devious I suppose. He proved to be very talented at goading Ludolf and he took great care not to alert Frau Leshnik. The guard was proving to be more than a match for poor old Ludolf and he knew it. Boris, too, had been surprised by the guard's boldness and Karl had not yet finished. "You have the nerve to call me scum. You, who have everything at your fingertips, you who have everything but give nothing back in return—you and your parents alike." He glanced around, his eyes boring into us. "Always keen to give out your orders aren't you—all of you. You send us into battle, not caring what happens to us, whilst you just hide and watch from a safe distance. You have always done this, your kind—you true Aryans." He smiled. It was not a nice smile. Then addressing Ludolf, the guard added, "Shove off, little coward, go and hide under a table. Leave the fighting to the likes of us, to me and my little brother. One day we will be dead, killed for the likes of you…TRUE ARYANS!"

Ludolf was not beaten that easily. He was angry now. "That's a laugh!" the tall boy had to stoop to face up to Karl, "A little rat like you has never seen combat. All you are good for is guarding these little girls. And you are doing a poor job at that."

"That's correct. At last, we agree Aryan," Karl growled and prodded Ludolf in the chest a second time. "We guard the little girls and the cowardly little boys—just like you."

These words clearly affected Ludolf whose hesitation revealed he was losing his nerve. The longer he took to respond, the bolder Karl became. Ludolf glanced at Boris and wondered if he could help; only a little help was needed to turn things around, since the guard could not face them together—surely!

You know, the awkward Boris offered no help at all. Instead, he gestured with a thrust of his hand for Ludolf to continue his pursuit for cigarettes. Dismayed, Ludolf turned back to face Karl. He was a little less confident this time, and all the other kids were moving closer to get a better view. Ludolf was determined to redeem himself. He could not lose face. After all, the younger boys looked up to him. He didn't know it, but they were counting on him; he represented protection, an unexpected father figure—him and Boris alike. At that time, no one realised how important this would be.

Ludolf was ready to make his move, but before he could utter a word Artur interrupted.

"G-g-go away. Sh-she is watching," Artur warned. It did not achieve the results he had desired. Instead, his brother Karl scowled at him, and both the bullies, first, looked at each other with a mischievous smile and then fell into fits of laughter. Artur had unwittingly provided the rebuke they had badly needed, a chance to even the score with Karl. Ludolf had been proving weak and now Artur's weakness had been revealed, a simple speech impediment, nothing more than a stutter was the poor guard's only fault, and it would be the downfall of Karl.

As expected, Boris seized this newly discovered advantage immediately and began to mock Artur's stutter. "G-g-g-g-go a-a-way. Sh-sh-she is watching," Boris said, his face beaming, he had more than evened the score; he was now in charge of the situation. The other kids were giggling and pointing, egging Boris on.

It was Karl's move. He was still scowling. Artur's face flushed red. He turned away quickly to hide his embarrassment, not only from the bullies, but from his own brother who he knew would be fuming right now. This was not a new problem for Artur, he had put up with it for years. His stutter had caused him untold misery, not just from the kids at school, but from Karl; his own brother had been the biggest bully of all. Unable to bear the taunting his younger brother experienced on a daily basis, Karl took it as a personal insult and had grown to hate his brother's impediment as if it was his own; this had caused much resentment between the pair and resulted in Karl dominating his younger brother to such an extent that Artur no longer did anything for himself without first consulting his older brother.

"Why you little spoilt—"

"Sh—shush, Karl, l-leave it," Artur wisely advised.

"Yes, sh-shush, Karl," Ludolf had found renewed courage and exaggerated the words much to Boris' amusement. They both laughed again louder than before. The children echoed them and craned their necks to see.

Karl was fuming. I swear I could see steam coming from his ears. In an instant of bad temper, he turned on his brother, "I told you, Artur, keep your mouth shut. Talk to no one but me."

"Yes, Ar-Ar, Artur k-keep your mouth, sh-sh-shut," Boris jeered.

"Stop it now, Boris. Stop it. Ludolf, that's not funny." I couldn't help myself. Poor Artur, he was so upset. I simply had to intervene.

"Shut it, Mona—keep out," Ludolf growled at me. I scowled in return.

It was Boris' turn to flush red; I knew he felt awkward. A feeling he couldn't fully understand, or wanted to admit to, but I knew the reason why. He wanted to tease the guards. He wanted cigarettes. But he did not want to offend me. I had discovered HIS weakness and despite the situation, it made me smile.

"No Ludolf," Boris warned. "Mona's right. And don't talk to her like that. She is in my Youth Group." Ludolf screwed up his face, clearly bewildered, his face a picture to behold. How difficult was it not to laugh at him, but somehow I managed to keep quiet. Boris had stepped in to protect me yet again. I could not remove the smile from my face. Gretl and Heidi joined me and poor Boris turned redder. I had a power over him—definitely.

Gretl nudged me knowingly. I gave her a discreet wink then turned to watch the guards. Karl was angry. He was after blood. Artur smiled though, showing his appreciation. I don't think he cared two hoots about the taunting—if only his silly brother could follow his example, perhaps his life would be a little less stressful. Despite being the younger brother, Artur was handling the situation much better than Karl, he was obviously more mature.

Meanwhile, Karl was so caught up in the trouble; there was no turning back for him. Boys and men—they're all the same! I watched Karl closely; it was clear to me he would not be beaten so easily.

Suddenly, Frau Leshnik released an annoying cough to announce she was still present and probably aware of everything that had happened so far. This helped ease the situation a little, forcing everyone back to their seats. Boris and Ludolf started whispering immediately; planning for the next little skirmish no doubt. Frau Leshnik had finally opened her wrinkled eyes and simply glared at us, I say us as she seemed to see every last one of us all at once, and every head turned away from her stare simultaneously. She sat back and lit a cigarette, then released a huge puff of smoke into the air—calm and in control.

My hatred for this despicable woman doubled in an instant. Personally, I think she would have been happier if a fight had broken out. Yes, she would have liked that. I was beginning to understand her; how she worked. She was disappointed on this occasion, there was no fight. But the peace was not to last.

Meanwhile, the train sped on. Mile after endless mile of beautiful scenery passed by the window; noticed by me only as it happens. I spent more of my time just gazing out, allowing my mind to wander into the clouds, my trance broken only by the occasional question that Gretl needed answering. It became obvious that she was also doing a lot of thinking.

"Where are we going?" she asked.

"No idea."

"Does Boris fancy me?"

"No idea," I lied.

"Does Ludolf fancy Heidi?" Her big eyes lit up and her smile was naughty and knowing.

"No thank you!" Heidi pulled a face.

"Does he fancy me?"

You get what I had to put up with!

Chapter 5
Pride

About an hour later I found my attention drifting out of the window again, watching as the countryside rolled by. There was so much of it, and it was both beautiful and interesting to see; I didn't think I would ever get bored with it. The train went over huge iron bridges, some of which were quite high and a little scary; we travelled through dark tunnels, which was quite funny as we couldn't get the carriage lamps to light in the dark, the little kids screamed and the silly boys made ghost noises, which, come to think of it sounded more like owls!

Every now and then Klaus or Magda pulled at my sleeve so that I could admire their drawings. Little Leni Koch had joined them and between fastening her hair grips, I had to admire her creations also. Our table was getting crowded, either one of them should move or I would have to.

Gretl had found a more peaceful table and had somehow fallen to sleep. Her head down on the table, she had endeavoured to make herself comfortable by resting it on her folded arms. I smiled as I noticed her dribbling onto her sleeve— big baby, I couldn't wait to tell her. Heidi was also sleeping, probably dreaming about Ludolf; I knew she liked him, despite her protests. Most of the other kids were in dreamland too; it must have been the rhythm of the train on the tracks. Frau Leshnik sat quietly, staring into space; she was probably working out horrid things to do to us. Whilst the two guards continued to smoke as they played cards. Something about this made me turn to Boris and Ludolf. I shook my head—it was plain to see they were hatching out their plans to cause mischief.

When I close my eyes, I remember that journey as if it was yesterday; my head leaning against the window, taking it all in. Field after field, forest after forest, little village after little village go by; rivers, lakes, hills and valleys, without end; our great Fatherland is immense you know. I don't really know why we call it Fatherland; it is just an expression we Aryans use. It is a place for only

48

perfect people, strong and proud all of us. Oh, here I go again, my mind wandering off the story. What a load of dribble fills our Aryan heads.

I saw lots of things as I watched, almost daydreaming through that window. Beautiful fields packed with different crops; green fields full of cabbages, potatoes and, I guessed—sprouts—yuk; fields of wheat and corn, not yet grown, soon to turn gold; fields of yellow flowers—not sure what that was; and some pastures full of sheep, cows, horses and goats, lazily chewing the grass, with every now and then a field left fallow, full to the brim with bright red poppies and other spring flowers—they were my favourites. These fields, simply left to go wild, were dotted with beehives, and though I couldn't see them, I knew there were millions of bees busying themselves on every flower, collecting the precious pollen, then returning to the hive to make their delicious honey—yummy, how my mouth waters just thinking about it.

Huge forests came into view, there was little else to see then, except trees and maybe the odd hawk that circled above them, they seemed to go on forever. Eventually though, the forests thinned out to be replaced with wide open spaces and scattered farmsteads. There were settlements of all sizes, though all small compared to even our little town, though some were large enough to have their own church with a steeple or a dome. Then I saw a village that had a medieval castle looking down on it from above a cliff—how exciting! Unfortunately, after that, there was little change in the scenery as I watched.

I eventually grew bored of it and thought about doing something else for a while. I attempted colouring with the little ones until they started napping too. I tried to sleep but couldn't drop off somehow. So I returned to my gazing.

But as the scenery past my window, strange things began to occur which reignited my interest. Little things at first, isolated incidents, nothing more; soon though, they became more numerous. I didn't know it at the time, but these strange things were a warning of things to come. If you allow, I'll try to recollect what I saw as best as I can.

What's that? I thought. Oh, it's just a deer running past, probably chased by hunters. Run little deer, jump the hedges; get away quickly. And what's that? Why, it's a man, he's carrying a child. He'll never catch the deer—silly man. Oh and there's a woman, she's lying in the field and is that a child by her side. How odd, just lying there—motionless!

More fields pass by, full of young turnips and cabbages, another poppy field full of bees, then more wheat and corn and then…Wait! Here are more people running, a whole group of them. What are they running from, I wonder? I can smell smoke, is there a fire? Where is it? Oh there it is, over there, a little fire burning. I'll be able to see a little better as the train nears.

You know something: that's not a little fire, it's a big fire; a whole house ablaze! Oh, I hope there's no one inside. How strange, there's another fire in the distance, and wait, behind that there is a third. That's strange don't you think? What's going on? There are lots more people running. Are they going to fetch water? They have no buckets!

It's okay, there are soldiers there. Lots of them! Possibly a whole regiment of them have arrived. But wait. They have their rifles out; they're no use for fighting fires. Bang!

"Oh…Dear!"

Bang—Bang!

"What's that noise, Mona, what are you looking at?"

I remember Klaus waking, how sleepy he was. I pulled him tight towards me, though I couldn't think why. "Soldiers, Klaus," I said as anxiety tightened my chest. I had an urge to stop my brother from seeing the activities outside but it was too late.

"What are they doing, Mona, those men lining up? They have guns. Look they are pointing them at those…"

"Oh dear—quick, Klaus don't look." Bang—bang—bang—bang. I was just in time to turn my brother's head, but I saw what happened in the corner of my eye. It was awful. What a shock to see. Oh how sad! They didn't look like it, but they must have been enemies! I wondered why they were here—in the middle of our lovely countryside.

"Have they been shot, Mona?"

"I believe so Klaus. Don't worry little Bro. It's over now." I needed to reassure my brother. I had no idea how this had affected him. I simply wasn't prepared for such a thing. I was too late—again.

"Quick, Boris, come here. You're missing it, there's shooting." I remember how Ludolf became excited with the shooting. That's boys for you.

"What is it, Ludy?" Boris rushed over, his face beaming with excitement—boys!

"They're clearing them out, Communists probably."

"Or worse—stinking Jews!" I remember it was Karl who said that and how it annoyed me.

"Who asked you to butt-in, Karl? Speak when you are spoken to, you little train guard."

That's it, Boris, you tell him. That thought really amazed me at the time. I didn't like Karl, but I would never urge Boris to be horrid.

"Why, you little spoilt…"

"I'm not that little," Boris replied. "I'm big enough to beat you," he said, as he stepped up close to Karl. Boris was in fact taller than Karl, almost a head higher. As he faced the guard he had to glance down and Karl craned his neck to look up. As the pair sized each other up, Boris increased his advantage by pushing out his chest to make himself even bigger. With clenched fists and eyes like slits, he scowled down at Karl, and grinned. "I am champion boxer for my age and weight in my home district youth group. I think you are probably the same weight as I am Karl—though you must be a foot shorter." The contempt for the guard shone from Boris' handsome face. "Well," he demanded. "What are you waiting for? Hit me Karl—if you can reach."

"Don't d-d-do it, Karl," Artur warned. "Frau Leshnik's watching."

"No she's not," Karl replied angrily. "Look she's sleeping again. Useless old witch."

"N-No, Karl," Artur whispered, "I am convinced she is watching; she is a very crafty woman. I know she is spying on us, taking it all in. She will report us."

"I don't care Artur. This little brat has insulted us. He has got it coming to him. I must teach him a lesson."

Boris laughed out loud. He too, was no longer concerned with the Frau. "Listen to your pathetic brother Karl. You're not big enough to teach lessons you little man. You will get hurt I promise you," Boris threatened, and without warning grabbed Karl's left arm and with one clever movement twisted it up the poor guard's back. Karl flushed red, dropping his rifle to the floor. Artur, in panic, quickly retrieved the rifle and struggled to push past his brother in an attempt to free him from Boris' grasp. But there was no room to manoeuvre and Karl remained a prisoner, and in pain. Boris had Karl in a very secure grasp; it would take someone stronger than Artur to prise him off his brother. "You are lucky I didn't punch you little man. I am not only a very good boxer; it so happens I am also an excellent wrestler. NOW give us cigarettes or I break your arm!"

Boris delivered his demand with an authority that could not be refused. I couldn't help feeling impressed. I didn't show it instantly, it would make his head even bigger than it already was. And I also wanted to spare Karl's feelings; after all, his pride was already in tatters. With one last effort, he attempted to free himself, but it was no use. Boris had revealed a secret strength of both the physical and mental kind. He didn't flinch, he was unafraid, he was the bravest I've ever seen him. I knew he was in the wrong of course, but my admiration for him had grown to the point that I could no longer hide it. I found myself staring at this impressive boy. He caught my eye and began to blush. I smiled, if only he could be brave enough to face me!

Meanwhile, Artur glanced at Frau Leshnik who hadn't even opened her eyes. I'm not sure if he wanted her to interfere or not, either way would be bad for the guards. I also felt the old woman was faking sleep; there was too much commotion, both inside the carriage and out. She should be here, dealing with this situation. Instead she was ignoring everything, shirking from her responsibilities; what a frustrating old hag she was. I promised myself that I would report her to my papa, I would record all her actions from now on—I would show her.

At last, Karl buckled; the pain in his arm was too great. "Okay!" he conceded. "Give him the cigarettes, Arty."

Artur sighed and reluctantly tossed the packet of cigarettes to Ludolf Brenner who demanded matches. Then, at last, Boris released Karl with a forceful push. Karl fell onto a seat and groaned. "Know your place, little guard," Boris insisted. "Next time I won't be so kind." Boris then returned to Ludolf, a huge grin on his face. Together they lit cigarettes and the carriage started to fill with vile smoke. Boris turned and caught my eye. I scowled at him, letting him know I was annoyed with him which made him lower his head. He didn't see me smile.

The commotion settled and everyone was now fully awake. Gunter produced some sandwiches—well, it must have been way past dinner time. The sandwiches, as expected, were triangular with the crusts cut off and I was instantly reminded of Mama. In seconds, the other kids began rifling through their satchels and soon an assortment of food was being unwrapped, including fruit, and buns and more sweets than was good for us. Klaus produced a package wrapped in brown paper and soon we were tucking into a feast. All troubles had been forgotten—for now.

With the carriage stinking of cigarettes and sausage, I returned to the view outside. Now well fed the younger children could not resist the mesmerising noise and motion of the train and were soon fast asleep. I was afraid to look outside. I could not shake the awful feeling that occupied my head and tormented me so. As far as I was concerned, the sooner we reached our destination the better.

There was also an uncomfortable feeling in the carriage too, the silence seemed to emphasise it. I can picture Karl's face now, fuming with anger and resentment. Boris had certainly not heard the last of this guard; he had made an enemy for sure. At that time, I could never have imagined the consequences of that little and insignificant brawl over cigarettes.

I aimed to sleep but it was useless, I could not settle. So I did my best to ignore my worries and instead I turned my attention outside. I dreaded to think what I would see, but there was little else to do now. Another huge forest dominated the view which went on for miles and miles, nothing but trees—a welcome sight. Then the forest dwindled as the others had done to a few sparse trees before a cluster of small farms came into sight, far off they were at first before some nearer ones appeared in view. Most of these seemed quite peaceful to be honest, but others were busy, the activity catching my eye and renewing the fears that I had tucked away inside.

As before, I saw lots of people scurrying about, running away in all directions. Something was going on, something awful, and no matter how hard I strove to ignore the commotion, I was glued to the window, compelled to watch, to witness these…these crazy things that were happening. I remember a crowd of people crouching in the undergrowth down beside the rail track. It was obvious they were hiding, but why? The train thundered past and they were forgotten as other strange goings-on took their place.

Soldiers appeared; lots and lots of soldiers, all with rifles. They had prisoners with them; men, women and children that resembled farmers and ordinary country folk. Then, more burning; houses, barns, schools and synagogues; all raging fires with huge flames and smoke billowing everywhere. The trees reappeared and blocked my view, allowing me time to think, to arrange my thoughts. The train veered away, entering yet another forest and now there was nothing but trees. It was all dark. I leaned closer to the window, to try to see inside the gloom, but all I could see was shadows between the trees; and above them, even the sky was growing dark with thick clouds of smoke.

For ages, the trees dominated my view, then as sudden as we had entered this great forest, we left it behind us. I hardly dared to look and as expected, there they were; the runners, the chasers, the captured and the damned.

I was thoroughly bewildered at what I was seeing. Were these people enemies? Had we left Germany and entered a war zone? Was this war?

I could see it all clearly now, it was all around us, on both sides of the train. Boris and the boys were excited, craning their necks to see and pointing at various horrors unfolding in front of their eyes. I was frightened. I was stunned. There was no denying what was going on outside. I did not know if it was a good thing or a bad thing. Whatever it was, it was unsettling.

As the train manoeuvred around a huge bend I could see it all. I could see how it ended…it was not nice. Thankfully the boys did not see, they were looking out the other side. I could not bear more of their excitement—it was all fun to them—it was wrong.

I saw, to my horror, lines of people, of all ages, marching in single file between the trees. There were mamas and papas carrying children and old people being pulled in carts, they were heading deeper into the woods. They were being herded together; rounded up, like sheep. I saw soldiers with guns and big dogs barking and snapping, pulling at their leashes to get to the people, they were everywhere; no one could possibly escape them.

The prisoners walked with their heads down, holding hands; though I couldn't see their faces, I knew they were sad. I saw this all in a few minutes as our train sped past. I didn't want to look then. But I am my own worst enemy, I just had to, I must do it, I must see.

The train turned away once more, following the rails around the wood and heading for the mountains. I still had time to scan the wood as we moved away. There were lots of people now, big crowds gathering. The soldiers were shouting orders and the dogs kept barking and snapping. The people were clearly miserable and frightened, most held their heads down and some covered their eyes. And I wasn't sure but I could have sworn they were removing their clothes. How strange!

Chapter 6
The Promise

Now we were heading towards a line of snow peaked mountains, the dense forests left far behind. The sun was shining but to look at the place, spring had not yet come here, from inside our warm carriage, it seemed cold outside. But more importantly, it was calm and…and peaceful. The beauty of this place could only be admired and taking it all in left little time to worry; my heartbeat settled and I finally began to relax. Outside there were no strange sights to see, no sad people, no soldiers, no fires nor guns. It all appeared so normal, what I would give to go back there, to go back in time. I would open the carriage door and…and jump right off the train.

It wasn't so peaceful inside. Klaus and Magda had joined forces with little Leni Koch and all three had come to pester me. They were so excited by the mountains, their imaginations going wild, and they had so many questions: Can we go tobogganing? They're so big! Will we fall off?

"No you silly things, we will not fall off." How they made me laugh. The upsetting scenes I had witnessed drifted further from my mind as I allowed myself to enjoy the company of the three children. Together we peered for a long time in wonder and amazement at the beautiful mountain scenery we were heading for. The questions came thick and fast as the little ones picked out interesting details as we approached the slopes.

Klaus pointed to a high path that snaked between the peaks and we were amazed to see a solitary building, probably a barn, perched up high. Surely people could not live on such steep slopes; even I began to think they must surely fall off. It all looked so huge to us, and so clean. The snow was so white and it covered everything like a blanket. How we wished we could jump in it, just feel it, ice cold, in our hands; or lie on our backs in it and make snow angels. The excitement had spread throughout the carriage; the boys wanted to throw snowballs of course, and the girls preferred to build snowmen. It didn't matter really. We just wanted the chance to get out there and jump all over the smooth white blanket, and simply—spoil it!

The train moved so close to one mountain that we could not see the top from our window, and trees began to dominate again—blasted things. Pine trees this time, they began to rise up the side of the great peaks. They were everywhere, all covered in deep white snow. Even the trees nearest to the rail track were covered in it, the snow falling from the branches as the trees swayed by the motion of the train.

There were lakes too, still frozen in places that resembled glass mirrors reflecting the mountains; I had never seen anything so beautiful. It reminded us of when we visited Herr Hitler in his mountain lodge, my little brother actually thought we were going to visit Herr Hitler again and started bragging, but I shushed him—we were not so important, and what would our leader do with so many kids running around his peaceful home. It would surely drive him mad and he needs time to think and make his plans.

As I gazed out, I became aware of the other kids, they were all so happy, their excitement growing, they were overjoyed. Snow has a way of doing that to a child, first when it starts to fall and then when it begins to settle. Later though, when your hands are so cold they hurt, that's the time when you wished you'd left it alone.

Klaus had changed his mind; he was now going to build the biggest snowman and Magda was going to build an igloo no less. Boris and Ludolf had forgotten their grown-up cigarettes and were threatening the biggest snowball fight ever. We all laughed and cheered. Boris said he was going to get me in particular— that he had unfinished business! I asked him if it was me, or Fleur he needed to deal with. He retreated yet again with a red face—what a wimp!

But then, in a crazy weird twist of fortune, our happy thoughts came to an abrupt end. It was the train, as it negotiated yet another tree lined bend it suddenly slowed down, this wasn't unusual, but we all became aware that it was turning away from the mountains and the snow.

Instantly, the air was thick with protests and the younger ones became very upset, nevertheless, the train travelled further away from the wonderful mountains. The snow-covered trees dwindled in number and soon the snow disappeared altogether to be replaced by the most ugly and dirty factories we had ever seen. Tall spires appeared next and these in turn, replaced by large buildings, all made from mud-coloured sandstone. We were approaching a town and from what we could see, it was very dismal and boring.

I don't know who was the most disappointed, the small girls or the big boys. Klaus was putting on his best sulking face. I assured him that we were probably stopping to refuel—that's all. Why would they move us from our little village to this awful place, surely it is a bigger target for the aeroplanes to drop their bombs.

By now, the brakes were screeching, a sound that grated through my head as the train quickly slowed down. The carriage went dark as it entered one of five magnificent steel archways, each with its own set of railway tracks running through it. The station was massive, suggesting this was a big town or even a city. The platforms appeared, protruding quite a distance out of the arches. I could see they were busy, just before the entire view from the window was blocked with steam and smoke. We all lurched forward as the wheels locked for the final time. My heart began to beat faster again and I took a moment to compose myself and take a few deep breaths, whilst willing my bad feelings to go away. I knew I was right, we needed fuel, that's all; no doubt we'd be heading back to the glorious mountains soon enough.

The carriage went dull as we entered the arches and it became clear that the place was bigger than anything we had ever seen. Way above us, huge iron girders criss-crossed each other to hold up the vast roof, fastened together with large bolts; the girders in turn supported by massive ornate posts, also made of iron and impossibly long, reaching to the sky. Everything had been carefully painted in vibrant colours that should never go together, yellows against greens, blues against reds and everything framed by white. Only the platforms themselves were left uncovered by paint, yet even they were clean, pristine, with neat painted edges—in white.

The kids grew excited; I have no idea what for. Again, the carriage became a riot of questions and petty quarrelling as they pushed to be the first to get off the carriage. Then an unpleasant voice filled the air.

"Children, children," Frau Leshnik had suddenly woken up. How she had kept so quiet for the entire journey escaped me, the woman is sub-human. She clapped her hands, demanding attention. Everyone obeyed and fell silent according to rule number one. She glared at us for an instant, then, satisfied she said in her ghastly voice, "We are just stopping for fuel and water. We will soon be on our way again." Every last one of us listened patiently until the irritating woman stopped talking, even then, we remained motionless and quiet—just in case.

Klaus tugged at my dress; he was itching to ask me a question. I shushed him, the slightest of shushes was enough to produce an annoyed peek from Frau Leshnik. Knowing what Klaus wanted to know I raised my hand to ask a question: contrary to rule number two—no questions. Frau Leshnik ignored me. I kept my hand in the air, inviting her anger—the awkward woman wasn't biting. Boris, and surprisingly, Otto, smiled openly at me with clear admiration on their faces, which made Gretl giggle. Frau Leshnik was alerted and it was my turn to smile as Gretl scowled at me for getting her in trouble—even though I had done nothing.

"You seem eager to break my rules, Mona, but I will not let you," the Frau growled. "Instead I will answer two of your impending questions," she added and I cringed. Gretl almost giggled again. "No, we will not be travelling for much longer. Perhaps an hour only before we reach our destination. And yes, we are heading for the mountains. You will be safe there. Now, everyone, return to your seats AND be quiet. We are not leaving the carriage."

Her words caused uproar as every single one of us was desperate to get off the train; I think that included the two guards who had already positioned themselves at the door. Little Leni, who had huddled up close to Gretl, secretly nudged her bigger friend prompting Gretl to raise her hand; a further attempt to break rule number two. We were joining forces. I secretly smiled. Gretl caught my eye and in an effort to stop laughing out loud she forced herself to cough. This worked well and saved my naughty friend from big trouble.

However, Frau Leshnik sighed before giving the poor girl one of her nasty looks, known to have turned many others to stone and radiating both disappointment and disapproval. "What is it, Gretl?" she demanded whilst shaking her head in exasperation. With Frau Leshnik occupied, I watched, amused, as the two guards slipped out of the carriage.

"Please, Frau Leshnik, Leni needs the toilet. I wouldn't ask, only I think she is desperate." Despite the carriage being so luxurious, there was nowhere to go to relieve yourself, well, not for the girls. The boys had been visiting the gap between our carriage and the next, which was full of war things, and they had been peeing onto the rail tracks. It wasn't such a good idea, as every one of them returned with wet pants. They didn't care of course—boys will be boys. But us poor girls had been crossing our legs for the whole journey, telling each other that we would soon reach our destination. We simply couldn't last any longer without visiting a toilet.

At the unexpected request, well, not so unexpected for anyone who had an ounce of thought for others inside them, which obviously didn't include the Frau who now made such a drama and began huffing and puffing at the inconvenience she now faced. Regardless, and as if some miracle had befallen us, the horrid old woman surprisingly relented and agreed to Gretl's request. She wasn't being kind in any way though, you see, even she had to answer to the call of nature sometimes, proving, at least, that she was human after all. "Alright, I could do with fresh air." She snapped her fingers. "Line up. Quickly now," she bawled and instantly the children left their seats, pushing and jostling each other; Boris and Ludolf gaining pole positions to be first off the train—as expected.

"Now, you've got ten minutes only, then back on the train. I would not want to lose any of you. Not yet anyway," Frau Leshnik added with a wry smile as she made her way to the door brushing Boris and Ludolf aside with that awful cane of hers, and with strength she shouldn't possess. The Frau opened the door. "Follow me," she ordered and stepped carefully off the train. We followed in an orderly fashion, trying hard not to push in front of her. When we reached the public convenience, the Frau directed the boys to their toilet; they raced off pushing through the door, poor Klaus in last place.

It felt good to stretch our legs, some of us running on the spot or bending at the waist, this is what Hitler Youth does for you, it made me feel proud. Then Frau Leshnik upset us again, well at least the girls, by ordering us to wait until she had finished in the ladies' room, she did not want any messy children anywhere near the toilet whilst she was inside, thank you very much. Little Leni crossed her legs some more.

I took the opportunity to explore. The station was a busy place. Our platform was full of people heading who knew where. Heavy suitcases rested by their sides as they chatted in twos, threes and small groups; mixed men and women, most of them soldiers or other war officials and businessmen. I caught the eye of an elegant lady, standing a little away from all the others; she puffed at a cigarette and smiled at me. Her hair was in the same style as Gretl's and her hat was of the latest fashion, decorated with a ribbon and a small colourful feather, it was simply beautiful, Gretl would love it. I returned the lady's smile and wondered where she was going. Many soldiers had left our train to stretch their legs also, I wasn't sure if the elegant lady was pleased or put out with the attention she now received.

The whole place was heaving. It was difficult to find a place out of the way; there were porters everywhere, pushing heavy sack barrows and generally annoying everyone; stationmasters shouting orders and train guards blowing loud ear-piercing whistles. Frau Leshnik was still in the toilet—so much for being back on the train in ten minutes. My curiosity got the best of me and I wandered to the edge of the platform to see what was happening at the next one. There were five in all, one for each set of tracks. Ours was platform two. Only one of them was behind ours, this was platform one of course. It was just as busy, with people climbing onto a recently arrived train. I wondered where they were going; it was heading the way we had come; did they not know about the bombs also heading that way.

In front of me were the other three platforms. The nearest of these, platform three was deserted of people, it was eerie quiet compared to our platform. It was full of wooden boxes in various sizes all stacked in neat but high piles, there was also all sorts of machinery, painted green and grey and there were huge wooden barrels of who knows what and crates of vegetables and clothing. There was everything here and it was all, obviously, waiting to be loaded onto an expected train; destined for the war somewhere or other, maybe east to Russia or west to the conquered lands there—France perhaps; what a wonderful place. How I wished I could go there and see the magnificent sights; the Eiffel Tower, the Louvre with all its treasures, the splendid Arc de Triomphe and not forgetting the beautiful Notre Dame Cathedral.

I've wandered again haven't I? Where was I—Oh yes. The next platform along was completely deserted except for one man busy sweeping it clean, a train must have just left; I wondered if they were heading for the mountains or the bombs. The last platform, platform five was quite interesting, probably the most interesting of all.

There was a train, obviously for cargo. It had those wooden box type wagons, the type used to transport goods or animals. They were quite big, bigger than any I'd seen before. They were old and dirty and battered, some had been hastily repaired with boards nailed here and there and most of them were a green colour, though the paint was flaking. I counted twenty of them, before the train trailed off around a bend and out of view.

The wagons had slotted windows and there were things hanging or sticking out of them. I stood on tiptoe and craned my neck to see over the blasted boxes that were stacked up on platform three.

I couldn't believe what I saw, I was absolutely astonished. The things sticking out of the slotted windows were arms, human arms! I could make out the hands now, clearly enough. Were they soldiers? Surely, our great army wasn't transported in this appalling manner. Maybe they were prisoners of war. Hmm, I didn't like the thought of our prisoners being treated like that either, but you know, as Papa said, these were hard times; this is war and in these terrible times, one has to act in ways that are not normal to them, or in ways deemed indecent; unfortunately in times of war one has to compromise his values.

As you know, I didn't always agree with Papa and I had my doubts about this. But it can't be denied that times of war are hard and we have to make changes and maybe do things we are not comfortable with. I had begun to learn this lesson; at this stage of our journey, I was blissfully unaware how important this lesson would become.

Perhaps it's not so bad for the prisoners, I remember saying to myself—I wasn't convinced; it did not look comfortable dangling your arms out of those windows like that. So why would you do it if conditions inside were better. There were many guards also, some sitting on top of the wagons; that must be worse than being inside when the train is moving. Just how dangerous are these prisoners to warrant so many guards?

There were other soldiers on the platform. They seemed to offer little or no help at all to the prisoners who were obviously wanting for something. I couldn't hear them of course, their platform was too far away from mine, but I recognised the arm movements—definitely asking for something—begging! Then, as I watched, I saw something I didn't like. I remember thinking what's he doing, the man with the officer's hat—the captain? He's just handing out something to the prisoners perhaps? But no, unfortunately he wasn't doing anything nice; he was in fact hitting the hands really hard with a stick.

Now I knew prisoners needed disciplining to keep them under control, I wasn't that naïve, but surely there was no need to do that, it wasn't as if they were doing any harm, after all they were locked in a cattle wagon. How cruel, I thought. I would like to speak to that captain. I had some choice words for him. I had heard from Papa what our enemies were saying about us. His type had given our great nation a bad name.

I was then, even more surprised to see our own guards, Karl and Artur on platform five; what were they doing there? I see it still. Simply thinking about it gives me goose bumps. Let me recall. First Karl walked over to the nasty captain with the stick, but Artur was frantically pulling Karl back…hmmm. You know, I first thought Karl was going to try to stop the nasty man beating the prisoners, I just knew he was a decent soldier—deep down. "Go on Karl, you tell him," I whispered under my breath.

Then I saw Karl and Artur salute the officer who now appeared to be shouting at them. I didn't like this man at all; from a distance he was all horrid and aggressive for no apparent reason. I watched as Karl began pointing to our platform; he was pointing to us. There was something urgent about his actions. My anxiety flooded back harder than ever, and for good reason. The sight of Karl pointing to me was to give me nightmares to this day, that was the precise point my fears came true.

Mistakenly, I thought perhaps he was explaining what we were doing here, reporting in on our progress or something like that. How ridiculous I was to think such a thing. Papa always said I was too soft; always thinking the best of people and that my head was full of these silly ideas, I would have to learn the hard way, he'd say. He certainly got that right!

What happened next made me uncomfortable. I watched the captain thrashing his stick and ordering his men to line up. Karl pushed his younger brother who stepped away with his head in his hands whilst the guards lined up in double quick time and then, all at once, after a quick command from their mean captain, they rushed towards the overpass. The captain had ordered them over the bridge towards our platform, their heavy boots made such a racket as they approached.

A shudder spread through my body, and the feeling was back, like something awful was going to happen; it was a pain in my chest like something had stuck in my gullet, you've had that feeling, like something is lodged tight in your chest, when you have eaten too fast! I swear at that moment a whole apple was choking me. I had an urge to run which instantly made me feel guilty, Klaus was not with me, he was still in the toilet; this had all happened so fast—I could never leave him.

Now I could hear the nasty captain shouting orders at his men. There was no need for that. Those Poor men! How awful, I thought, to have such a horrid commander. How absurd I was to think these things. It was all in my head wasn't it, these thoughts of doom and gloom. You see, we were not in trouble. It was just my imagination—that's all.

It seemed mere seconds before they arrived on our platform; our glorious soldiers. I will never forget the sound of their heavy boots coming down the steps of the overpass. Now my urge to run had gone altogether—I was frozen to the spot. Suddenly, a warm and slightly wet hand grabbed hold of mine. I glanced down and there was my little brother Klaus, scared to death—did he feel it too! I offered a reassuring smile, but I'm not sure it helped. Then HE appeared at the bottom of the steps—the nasty captain. Here was my chance to give him a piece of my mind. You know what—I was dumbstruck. He approached quickly, his face stuck in a sort of scowl, like a vicious terrier. All I seemed to notice was his large gums and crooked teeth, even from a distance.

"You, you, stop there." The captain shouted his orders in his whiny irritating voice, it sounded strangely like Frau Leshnik's, and like her, he was rude and arrogant—perhaps they were related, I wouldn't be surprised. I couldn't work out who he was talking to? There were only Aryan people on the platform and us kids of course; surely he wouldn't speak to us in such a fashion; but there was that feeling again, chilling me to the bones.

I stood on tiptoe to see who he was bawling at, my nerves on edge. But just then, the soldiers pushed past the curious crowd and within seconds they had us completely surrounded—like criminals! Each soldier had his rifle at the ready as they loomed over us children like huge school bullies. My feeling of dread and doom had been correct all along, I simply knew it somehow. Now in an instant we were all consumed by terror. The girls screamed and instinctively we clung to our friends in small clumps, all fearful and wondering what we had done wrong.

Then, to our total surprise, the soldiers started pushing us in a rough manner, herding us together; you wouldn't treat animals like they were treating us! Boris and Ludolf protested and were pushed even harder. Boris was enraged and retaliated, pushing one soldier back, before a second soldier appeared from nowhere and slapped him hard across his face. A red weal coated his entire cheek, it was awful. Poor Boris, I thought. But he was not broken, it would take more than a slap to defeat Boris; he was a champion fighter, both boxing and wrestling, albeit junior champion. Nevertheless, he still had fight left in him yet—his defiance was magnificent.

"You'll pay for this," I heard Boris scream at the soldier, his hand rubbing his sore cheek and anger in his eyes. The soldier, a strong looking man with a huge jutting chin, faced up to Boris, much like Karl had done earlier, but this man was meaner than Karl, he was more experienced. He could see Boris meant trouble for him and so he would finish Boris quickly and before the boy could react, the soldier jabbed his rifle butt into Boris' face—that was unexpected. The children that saw this screamed as poor Boris fell to the floor in agony, his lip bleeding badly, his nose surely broken, his face a rush of blood.

We were thoroughly shocked. What was happening? It was all so fast. The rest of us screamed in protest and horror.

Poor little Leni had somehow separated from us and was shaking with terror, her screaming pierced the crowds who had begun to watch the spectacle developing before them. Her screams didn't save Leni from a horrid soldier who noticed her and quickly dragged her by her pigtails towards the rest of us. He pulled her so hard that her legs almost lifted from the ground. Leni shrieked in pain; her lovely pink ribbon had fallen to the platform floor along with a clump of her hair. "You are bad men," she cried, "get off. GET OFF ME!"

"STOP IT, stop it, please," I shouted and ran to the poor little child, pushing my way between her and the mean soldier. He raised his hand to slap me and in my surprise I almost vomited, for I couldn't believe what was happening to us, it was a nightmare. I knelt to embrace the little girl who had finally come to my arms. I held her tight and moved backwards away from the soldier's reach.

Suddenly the captain's unmistakeable voice was heard above all others and everyone stopped dead. Leni clung so tight that any other day I would have fainted, but today I had other things to contend with and so allowed her to push her face into my shoulder, shielding her eyes from the terrifying events now unfolding around us. Klaus too clung to me and all the others started to gather around in a tight bunch.

The platform had gone completely silent. People glowered at us as we huddled together whimpering and sobbing. Most of us were crying out for our mamas and papas, if only they knew what was happening to us. My mind was racing, and where was Frau Leshnik and—and our guards?

I spotted a bystander, the elegant lady who had smiled at me earlier. Perhaps she will help us explain this mess to the captain. It was all a mistake—surely! I caught her eye. Suddenly the kind eyes I expected had turned wicked. I could barely look at them as she glared hard and disapprovingly back at me. How could she change so much, from kind to wicked in an instant—WHAT HAD WE DONE?

Just then Karl and Artur appeared. Oh, thank heavens, now all will be sorted. Artur had a worried expression but Karl was smiling; I didn't like his smile at all, there was menace in it. His eyes searched for Boris and Ludolf and it all came clear to me.

"These are the children, yes?" the wicked captain demanded.

Karl answered quickly. "Yes. Captain, these are the runaway Jews."

I couldn't believe my ears. We are not Jews. I wanted to shout out my protest, I wanted to explain who we were—look in our cases, you will find our uniforms, our Hitler Youth uniforms—how can we be Jews? But for some unknown reason the words would not come out; they stuck in my throat, held back by that, God damn, apple that was hurting me so much. This was incredible, like a dream. I peered at the other children in turn. Every last one of them had been stunned by Karl's accusation—we were not Jews!

I caught Artur's eyes, surely he would speak up on our behalf, but he was afraid, clearly afraid of his brother and of the trouble he would get into if he disagreed with him. It had gone too far for the brothers; this wicked plan of theirs, or should I say Karl's, for I was certain Artur was innocent—he was not wicked, anyone could tell that. They could not turn back now or…or they would be in big trouble themselves. It was surely no more than revenge for what had happened in the carriage—the cigarette incident—I was certain of it. How could Karl do this though; if this was his way of revenge then it was all too much.

I looked at Artur, I could almost feel the young guard's distress. I knew then that he had no part in it and he liked it no more than we did. He was in turmoil, not knowing which way to turn. I urged him to do the right thing but in his shame he could not look at us. There was that feeling again, worse than ever; the apple hurting my chest now accompanied by daggers piercing my stomach. I did not deny this pain; I had a feeling I was going to get used to it.

I knew we were in big trouble. My heart sank as Artur confirmed the lie with the simplest nod of his head. Both the captain and Karl scowled at Artur's hesitation. Then Artur caught my eye and instantly turned away. I wanted to plead with him. This was his chance to make it right, or, or he would regret it—forever. But again, something inside held me back; something warned me to keep quiet, that it would be no good to try.

I couldn't help myself. Boris had fallen silent, afraid to say anything more and Ludolf was visibly shaking with fear; such babies, they had caused this mess, but to resolve it, it was down to me. Someone had to at least, try. "Artur, please help us," I uttered in a voice barely above a whisper. "Tell the truth, please Artur, this is a mistake." I turned to the captain with my pleas. "Please sir. We are not Jewish children. We are Aryan, every last one of us. Our papas are generals."

"Silence," he yelled. "There will be silence."

I froze, staring directly into Artur's face. He had heard my words and as his wide eyes met mine, I thought he was going to save us. A simple word was all that was needed. His mouth opened to speak, but he had no voice. "Artur," I pleaded again and for a second Artur hesitated; he was going to help us. But Karl was watching and stepped in to prevent his brother from speaking out, grabbing Artur by the collar and pulling him away; freeing the weakling from his misery and releasing him from his duty to us children. Our only hope melted away with Karl's angry voice. "Come Artur," he demanded of his brother, "we need to get back to our post."

"What post?" I shouted. "You have no post. You have no one to guard anymore, how will you explain this to your superiors? How can you lose eleven children?" I had thrown all caution to the wind. I would regret it.

I felt a burning sensation spread through my face, everything turned black and I began to sway. "Silence!" the captain commanded as Leni and Klaus clung to me screaming. I came round, and though dazed, I was amazed to find I remained standing. Spots floated before my eyes, my ears weren't functioning properly either and so I ignored the captain and searched for Artur. It was too late, our guards were walking away, but they did not turn their back on us altogether, at least Karl didn't. He turned and glared at Boris and Ludolf; triumph shining from his small brown eyes.

"Know your place little rats," Karl snarled and at that moment, I realised he had doomed us all; his revenge was swift and ever so easy, a treacherous act to match no other. I remembered Uncle Heinrich's words. There are treacherous people about, trust no one!

Now as I recollect what happened, I am still, to this day filled with horror and dare I say it—hatred. Seeing our guards turn their backs on us and walk away like that was the worst act I had ever witnessed. How could they? How could they have failed at their duty as both guard and human being!

Yet, even now, deep down, I do not totally blame the two guards. They were young men and they were reacting to their circumstances. Circumstances created by the crazy world we lived in, the strange ideas we harboured. Our Aryan ideals: our papa's beliefs; Uncle Heinrich's notions; Herr Hitler's values; from boys like Boris and Ludolf with their arrogance, to men like the whiny captain, eager for power and constantly searching for approval and never questioning orders; and to women like my very own mama, my dear mama, so kind and gentle, but refusing to open her eyes to what was going on in the world.

"Move them," the voice I had come to loath pierced the air. I can hear it as clear in my mind now as it was then. It still continues to terrify my soul. Suddenly, we were prodded and manhandled towards the platform bridge. All around people frowned and pointed; their faces full of hate for us. I pulled Klaus to me and held Leni tight, how they sobbed so. Up and over the bridge we were quickly marched and down the other side to the far platform—to platform five and the ghastly train stationed there. Leni was small but she grew heavy quickly, I almost fell down the steps but managed to keep my footing as I entered the new platform. I was greeted with the sight I had feared most of all—the open door of a cattle wagon.

As I approached, our horror only worsened by what we saw lurking inside. The apple lodged in my throat began to throb, and the daggers in my stomach turned, the pain spreading throughout my body, all fired up by the appalling scene inside the wagon. It was full to the brim with people; poor miserable people. The same ones I'd seen earlier in the woods. There must have been fifty, no, a hundred of them crowded into the dark and stinking wagon. They too were terrified. They made no sound but for the occasional whimper and moan; they were broken people. What evil was going on here?

One by one, we were lifted into this strangely silent box. Even Leni and Klaus seemed calm somehow; we were simply stunned. Though this thing was huge, there was little room inside. Regardless, the miserable people who had been packed inside somehow managed to squash together, a combined effort to allow us a little room as the wagon doors slid shut. We children screamed then, but we were the only ones, everyone else had grown used to the darkness that completely surrounded us and the smells that assaulted our nostrils; sweat, vomit and worse! Complete and utter fear ruled here. I could feel the other children huddling around me, tense and shaking. I couldn't help repeating the same questions over, and over again in my mind—what was happening to us—and why, why, WHY?

Mere seconds had passed, yet it seemed an eternity already. Then, surprisingly, voices were heard outside and soon the heavy bolts were unhooked again and the door slid heavily to the left. It was reopened to allow light and fresh air to flood in and the entire wagon seemed to gasp for the air. The pain in my chest was now caused by relief, and I almost fainted. Had this all been a joke? If so it was a bad joke—very bad, but even so, I was prepared to laugh, no matter how tasteless the joke was, because standing tall in front of us was a wonderful sight, Frau Leshnik stood between two soldiers, her face stern and unmoving, proud and fierce.

Was she responsible for the joke! Was this a crazy thing she had conjured up to discipline us—was she mad! Though she had come to rescue us; I had made up my mind to hate her forever, I would never forgive her for this.

I sighed, what a wicked joke from the most wicked of witches. But still no words came and no laughing, everything seemed to stick in my throat. I was consumed with expectations; they were not fulfilled. I stared silently at Frau Leshnik, awaiting her sarcastic words, which would surely deliver a comforting sting. My body shook, visibly now, harder than ever. Time stood still. Come on, Frau Leshnik, say something!

At last, the mounting tension was released—it was replaced with shock. I watched incredibly, as two soldiers began to lift Frau Leshnik into the wagon, I watched anxiously as she dropped her cane; I had never seen her without it. She didn't protest! Why did she not protest? This was not like her.

Inside the wagon, she turned, and stood still as stone, she glanced at me for a second—a million unsaid words. She scanned us all, counting us, making sure we were all present; even now, she would leave no one behind. When she was satisfied with her count, she turned to face the door and scowled hard at the captain. He glared back at her, idly stroking the polished wood of the Frau's cane. He held her gaze for what could have been only a few seconds, but, again, it appeared longer. Of course, the Frau was a master at dishing out disapproval with her eyes, and at last, the whiny captain wavered.

"What are you looking at, you filthy Jew?" he demanded and turned away, thoroughly beaten by the old woman.

"A dead man," Frau Leshnik replied with a calm, acidic tone.

The captain laughed, his high-pitched giggle filling the wagon, no more than a show put on for his soldiers. But he couldn't hide his discomfort from the precise and carefully chosen words he had just heard.

The wagon door shut again and just before the dark completely consumed us, I saw Leni clutch Frau Leshnik's hand. Somehow, I was not surprised to see the Frau squeeze that little hand tightly. My suspicions had been confirmed; I knew she had goodness inside of her.

Then a whisper: a curse, "I promise you; you are a dead man."

Chapter 7
The Witch and the Rabbi

Except for the shaking, we all stood perfectly still. Not a word was uttered. No sobbing. No moaning. Complete silence. Complete darkness. I think we were all in shock; not just our gang, but everyone in the cattle wagon. We were so squashed, crushed tightly together, and I don't want to be rude, but some of the people stank of body odour, sweat and urine, smells so strong that they made me retch.

Plus, on top of that, there was the smell of farm animals; pigs and cows and sheep had occupied this wagon before us and it had definitely not been cleaned out, the floor was carpeted with straw and dung—disgusting! The contrast between this cattle wagon and our luxurious coach could not be dreamed up. Our wonderful lamps were now replaced by small cracks in the wooden panels that barely allowed any light in from the station outside, and in place of our comfy seats and spacious tables there was…well nothing! Space itself here was a luxury, with at least eight people using up the same amount as one of our tables had done in the coach.

Before too long, the silence was broken. First men shouting orders and commands somewhere on the platform but these voices, soon drowned out by engine rumblings accompanied by a vibration that seemed to infiltrate my bones, whilst clinks and clanks hurt our ears as heavy metal parts clashed. This in turn was replaced by hissing of steam, some of which entered our wagon, and next screeching of wheels threatened to deafen us as the great iron things skidded on the tracks, and then finally, a long sharp whistle announced our departure from the platform. That was it then, there was no getting off this thing now. We were trapped with no idea where we were heading.

The powerful sounds seemed to enter our bodies, they hurt us, they ached; they sealed our doom and made everything real somehow. One other thing, they shook us out of our solemn trance just before the wagon lurched forward. As one, every person inside, jolted to one side of the wagon, to the left, and then back again, some people fell to the floor pushing others with them. Those crouching on the floor were trampled, likewise, the people leaning against the walls were crushed and the screams hurt our ears again before they died down to curses and moans, finally dwindling to crying and whimpering.

There was no time to recover as a second jolt set the train slowly in motion. Again, we all lost our balance, leaning or falling towards the back of the carriage this time. Again, many people were hurt, mainly having suffered minor bumps and cuts, but I was certain others had been hurt quite badly. Otto, Gunter and Magda had ended up in a heap amongst some other unfortunate people. I could hear Magda crying out in pain. They would have made a sorry sight, if only I could see them. We all scrambled in the darkness to help our friends. Eventually, my groping hands found Magda and I pulled her up onto her feet, her face covered in a sticky substance that had to be blood.

"Help me Mona," the poor girl begged. "My head hurts so, and I can't open my eyes."

"Shush Magda. I have you." As I sought to comfort her, I plucked a handkerchief out of my pocket, first using it to wipe the blood from my friend's eyes and then pressing it hard against her head. She quickly quieted whilst everyone else were finding their feet. Yet again the train lurched as it crossed tracks and again some people fell, but not as many went down this time, most of us it seemed had braced ourselves for further impact, people learn fast when they find themselves in dangerous situations!

The train gathered speed and the chug-chug sound it made increased in the background. The noise that dominated now though, was the sound of tears; women and children mostly and I also heard a baby amongst the racket—poor thing. How could this be? How could this happen to decent people, to women and children? Were there not rules for this sort of thing, sort of codes of conduct? I thought I had read about such things but perhaps I was wrong. What I did know is that I would never forget this place, these terrible noises, these awful smells, the beginning of a nightmare.

Though I had hurt myself in many places, I was determined not to cry. I'd bumped my head against someone with a harder head than mine; it's funny how it always works out that way. I had an awful thought it may have been Magda that I had collided with and that I was responsible for the cut on her head, but I was blood free, so it couldn't have been me. Though I had bent my fingers back, a little too far somehow, and now, as the commotion was beginning to settle, they began to throb. I wanted so much to cry, but I had to put on a good show for Klaus and the little ones, and so I bit my lip and hid my pain, it brings tears to my eyes just thinking about it.

The train was moving smoothly now and had left the station far behind. Rays of light now filtered through the cracks between the wooden planks, illuminating the wagon with strips of daylight chock-full with dust. We were not in total darkness anymore, more of a grey fog. The dust swirled around our faces, before invading our mouths and irritating our throats in this already dry and hot place. We began to cough and sneeze, bodily functions that are normally ignored, but not here in such close proximity to other people, and when every sneeze brings pain to already broken heads, people start to cry again. At least, the dusty strips of light allowed us to see each other's faces—a little comfort I suppose.

I looked down at Klaus as he buried his face into my body, so tight he clung onto me, I nearly toppled over. Scared of the dark at the best of times, my little brother was clearly distressed—poor thing. It was then I pledged to always be there for him…and the others too, we simply had to stay together, to protect each other, and it must start now. I could just see Heidi; she was a short distance away, separated from Klaus and me by the constant jostling of the crowd. I reached over to her, nudging two squashed prisoners away as gently as possible I managed to grab onto the girl's cardigan. With all my strength I pulled her towards me, upsetting the two prisoners who were annoyed at first, but then realised what I was trying to do and as best they could, the pair helped Heidi through the gap. Heidi nearly fell over in the process but her expression was full of gratitude, I think I had made a new friend.

Then I glanced at Frau Leshnik. Both Leni and Magda had flung their arms around her and, incredibly, she had pulled them close to her. With her arms tight around their shoulders, the old woman was determined not to fall, despite not having her cane. The Frau seemed more sure-footed than anyone, perhaps it was the anger that held her upright, for I had never seen her so mad. She was infuriated, and I guessed more than a little bitter and desperate for revenge. Her face hid her true feelings; I could see it. The old hag was actually showing concern for us all. It was probably killing her inside to reveal such thoughts, such emotions. She was definitely not the witch I had thought she was. A tear of…can you believe it…joy, appeared in the corner of my eye when I saw her standing there—all human!

Our eyes met. She glanced at the children then back at me. I knew exactly what she was trying to say. I needed to be strong; we needed to be strong—for the sake of the little ones and for some of the bigger ones I suppose. I realised then just how serious this situation was and I had also discovered something about the Frau; she cared about us! How wrong we had all been about her for all this time. I reminded myself that it was all her fault. That she was the reason we were in this predicament and not playing in the snow, as we should have been doing right now. There was no denying the Frau was to blame I guess, the act she put on—her horridness had led us here. We all make mistakes…don't we? It's just that some mistakes are bigger than others. We must be prepared to forgive…I suppose.

Yes, it was all nothing more than an act all along. I had discovered the Frau's weakness and she knew it. She half scowled and half smiled. I returned a half smile, it was all I could manage in the circumstances but it was a little comfort. I had quickly learned that comfort can be found in the most unexpected places; an important lesson learned. I had made my mind up to forgive her and this alone, provided yet more comfort.

I wanted to thank Frau Leshnik; she hadn't deserted us after all. But I could not speak. I remained overcome with shock and bewilderment; even Boris and Ludolf were mute. Boris' face was a mess of blood and bruising, his nose didn't seem right somehow; I think the soldier's rifle had broken it and every time the light caught his face his poor eyes seemed to have swollen further, they were almost shut. How I wanted to hug him, he was so brave…and stupid—oh Boris! Ludolf had a huge cut to his forehead; he was the most likely candidate to have clashed with Magda I suppose. He made me smile when he accused me of having a rock-hard head! A moment of unexpected pleasure, that couldn't last.

I played the events over and over in my mind. I just couldn't understand how suddenly our fortunes had changed. One minute we were travelling in a luxurious coach that we had been lucky enough to have almost to ourselves and we were heading for beautiful snow-covered mountains, a place we were to find safety and to have lots of fun. Yet now we were huddled in a crowded cattle wagon, accompanied by strange people many of whom were injured, and we had no idea or inkling where we were heading and I definitely doubted very much that the word fun would apply.

I closed my eyes to shake away my thoughts, I dared not contemplate them any further, they simply upset me too much, they lowered my spirits—if that was possible. Of course, I had to stay strong. I did not know if I was up to the task.

Then, and at last, a sound filtered through that, surprisingly, I was glad to hear, a sound that I was longing for—Frau Leshnik spoke to me.

"Be strong, Mona, remember who you are." To her credit, she did not wait for an answer. Instead, she addressed all the children. "Children, stay calm. Remember who you are. There has been a big mistake here. It will all be sorted out soon enough and that miserable little captain, that insignificant cockroach, will pay—mark my words." She lowered her voice and uttered, "Mark my words, he will pay. I swear to you."

"Your words are comforting to us; I applaud you Madam." This strange voice, soft and strong, astonished us all, including Frau Leshnik. I turned as far as I could to see an old man smiling at me. Well, I think he was smiling. I couldn't see his mouth because he had a huge beard that was made bigger with curly ringlets running through it. Though his eyes were dark and also in shadow, I just knew they would be kind somehow.

Frau Leshnik scowled. She could barely see the man from where she stood, yet still I reckon the ill will radiating from her face reached him. "And who are you may I ask?" Again, the old woman surprised me, I almost smiled as Frau Leshnik returned to her usual mean self. The wicked old witch had resurfaced as if turned back on with an invisible switch.

"A fellow prisoner, Kauffman is my name, Rabbi Kauffman."

"A Jew then," Frau Leshnik said with a disapproving tone.

"A Jew...Yes—but also a German."

"You may deceive yourself, Mr Kauffman, but you cannot be both Jew and German. Not anymore. NOT these days."

"Sadly, it seems you are right Madam, in one way," the Rabbi replied, his left hand combing his beard as if thinking out his response. "But in another way you are also wrong. For just because someone in authority has declared it so, it does not mean it stands." He remained calm and smiling. I was amazed at how easy it was for him to contradict the Frau when all others had given up.

In contrast, Frau Leshnik was annoyed to the point of bursting, making no effort to hide her feelings; this was nothing new of course. I only wish it had occurred in better circumstances, such as a dinner party; how we would have all enjoyed the spectacle. Yet here, in this dark place, any minor upset would only hurt us even more. The Frau was boiling over, her hold on the little ones was growing tighter, I was afraid she would choke them. "That someone you speak of is our Fuhrer, Herr Hitler; and you must believe me when I say, whatever he declares, stands quite firmly, as you will find. I correct myself, as you are finding out this very moment."

"I am confused, Madam," the Rabbi said. "Do I hear approval in your words for Herr Hitler?"

"Of course you do."

"Mmm," the Rabbi fingered his beard, pulling at the curls. "But yet here you find yourself, tightly crammed into a cattle wagon, loaded with innocent Jewish people, being carted off to who knows where, like criminals, with no reason and no crime to answer for."

"As for innocent—well, we all have our ideas regarding such things." The Frau glanced at us children. She pulled Leni to her and reached over to stroke Gretl on her shoulder. A flash of light lit the wagon, which had fallen silent— not even a cough to be heard and for a mere second I could see the boys gazing at the Rabbi, eager, yet afraid to hear his words. The Frau had not yet finished. A slight movement, a mere twitch of her head and all attention fell back upon her. "These children for instance, they are entirely innocent, caught up in some dreadful mistake."

The wagon remained silent—it was eerie. I could not see them, but I was aware that every person crowded into this awful place was listening, and probably not approving of the Frau's words.

The Rabbi replied, it was more of a, how do you say, a reproach. "Yes, your children are innocent, as are ALL the children in this wagon." There were sounds of appreciation following the Rabbi's declaration, mere murmurs, but they were there, and the Frau took note. "These women in here, they have committed no crime, neither have the men. I know them all personally: bakers, tailors, grocers and jewellers. Some are teachers and others professors; my friend Herr Steine is an eminent surgeon and his son was top of his class at medical school. I myself have been a Rabbi for nearly fifty years. I have practiced my faith in the little village where I have had the pleasure to live alongside all these amazing people who find themselves mixed up in a horror that has nothing to do with them."

"We have lived together in our village for many years—I have totalled seventy for myself. We have lived our lives peacefully, keeping our business to ourselves. We have both loved our neighbours and welcomed strangers into our homes. None here have ever committed harm or indeed, any sort of crime nor harboured the desire to. Indeed, we are all innocent here, Madam. I can say that about all these people. I can say that as a fact and I can say that from my heart, though I can't speak for you of course."

I could almost see steam coming out of the Frau's ears yet she did not reply. The Rabbi waited a few moments to allow her to collect her thoughts and as none were expressed he continued, but gentler this time, his voice low and calm; almost understanding that we were in the same predicament, the very same mess as they were. "You say there has been a mistake? I say no, this is no mistake. This is a calculated travesty of justice. Yes, a great injustice I say, yet no mistake. Mark my words—this is malice!"

There was another pause without response before the Rabbi continued. "For you well know, Madam, the German authorities, the true Aryans, they don't make mistakes lightly. They are too busy carrying out the wishes of their great leader, Herr Hitler. He is so great that his wonderful Master Race do his bidding without question. That is why all of us, we so-called Jewish criminals are here. I suspect you'll agree with that—yes?"

I was amazed at Frau Leshnik's reaction; she nodded. What was the Rabbi saying? Had Herr Hitler been wrong? Were we, the true Aryans, simply following blindly without question? Had Frau Leshnik just acknowledged this? How could that be?

Still the Rabbi pressed the issue. "But yet, you and your little group of children are here also. You are not of the Jewish faith, that I know for certain. You are not Communists either and I suspect with the age of your group you are generally of no political opinion. I cannot see the threat that you pose to the great Fatherland." The Rabbi paused for thought and to untangle his beard again. "A mistake you say. Perhaps there is a slight chance of that, in your case. But I still say no—this is malice—most likely."

Frau Leshnik remained silent and lowered her head, annoyed with her lack of vigilance. It was obvious the Rabbi had worked out our identity. How weird this was. Here we were, stuck in a cattle wagon with at least a hundred other people, all of whom we had declared our enemies. This situation didn't look so good for us at all. My grip on Klausy tightened and I pulled Heidi closer too. Both of them were listening intently to the conversation and both, my little brother included, were aware of the significance the words were to our situation.

Frau Leshnik gently nodded her head, she seemed to stare blankly into space as she pondered the Rabbi's words; words I had agreed with instantly. This was malice and I had witnessed it on the station platform in the eyes of the elegant lady; I had seen it in the nerve-racked face of Artur. I had heard it in the vicious laugh of his brother Karl and finally in the orders to close the wagon door on us, sealing our fate.

The Rabbi Kauffman's voice had no hint of malice, and his eyes were gentle; as were all the other eyes around; why even the Frau's eyes were softening somehow—glistening—sort of. He remained steady on his feet and his words were just as firm, his support for us was obvious for all to see, deliberately making no reference to our Aryan background. He graciously smiled at the Frau; sympathising with her—with us.

Frau Leshnik scowled. She could never accept this, this logic, from a man such as him. I could almost feel her turmoil, the fight inside her, after years of hate that she had nurtured against such people; here she was, listening to reason, from…our greatest enemy. She closed her eyes and shook her head, as if to make it all go away whilst all present watched her every move, eager to hear her reply—her explanation. How this conversation troubled her so. She simply could not find the words.

The Rabbi sighed. "I do not know why you are here. What I do know is that, like us, you are considered enemies of the Third Reich. I say this to you Madam, for I know this to be true. It is by no mistake that you are here," he repeated calmly. "In fact, it is the total opposite, and I suspect you know this Madam." He stared hard into Frau Leshnik's face, daring her to contradict him. But the Frau had no words of her own. Instead, she hung her head in the darkness, her right-hand stroking Leni's hair and her left gripping Gretl's shoulder.

"It seems someone wanted to be rid of you, just as someone wanted to be rid of us, and it is all too easy to get rid of someone you dislike these days. Like the rest of us here, you have been carefully chosen to be a passenger on this train for there has been much debate regarding the matter of who travels on this line…though none of us here were consulted."

A strip of light crossed Frau Leshnik's face and in that instant, I saw the disapproval that shone in her eyes. Was it the man or his words that she didn't like or the simple fact that he was making sense and making her see the logic of his words? At last, she spoke out. "You are very free with your opinions Jew;

opinions that were not sought after. I am not wrong in this," she said. "You will see that I am right when this matter comes to a close."

I couldn't believe what she was saying; she knew all too well that the Rabbi was correct, she was just being awkward. I had seen her do this before; the stubborn old woman never lost, no matter what the subject, no matter what the stakes, no matter whom she argued with, or how wrong her ideas were. Yet, as Frau Leshnik opened her mouth to offer more folly to support her argument, her resolve suddenly faltered, melted away into the dust. She started her sentence only to let it disappear into the darkness. "We are not like you, we are not…" she uttered and then abruptly lowered her head again unable to meet the Rabbi's gaze.

"You are not Jewish, I say again Madam, this is obvious to me. Yet you are proud. A fierce political enemy of the Aryan race most likely. Not so these poor children, innocents caught up in your political beliefs—maybe?"

Frau Leshnik looked at the Rabbi, half furious, half tearful. The irony of his words hit her like bullets fired at close range. There was no denying that her political beliefs were the reason why the Jews were here, but they had not brought us here. It was her stubbornness, her unhelpfulness, her pig-headedness that had brought us here. If she had only intervened between Boris and Karl, this would not have happened and we would be back in our comfortable coach right now. The Rabbi had offered her a way out, a way to deny her mistakes, a way to avoid blame.

"Damn you, man," she mumbled. I could barely hear her. Then nodding, she conceded, "Yes, —yes you are right. Political beliefs yes, and prejudices of one form or another have led to this mess we are now in—all of us. At that moment, I was convinced she would accept his offer, his way out; for an instant, I was racked with anxiety, desperately not wanting my old hatred for her to return would she abandon her responsibility, would she destroy our new-found respect, had she betrayed me, how could she. The answer was NO. The Frau was bigger than that—she did not disappoint me—she confessed." "I could have done more to stop this; I could have intervened when I had the chance. But I stayed silent, secretly watching as boys quarrelled…in our case anyhow."

"The winds of Heaven change suddenly, so do human fortunes," the Rabbi professed.

The Frau retorted strongly. "I don't believe in fortune…and chance. I think we make our own fortunes. Our deeds determine us as much as we determine our deeds."

The Rabbi nodded, "I am in danger of agreeing with you Madam."

Frau Leshnik ignored him. "Already I regret my actions, or lack of them; yet I suspect the hardship has barely begun. We have more important things to worry about now. We had better prepare ourselves." Her voice trailed off and our eyes met for a fraction of a second, long enough for me to notice a significant change in her.

"You know where this train is heading."

"I have knowledge of such places." She glared at the Rabbi and then at us children. "Ask no more of it." She lowered her head and hid her eyes.

Her voice was almost pleading, it disturbed me; like, someone had stepped on my grave. The Rabbi acknowledged her request and the whole wagon fell silent again.

I pulled Klaus and Heidi closer still, whilst a thousand questions buzzed around my head. I had never felt such intense feelings before, such uncertainty. I was in turmoil, and every second that passed, the train rolled onward, taking us to an unknown destination and whatever awaited us there.

The sound of the train on the tracks dominated now and we moved on. For hours, we travelled. Though there was no way of telling the time, I guessed it must have been early evening by now. It was growing darker inside as outside the sun began to descend forcing our eyes to adjust to the darkness, allowing us to see shapes and ghostly silhouettes only.

The silhouettes were very miserable people. Many still standing, trying hard not to fall. The children and the elderly were allowed to sit as they pleased, whilst the healthy adults took turns to stand for as long as their legs held out. Others, whose aching muscles had failed them, were being propped up by their loved ones. Even those occupying the space on the floor, among the animal dung, did not find comfort.

An old man lay alone, abandoned. He had more room than most and he did not need it, having died a while ago. His only family member, a young girl sobbed silently, wrapped and comforted in the arms of a total stranger.

Many others wept; there was little else to do as we raced towards our destination and our fate. I remember thinking, the chances of completing this journey at all were slim. Despite the draught pushing through the holes in the walls, the heat was unbearable and would surely take its toll on the weak, and the smell was now rancid. Most children, including a few members of our party, had wet themselves; and there was an unmistakeable odour of poo and vomit.

Our group of children were allowed to sit for long periods, but Boris and Ludolf took their turn to stand with the adults. I had somehow managed to kneel on one knee. Klaus knelt close to me and the smaller girls were being cuddled by Gretl and Heidi. We were all so uncomfortable, I could barely feel my legs, and my back ached so much. Otto had also been standing for quite a while and had realised there was no place for him to sit. I could see the poor boy's legs shaking. I wanted to hug him but I could not reach. Ludolf also noticed Otto's distress. He spoke to Boris and both the big boys placed their arms around Otto to hold him up. Otto was so pleased, and a little surprised at this sudden act of kindness, especially from the two notorious bullies who normally terrorised him.

Frau Leshnik nodded her approval and then glanced at the Rabbi. Though I could not see him, I knew he had offered a smile, which surprisingly, from the look on Frau Leshnik's face, was received with a hint of gratitude; yet again, the Frau proved surprising.

Another hour passed and now the sound of people moaning was dominant in our ears again. Our limbs ached so much we could barely stand it, and the odour in the wagon kept getting worse—intoxicating, we were barely able to breathe now and although it was cold and dark outside, we were so hot, packed tightly together. We were literally suffocating, yet still, when the light caught his face, I saw the old Rabbi continued to smile.

All crying had stopped, it sapped our energy, and some of the younger children had cried themselves to sleep. It seemed this journey would never end; how I longed for our nice carriage with the comfortable seats, the tables and electric lamps and most importantly, the windows.

Then, at last, after many, many, torturing hours, the engine whistle sounded again whilst the train's brakes rammed against the many spinning wheels. The intense screeching sounds returned to torture our ears and the train suddenly lost speed. The carriage jerked and those standing lost their balance, and once more, many people, Boris and the boys included, fell to the floor.

It was chaos! Otto had fallen on top of the other girls; his elbow had clashed with Heidi's forehead and his fingers had poked Leni's eyes. There was a time when he would have done this on purpose, but this was not that time; oh, how we wished it was. The other boys were in a tangled heap and Frau Leshnik had fallen into the steady arms of the statue-like Rabbi: the only person who remained on his feet.

Screams and moaning returned as fingers and hands were trapped, heads were bumped and bodies were painfully squashed. For an eternity, the sounds of pain continued to be gradually replaced by the return of moaning and sobbing. At last, even this stopped, and the only sound I was aware of was the anxious pounding of our hearts.

The train continued to move. Would we ever stop? Did we want to stop! Yes we did, and no we didn't. The choice wasn't ours. The wagon slowed and the screeching wheels were stilled.

We had begun to untangle ourselves from the pile of misery when the doors were slid open. We gasped as fresh air rushed in, followed by a cloud of dust and then bright lights that smashed into our sorry eyes. At last, it seemed, we could all get out of this awful wagon.

But I will never forget that moment. We, being nearest to the door, witnessed a vision of horror!

Chapter 8
The Separating

Bright lights shone into the wagon, so bright that it was impossible to see the dark sky that surrounded us. After suffering the darkness for so long, we were blinded at first, but as our eyes adjusted to the glow, we saw rifles pointed our way. Rifles held by three very scary looking soldiers that stood silently in line. Their expressions blank and uncaring—almost bored, this was simply another day for them. Three others, even scarier than the first, held back the most terrifying dogs any of us had ever seen; all teeth and snarls. Someone yelled orders at us, most of which we couldn't understand and so we just stood still—huddled together—bewildered and petrified.

Klaus squeezed my hand and I peered down at him, he shook like a leaf and he had wet his pants. "Have our enemies got us, Mona?" he asked through chattering teeth. "Are we their prisoners now?" I could feel him tremble as he clung tighter to me, desperate to hide behind someone, but I provided little cover for the poor boy, and even less comfort.

I could not lie. "It seems so, my little brother," I said as I pulled him closer. "We need to be strong in the face of our enemy. At least, until our papa comes to rescue us," I added without a hint of conviction.

Klaus seemed to sense my uncertainty. "He'll come, Mona, I'm sure of it." My little brother glanced up at me, his eyes glistening over, ready to burst into tears. How brave he was then.

"Yes, Klausy, you are right of course." How I wished Papa would come and end this nightmare soon. Though I prayed hard I knew it would not be soon enough, he was needed right now. Every second he delayed would be bad for us. He would be so angry of course—when he found out what had happened to us. There would be—how do you say—hell to pay!

At last, a soldier of some rank approached, a sergeant perhaps. He was calm and seemed to know his business. He was a tall man, brimming with Aryan confidence, as he stepped near the wagon door, the dog handlers fell backwards to allow us room to climb off the wagon. The sergeant spoke politely but with authority, instead of shouting orders he made a request for us to get off the wagon—he even said please—with a smile.

But as other wagons further down the train began to empty, rows of miserable people trudged past in lines of two or three abreast depending on how many friends or family members they had managed to grasp hold off. They veered towards us in their attempts to give the snapping dogs a wide birth. This left us even less room to exit the wagon despite the polite sergeant's efforts. I watched as he signalled something to one of the guards who repositioned his dog so that the oncoming crowd diverted away from us. Pleased, the sergeant then beckoned to us to alight.

It had not rained here and the dry ground produced clouds of dust as the people marched by. The dust rose higher, finally reaching our faces and irritating our eyes. It was time for us to make our move. But we all stood still, awaiting someone else, someone braver to take the first step. The endless line of prisoners (because now it was evident that we were prisoners) continued to march past, almost enticing us out of our wagon, a place that had caused us so much pain, a place we had hated so, but yet a place we could not bear to leave—it had become our place of safety.

Those that had left their safe place held their heads down, some closed their eyes tight shut, not daring to see what they would encounter next. They clung on to each other, the bravest leading the weak. They were all brave to me, much braver than us. I watched; my heart broken as they moved forward, their hands clutched tightly to loved ones, with terrified expressions of uncertainty carved into their faces.

Now, at either side of these people, guards shrieked orders. Some in German, but I also heard other languages, which I didn't understand. And there was much kicking and punching whenever a prisoner came into reach—the guards were proving to be very cruel indeed. Other guards allowed the vicious dogs to snap at legs; and some, even more sadistic than their comrades, used the butt of their rifles to hit people in the face, for little or no offence at all. Many people walked past with blood streaming from their heads, others struggled with the sick and injured, whilst some clung tightly to more than one child in their arms.

I couldn't believe my eyes. Such cruelty—was it possible? A thousand questions crossed my mind: What was happening here? What was happening to us? Were these German soldiers doing this to us? Or were they our enemies? How had this come about? If only our papas knew what was going on, they would surely stop this atrocious behaviour and put an end to this awful place—this prison camp!

The polite sergeant moved closer and glanced up at us. As he stepped out of the light, I could see his face clearly. He had nice eyes and he continued to smile. Though looking back, I'm not sure if he smiled through kindness, the word does not apply here. He was merely coaxing us out with as little effort as possible, using language that seemed kind, but there was an edge to his words, which caused us to hesitate. "Out, out, quick, quick…please," he added and despite his calm voice and kind eyes, apprehension spread through the wagon. No one wanted to move; like me, my fellow travellers did not trust him, all preferring to stay in the cramped misery we had known for the past hours. I watched as the Rabbi closed his eyes in silent prayer, then he pushed his way to the front of the wagon.

Immediately, others started to follow the Rabbi, this wonderful man. He moved forward with a purpose, which was to move this nightmare forward, to face the next stage. His movement caused a stir; a ripple that awoke those people frozen solid at the front, hesitant, doubtful and cautious; unable to move their aching legs. The Rabbi was clever, kind and brave, his smile was sad as he gently nudged his country folk out of the door…to face untold horrors.

There were no steps to negotiate, no ladder, not even a box to help us climb down from the train—just a three-foot drop to the ground. Leaving our wagon would prove hard, as did entering it. Many hesitated at the door for a few seconds before those surging forward from behind forced them to take the leap. Many weak legs buckled on landing and many ankles bent too far. The sound of pain dominated once again and above all this, the polite requests from the calm sergeant had now been replaced with vicious orders accompanied by the cracking of a whip.

We had become sheep, lambs following each other to what—to the slaughter is the end of that phrase—I shuddered. Then, as I reached the door, I began to panic. Klaus clutched onto my left leg, which caused me to overbalance. The drop neared too quickly, leaving little time to prepare—to think. I got it wrong. I lost my footing. It was too late to compensate and I fell the three feet to the hard, dry ground pulling my little brother with me. I landed awkwardly, my knees and shins taking all the impact from the ground, which had proved to be littered with sharp stones, instantly removing the skin from both knees and shins in turn. I swallowed my pain. There was no time to cry as other people were dismounting from the wagon behind, threatening to trample Klaus and myself. I lurched forward, dragging Klaus with me and, finding a little space, I pulled him up onto his feet. Gretl was immediately behind us; the others were lost.

It was crazy. Distress and panic and anger that I'd never experienced before ran through me, causing my whole body to tremble. I quickly glanced around, in an instant I had somehow discerned where all the other children were. Boris was brushing himself down, having been trampled to the ground, whilst the other big boy, Ludolf, had managed to pull little Leni and Magda to him; he was proving to be a very brave and thoughtful boy. He also stood a head taller than those around him, which seemed to draw others, even strangers to him. Without realising, Ludolf was displaying his leadership qualities. I for one had decided to move his way. The other boys were huddled tightly around Frau Leshnik. I couldn't see Heidi at all.

Boris forced a path my way, his face was furious. I could see he was going to do something. I opened my mouth to stop him but it was too late. Without warning, he jumped towards a guard, screaming insults into his face.

Instantly, two other guards pounced on Boris, beating him ferociously to the ground. The crowd around him fell back screaming. I was horrified and shielded Klaus' eyes as blows and kicks from all three guards fell relentlessly on poor Boris. Other guards raced forward; surely this was the end of Boris. Mercifully, they ignored the fight, but began bawling orders and prodding people with their rifles. The whole group, the total occupants of the wagon, were now herded forward to join the lines of marching people.

We passed the guards who continued to beat and kick poor Boris. I was consumed with pity for him and also with rage. Someone would pay for this atrocity; someone would be brought to account—my papa would see to that!

"Mona, Mona, wait." I scanned around and saw a tearful Victor racing to catch up. He had separated from the others, only a few metres behind, but, it may have been a mile for all the difference it made to this terrified boy. We slowed down and as he reached us, Klaus urgently clutched his hand, both boys feeling instant relief and comfort.

The once polite sergeant had turned into something evil, yelling at us and thrashing with his whip; some sort of riding crop. I had one just like it back home, but never was it intended for use on people. The crowd surged away from his reach, and we continued forward but at a slower pace to allow the others to join us. Heidi appeared from nowhere, thank heavens, and pretty soon we were all together, linking hands tightly, all except poor Boris who had fallen behind. I stood on tiptoe to search for him, but he was nowhere to be seen; how I hoped he was not still being beaten.

We followed the crowd or rather we were dragged along with them, passing many empty cattle wagons as we made our way forward. Though we tried not to, we also overtook many sick and injured people, some beaten so badly they could no longer walk unaided. There were those that were worse off still, I turned Klaus's head so he would not see the dead bodies piled at the side of the last wagon.

Eventually, and thankfully, we turned away from the train, crossing the rail tracks to a fenced off sort of yard or compound, it was all dust and bare earth. A high wire fence, topped with barbed wire encircled it and a little way in the distance I noticed towers, with guards and yet more lights. Again, we were squashed in as those in front of us came to a standstill and those behind pushed on.

Then, the next horror to show itself! Above the screaming of the guards and all the moaning and crying, we were aware of other voices. At that time, I wouldn't have thought it was possible to be more afraid, but our fear ascended to a higher level: DREAD. The new voices were similar to the others; they screamed like the others, they demanded obedience like the others, they were full of hate, yet there was one very subtle difference. They weren't chaotic and unorganised; they had a job to do; they were well trained and efficient.

What now? My chest heaved and ached with every step that brought us closer to the commanding voices. I couldn't see what was going on at first but as we approached I managed to crane my neck above the others, what I saw was horrific. There was a row of small tables; a senior officer sitting at each, with a common soldier ensuring the prisoners approached him in single file. A quick examination, barely a glance and the order was given. "You to the left. You to the right, you to the left, left, left, right; you to the right also." They were separating us. Why, oh for God's sake, why?

I sighed deeply, then remembered my poor little brother still clutching my hand with all his might, and the others, with Boris gone, they were looking up to me, and perhaps Ludolf, I just knew it. Some of the boys clung to Frau Leshnik, she was proving to be useful—thank heavens! I Needed her support, I felt so much responsibility, just a girl who desperately wanted nothing more than to cry. I needed to cry. But I would not. I simply could not cry. Not just yet at any rate.

Right now, the old woman pushed in front. "I'll go first, Mona," she said urgently and offered an almost reassuring smile. It didn't lift my spirits I'm afraid. I wanted to say be careful, but she had already reached the commanding voices. "Heil Hitler," I heard her say as she raised the appropriate arm salute; the perfect Nazi had returned.

To my amazement, the orders ceased and the line came to an abrupt halt. Frau Leshnik stood in front of a commanding officer, a tall man, smart in his uniform, which was adorned with emblems of high rank. How he reminded me of Papa, so proud and strong. He could have been Leni's papa for that matter, or Victor's, or Frau Leshnik's son—if only. No doubt, somewhere, this officer had children of his own who were safe and warm in their homes or at school or in their mama's loving arms—just as we had been such a short time ago. He glared down a long thin nose through wire spectacles, with a mixed look of amusement and annoyance. I held my breath. He returned her salute; could this be going well? Then he said in a surprisingly polite voice, "You salute well, an old soldier—yes?"

"I have served my country for many years and have risen to a rank much higher than," she paused and then that awful patronising tone of hers returned, accompanied with a smile that offered nothing but contempt and distaste, "You—Obersturmführer." If the officer was prepared to hear her out before, there was no chance of that now; he was clearly offended. In one stroke, the Frau had ruined everything, why couldn't she just be nice? I knew then that she would make things worse, if that was possible. I watched, horrified as the officer's thin lips turned from a smile to a grimace and his pink cheeks flushed through crimson to purple.

Frau Leshnik, ever ignorant to how her tactless words had been perceived, continued in the same manner. "There has been a definite act of malicious intent here, I demand it is put right immediately." She punched her fist down hard on the table and then stared, harder into the officer's cold, almost black eyes—

daring him; a direct challenge to his authority. He remained silent…for a fraction of a second.

I remember urging the Frau to say her name, to introduce herself; just mention the name Leshnik, the name that terrorised the east, surely that would be enough. I whispered her name, then again a little louder. "Say It. Say your name—Leshnik." She could not hear and I urged a third time. "Say it—Leshnik."

But it did not occur to her to do so. She was full of confidence, full of self-importance. In her day, the Fraulein had indeed risen to a high-ranking army officer. But it was doubtful that she had achieved what she claimed. Whatever level she had reached, was surely to blame for her attitude towards all others deemed beneath her and the cause of the trouble we now found ourselves in, which, any moment was going to get worse. As far as the Frau was concerned, people of her rank did not have to explain themselves—it just wasn't done. "Now bring to me your commanding officer and we will sort it out," she demanded.

The officer's eyes widened and his face almost exploded, I could see his nostrils flaring and pulsating like a mad bull about to charge. But Frau Leshnik remained oblivious to the danger, holding her ground and her stare in a firm and extremely irritating manner. This was nothing new to her, having upset so many people in her lifetime, and this occasion was no different to her despite the peril that we faced and she had forgotten.

The Frau didn't flinch, not even a blink. I asked myself, was she actually seeing what I was seeing, what everyone else around us was seeing or did she simply possess nerves of steel? "Say your name," I urged, to no avail, not from the Frau at least. It was Heidi who took up the cry. "LESHNIK," she screamed, and all around her were astonished. The guards searched for the only voice in a sea of silence, and it sounded again, "Leshnik—Leshnik. She is Herr Leshnik's mama."

For an instant, the brave voice distracted the officer who paused—had he heard the name. Then, orders were bawled and the guards entered the crowd. "Shush I warned. That is enough." Heidi had proven her bravery and now to show her sense she turned away and crouched into Gretl's shoulder, pretending to sob. Luckily, for Heidi, the approaching guards had not fully committed to the search and soon gave up, turning their attention back to the captain and the Frau and the promise of entertainment.

The officer, who did not share the old woman's incredible self-control, was twitching like a man on fire. He seemed to rise in height, his face contorting with anger; teeth gritted, he breathed fast and hard. He closed his eyes for a fraction of a second, and that was when I realised it was all over for us. The captain was about to erupt—he did not disappoint and to, even, his own guard's disbelief he slapped Frau Leshnik across the face with such a force that she fell to the ground like a stone. The whole place fell deadly silent. Not a murmur as we all held our breath and stood motionless. Magda was the one to break the silence and bent double to vomit. I swallowed the bile that rose in my mouth and watched sadly as Heidi allowed tears to run freely down her cheeks. What next?

We watched in utter shock as the officer quickly composed himself; closing his eyes again for an instant before straightening out his tunic. Then, in fury that I have never witnessed before, he began screaming orders.

Instantly, the place erupted with activity. The separating began again whilst other prisoners, this time dressed in dirty striped clothing, appeared and began to drag Frau Leshnik off, their task made all the harder by the line of terrified people eager to pass them and be separated.

The separating process was efficient to say the least; within seconds, loved ones were parted, families were torn asunder, parents pulled from their children, husbands, their wives, friends and lovers split apart, never to meet again. A scream and a push, and job done! A simple thing it is to separate one person from another, yet it results in irreparable damage and untold grief. Of all the atrocities I would later witness, this was the moment that sickened me most of all. I had been separated from Mama, and now I faced losing little Klausy.

Magda was pushed forward, alone and scared, a quick examination and she was forced to the left. Leni then found herself at the front of the line, what a sorry sight the poor little thing made, her eyes wide, her voice lost. She too went to the left and I was relieved to see her join Magda. They were alone though, for mere seconds only, but so afraid, they might have been abandoned—how I felt for them. Seconds later, Heidi was pushed forward. Perhaps she could join the little girls. I prayed then, harder than I had ever done so far, my new friend was pushed to the right—she was now all alone too.

Klaus and I were next in line to face the officer. I gently pushed my brother forward, not completely releasing my grip on his shoulder. "Go on," I urged, "have courage." Then I prayed again as my brother stood straight and tall whilst the officer scanned his little body, scrutinising and judging. It only took an instant for him to make his decision and my brother began to step to the left. But I held on to him. How could I release my grip—to lose my brother! That could not happen. I challenged the officer, my eyes pleading and for a moment, just one moment, I thought we were going to be okay, but it was not so.

I heard the word 'RIGHT' and time stood still. The officer smiled and the extent of his evil revealed. The well-practiced guard placed his big rough hands on each of our shoulders and began to pull us apart. I felt dizzy and my head began to spin—I was about to be separated from my brother, him to the left and me to the right. This was unthinkable.

I couldn't explain how I felt at that moment. A torture I could never have imagined. A flush of nausea rushed up my body in a wave; I could pinpoint the moment it reached my heart, and at that very moment—I exploded. "NO, NO, NO," I yelled and began to fight off the guard like a girl possessed by demons: kicking, screaming and biting with all my soul. I had become a maniac, driven by lunacy. I kicked and punched. I slapped. I scratched and I spat.

Such was my performance that indeed the guard must have thought I was from a lunatic asylum. He had lost his cap and his tunic had come unbuttoned; scratches bled on his cheek and his face was flushed with exertion. He stepped back from me to gather his strength and at that moment, Klaus was back with me, holding my waist as tight as he could. Then the guard returned with renewed vigour, his arms around me, this time his grip was firmer and no matter how hard I fought him, how hard I pulled away from him, he would not let go. Klaus and I fought together—united to the last. We were losing!

But then, I heard the officer's voice again, filtering into my ears, into my sub-conscious. The voice was calm again and full of reason, it made perfect sense. The guard, by now, held me firmly by the neck, threatening to choke the life out of me. My eyes became blurry but I could make out the tall figure of Ludolf pushing forward, he was talking to the officer, he was pointing at me. I called to him, and he shook his head, I was angry—confused. Then a miracle happened.

An order was heard; it was short and sharp. It was very simple and said with indifference. "Let her go." Had I heard correctly, was this a joke. Then came the confirmation and I allowed myself to cry—finally. "She is mad. Move on to the next." The relieved guard almost threw me towards my brother—to the left! Instantly I relaxed, my entire body crumbling and weak. I inhaled deeply, shocked and bewildered, what had just happened—had I won this battle. Had Ludolf reunited me with my brother—clever Ludolf. Yes, I had won—we had won, my brother and I would stay together, it was thanks to our brave friend

Ludolf. Klaus was so relieved. I felt his little hand tug my dress. I glanced down at him and as our eyes met, I broke down into more tears, sobbing uncontrollably. Our separation had lasted barely seconds, but even this was far too long. I vowed it would never happen again.

The guard had continued his despicable job. As my brother and I stepped away, I could hear him joking with the other guards who laughed at his defeat and in my stunned trance I heard him retort playfully. How heartless! This was all just a game to them, of no significance at all, yet to me this separating of loved ones was a crime worse than murder. I would surely wish to die than lose my brother and if these vile men, these monsters, were faced with the same thing, perhaps they would not take it so lightly. How they laughed, how they joked with each other whilst we were treated like animals. I wanted to scream but something inside warned me not to, I must calm down, immediately, and…and take stock.

I was left shaking with rage and though I continued to sob, I realised my tears were of relief, whilst an incredible pain developed in my head; I reached up and pulled out handfuls of loose hair. Yet I had no time to think about the pain, I had responsibilities; I was only too aware that the little ones were watching my every movement. I shook away the tears and held my head high, how I managed this was beyond me; I had just experienced the worst moment in my entire life—so far! I grabbed hold of Klaus and hugged him so tight that I believe I hurt him.

Only the grip of Magda and Leni, who both now clung so tight to my neck that I was in danger of choking a second time, helped release Klaus from my painful clutches. Despite my efforts to hold them back, tears returned and ran freely down my cheeks and I openly cried out loud, my entire body shaking. The little girls joined me, and Klaus threw his arms around my legs, he too bawling like a baby.

I took a deep breath in and shook my head; perhaps to clear it, I don't really know. My wits returned. I needed to find the others, what had happened to them. I stood on tiptoe to find out and there they were, to the right: Ludolf, Victor, Gunter, Otto, and Gretl; they had all joined Heidi. I was so pleased she was no longer alone—yet my heart was breaking. Slowly they moved further away in the opposite direction. I watched as Gretl turned around; I could see her bobbing about, searching in vain for us. I'm not sure if she did see us, but she waved anyway and I waved back. I wondered why my friend had gone that way. I had a sudden longing for her, for all of them; it was a longing I had never felt before.

This was a time of crazy, vivid feelings. I did not know then, how could I have, but I would never see my best friends again!

We needed to move, to follow the crowd, to mingle and hide amongst them, anything to get away from the guards. It was awful, but we could not be associated with Frau Leshnik, she was in big trouble and there was no way we could help her now. So I pushed my three children forward and soon we were lost.

There were many small children in our line, many of them alone, all going in our direction; where that was, we had no idea. We had many old folk with us too. In fact, they were all old folk and little children, the ones that appeared healthy were no more than nine years old, the older ones I noticed were either very short and weak, or ill, or disabled somehow, in wheelchairs or wearing leg braces; others wearing slings or plaster casts to support broken bones. They all joined our line, a line of outcasts that nobody wanted, that no one needed, and that thought, that one little thought that had suddenly popped into my head, absolutely horrified me.

The bigger children, the healthy and more useful ones had all marched off to the right, unless that is, they were injured or crippled in some way or considered crazy like me; then they were with us. I searched for Frau Leshnik. Surely she had joined our line. But the poor, stubborn, old fool was nowhere to be seen. How I worried for her…For all of us. There were other emotions too. I was angry for a start, angrier than I had ever been before and I was hurting of course, not just physically but mentally. This whole mess seemed to have been created by Germans, my own people, the ones I trusted and loved. I was puzzled, and I wouldn't solve this puzzle for some time.

What I did know, was that I was now the head of our little group. I had to take charge; there was no one else for it. The little ones were lost and desperately needed someone to care for them. Thank heavens for Hitler Youth camp—I was ready; I had to be. "Come, children," I said. "Hold hands tightly, our group is getting smaller. We must stay together and look after each other, so that we can stay safe. Do you hear?" Three pairs of frightened eyes gawked up at me and nodded. "Good," I said. "We are a little family, hold on to each other's hands tightly…and never let go." Though I said these words, I had no faith in them. The opposite was true, I could feel it in my heart; my whole body racked with a spine-tingling feeling. I had felt this feeling from the very beginning and had struggled to dismiss it. It was a warning that I should have heeded, it was a friend and I would no longer ignore it.

I was so afraid, but I could not let on, someone had to be strong, and though I didn't feel up to it, that particular job fell to me. We were captives of some evil men and we were in terrible, even mortal danger.

I manoeuvred myself to the edge of the line so that I could see where we were being taken. We were heading across a large bare area, as big as a football field, all dusty and dry; no grass had grown here for a long time. There were more fences made of wire, as high as the first I'd seen and topped with barbs, in fact there were fences everywhere, and scattered here and there were more towers, high towers with yet more guards and big bright lights that made the night seem like day.

It must have been getting quite late by now, yet there were many people around, all dressed in striped clothing, busying themselves here and there with rakes and wheelbarrows; every now and then one of them dared to glance up at us with sad expressions and teary eyes. Beyond them I saw a large wooden fence with huge gates, all topped with many rows of barbed wire, they'd found a use for that stuff everywhere here. It seemed darker over there, as if light wasn't needed; the spotlights seemed to avoid it.

We were heading for those gates. A long line of miserable people, the very old, burdened with the very young, the sick and the handicapped. All moving slowly forward, a shared reluctance to reach their goal: those very scary gates. What was beyond them? A place where even light didn't reach, a place for monsters—Hell maybe! It was all I could think of—there was that apple in my chest again!

As the first of the column approached the gates, some of the resident prisoners of the camp, were forced to open them. This did not look good. I half expected some fierce creature to spring out and gobble us up. It didn't happen. Nevertheless I felt a flush of blood rush to my head and I became all hot and flustered, any moment now I would vomit. Somehow though, I held it all back, forcing the vile taste in my mouth back down, in my efforts to hide my true feelings from the children.

Just listen to me talking about the children, about MY children, as if I was no longer one of them—how quickly we adapt when we are facing unknown perils. I glanced at Klaus and smiled at him. A reassurance: a blatant lie. I had to do it I told myself, I had good reasons; I looked around at my fellow prisoners in the line, every last one of them scared and sad, all had lived through the horrendous train journey, all were hurt, dirty or ill. Like my little brother, every one of them faced a very uncertain future, and right now they all needed reassurance; if it came in the form of a lie, so be it. Klaus returned my smile and so did the two girls, their smiles were strained; they were not good liars. Had they seen my lies? As there was little else I could do, I closed my eyes and began to pray.

My prayers were interrupted by Magda asking the whereabouts of the others. I did not know. "And Frau Leshnik?" I did not know that either. "And what about Boris, and where are we going," I did not know. "And, and," she kept on. I DID NOT KNOW!

The line made slow progress, but the gates grew bigger. The front of the line was already entering. What was behind those gates? What was there, waiting for all these old folk and children? Perhaps it wasn't all that bad, just my imagination that had run wild, I was fearing the worst—that's all; I had done this before, and I had been right. I knew one thing for certain—it was quiet behind that fence— too quiet. What were we walking towards? The suspense was killing me—how was I keeping myself together? As one, we all seemed to tremble, as if someone had walked over our graves, all of our graves—all at once. Don't be stupid I told myself. Soon we would know. Soon we would be through the gates, and everything would be fine…and…and we would all laugh at how silly we had been.

Yes, it would all be okay—wouldn't it? I could not convince myself! With every minute bringing us closer to those gates and every second my imagination rising to a higher level; there was a monster behind the gates, there had to be, and we were being marched straight to it—fed to it like helpless lambs. It would devour us for sure. What to do? What should I do? Should I tell the kids to run for it? Should we fight? Think—think Mona. There was no hope. We could not win. We had no chance. I had to face it—it was all over for us; we were done for. My mind was in turmoil, I could not think; I did not have the answers, I had failed the children—what was I supposed to do?

Then, a miracle happened: it had to be a miracle. When I look back now, I know it was a miracle. There was no other answer for it. This is what happened; let me tell you, let me tell you my miracle—they do happen!

I was startled to hear someone calling my name. How could that be—surely I had gone mad. It was the voice of a girl—an angel! Had I died already, had the monster devoured me? I could hear an angel, but this was not Heaven—certainly not. I looked around but I couldn't see who was calling. Then a lone guard strode up to me, from nowhere he appeared. He was tall with a huge face of solid features, both his nose and chin were created from straight lines and sharp angles, he was in need of a shave and as he spoke he showed two rows of pristine teeth, though his breath was a little stale. His eyes were dark brown, shaded by thick eyebrows and the peak of his cap. Without warning, he placed his rough, dirty hand on my shoulder and pulled me out of the line. "Come, come—" he demanded in broken German.

Klaus and the other children instantly screamed and clung on to me with all their might. But the guard, hindered by his rifle slung over his shoulder, strived to push them back into line. Despite being half his size, I joined the protest. If the little ones were willing to fight, I must join them. I would not be separated before and I would not be separated now. But the man was strong, much stronger than the first guard; he was committed to his task and I was quickly losing the will to fight back. The earlier unexpected spirit I had possessed had now deserted me and I simply could not find the will to defend my little family any longer. It wasn't that I had become weak all of a sudden. I simply did not see the point in going on—what with all these horrid monsters around.

But there was something different this time, there was something else holding me back and allowing him to get the better of me. At first, I couldn't place it, but then I realised, it was his voice. He was speaking to me you see. Somehow, amongst the horror, I grasped he was actually speaking to me and not shouting orders; he was almost pleading and I could see that he was concerned and sincere, it was in his voice, but also in his eyes—he was warning me! In the commotion, his words had been difficult to understand but at last I began to realise what he was trying to say to me. "Go, go," he urged whilst tugging at my sleeve. "Work! Wash clothing," and then the all-important word, "LIVE!"

His message was startlingly clear and in an instant our destination had been confirmed—monsters do exist, and I wasn't surprised by the revelation because, deep in my heart, I knew this extraordinary journey was taking us to a terrible place and would most certainly end in a bad way. We had already experienced some horrendous conditions and treatment; no, there would not be a happy ending for us now. Yes, we were definitely heading towards a monster, we were going to our death and…and this man was offering me a chance to live. I must accept. I could not refuse—could I?

I was faced with a difficult choice—a horrendous choice—can you imagine it. I was so afraid. What if I had made the wrong choice? How ridiculous of me, how absurd. You see, there was no choice at all—not for Mona Lange. The offer was for me only. I most definitely would refuse it. Not without Klaus. Hadn't I already promised never to be separated from him, and now, of course, I had the girls. I would not leave them, nor my little brother. If they were going to face their doom, then I would be tightly holding their hands, there was no doubt about that. We would face our perils together; I had made my decision, I had chosen my path. So despite his pleas, and the fact that I was giving away my last chance to survive, I fought the guard with renewed vigour.

The poor man, this guard that was attempting to rescue me for reasons known only to him, could not afford the commotion we were creating. His fellow guards had seen what was happening and were laughing at him, seeing him as a tormentor and not a saviour. He protested; a vain attempt to stop me fighting back. He was alarmed and confused, I could see it in his face, he needed to seize control, he was quick, he was urgent, but he only had seconds to succeed; that is all he'd allowed himself before he gave up.

Of course, when that moment came, the moment he stopped saving my life, my eyes flooded with tears of… relief, regret, and disappointment simultaneously. The guard had given up his rescue attempt and walked away— just like that! I almost pleaded with him to return, to continue with his efforts— I would give in soon—keep trying I urged and was consumed with guilt. Come up with another solution, one that includes the children—PLEASE!

What did I expect; I had thrown his goodwill in his face and I had wounded him in front of the other guards who now taunted him incessantly. I watched him closely as we moved away, to fall back into line, the children clinging so tightly to me that they almost brought me to the ground. I had mixed feelings then; he had given up and I was torn in two. I wanted to save my own life. Of course I did, who wouldn't, but I had made the correct choice. I was back with Klausy and the girls, and I had not deserted them. I was pleased with my decision; I was proud of myself; indeed I really was their mama for now and always.

A good mama will do all she can to protect her children. There was one thing left for me to do. I needed to break the silence, it would not hurt after the commotion we had just created, and after all, the only guards watching, were the ones who had been amused by the spectacle. Using all my strength, I called after him, "Please sir…Can you not help all of us?" But he had not heard me, he was moving away fast; every moment, every step, taking him further from us and our last chance to live. The children had not recognised the significance of what had just happened and they remained oblivious to what awaited at the end of the line. We were alone again and now had to face our fate beyond the gates, once and for all. I closed my eyes and asked God, "Please make it quick."

But God was not ready for us just yet. I dared to glance at the retreating guard and watched as he was approached by a girl in striped clothes: it had to be a girl, so slim and so small. She was the voice I'd heard calling my name and now she urgently pleaded with him for something. She was obviously very brave and somewhat forceful, arguing her case in a frantic manner. He argued with her just as ferociously and I expected him to hit her, but he stayed his hand. I remember thinking how strange it was that he was actually listening to her at all, when violence was the preferred answer in this place. It was obvious he was trying to dissuade her, but yet she had some sort of power over him and he gave in to her will.

He then took hold of her in a rough manner and marched her over to another guard, his superior. That was the kind of treatment I had expected all along; so nothing strange after all. After a short discussion with the superior officer, perhaps a sergeant, the girl was then pulled by the guard towards the line. Oh dear, was she now in trouble, had she talked her way into the same fate that awaited us? I watched in horror as they headed straight for me. Oh no, I thought—what now?

They say you never know what is around the next corner and I can say this is true, for as the pair approached and my eyes focused on the girl dressed in her shabby striped clothing, my dread changed to amazement. For despite her short hair and thin face, I began to recognise her. I began to feel happy. Can you believe that? I certainly couldn't! Neither could I believe my own eyes. Surely not! It was impossible: it was Ola, my Jewish friend from home—MY MIRACLE!

"Mona, Mona," she said urgently as she approached. There was no time for the pleasantries of reunion. "You must come NOW." I tried to hug her, but she pushed me away. "NO, not here," her voice was harsh and curt, not the friend I had once known.

"Ola, what is happening, what is this place?" I scrutinised her, taking only seconds to see how she had changed. Her manner was urgent where once she had been calm, her face hardened by stress and hardship, her once sparkling eyes, overflowing with love and fun, now dull, but yet, proud and determined still. My old friend had shrunk in size, a mere shadow of what she once was, and her stick-like arms appeared even thinner underneath the overlarge camp clothing. What had happened to the beautiful vibrant young girl who had been my best friend, who I had had so much fun with, who had looked after me and taught me so much, and how had she come to this place? It seemed so long ago now, but it was not even a year ago since I last saw her—surely!

Ola grabbed hold of me by the shoulders. "No time for that now Mona, come, come now. If you pass those gates, you will never be seen again."

I KNEW IT! Those gates meant danger—even death and we were only twenty paces from them. The line had slowed as people started to go through, only one gate had been opened fully and beyond the gate people were undressing. In my mind, there was only one reason for this; they were being fed to the monster, and it was always hungry.

"No, Ola." I pulled away from her and protested. "I will not leave these children."

Ola smiled. Though she seemed hard and unkind in her manner, for an instant, her former beauty returned and her eyes teeming with a fire I had never expected. "I know that, Mona—silly. Do you take me for a fool?" She shook her head in annoyance. "I know you too well, you would never leave them. It was never my intention to leave the children." She glanced at the guard. "That was this big lout's fault." She smiled. "I can't blame him really, he barely understands anything; he's not the brightest, but he will have to do." The guard stared blankly, a confused expression on his face that mirrored my own. Ola shook her head. "You are as dim as him," she said to me and then I heard the words I needed to here so desperately. "Bring them, I have work for you all, I think we will get away with it…Yes it's worth a try."

Right then, I had no idea what my friend was figuring out inside her head, but I didn't care, whatever she had in mind had to work, it simply could not fail, and anyhow, what other choice did we have, we were twenty paces from death! "In this place work means life—for a short time anyway," Ola added, then without waiting for a reply, she simply pulled us out of the line, and the guard, understanding his duty, jabbed his rifle in my back, though not as hard as I expected. "Don't mind Gregor," Ola said. "He plays his part well; he is only acting when he hurts you, putting on a show for the others. Keep away from them, especially Ardit, he has an eye for the girls, especially the new ones. But Gregor—he loves me."

"He does?"

Ola stepped back and glanced at her body, with arms open she indicated, "How can any man resist?"

I smiled at her and her hard face, now rapidly softening, could not help but smile back. I knew she wanted to hug me, but dared not reveal that we were acquainted. It turns out she had been sent to find workers for some sort of sorting shed, where clothes were washed and put back into good use. Ola was supposed to choose healthy prisoners but had decided to take from the line of people doomed to immediate death. She was so smart. It was just like her to do this thing, this wonderful deed, she had chosen to save a few lives, and by chance, by a miracle, she had saved ours.

Now we would have to play our part, we must do her proud. The old Ola was still there hiding inside this hard, purposeful shell. She had rescued us all in the selfless manner that she had possessed when she first took me into her life. I felt a great relief overwhelm me. I had a friend again, a mentor and a teacher. I felt hope returning and my burden of protecting the other kids had instantly halved. "I love you, Ola," I whispered too low for her to hear.

She turned again as her hand fell from my arm to grasp my hand. "I love you too, Mona," she said. "And you too, little Klausy, did you think I'd forgotten you."

The guard said something, his voice urgent and Ola replied, "You are a big softie you know," she replied to him. Then she turned back to the line and politely addressing an old woman clutching a young girl in each hand she softly said, in the most persuasive voice I have ever heard, "Follow me, Grandma, and live."

Gregor offered the faintest smile and pulled the old woman out of line.

"Don't be afraid of him, Grandma. He may have an ugly face, but he is your saviour."

Six people doomed to die, led away by two angels. But many more were left behind. The relief I felt was tainted with guilt. Ola looked at me, her eyes searching my soul. "You cannot save them all, Mona. We do our best. If you want to survive here, you must close your eyes to it, you MUST get used to it."

Chapter 9
Ola the Unbreakable

You know who I am, surely. It's me, your friend Ola. Okay, so I have lost a lot of weight, food here is awful you know and such very small portions. I also do a lot of exercise, you must keep fit here; standards are very high and if you don't meet them, you will either be kicked out or carted out—whichever ill luck gets to you first. I say exercise, of course I'm joking—just kidding that's all; I have such a bad sense of humour, my papa used to scold me about it all the time, but Mama used to giggle—how I miss them.

What I mean to say is—work, hard work. I wish I could add honest hard work but that's impossible. My job—scrubbing clothes clean. I do this every single day, from very early in the morning to exceedingly late at night. I'm sorry I cannot tell you the exact times because I don't know, I haven't known the time since we arrived here. It is always dark when we finish our day and daylight is just breaking when we start, they are the only times I need to know; when it is dark and when it is light—what difference does it make anyway?

I love the early mornings. There is always morning dew around and that nice, fresh feeling in the air. You know what I mean—before the stench of death takes over. It reminds me that there is still a God. There must be; after all I have just been promoted to Angel—fancy that! An angel surrounded by demons, that's for sure.

The clothes washing goes on all day long for many hours, and oh yes, I forgot, we were discussing honest work I believe. How can it be honest work I ask you when all the clothes have been stolen! Yes, that's correct, stolen from the new arrivals who are either put to work—they are the lucky ones just like us, or marched directly to their death—the not so lucky! No, there is nothing honest about my work I'm afraid to say.

Let me tell you a little about me and how my family and I came to be here. My papa was a tailor. He was a very good tailor—excellent even. His business was thriving to the point where he needed to take on more staff. It had been a family business from the start, going back many generations on my papa's side of the family. We had lived on the same street for many years, as far back as 1860—I believe! We were still a family business; Papa would do the measuring and sewing of course, but Mama and I would do the cloth cutting; not to mention the fetching, carrying and packing. There was also the stock-taking, book-keeping, cleaning the shop, making the tea and tidying up and just about everything else you can think of. Do you get the picture?

But Papa was the boss—definitely; except that Mama made all the decisions…and she was in charge of the money. Yes—Papa was the boss; it was his business—haha. How I loved him.

We all busied ourselves at the shop. Even my little brother Jan would help where he could. Papa always rewarded him with a few coins to buy sweets. Jan was always so pleased when he received a reward, his little face would light up with pride and he would race off to meet his friends at the corner shop. He would always share his pocket money and treat them all with sweets. Jan was such a nice little boy.

Frau Weiss, the shopkeeper, was a lovely old lady too, how she made a fuss over my little brother, always giving him more sweets than he could afford. My papa was aware of this and often gave her a scowl accompanied by stern words, playfully of course. "You are spoiling him old woman and you are making yourself poor at the same time." Papa's protests went unheard and Frau Weiss would argue it was Papa doing the spoiling by giving the boy the money in the first place, only he didn't give enough. Papa would smile and then present her with a little gift—a scarf or a handkerchief. She would get all upset over his kindness even though she expected the gift—what crazy folk I lived with. Papa would say it was nothing, made from leftover cloth—rags, nothing more. Frau Weiss would scoff and say she was receiving nothing but rubbish, as usual—and would then hand me something nice from her shelf, often expensive perfume stating it was not in fashion or it smelled off; just in case Papa disapproved. As we walked out Papa would moan that the old woman wanted his daughter to smell like bad eggs. She would be left alone laughing.

At the first chance I got I would share the perfume with Mona of course. Mona Lange was one of my best friends. I liked her so much. With me, she was shy and very much how a girl should be, a proper little lady. But I had seen her play football with the boys and she also had a boyfriend. Though she denied it, she couldn't hide the fact from me; I knew her too well.

I finished school at fifteen years old and was preparing to do further studies. I wanted to be a scientist! Papa often laughed and said I was dreaming. Women could never be scientists, he'd tease. They don't have enough grey matter; he'd say whilst tapping his head. That was Mama's cue to throw something at him. Make some perfume that isn't off he'd say, you will make your fortune. I did not tell him what a good idea I thought that was—how I wished I had.

I was determined to make a success of my life. I was already a very good maths student, the best in my year at school and much better than Papa; the reason why I always checked his accounts for him—which I might add were often wrong. For this, Papa would often surprise me with a new dress that he had made, often out of 'spare' material. I knew this to be a lie as we had no spare material—I should know, I did the books. Silly Papa, he would never be a rich man. I imagined both he and Frau Weiss begging on the streets someday, her wearing all his scarves and him eating her sweets. Money did not matter to him, nor to us either. We were so happy, and happiness, Papa would say, was the best form of wealth. He used to say lots of clever things like that, my favourite— 'You cannot get into Heaven with a bag of gold you know, all you need is a smile'.

All was going well for us really; everything was just right. We all loved our lifestyle and our little town with all our friends and neighbours. But things started to change. I don't know why things can't stay the same, there's something about people, about humankind, something that makes us spoil the good things.

The changes seemed to creep up on us, slowly at first but then things began to gain momentum. We started to get funny looks from people on the street; they were mostly strangers so we did not mind too much. Soon enough though, our friends and neighbours also started to shun us; little things, like crossing the street as we approached and ignoring our greetings. Papa's business began to suffer also with a sudden drop in new orders and orders already placed being cancelled at short notice and without reason and…and very few people came through the door.

I wasn't sure then what was going on or what we had done to deserve such treatment, but I believe Mama and Papa had some idea and they did all they could to try to protect me from the evil times that were approaching fast. For instance, they often hid the daily newspaper from me which told of the growing hatred towards our people—the Jews, and sometimes when Papa came home with dirt on his clothes and even spittle, he always had an excuse for it. I think he knew that I could tell he was lying—even though they were only little white lies—bless him.

So I took matters into my own hands and bought a newspaper from Frau Weiss, at least she still offered a smile. The newspapers had annoying illustrations showing how frightful the Jewish race was. I remember screwing the newspaper up and tossing it away and as I rushed home I began to notice awful slogans written on the walls of shops and houses that I knew belonged to Jewish people.

It was hard to believe at first, how our neighbours had suddenly turned against us, after so many years. How could such a thing happen, how could our neighbours be so horrid when we hadn't done anything to deserve the way they were behaving towards us; when we had been friends for so long—can you imagine? I have to be fair though to the good people around. Not everyone hated us you see. Some friends remained loyal; Frau Weiss for one. This wonderful old lady continued to welcome us into her shop despite the angry looks she, in turn, received and despite the locals boycotting her shop. She didn't care, she announced one day as she packed up her things. "I'm going to Australia to live. I have a wonderful son with grandchildren I have barely seen." With these words she dumped a huge box of sweets on Jan's lap. "You should all come with me. I will pay and that fool of a papa you have can sit on his fortune. Money is for spending," She added with a naughty smile.

Papa replied by paying for a huge leaving party for the old lady. That was a happy day, one of the happiest I can recall. Many people attended, mostly Jews, but a few good Germans—none who would call themselves Aryan. We ought to have gone to Australia with her; the offer was genuine but politely declined.

As expected, things only got worse for the Jews in our district and soon it wasn't safe for us to go outside. We had to sew yellow stars, the Star of David with the word Jew written on it, to our coats, which we had to display whenever we were outside so that people could avoid us, or stop us entering their shops and cafes or, if inclined to do so, generally abuse us. This had been going on for quite some time in neighbouring countries such as Poland but it was new to us in Germany. We were all quite upset about it I can tell you. Jewish people became frightened and started seeking each other out. Mainly to try to figure out what was going on and what we could do about it. However, when the authorities heard of this they soon forbade any gatherings of Jews.

Each night, I would curl up in bed, worrying about our situation. I had wanted to continue my studies but it seemed that my dreams were over; I would never become a scientist and perfume would always stink like bad eggs. If things carried on this way, all I could do was work and live in Papa's shop, which must surely go out of business soon; all we were doing lately was sewing on those ghastly yellow stars that marked us out as some sort of disease to be avoided.

One night, as my mind raced through the horrid events of the day, I was so upset that I couldn't sleep at all. Instead, I turned to my favourite book, The Last of the Mohicans, and began to read. It was such an engrossing story, about two young girls, two sisters named Cora and Alice Munro, who go to visit their papa in the wild forests of Canada. How I wished we could go there; surely we'd be safe and happy and prosperous. But it wasn't safe for the two girls in the book. It appeared we weren't the first people to experience hate. The story told of deceit and treachery and led the girls on a very dangerous path, they would have to be strong and fight for their very lives. I had just read how they were kidnapped by a band of ferocious natives. I was afraid for them…and that was when I heard commotion outside my bedroom window.

Like the girls in my book, I had to be brave and dared to sneak a peek through my curtains. I was horrified to see a group of soldiers at our door, kicking at it. The soldiers of our brave army had grown quite menacing towards us Jews lately, but we thought if we kept our heads down, kept a low profile, we would be left alone. These soldiers hammering at my door had become the bad men in my book; menacing and determined to hurt us. Already, other Jewish people were being herded down the street, just like cattle; they had been dragged from their beds with little time to gather their belongings. On seeing this, I grew nervous and in panic I couldn't think straight, I had no idea what I should do. Inside, my heart pounded—I was useless.

I had to do something fast. Warn my parents immediately. But it was too late, as I saw to my horror, Papa being dragged into the street by soldiers who were very rough with him. He fell to the ground quite hard and my heart broke to see my beautiful and gentle papa treated so.

Mama followed Papa out of the door, she was screaming in sheer panic. Hysterical she was, shouting out to Papa, shouting out to the soldiers to stop; calling out my name—Ola, Ola—help. I was horrified. Inside my body I had turned to jelly, my head spinning. I pressed my face hard against the windowpane. I wanted to shout out, but I had become dumb. I could hear one question going around and around in my head: What to do—what would the girls do, Cora and Alice?

Then all of a sudden, my bedroom door was kicked open, soldiers rushed in and grabbed hold of me roughly by the shoulders before dragging me onto the landing, my feet hardly touching the floor. Jan was being carried down the stairs, he was kicking and screaming but I stayed silent, I just needed to get to my family and I seemed to know that the only way to do that in one piece, was to keep calm. "Please," I said, "it's alright, I will come, I will follow—don't hurt us."

We were thrown into the street. That's when the soldiers let us go with a simple point of a finger—down the road—go that way. We ran as fast as we could and soon we were reunited with Mama and Papa who were so relieved to see us. We were all bewildered and…and devastated! We had left our home behind and all our possessions—what were we to do now. I will never forget the worry on Papa's face; it said a thousand things—all crazy and scary. There were so many questions to answer then: What was going to happen to us; how will we live now? Without a livelihood, without a house, without our little tailor's shop. As we moved down the street, we were joined by other Jews and behind us, we could hear our house being vandalised and all our furniture being smashed and all Papa's suits being destroyed.

None of it made sense; what was the purpose of this? How could people be so cruel? Despite the late hour, many of our neighbours were watching the commotion through their windows, hiding behind closed curtains. They did nothing to help us, some were even cheering on the soldiers; how quickly they had turned on us. Papa muttered how they were all the same and I immediately thought about Mona then. My good friend Mona, she was not the same at all; she was nothing like these people. She was good and kind, she was my friend and she would be livid if she could see this, this bizarre thing, this shameful spectacle!

We were rounded up with all the other Jews and marched down a maze of streets, finally ending up in a large yard surrounded with high brick walls. It was damp and cold with little protection from the weather. There must have been two or three hundred people here, all clumped together in their family groups. Like us, they were all dumbfounded. Stunned, they sat on the ground, quiet and afraid. The only belongings they had were the things they were able to carry with them.

In our case, we had nothing whatsoever; I was wearing my night dress. Papa was the only one wearing a coat and he shared it so the four of us could huddle closely under it in the cold night air. It was inadequate, but we loved Papa for it.

We stayed in the yard for the rest of the night and most of the next day with no food and drink and by the time we were moved on, many were ill and weak. Some of the older people were spared the journey to Hell inside the cattle wagon. I did not know what had happened to them at that time, had the cold got them or had they died of fright! Whatever the reason, they had escaped the nightmare that was to come.

We entered the death camp in the same manner as Mona and the children, a long train journey followed by the separating process. Papa urgently explained we were a family of tailors in a brave effort to keep us together. Thankfully, he had taught me how to sew and mend clothing well and so the two of us were sent to the sorting shed. We would mend clothes but we could never mend our broken hearts. You see, there was no place here for my little brother Jan, no matter how much Papa pleaded for him. Mama—my brave mama, would not let go of Jan's hand and so, without a single word of goodbye, half of my family walked in the direction of Mona's monster—we never saw them again.

It was too much for Papa. One day he kissed me tenderly on the cheek and I knew this was goodbye. I remember the sadness in my papa's eyes as he explained how a bullet was only an instant of pain and then all the suffering is done. He simply sat down on the hard dusty ground and refused to move. The bullet did indeed deliver a quick end for Papa. It was the hardest thing I had ever seen—so far.

Papa lasted only a few days before he died from his broken heart, I still live with the pain of mine. I knew Papa hadn't made the decision to leave me without weighing up the consequences. He needed to be with Mama and Jan—they needed him. I was stronger, or at least Papa thought I was. I would become Cora Munro or Alice. I would be brave—I would face my nightmare—I would survive. This terror could never last I knew that much for sure. I had made my mind up. I would make it my responsibility, my mission to tell this horrendous story to the whole, wide world.

Chapter 10
Ardit and the Black Knight

I was five when I first met her: the love of my life.

Before she arrived, there was very little to do in my village, it was very small you see. A tiny settlement in the middle of nowhere, no more than a clearing on the mud track that brought scant traffic from way down south and on towards the great Ukrainian city of Odessa in the north.

It was so quiet here, so peaceful. Surrounded mostly by a huge forest with a few small fields of vegetables, mainly corn, and the odd orchards laden with apples and pears, all kept free of weeds by the very hard-working villagers. They occupied the nine tiny cottages that were always in need of repair and the two larger farms found a little way along the track in the distance. This was Moldavia, at least for now; our part of it had been disputed for many years by the many nations that surrounded us; and others from afar.

Life was hard here. Each day brought back-breaking hard work for the adults working long hours in the fields or gathering wood in the forest. If the harvest failed, which often it did, the forest would provide berries, mushrooms and game—but not always.

I was the only child in the village in those days. Illness and poverty had claimed the rest. There was no one to play with; I was so lonely. Each day I wandered around aimlessly, spending hours exploring the forest, I left no stone unturned as I searched for small creatures and strange fungi or I would swim in the stream, there were many deep pools that had formed naturally. My papa had put up a rope swing over one of them for me to play with; I had hours of fun with it, launching myself from a great rock and splashing into the water. On occasion, Papa and some of the younger men would join in, the water was so fresh and clean, but very cold. These were rare occasions and we were warned not to do it. You see, we were a very superstitious people. We should avoid the forest if possible, only entering for wood and food—nothing else, especially fun. The older villagers did indeed keep clear of it—it was cursed. It was cruel. Witches lived in it, with their pets—the monsters! Let me tell you more.

Hundreds of years ago, far too long for anyone to remember the date, the forest was a dark and lonely place, occupied by an ancient witch, a tree spirit known to the people that lived here at the time, the Bulgars, as Baba Yaga. This evil old hag was said to be as old as the forest itself. She was ugly beyond reason; her face full of black warts, her back bent almost double, her head, bald with a few strands of long grey hair that reached down to drag in the mud. She was the voice of the forest, the very essence of it. She had many rules that must be obeyed. Anyone who didn't obey, first felt her cane; a gnarled and ancient tree root said to have been taken from the oldest tree for hundreds of miles. It was a Grandfather Yew that could be found in the very centre of the forest; a place full of magical folk: of pixies and fairies, goblins, elves, imps and demons, and a myriad of amazing creatures. It was a place where no one dared venture. Baba Yaga was charged with protecting the forest at all costs. She spent many hours keeping intruders out. It was rule number one—keep out of the forest.

The hag did not work alone, her burden shared with the Leshy, a huge man-like monster that could change shape. Some said the Leshy was the first-born son of Baba Yaga, no one knew if this was true of course, or if Baba Yaga had given birth to other children. Some said she was the mother of trees, and therefore had millions of children—who knows! What is known is that when summoned by Baba Yaga, the Leshy would come forward to avenge the forest. Many had encountered this pair who had been named evil, though it was their nature to protect the forest only. Fair warning had been given. The rules were known to all local people.

Yet invaders from foreign lands came in their thousands: Dacians, Romans, Goths, Huns, Turks and Mongols. All came to settle and if they were to succeed, they needed to harvest wood from the forest—to destroy it. They met the wrath of the Leshy in their hordes, thousands perished and eventually, new residents learned to treat the forest with the respect it demanded.

People began to settle again and an age passed with man and forest living in harmony. Wood was collected, it was needed for building and burning, but only that willingly given by the forest was allowed. Eventually, as generations came and went, the witch and the Leshy fell into legend.

Newcomers arrived, hailing from Bulgaria. These people, like all others before them, were fierce and powerful, and like all conquerors, these people were not afraid of mad witches, they did not believe in monsters and they heeded to no rules but their own. So, disregarding all warnings they set about the forest with their newly sharpened axes and a large community began to grow, the largest ever to settle in the area. They began to prosper. The village continued to expand as streets began to form and a market square became the centre of attention. A church was erected and each new house was bigger than the last. The village was now a town, much to the detriment of the forest. The people became rich and proud, and they forgot about the curse, and the witch and the monsters that protected the forest; they now entered without fear or caution.

Enough was enough! It had to happen, she had to come. She did not work alone. It is said that an old woman wandered out of the forest. Old and ancient and bent double, held upright by a gnarled and knotted old stick of Yew and dressed in garments that resembled leaves and vines. Where had this woman come from? There was no road into the forest from the direction, whence she had come. How had she survived deep in the dark forest?

The entire town came out to see the ugly old woman whose face was covered in warts and whose hair dragged in the mud. On sight, the oldest in the town remembered a name—Baba Yaga was whispered. The old witch heard the whisper and laughed. Ever so slowly, she made her way to the little town and upon entering the market square, she stood motionless, scanning, observing and taking in every detail.

A huge crowd gathered, and finally, a town elder challenged the old woman. "Who are you? Where do you come from? What do you want?"

Ignoring the questions, the hag offered a hint of a smile and spoke at last. "There was once a time when the land was covered in trees," she said, her voice hoarse, but deep; blessed with wisdom and sadness. "As far as the eyes could see they grew; on every hill, in valleys, moors, marshes and dells. Dense they were, their branches entwined hugging their neighbours, lush and happy. No space for bush to grow or fern to flourish, nowhere for flower to bloom, nor bramble to roam. No hideaway for a mouse to run or rabbit to burrow. Only birds shared this place, gliding through the blue skies and settling on the arms and fingers of these mighty trees, reaching ever further towards the Heavens."

"Then from the ground they came: the elf, the fairy, the giant and the dwarf and they paved the way for the worst of all—the man. Left unchecked, the man spread across the land, like a disease, a canker, killing all in his path for all he knew, was how to destroy. And so I was released. Some call me witch, others hag, fewer name me Mother of Trees. My purpose: retribution."

The people gawped in amazement and fear. She stepped closer and offered another smile, this time, her mouth opened wide, revealing gums almost bare but for a few sharp thorns serving as teeth. "You will continue to destroy. That is the purpose of mankind. And you shall pay, for I shall see to that." Then, with her stick, she rapped on the great wooden door of the church and warned, "For that door there is a price—the most terrible price." The townsfolk watched in wonder and alarm as the church door split asunder. Entering the church, the old woman pointed to the wooden beams of the church roof and called out again, "For those beams a price will be paid." Without warning, she tossed her cane into the roof and every beam that was touched by it cracked from end to end. The terrified townsfolk ran for their lives as the church began to crumble.

Next, the old woman began to wander around the town, down every lane and into every yard. At every house, she pointed out the price that must be paid in return for the timber that had been stolen from the great forest. The strangest thing is—she spoke only to the owners of each dwelling. The poor folk watched in stunned silence as every tap of her cane wrought destruction to their beloved homes.

Talk of the curse began to spread and of course, the townsfolk became nervous, demanding answers from the woman, "Is this the price you seek, that we should lose our homes?" a brave woman asked. Baba Yaga offered a final smile, "There is another to come, and he will take what is owed." Hearing these words, the townsfolk ran to hide, some to their homes, and others, in their panic, to the forest—there would be no safe place there. The wealthy returned with bags of money, anxious to pay their debt. The old woman ignored these fools and moved on, continuing her dire warnings at each house she came across.

By now, hysteria ruled, women were on their knees, praying; children cried and men argued and cursed. Baba Yaga wondered around for an age, leaving no dwelling, barn or fence untouched by her witchcraft. At last, finally satisfied, the witch laughed out loud, a sound that could be heard for miles around, a sound that was also a summons. "He will fall upon you. He is my son; he seeks justice for his kin; he is the wrath of the forest." Her final words left the townsfolk fearing for their lives. Pleased with her work, Baba Yaga wandered back into the forest from whence she had come, leaving the town in ruins.

After many meetings held by the town's elders, the townsfolk retreated to their shattered homes, all doors locked and all windows shuttered tight. That night, the wind howled and snow fell out of season. The sun rose only to be covered over by the moon—a sure sign of doom. Great trumpets sounded in the distance and alarm bells responded. The frightened people opened their doors to a very dark day and froze in horror as a man in black, a huge knight, rode slowly into town on his great charger; behind him, a column of riders wielding swords, spears, and flags bearing the face of the devil. The Leshy takes on many forms, and he had come to avenge the forest. All would pay!

I am here to collect a debt, the black knight announced, and when all the gold and silver and pennies were piled high at his feet, the great knight glanced at it and declared that it did not suffice. The town was searched for anything of value and soon enough a pile of silver plates, candlesticks, crucifixes and even buttons, joined the gold and silver coins. Silence fell as the elders waited in dismay for the great knight to speak. "It is not enough," he growled and a shudder ran through the whole town.

In desperation, the townsfolk fell to their knees and began to plead for their lives, for though they were uneducated, every last one of them knew what was to come. The havoc that followed had not been witnessed since the time of the Mongols and when, finally, the knight and his men rode out of town, only a handful of survivors remained to tell their tale. The cursed forest was feared once more.

Years past and again, the curse was largely forgotten, kept alive by a few vigilant people determined to ensure the existence of their families and descendants. Time after time, the forest was violated and time after time, the forest was avenged. Tatars and then Hungarians experienced the terrible curse and many towns and villages rose and fell, as the Leshy in its many forms returned to collect the debt owed to the forest mother. No army could stand against the mighty beast, all would bow and all would pay.

Finally, my own ancestors, descended from the people named Rus who had come out of the east to make a new life here. The Rus were careful people, exceedingly superstitious. They had heard of the Witch and the Leshy Knight, they vowed to protect the forest at all costs, for it was the only way to survive.

Of course, my people needed the forest for building material and for fuel and so they were very careful to take only fallen wood from the very edge of the forest, always cautious not to cut from the living trees. So far, their vigilance had kept the old woman satisfied and she in turn had kept her son, the mighty black knight at bay.

That was my favourite story, and though I say story, we all believed it to be true. My greatest wish as a young and lonely boy, was to see the elves and fairies, and the giants and trolls, and most of all, to meet Baba Yaga and her fearsome son, the Leshy. I do hope you enjoyed my story. Now where was I—Oh yes, let's start here.

Sometimes the adults gave me chores to do. They kept me busy when I was bored. It was never hard work, but the chores were dull. Most times, I was sent to help the older people in the village, especially my grandma. I helped her make many repairs to her little house. Then we would enjoy hot milk and biscuits that she would bake especially for my visits. That is when I heard of the Leshy and his mama the witch. Grandma would make me promise, to Almighty God no less, that I would believe in the curse. "Never forget it—NEVER," she would scream whilst shaking me with both hands. Of course I promised her, each and every time—I would never forget.

Disease took my grandma; it had to come, she was ancient after all, for twenty years she had been waiting to be reunited with my grandpa. The little house was left empty and cold, there were no more biscuits and no more horror stories, and no more promises to be made or kept. It remained empty for a long time and with no one bothering to make repairs, it threatened to fall down.

I was bored again and returned to my chores, despairing that life would never change in this miserable little place. It did change: in a big way. It arrived suddenly; in a truck packed with furniture. I was delighted to see it; automobiles were rarely seen in the village. I was allowed to sit in the driver's seat where I convinced myself I would become a great truck driver and drive wonderful new trucks all around the world. The truck was unloaded in a hurry and I was saddened to watch it race off down the hill. It left a pile of furniture behind, accompanied by a man and a woman and…and a little girl.

Katya was six. Our eyes met and we stood in silence and wonder. She smiled and her hazel eyes sparkled in a pretty face surrounded by long mouse-coloured curls. My family clasped hands with hers, and we ran off to play. We had such a wonderful day exploring all my favourite play areas. I had so much to show her and at the end of the day I was exhausted and, though I did not know it then, I was in love. Katya had brought summer with her and soon the fields and hedgerows were bursting with flowers of all colours. From that day, life was good for me.

Katya's papa was named Axle. He was a giant of a man with a huge beard and a head full of long black hair. His arms were as thick as tree trunks and his hands were the biggest I'd ever seen, yet he was a gentle man, a craftsman and not a fighter, as was expected. He turned out to be a carpenter, a very skilled one at that, and pretty soon he'd created some wonderful furniture from wood donated by the village elders. I spent hours watching him and he taught me how to use his wonderful tools, many he'd actually made with his own massive hands, such as his selection of mallets, his wood chisels and spoke shaves.

Anoosha was Katya's mama. She was quite tall for a woman. She was slender and elegant in her manner. Anoosha had beautiful black hair which she wore loose; for a mama she was quite pretty. Katya obviously inherited her beauty as her papa wasn't the most handsome man around. Anoosha mostly helped with the furniture making, her task consisted of polishing and cleaning, but she was a very intelligent woman, it shone from her eyes, a sparkle that ensured she kept our attention when she spoke. She had received an education! This was a rare thing in these parts, leaving her studies only to follow Axle to a new life, where he could make his fortune.

Eventually, the pair took on an apprentice for the workshop, which allowed Anoosha to open a school and put her talents to good use. The school was exceedingly small of course with just the two of us kids around, but later some adults attended when they had time; and also, Axle began to show all the menfolk how to make furniture. Pretty soon, the village was making cartloads of the stuff, mainly chairs, but also tables and cabinets; we were also getting brighter in the bargain!

Axle was a good man and encouraged many of the village folk to get involved. Soon word began to spread far and wide about our furniture and we were very pleased when people from other villages and towns arrived one day to purchase it. More orders came in from even further afield and soon the furniture was being exported great distances, mainly by horse and cart but the occasional truck turned up now and then much to my delight. With the growing success now shared by the villagers, Papa announced that I could begin my apprenticeship immediately. I had already gained some knowledge and was disappointed when I had to start at the very beginning of the process, collecting the fallen and dead wood from the forest.

113

At this point of my tale, I need to remind you of something, something that I could not forget, because I had made so many promises, both to my grandma and in front of God—the curse!

Wood was now in great demand and as we used up the wood that had been given freely by the cursed forest, like many other people before us, our attention soon turned to the living trees. When Axle heard the tales of woe that had befallen these parts at the hands of the Baba Yaga and the great Leshy, he laughed it off—just like that, and just like the Turks had done and the Mongols and the Hungarians and the rest, Axle declared the curse to be nothing but superstition and coincidence. He was very convincing and when Anoosha also dismissed the stories as old wives' tales, my neighbours began to listen and even agree.

Katya's parents were a formidable pair. We all admired them—we all believed them. It didn't take long to convince us that the only way forward, if we wanted the village to prosper that is, was to dismiss our superstitions and take a few select trees from the forest. It was decided then—what harm could it do, we would choose trees that were dying and that would soon be available to us anyway. This would not only provide the raw material for our newfound craft, but also create more land for farming and expanding the village.

Though the village elders agreed, the only person to step forward with axe and saw was Axle, and with a broad smile on his face, he chose a tree. He did not choose wisely! Ignoring the dying and diseased trees, the big man chose a magnificent elm tree that had guarded the gate to the forest for centuries. This tree had witnessed the destruction of many a village and town, it had been forever present, part of our very lives. As the axe sliced into the huge trunk, the people of the village sighed—it was too late to change our minds now. The great grandpapa elm came crashing down to the ground. Soon we would find out if the curse was real or a myth of old.

Days turned into months and even years past without any evil event falling upon us. The villagers began to relax—but not entirely. I worked long hours alongside my papa who turned out to be really accomplished at making chairs. I also made progress and soon moved onto the next stage, which was more interesting—shaping and sanding chair legs. By the age of nine, I could fashion a whole chair from wood freshly cut from nearby trees. Our success encouraged other people to move into our village and by the time I was twelve, the little place had doubled in size.

All the new homes were made from wood from our forest and fashioned in our workshop which by now dominated the village, yes, that's correct, we had expanded into making doors and window frames and simple planks for flooring and walls, and roof tiles and fencing and ladders and wheelbarrows and carts and everything else needed to build a house and home. Though Axle was the boss man, the ownership of the business was shared by all the main families in the village. We prospered, and our fame spread far, and wide.

I loved the work, the smell of sawdust, the wood chippings littering the entire village, the finished products that were displayed for all to admire. All the men employed as carpenters tried to out-do each other and so we all continued to improve at our trade and our products, even a simple wooden lintel became as ornate as it could be before it was utilised for the purpose it was made for. Carvings began to appear on things from chairs to doors and our designs grew more intricate as the years sped past.

Katya also worked in the wood shop. She wasn't half bad for a girl. All the women helped in one way or another; in fact, most of the villagers were involved when they weren't tending the fields.

The new residents of the village and the merchants that visited brought more children. Now, at last, we were able to play games such as football and hide-and-seek, after we had finished our day's work in the workshop of course. Katya was always on my side; she was my best friend; we were inseparable. I saw her as my girl. You know what—one day we would be married. We had said as much and agreed it would be so. It makes me smile when I remember how happy we were then.

The curse was forgotten along with my promise to Grandma, it was something from the past and we were only looking towards a wonderful future. The carpenter's shop kept on growing in size and we all had enough money to buy food to supplement what we could grow ourselves. Indeed, as we felled the trees for the woodworking, more fields were created just as Axle had said, and soon there were cows and pigs and goats all over the place, we wanted for nothing.

We continued to build new cottages and as soon as they were finished they were occupied by new arrivals to the village. The school grew in size also and a second workshop was built to provide work for the newcomers. I increased my hours in the workshops and the beginnings of an accomplished carpenter began to take shape. Also taking shape, a church and a town square—you heard me, our village was now a town—we were townsfolk now and our town was given a name—Woodville!

Just after my thirteenth birthday yet another family, who had heard of our success, moved into Woodville; another carpenter, attracted by the work and his seamstress wife, they had five sons no less. A baby, two small boys and two that were slightly older than me; both had fancies for Katya. Every time she smiled at them I was hurt inside and, on occasion, I found her alone with them—this was the worst of times.

Though Katya often reassured me that I was her best friend, I often felt angry. I was racked with jealousy you see; I couldn't help it. Without realising, I had become quite possessive. No wonder, with so few girls of our age around for miles. Papa just laughed and said it was all part of growing up. He warned if I wanted to keep Katya for my own then I would have to claim her and fight for her. He wisely advised that as there were two of them, I must not run into trouble blindly or I would lose. I needed a plan—that was the key to success.

I could always count on Papa for sound advice and so I made my plan. I would move fast and sort both my problems in one day. First, I would tackle Yoet. He was the younger of the two and I reckoned the easiest to beat. Yoet liked to make eyes at Katya when she finished her reading lessons. I watched as she left school and strolled towards the field where we had put up a swing, of course Yoet wasn't far behind. My plan consisted of this: walk up to Yoet and smack him in the face. Not much of a plan you say and you are correct.

Yoet turned out to be a marvellous fighter for his age, years spent sparring with his older brother had seen to that! The fight lasted ages and on many occasions I felt I was losing. There was no shame in that; Yoet was a year older than me—at least. I did not give up. I had fight left in me and so I continued with renewed vigour and you know what, my persistence won the day, as eventually Yoet had no more to give. I can still feel the moment when his strength left him and I sensed my victory.

Despite this and the fact that I was thoroughly exhausted, I gave Yoet a final clout—just in case he had any more ideas and to make sure he didn't put them into action. Yoet got the message clear enough and never made eyes at Katya again, though we included him in all our games and sports—we were still lacking decent numbers for a football team after all. He had been defeated, and by a younger boy, but he submitted admirably and had earned my respect and friendship forever.

I was now prepared for Petru. He was bigger and stronger than Yoet. I had my doubts he could be beaten but the stakes were higher for me—Katya was my girl. Then good old Papa's advice helped once again. "Love is always worth fighting for. I fought off six of the strongest for your mama." He broke off as Mama clouted him for lying. "If you believe she is worth it, go get her." I recall I began to speak but he shushed me. "If she loves you, it will not matter to her that you lose at least one battle. It is the fight that counts."

Petru was not only the oldest; he was the most cunning of the brothers and often led Katya away so they could be alone. He was turning into a young man, with fluff on his face and she was shaping into a fine young woman. I was so jealous—I hated him for trying to steal her away from me. I remember looking at him and thinking how huge he was. Well he was tall but also very lean, like a bean pole, but there was something formidable about him, perhaps it was his wonky eye that made him look fierce—I wasn't sure. What I did know, was that he was after kissing Katya; eventually he would succeed. I was determined to do something about it. So, I put my plan into action again—to walk up to Petru and smack him in the face—harder than I had Yoet…I hoped. This I did and remember closing my eyes to receive the expected beating. It did not come. Petru had been knocked out completely by my blow. I had got lucky!

Katya told me off but I knew she was impressed. As a consequence, all the kids in Woodville were now afraid of me. From then on, I kept a scowl on my face, to look tough and keep Petru at bay. Though, inside, I remained a nice boy and allowed all, including Petru to join my newly formed football team. He became the best goalie in town.

I had now reached the age of fourteen and I was madly in love with Katya. Not only was I a skilled carpenter but I could read and write better than most and I had already put some money aside and both my parents were very proud of my achievement. Woodville had increased in size and we now had a considerable football team, which I coached and managed, appointing Petru, the second-best footballer, to be captain.

To demonstrate how proud he was of me, my papa presented me with a piece of land at the edge of the rapidly growing town. I was now a landowner and Papa pointed to a huge pile of wood planks. "You know what to do son," he said with a smile and within hours, I had designed my own house which I intended to build, without help, though plenty was offered.

Katya too, was excited and both her mama and papa approved of our courtship and though our marriage was not formally arranged we all knew it was certain. I had a wonderful future ahead of me, I worked hard, eager to finish my house and marry the girl I loved; a date was set just after my fifteenth birthday. The house began to take shape. I worked alone only allowing my friends and family to clear and prepare the garden and fields that were to house a few goats. At last, I stood back to admire my house.

My papa placed his hand around my neck and as he pulled me close, he rubbed his knuckles playfully across my head. It hurt but I was glad. Next Katya's papa and many others lifted me high above their heads and soon I was surrounded by all the men, women, and children of the town who sang songs and brought gifts. The entire house was stuffed with wonderful, handcrafted furniture and then I was ushered outside. My eyes were covered and when I was allowed to open them, I saw the delighted face of Katya staring up at me. It was the happiest day of our lives.

Not a week later, a truck pulled into Woodville to take away a load of planks. Inside the cab sat an old woman, her grey hair mostly covered with a black scarf. She turned and smiled; a toothless smile surrounded with a wrinkled face covered in black warts—it sent shivers down my spine. The driver announced that the great people of Germany had invaded the vast land of Poland. "This would mean troubled times," he warned.

My fifteenth birthday arrived and Katya and I were wed soon after. Life in Woodville continued to flourish and happily our first baby was on the way. Except for the increase in orders for wood, either for building or for burning in the metalwork factories that had sprung up in the huge cities of Russia, Poland, Romania and other great places that surrounded us; the war in distant lands was mostly forgotten. But as the truck driver warned, we, in our rural paradise, would not avoid the horrors of war that were approaching fast. At last, ignoring his mama's tears, my best friend Petru, packed his bags and set off to war.

He had no need to bother, for soon after, the war, which was now engulfing the entire world, came up the little mud track and paid a visit to Woodville.

They arrived early and were greeted by the field workers who were always the first to rise in the morning. There were hundreds of them, all in brown, as if they had risen from the mud, and all carrying rifles. I wasn't sure at first but soon realised they were mostly Romanian soldiers with some Nazis. The field workers offered no threat, yet they were beaten and rounded up like goats. Almost immediately, the usual calming effect of the dawn chorus was replaced with screams and shouts of protest.

Within seconds, every man in the village was outside to investigate the commotion and they too were instantly rounded up. An expensive black car arrived, closely followed by trucks crowded with more soldiers. A tall man climbed out of the car, he was clad in black, trimmed with shiny metal finery. His face in shadow: his eyes dark. Images of the Black Knight of old appeared in my mind—the great Leshy had arrived as promised; death had come at last to claim payment for the forest. Grandma had been right all along.

No sooner had these vehicles screeched to a stop did the soldiers jump out and scatter through the town and all the while, the Leshy bawled his orders; never had I seen a man command so much authority. Many people ran away to be pursued by soldiers. As they disappeared into the forest where the great elm had once stood, screams were heard, I saw no one return. At the sound of the Leshy's voice, all the women and girls that had not run away cried in despair and the men backed away to crouch in doorways; even his own soldiers flinched as the Black Knight barked out his terrible orders.

The soldiers kicked down doors and further screaming came from every cottage and then that sound we all dreaded—a gunshot! The townsfolk fell silent for barely seconds before the sound of wailing and moaning choked the air—someone had been killed. More orders followed and we were all revived from our trance before being shoved into small groups, surrounded by guards. I was separated from Katya who had been dragged out of our cottage along with our baby girl. They too were herded together with other women including her mama and papa. My own parents were huddled in a third, smaller group a little way off. I watched in anger as flames licked at the carved lintel of my cottage door.

"Identify the Jews," the Leshy demanded. "Identify the Jews and the rest of you will be released." We were all petrified, not a word was uttered; we were stunned and bewildered. "My name is Leshnik. I am the commandant in this district. You will obey me and no one else. Is that clear?" Complete silence followed as the commandant—as the Leshy—as the Black Knight expected. "I am in charge of this district which must be cleansed. Now bring me the Jews and the rest of you can get on with your dreary lives."

Again, there was no answer. I watched as Herr Leshnik's face grimaced. He was losing patience by the second. He nodded to a soldier, perhaps a lieutenant, I could not tell. A simple nod, nothing more; that was all it took. A second shot rang out. It was harmless and fired into the sky and everyone fell silent. The demand was repeated. "Bring out the Jews." The continued silence was unacceptable and a third gunshot deafened our ears…Yoet fell dead! The screaming lasted for only a minute before a fourth shot, also fired into the sky quietened the folk of Woodville, each and every one of them searching for the victim.

"You will bring me the Jews or you will all die one by one." Herr Leshnik glared at us all, his eyes burning into every last one of us. "It means nothing to me. It is completely your choice."

Then I heard a voice that broke my heart. "Please sir…Our town is poor, there are no Jews here." I prayed that Papa would say no more.

"Nonsense. That is a lie. This is a wealthy place. The name is recognised for miles around when other towns are forgotten. You have a thriving business here. Therefore there must be Jews around. Wherever there is money, there are Jews— yes? Now, bring them out."

"Please sir," was all Papa could say before he collapsed to the sound of a gunshot. I screamed and pushed towards him. But I was stopped by the butt of a rifle that sent immense pain through my head; I sensed myself falling before I was covered in blackness and silence. I did not see what happened then but the tale I was told both sickened and enraged me.

A second man was shot dead, an old farmer and next in line was his ailing wife. But before she was executed, Katya's papa, Axle, held up his hand and lied. "I am a Jew. I am the only Jew in Woodville."

Katya then made a fatal error, and screamed out the word. "PAPA!"

"Bring out the Jew," Herr Leshnik ordered. "Bring out his daughter also," he announced, "I see she has a child. There must be a husband somewhere." Katya's protests were fruitless as she was dragged into the open. But the Leshy Leshnik was not yet satisfied. "I am lacking a wife for this Jewish man. I am lacking a husband for this woman," he announced as Katya and her papa were pushed forward, "and there must be other family members. It is well known that Jews have large families—yes? I am lacking another Grandmama at the very least. I have a papa for the girl but no Mama."

It took another rifle shot and a dead farmer's wife. Axle sighed. He had failed to save her after all. He had endangered his family for nothing. But the stunned townsfolk were not without their wits by now. The three dead were identified as Jews and offered as payment; Yoet, a father for the baby, the farmer and his wife, a grand-mama and a grand-papa. A fourth body was brought from the woods—an elderly woman, and the Leshy smiled.

A silence fell and the townsfolk held their breath—had payment been made! Only the Leshy had the answer and he too remained silent, in deep thought. Nerves were racked, tension mounting. It was too much for Katya's mama, who then made a fatal mistake. Desperate to be reunited with her family she stepped forward as the missing mama. The Leshy smiled; it was full of evil intent.

"That makes four grandparents, two parents, a young man and his wife. This Jewish family is not large enough. You people are lying to me…Where are the uncles, the aunts, the cousins?" He clapped his hands. "Bring them out—NOW."

Complete stillness: absolute silence.

"You have made your choice then—good," Herr Leshnik announced. "This group here," I'm told he pointed to my group, "is free to go. These other two groups are clearly Jews. Bring them." With these last words, my entire world crumbled. In an instant, everything we had worked hard to achieve in our little paradise town was lost, and my darling Katya, the girl I had loved since I was five years old, the girl whose heart I had won in battle as a boy had gone from my life, along with my baby and eighty-three innocents.

I woke in pain that ravaged my head, a pain that dwindled with time. Yet the worst pain, that in my heart, that threatens to kill my soul will never subside, not until I find my Katya.

"I swear my darling Katya that I will find you. I swear to you Herr Leshnik, that I will find you also. I know what you are. You are the son of the witch; I have seen her and I will find her again. You are the Leshy, you are the Black Knight, the Monster. You are a mighty foe. But I…I have a plan!"

Chapter 11
The Sorting Shed

It seems that there is trouble and hardship everywhere these days. Mama used to say that what we experience in life shapes the way we turn out in the end. Having now heard Ardit's story I can understand why he is like he is. Of course you do not know yet, but Ardit has a bigger part to play in my tale. You will hear of a bitter man who is constantly searching. His search leads him to the camp, where he puts his plans into action. He does not trust anyone and refuses to make any friends. For that reason, he is not trusted in return, especially by Ola who believes he has an unhealthy interest in the new girls that arrive. My friend believes his intentions are dishonourable. But we know his reasons—don't we? We know what he is looking for—the love of his life! We would do the same, I'm sure of it.

Anyhow, guess what? I have not only digressed but I am jumping ahead! Back to my own tale.

We had dwindled in number till there were only four of us remaining of the original eleven that had set off in the rain on that miserable day; myself, Klaus, Magda and little Leni. I wondered about the others for a long time. I worried so; I missed them so. I had realised how important they'd been to me; how important we had been to each other. Things would never be the same. I learned that they had been put to work; hard labour of some kind or another, in one of the many factories that surrounded this evil place. I imagined how hard things must be, the days crammed with hard work, and the nights—well, they must be so exhausted. It must have been hard for them. I longed for news. Were they all alive? Or had some of them fallen? I couldn't bear to think. Was it better for me to forget them? Or should I keep them alive, at least in my mind. But of course they were alive, deep down I knew this to be true. They were useful, and if you are useful here, there is a chance to live.

I guess we were all useful for a short while, until we became ill or too weak to work, until we were dying—either from disease or hardship or…torture. Then we would join the other line of people, the line walking to the left, towards the gates of no return where the monster waited with its sharp claws and snapping jaws. I wondered if Ola's brother, little Jan, and her mama and papa had gone that way also. Of course they had, I knew this was true, though my friend had not mentioned them at all and I did not dare ask. Ola would not trouble anyone else with the sorrows that she had experienced. That was just like her.

Our little group had been more fortunate than Ola's lot, and it was all thanks to Ola herself. After our miracle, and I say it again, because it was a miracle, I am certain of it, she had rushed us through a series of fences and walls to an enclosed yard. The place was as big as a school gym I guessed and was covered by a rusty tin roof supported by iron beams that were just as rusty, it didn't look very sturdy to say the least. The walls were made of wooden planks, they were rotting and broken and many were loose; big holes allowed the weather, whatever it was, to enter.

Beneath this shelter, many young women and girls were busy at work. Some were sorting piles of clothing, which made the place resemble a huge jumble sale. There were giant heaps of garments of every size, colour and design; brand new clothing still with labels on and old rags full of holes. There were dresses, skirts, blouses, shirts, trousers, socks and undergarments and hosiery of all sorts. The variety was immense; I had no idea there was so much choice, the entire collection reaching as high as the ceiling of the building.

In the centre of the large room, there were other women separating jewellery and pocket watches and spectacles which had been strewn across a simple wooden table. There were also rings, necklaces, earrings and even the odd tiara. Cufflinks, badges and buttons, hip flasks, cigarette cases, and buckles, covered every inch of the next table along, and a third table was laden with wallets and purses, all ready to be plundered. In fact, there were all sorts of odds and ends being separated. It resembled Aladdin's cave in here, the people that ran this place obviously liked order.

Yet more girls, in the far corner, sorted shoes and hats, gloves, belts and braces. Again, huge piles were forming and other girls were packing these away into boxes, securing them with string and labelling them to be shipped out. Shoes were tied together and the more expensive hats were also packed carefully; whilst the cheaper things, the cloth caps and scarves were simply thrown into hessian sacks. I watched as the full sacks and boxes were loaded onto carts and taken away to be put to good use, I suppose.

I stared in amazement: soaking in the scene. There was a stack of scarves, another made up of umbrellas, yet another of handbags; over here a table full of bow ties and another stacked high with socks. Whatever a person required for every day, ordinary life, could be found here, heaped up in huge cones— mountains! I couldn't believe it, there was a grotesque collection of spare parts— for people; you know, fake legs and things, sets of teeth, wigs and even glass eyes!

It was a very busy place indeed, a factory for sorting things. But where had it all come from?

The nearest girl to us was emptying the contents of wallets into large white trays, which were quickly taken away by the guards and delivered to eagle-eyed soldiers who sat quietly at small tables under a three-sided shelter. These men checked the money, and more separating took place, and coins and notes from all over the world started to form, guess what, more piles. Money bags arrived and the cash was double counted before being ferreted away, never to be seen again. I could not help thinking this was wrong and you would have to be stupid not to realise where this stuff had come from. It was of course, stolen from the people who had accompanied us on the train.

Not only belongings and valuables were being pilfered in this place. Another table was surrounded by officers searching through documents. Personal things like passports and business cards as well as bills, contracts, bank books and all sorts of papers. Identities were lost here, entire lives were wiped from existence, and whole communities lost forever.

I only glimpsed this scene for mere minutes but I knew this was big, this was important. These items represented hundreds of people, maybe thousands. I did not dare to think about the owners of these things, these trinkets which had been so precious. But something told me I already knew what had become of them. In such a short time, I had learned so much, I was barely a resident, but I was becoming an expert.

My mind conjured up images of the monster as we slowly walked past the busy soldiers and their stash of money; obviously the monsters that lived here were expensive to keep. Our nerves were on edge, but we had no need to fear these men, they were engrossed in their activity, eagerly searching and counting and adding up their valuable hoard. They had literally become Aladdin in the cave. Yet, I had a feeling that none of it was theirs to keep.

Ola led us through a door to another sorting room, bigger than the first. It resembled a huge barn, the corrugated tin roof held up with wooden beam posts. It wasn't much and though we didn't know it at the time, this building would become a place of safety for us, though our lives would be hard, we would be warm and dry and if we behaved, this place would secure our survival. Compared to all the other prisoners in this hell of a place, we had been very lucky indeed.

The barn was where the larger items were initially sorted, where suitcases were emptied and searched and clothing was washed and mended. After which they would go to the place we'd just walked through next door for more careful scrutiny and packaging. It was just as busy here, perhaps more so. The major difference between the two vast spaces was this one lacked the protection of walls. Ola stopped us and immediately the younger children collapsed to their knees. "Welcome to the sorting shed, though some of us prefer the name laundry. Despite the fire at the far end, it is a cold place, especially in winter. But at least you will be dry." Ola attempted to reassure us with a smile whilst I tried to get the children back on their feet but Ola promised they were safe for a short while.

At last, some of the young women busy at their work, stopped for a few seconds, offering half smiles, but even here, the guards were keeping a watchful eye on everything that happened. Gregor whispered something to Ola and our brief respite was over. "Come, children," Ola announced. "Let me show you your duties."

Despite the guards, compared to the rest of this evil camp, the atmosphere, dare I say it, appeared more relaxed, less urgent, if you know what I mean? The workers busied themselves without rest, yet there was no sign of tension anywhere. There were only a few guards and they looked bored more than anything, being charged with keeping an eye on the thirty or so young women and teenage girls was hardly a hardship I suppose, though the girls were not much to look at, with their heads shorn close to the scalp and all wearing dirty striped uniforms.

The older girls and women were busy dunking clothes into metal bathtubs overflowing with hot water, there were soap suds everywhere. At the far end of the barn, a huge log fire burned beneath giant metal pots and every few minutes a younger girl dipped two metal buckets into the pot before struggling to the washer women with her heavy load. The task needed skill and strength; the poor girl had neither and before she deposited the hot water into one of the waiting bathtubs, she had lost most of her load. I noticed she had many red sores and blisters on her hands and forearms, some looked infected. The scalds must have hurt her so; the poor thing was desperately in need of medical attention.

"Poor Carmel," Ola said simply, "she needs help—yes. That is what you will be doing Mona. You will fetch water to me and I'll be washing the clothes. It will ease Carmel's heavy burden, make life a little easier for her. Some of her burns will heal but you will acquire some of your own—you can do it Mona; I know you can. The younger children will be over there in the corner." Magda started to protest but Ola instantly shushed her with a strict look that said she would accept no nonsense. "No fuss! Your task is to remove buttons from un-mendable clothing. You will be safe, little one, and you will be able to see Mona at all times. If that is, you behave yourself and do what you are told."

The children stared at their feet until Leni found courage to look up. "Will I be able to do it?" she asked, tears welling in her eyes.

Ola, kind as ever, nodded. "Yes little one, of course you will. There are others over there who will teach you. Just work hard and you will be alright. You have the best job in the camp; the rest of us will envy you." She smiled again and Leni returned it. "Keep your nose to the grindstone. I will look after you, you are my responsibility now."

"But!"

"Shush Leni," I said. "Ola will show you what to do, it will be easy."

"But Mona."

"What is it Leni."

"What is the grindstone? Where will I find it and will it hurt my nose?"

We laughed too loud and a guard some distance away glanced at us for a second. He soon lost interest. Ola sighed, "Phew," she exclaimed. "We are going to have fun with you little one." Leni smiled; her hands clasped behind her back as she swayed from side to side shyly. Ola smiled again and lifting Leni's chin gently she said, "How beautiful you are. You are also very lucky to have Mona."

I reddened. Ola always did this to me. "Thank you," I said. But I had a pressing question. "What about Klaus, there are no other boys here; will he not stand out and be noticed?"

"Gregor will sort it out with the other guards and kapos, Mona."

"Kapos?"

"Yes kapos, the guards Mona, you have a lot to learn. They are our guards; they are not Nazis like your…" She was going to say papa, I felt it like a sting. Ola smiled again and continued. "In this camp, all the officers belong to the Nazi Party but most of the guards are foreign soldiers. There are also the kapos. These are prisoners, just like you and me, but they help the Nazis, and in return they receive better treatment—food and such. Gregor is a guard whereas Wilhelm is a kapo," she said pointing to a short fat man who for all intent and purpose looked just like a guard but without a rifle.

"The shed is run by a sergeant. He is a Nazi; he is also a crook who steals at every opportunity. We call him Captain Crooked; we have promoted him. Just remember, all of them, except for a few like Gregor, are really horrid men. Watch out for Ardit, he is especially horrible and he is especially interested in the girls and women. He seems to ogle all the time, especially at the new ones, the healthy ones that arrive and also the very old ones, he examines their faces quite closely and I don't yet know why. It puts me on edge—be careful of him." Ola grabbed hold of my hand and squeezed. "If he comes to you, just keep calm and do not speak. His interest never lasts long. He is searching for something, for someone in particular, and when he finds them…May God help them!" My friend's voice had taken on the same urgency as when she pulled us out of the line. "I hope that day never comes, I pity the poor girl he settles on. Or the old woman he seeks. No doubt he already has his eye on you. You are far too beautiful to be around here Mona."

I blushed but I heard her warning clearly enough. "You need to fit in, Mona, the sooner the better, for all of your sakes. Look around, Mona. None of us have any hair and we are all skin and bones. Before long, you and Klaus and these two girls will look just like us, so you will not be noticed. At present though, you stick out like a sore thumb. We need to start your transformation immediately."

"We do?"

"Yes, follow me," Ola ordered and set off towards the corner of the barn. We followed her like baby ducks waddling after Mama duck, without question. Our angel led us behind a huge pile of dirty clothing and as we stopped, we noticed we had acquired another duckling. The girl introduced herself as Tatiana who, in her normal life had been training as a hairdresser. She was a little older than Ola but it was obvious she was lower ranking; in this place, all the women and girls here looked up to Ola. Tatiana was the best at removing hair, she was fast and she would only leave a few sores where the blunt scissors cut into our heads. "Don't worry about the scabs," Ola said, "they make you look like you belong."

All four of us stood motionless with horrified expressions. Ola smiled. "Not only will we cut off your hair, we will cover your face with ash from the fire, that will make you as grey as the rest of us. There is no time to lose, we must not delay; there are worse men than Ardit around here." Ola grabbed my hands and shook them, I examined her face as I absorbed her words, she winked and I smiled. "You have no choice in the matter. If you have nothing to lose, you must try everything."

My friend's warnings filled me with anxiety. I nodded and cleared my throat; the words I managed to utter were no more than a whisper. "Of course Ola; we will do exactly as you ask…won't we children." The look I gave the kids did the trick. There were no complaints as all our beautiful hair fell into a golden pile on the dust covered floor before being carted off to the fire.

"Good." Ola's face showed she was satisfied with the results. Her next command was aimed at my brother who listened intently. I could see he was eager to please. I was proud of him, he was showing courage and sense, it was obvious to me that he had understood the danger we were in. "Klaus will be the one that brings in the wood for the fire; there is a stockpile just beyond the wall. It's an old-fashioned way of doing things; boiling water on a fire. But they have lots of free labour, so they don't care how they do it, as long as the job is done." Ola stopped for a brief instant and sighed. "Fortunately for Klausy the job is vacant."

"Will he be safe?"

"I cannot guarantee his safety, Mona. You know that by now, you are a bright girl. But it is the safest job for any boy of his age. Come to think of it, there are no other boys his age in this camp!"

"But—"

"But what? Mona!" It wasn't a question, more irritation. This girl had saved our lives. She did not expect thanks, I knew that much. But she did expect more of me. It was clear she needed me to understand. This was the only way to support her, to support her to save us. I had to remember not to disappoint her. She needed someone with determination, someone strong; someone with fire inside. I already knew what she wanted to hear, but there was one last question eating at me. I had to ask. "It wasn't safe for the last person who brought in the firewood…was it Ola."

Ola released a sort of sob, and then quickly checked herself. "The job didn't kill her Mona. Poor Bibiana died of fever. She was so weak, you see. Hunger is a bigger enemy than the Nazis sometimes. When we are weak, we become ill." She turned to the children. "Do not refuse any food that you may be offered, even if you do not like the food. Someone else, someone close to you, will make use of it. Do you hear?"

The young ones nodded but I was feeling so guilty then. Sorry was all I could offer. Yet to my surprise, Ola smiled. "If Klaus works hard and keeps his head down, he may live till the end of the war. It WILL end, it has to. Who knows, we might be rescued if we are lucky, and the Germans are beaten of course; evil can never win."

My face must have been a picture. I was confused of course. Here I was, listening to my best friend talking about my own people losing the war, and I was sort of hoping for this to happen, in fact I was praying for it. Ola kissed my forehead. She seemed sad. You know I think she was doubting her own words, but she never let on. "The important thing is that you are both alive and you can meet up many times in the day. For now, that will have to be enough." As we stared blankly at her, another girl brought a bucket full of ash from the fire and immediately set about rubbing it into our cheeks. By the time we had finished, we resembled ghouls. Klaus smiled; his eyes and teeth almost shining out from his grey face. The girls giggled.

"That's enough laughter," Mona said. "And I must warn you. Do not let on that you are family or friends. Do you understand?"

Again we nodded to the girl who had saved us from a hidden monster. "Thank you Ola," I said, then instantly broke down in tears. "You saved our lives." Ola, also in tears, then risked a quick hug. The other kids joined in too, a brief moment of comfort and relief, which we all needed badly. Ola was the first to come to her senses, aware that we were arousing interest from the guards.

"You need to change your clothes. Here we are in a barn full of clothing, but none of it is suitable. We must send elsewhere for your stripes, don't worry, I will have them here in no time," Ola promised. "We must get to work," she urged. "These guards are lazy, and mostly leave us alone. But sometimes they get mean, and they don't need a good reason." She summoned a small skinny girl over, at least I thought she was a girl, she was totally covered in dirt, from head to foot. "Hannah here will show Klaus what to do. She has been here forever. Hannah never washes do you Hannah." The girl nodded. "Instead she blends in with the place, especially the woodpile. Most days we hardly see her, such a clever girl." Ola had grabbed the girl by the shoulders and playfully shook her. "She has turned into some sort of wood elf—Hannah the elf!" She glanced at Klaus, her full attention on him. "Klausy will become an elf too." This was not a request; this was an order. Without waiting for an answer, Ola turned to the girl and gently shoved her away then she ushered Klaus after her; and without question he instantly did as he was told and scampered off after the little elf girl. I was amazed and dare I say it—delighted. I had misjudged my little brother; he had understood the situation better than I had thought. He had gone to work without complaint, and inside, I felt my anxiety lift a little—just a little.

Magda and Leni were also surprised by the ease Klaus accepted his new duties. His example was not wasted and both girls held hands, smiled at each other and strolled over to the corner of the shed. Other girls were waiting for them and soon they were up to their eyes in dirty old clothes, tugging at buttons. I watched them for a second or two before picking up two metal buckets and marching to the boiling water above the fire. I don't think I had ever seen a girl more grateful of my presence than Carmel.

Tears fell from my eyes; tears of relief or despair, I could not tell. How lucky we had been, we had escaped death, I know I am repeating myself, but I can't believe how lucky we were to meet Ola at that moment in the line marching to the left. Despite the existence of this awful place, I now know there must be a God watching over us. I later found out that Ola, my amazing friend, had already visited the line heading for the gate earlier in the day. Unexpectedly, she had been ordered to choose additional workers for the shed, a second batch of those arriving by train. This was irregular, but not enough workers had been selected earlier; I like to think this was because Frau Leshnik had caused a fuss and upset proceedings. Of course, I would be eternally grateful to Ola, we all owed her our lives. But I also felt I owed the Frau a little gratitude as well—how would I ever thank her?

Filling buckets with boiling water turned out to be exceedingly hard work; the buckets were quite large and had to be filled to the brim. This made it quite dangerous as I kept spilling the hot water down my legs. Luckily, my knee length socks helped prevent some of the scalds.

Though hard and tiring work it did not require brains and so I had plenty of time to think and ponder over our situation. The questions were always the same: just what was going on in this place? What were all these people doing here and where had they come from, surely they weren't all our enemies; and why were we here, how did it all go so wrong? Was this a nightmare, would I wake up soon? The answers didn't come as easily as the questions, instead I came up with my own, rather illogical solutions, that only served to provide false comfort: This is a dream—I will wake up soon; surely this was nothing but a test, some Hitler Youth Group test of strength, it would end soon enough; it was all a mistake, the error would be noticed and someone would pay!

If it was a dream—a nightmare, it was a long one! We seemed to work for hours. I was soaked through and my dress had singed at the edges and I had scald marks on my wrists and knees. I did not know when our day would end. Then, at last, Ola approached with a bundle of striped clothing, the same ones that everyone was wearing. We hid away, out of sight behind the pile of clothes, the others were already there and we all quickly changed. The garments were disgusting, but at last, our transformation was complete and at least the striped rags would provide better protection from the hot water than my dress had done.

Again I admired my long-time friend. Ola was different somehow, a different girl. She had changed from when I knew her before; no longer the fun-loving girl who had shared jokes and secrets with me; she had become a grown up. She was determined—yes she had acquired a mama's determination—a determination to survive, and she would ensure her friends would also survive. I could see this inside her and so could all the others. She was clearly in charge of the laundry area even though there were older girls and women around. Ola possessed strength; she was an inspiration. Everyone loved her and accepted her as their leader; we were no longer alone; we had joined them.

Klaus and the two girls examined their new clothes and exchanged horrid looks. They were unrecognisable to what they had been a few hours earlier. I almost laughed when Klaus showed me, his new clothes were so large, he had to roll up the sleeves and the legs and use string to secure the waist. He spread his arms as if showing off a new suit, as if he was going to a wedding; there was nothing else to do but laugh at each other. "We are a football team," Klaus announced and again we laughed. Ola scowled at us and the children rushed back to work. Their clothing along with my dress was taken for washing, never to be seen again.

"Now we are all the same," I said. "Now no one will see us."

"I hope not," Ola replied. "You should have changed into stripes before now. You have already caught the eye of Ardit, the most vile guard in the shed, but even he is a hundred times nicer than the Nazis—they're nothing less than evil!"

The Nazis were of course the Schutz-Staffel, the defence corp. Known as the SS for short, who were Herr Hitler's favourite soldiers and were supposed to protect the Aryan people—what a joke! Thoughts of my papa entered my mind. How proud he was to be an officer in the SS, Herr Hitler's elite army. Even then I remembered thinking that surely they had nothing to do with this terrible situation we were in. I had to stop kidding myself—anything was possible. "I have to do all I can. I have to protect them somehow."

"You are a good friend, Mona, they are lucky to have you. You are a survivor."

"I must get back to work," I said as I returned to my buckets. "Thank you Ola. You are definitely an angel. Which means there must be a God; I was beginning to doubt it"

"So are you Mona; an angel and a leader. I'm not so sure about God though."

Chapter 12
Fading

Mama was brushing my hair whilst Klaus zoomed around my room with his toy aeroplane. It was a British Spitfire. The German plane, the Messerschmitt had been shot down and now lay discarded on my bed, though it was the pride of the Luftwaffe made no difference to Klaus, he loved his Spitfires. I teased my little brother—you traitor, and laughed at his protests and excuses. Mama winked at me as Klaus explained why the Spitfire was his favourite plane. "They paint a huge mouth with fierce teeth on the front Mona, it looks like a shark." I had no time to argue as instantly we were at the gates of our little school.

Mama was chatting with the other mamas. They all had beautiful blonde hair and large, perhaps over large, blue eyes; every one of them stood tall and proud. I nibbled at a jam sandwich, it was triangular and most importantly, it tasted wonderful. I was happy, I was calm. I was floating on the clouds. Boris smiled at me with his beautiful white teeth and I hugged him, his strong arms wrapped around me; holding me tight, I was safe and sound.

Then my boyfriend's grip loosened and he disappeared, in his place stood Frau Leshnik, her face, full of black warts and a sort of woody feel to it, was a stark contrast to my handsome Boris. Even the old woman's grey hair had taken on a green tinge as if she had become a sort of creature of a forest—a woods witch. She offered a sarcastic smile with her ugly thorn-liked teeth and, at the same time, the school gates began to change in front of my eyes. Now looming above me were huge black wooden gates, behind which, came a deafening roar whilst acrid smoke rose up to clog my mouth and sting my eyes. The smoke formed the shape of a man, a great knight on a huge horse. His eyes searched for me and an ice-cold chill made me shudder before the knight changed shape again, this time, a tall man in a Nazi uniform screamed out orders. The gates began to open and a second chill spread through my body. I could rest no more.

I sat up. It was dark and cold, but there was much movement, much goings on. The scene had changed, yet my eyes still stung and my mouth was clogged, my throat dry and sore—I was coming down with something, probably a cold that's all, and in my mind I prepared myself for the worst battle of my life; for here, a simple cold was a notorious killer. My sudden movement had stirred the others, Klaus and Leni clung hard to me, Magda holding tight to Leni; they all looked at me, bewildered.

The smell of the place hit me then, the sour air, the salty tinge of urine, of vomit, the indescribable smell of sickness, so much sickness and above all this, the undeniable stench of death—musky and stale! The dream had turned into a nightmare, and the nightmare continued. Was I still sleeping? Afraid not! That would offer hope, a chance of waking up in my own bed. I rubbed my eyes and shivered.

"At last, you're awake." Ola's voice had magical powers, uplifting somehow. Even here, of all places, she had the power to give happiness and…dare I say it—the hope I was craving.

"You let me sleep."

"Why not? Only a few minutes more than usual, you deserve it. It's not like we have to get ready for work is it Mona. We only have the one set of clothes," she said playfully whilst splaying out her overlarge stripy top. "My pyjamas are also my work clothes, and my evening dress, and my ball gown—How I love these clothes, thank you Herr Hitler for such a lovely gift." She giggled and we all caught her irrational mood. How could she be so jolly, the girl never stopped amazing me. "Time to brush our teeth little Klausy and wash our faces girls." The children didn't know whether to laugh or worry for Ola's sanity. Their faces were actually funnier than Ola's mood. "Come on Magda." Ola continued, "Put your best perfume on." She placed her face into Magda's stripes and added, "Aah lovely, you always smell so nice." Magda almost squealed with laughter and more of it came from all over the hut. I was stunned, though it was sporadic and weak, it was definitely laughter; a rare thing here, another sign of Ola's magic at work.

But some had not laughed and Ola would not allow that. She grabbed the girl on the next bunk by the waist and began to tickle her. Aliona was her name, she was around thirteen years and she had begun to fade of late. I bet you have never heard that phrase before—to fade. I have made it up myself, essentially it means to give up and die, either in your head or your body, it is a failing of both mind

134

and muscle strength. I had begun to notice these symptoms in the people around me. It was as though they had given up the will to live. First of all, your strength started to fail and next came ill health. When this happened to you, you had little time left in this world. It didn't make me feel sad. It offered a way out of this place and an end to the daily suffering. I had named this slow decline fading; it was altogether nicer to hear than dying.

Aliona released the weakest laugh as Ola's broken nails dug into her. "Do we have to wash Aliona—no let's not bother today, let us all be naughty and go to work scruffy and stinky." This time Aliona tried harder but both Ola and I knew this was not enough to save the girl. I could see Ola's disappointment, but I remembered the words that had become our mantra— 'You can't save them all'. Ola turned to Leni, "How about brushing our hair, little Leni." Leni shook her head. "Of course not, how naughty we are especially after eating so many sweets last night." She winked. "How lucky we are. Straight out of bed and straight out the door…and sometimes, if we're really lucky, the sun is already up before us."

Ola then sprang to the door with energy she should not have and opened it wide allowing cold and fresh air to flood in. Outside it was pitch black. "Oops!" Ola said, "The sun is late today. Perhaps it will greet us tomorrow, or the next day, soon anyway, when summer returns. For now, we will have to go to bed in the dark and get up in the dark."

"Ah yes, summer. Will it ever get here?" a voice called from way back down the hut.

"It won't be long now," a second voice answered. "I think we are in May, aren't we? At least I think so. The sun is only around the corner. I fancy lying on a lounger to catch some rays. I hope I didn't forget to pack my sun lotion; I wouldn't want to burn."

Now it was Ola's turn to laugh but before she could comment, someone else, further down the hut asked, "Does it come here?" and pretty soon the hut was full of voices debating the subject as they began to climb out of bunks and make their way to the door. I smiled at Ola. She had stirred everyone into action. How I wished I was like her; so strong, not just our leader, but the leader of the whole hut. "Come Aliona," she called and offered her hand, "you can work beside me today."

Outside, two men approached the door pulling a heavy cart. "Bring out the lucky ones," Ola shouted. "Their chariot to Heaven is here." Four prisoners had died this night. Four poor souls who had given up the fight, who had decided to exchange this hell for paradise. We did not mourn them. Their suffering was over—we envied them.

Those left behind followed the cart towards the parade ground. Here we lined up whilst the kapos counted our numbers and ran like little rats to the Nazi captains with their totals. In full view of the captains, the straight and equally spaced lines of captives offered nothing to hide behind. With all our weaknesses exposed, this was a perilous time of the day and many of the ill were dragged out of the lines and carried off to feed the ever-hungry monster. The first couple of times we experienced this I was so worried for Klaus and the girls, but now that we had gained experience I could tell who would pass the test and who would fail. Our little gang were fit enough and we all knew it. Aliona was not so lucky, and as she was taken away I noticed a single tear run down Ola's cheek. In her mind, our angel had lost another one to the monster. I would later remind her that she had made Aliona's last morning a happy one.

Today and for the twentieth time our small group passed the inspection as we had expected and after a meagre bowl of soup we soon found ourselves hard at work in the laundry. How tedious it was, the same tiresome task, the same movements, hour after hour, day after day and what would be month after month. How many times had I already filled my steel buckets with boiling water from the huge cooking pots I could not guess. How many scalds covered my limbs— at least a hundred! How long before my strength gave up on me—a little less each day; and how long could I go on…before I began to fade—surely not very long now. Carmel had lost her fight over a week ago; she had not been replaced. My future looked very bleak.

Klaus was doing much better than I was. I had to smile when I saw him. So small and so skinny; his hair cropped close to his flea-bitten scalp and his dirty clothes falling off him, both sleeves and pant legs turned up to fit better. His beautiful face was so dirty these days; I hadn't seen it properly since we had arrived. Yet he carried on without complaint. He seemed to have found a source of energy known only to him. Even smiling now and then as he piled the wood on the fires; smiles that earned him treats from the guards which he shared with the girls.

Ola had been right all along, Klaus blended in well, it was impossible to tell him apart from the two girls; all three resembling scruffy little orphans straight out of the pages of Oliver Twist. How I loved that book and how I used to love reading. As it happens, we often find books hidden away in suitcases. But we are not allowed to read them; even if by some miracle we were allowed to read, I don't think we would have the energy to do so. Every spare minute we had was used for eating and sleeping—the two things that kept us all going.

Magda and Leni were fairing even better than Klaus. At least, they got to sit all day, often surrounded by soft clothing that was far cleaner than they were. On more than one occasion, as I returned to the cooking pots, I would see them rub their faces into the garments, remembering lost comforts and homely smells. Klaus and I on the other hand could only smell smoke and burning skin, of course we didn't resent the girls their good fortune; we thanked God for it.

Ola and her washer women (as she liked to call them) spent all day kneeling in front of tubs, rubbing clothes up and down to clean them on scrubbing boards. They were probably the cleanest prisoners in this camp, smelling of rose-tinted soap, but they were always sodden. It was backbreaking work and each day the small team moaned of their aches and pains as they returned to the huts. No sooner had they eaten, they would fall fast asleep, utterly exhausted, yet sleeping in wet clothes was fretful and cold.

Though Ola cared for her girls, the continuous work with little rest and even less food meant they did not last very long as a washer woman. Ola often came home...oops! I said came home. I should have said returned to the hut...but I suppose it is actually our home now. It might not be comfortable, but at least it's a place to rest and sometimes, very occasionally, as you have heard, laugh with our friends. Most importantly, the hut is a place where we can come together as a family.

Oh but where was I—oh yes, Ola often returned to the hut in a distressed state after one of the girls had collapsed and been carted away. I hated to see my friend upset but it happened all too often. There was, in fact, only one other that had lasted longer than Ola herself, her name was Eva and she had sworn to herself that she would live forever. How encouraging, Eva was a positive example to us all. Magda particularly admired her; they were becoming close friends. We all believed Eva. When we had all gone, there was no doubt she would surely be the last one left in this place.

If you stood back and watched the shed workers going about their business, you would think we were some kind of machine, all wound up like clockwork toys, every one of us doing the same task, the task we had been assigned, over and over again. The constant repetition of movement started with Klaus bringing in the wood and depositing it on the fire before he left to collect more. Meanwhile, I would bring water for the tubs that hung over the fire, back and forth, all day long. The fire would heat the water and when hot enough, I would dip my buckets in and move the water to the washing tubs where Ola and her washer women would scrub and scrub, on hands and knees. Their bodies were in constant motion, pushing down on their scrubbing boards with straight and strong arms; their waists bending with every push and then straightening back up—clockwork! Other girls then took the wet clothes outside to hang them on long lines to dry. Once dry, more girls folded and packed them neatly into boxes and then finally, men came and took them away to be shipped out. Then the process would start over again with the arrival of the next train of prisoners who were to lose all their belongings and valuables.

But like clockwork toys, we would, as one, begin to slow down until at last, the invisible key slotted into our backs, stopped turning altogether. We would then start to fade. If we were lucky, the key would stop during the night, during a wonderful dream.

Chapter 13
The Remarkable Rise of Fraulein Leshnik

Okay. So, you want to hear my side of the story, do you? You want to pry into my business. Um…nosey, aren't you. It's not good to go sticking your nose into other people's business you know; it's one of my rules—if it has nothing to do with you—keep out of it! Actually, that's one of my grandmother's rules; she was the one that raised me. I never knew my mother. Come to think of it, Grandmother as I addressed her, used the same rule for many things: keep out of my room, keep your nose out of my books; keep out of my closet, keep your hands out of my jewellery box; keep off the grass, keep off the road, KEEP OUT OF THE FOREST! She was such an evil witch!

Never mind. I can see why you want to know what happened to me; I am of interest yes. It will set the record straight I suppose; make the whole saga complete. How could you not know what I got up to, after all I am one of the most important players in this tale!

I am Leshnik—Fraulein Leshnik. I am a great leader, descended from a very old family—as old as the hills and the forests! I am a politician; I am a teacher. I am proud, I am powerful, I have a great mind and I put it to good use. I am a staunch member of the Nazi Party; I was there from the start. I have socialised with those at the highest level—my level. I am Aryan through and through, the greatest of the greatest.

Everyone addresses me as Frau Leshnik. Except my son of course, I am plain 'Mama' to him. For your information and to satisfy your insatiable curiosity, my first name, my Christian name, for I am a good Christian, is Delma; it means noble protector—pah! What a load of rubbish that turned out to be.

It is only right that I should tell you a little of my past life—yes? In particular my rise to power and how I became a prominent member of our society—an elite society at that.

Our great empire, the empire of Germany had been forged in the year 1871, well somewhere around that time; after outclassing and defeating both the French and the Danish on the battlefield. Before that, the German people, the true Aryans had been scattered in smaller provinces such as Prussia and Bavaria. The majority of Aryans lived in Prussia and this is where I was born of course. All the greatest Aryans came from this region; we had our own prime minister and even a king. It was only right that the leaders of the new united Germany, the place we now call Fatherland, hailed from there. We had great leaders then as we do now, the Prussian king, William was his name, became Emperor of all Germany. He ruled with the aid of the Duke of Lauenburg, the great Otto Von Bismarck, also known as Baron Bismarck and whose cunning and expertise had helped us thrash the Danish. The Duke took the helm of our wonderful new Germany. A few years later, I was born.

But our brand-new country was not without its teething troubles you know. We were a country of mixed race, not only Germans were occupying our territory. Polish and Jews and many more people, from different regions that bordered our lands, wandered across our borders. Do you think we Aryans would put up with that for long?

Political parties and various religions, of all sorts, sprang up and the law and governance of the land was under threat. Baron Bismarck was determined to get it all under control and to do that he needed help. That is where my own father comes into the story. He was a strong man, tall and formidable in his black suit and hat. He carried a cane you know; it had a sword inside it and I believe he actually used it sometimes.

Father was a very clever and cunning man, rising up from, dare I say it, very humble beginnings. His own father had been a mere forester, making a living deep inside a forest far off from Germany. He had died young, under mysterious circumstances, but his wife, my grandmother was a very capable woman, she was also very cunning and had realised that the way out of that forest, where our family, our ancestors had lived for many generations, too many to count, was to gain the acceptance of the Prussians, to become one of them. So grandmother worked hard, saving all she could to ensure her son, my father, Jeugen Leshnik moved in higher circles. Education was the key, of course it was. Grandmother counted her savings and realised it was not enough and so, one morning, she left the forest; she did this often, her only explanation—to collect a debt owed. She returned with a sad expression and enough money to send father to college.

It was a start, and my father would make the most of it. He possessed an intelligence that surprised even grandmother. Father had set his sights high; he would become a politician. Well actually, after graduating with highest honours he could only gain employment as an aid in the local council offices, it seemed background and breeding were of utmost importance in this new society and father possessed neither. This did not worry father, his marvellous ideas and novel views impressed all around him and soon saw him rise through the ranks. Higher and higher he rose, leaving all others in his wake until eventually, you will never believe this, he was invited to join the small group of personal aids to Baron Von Bismarck.

Is that enough of Father? If truth be told, the man grew so old and cantankerous that I could barely stand the sight of him in the end. But I suppose I should be grateful for the opportunities his success granted me. Grandmother passed away. For some weird reason, she was returned to the forest of her ancestors and was buried quite deep without great ceremony. With her out of the way, my father, who had almost forgot that I existed by then, had no option but to pay more attention to my needs.

What I wanted most of all, was to mingle with Aryan society. After great persuasion, he finally agreed to take me to an important state ball. It is here that the real governance took part. Here, where the big decisions were made, where partnerships were formed and important alliances forged.

Believe it or not I was a beautiful girl in those days. I was twenty years old and though it wasn't all that important in the early days, I was definitely a true Aryan in every way. I know what you're thinking—what happened you say? Well listen to me and take heed. Too many dinner parties, too much wine and the awful addiction to cigarettes happened. How lucky I am to be denied these extravagances these days.

Now, in those days; well I say in those days, it is not so different today believe me, a woman was a thing to be admired; to be paraded around, to be seen but not heard, definitely not heard. But do you think that I, Delma Leshnik would agree to that rule—not a chance. In fact, the opposite was true. I spurted out my opinions at every opportunity, whether it was wanted or not, I didn't care. Whenever a crowd larger than two occurred I would be there, occupying the centre of attention, having my say—haha!

You know what? My opinions were good, they were more than good they were excellent—and I enjoyed sharing them. When father heard them, he did not approve of course, how could he, women's opinions were not heard in public, it simply was not done. But though he did not encourage me, neither did he place a gag in my mouth.

I took this as approval and continued. Later I realised that people were not only listening to me, but they were quoting my words, repeating by ideas, making my voice heard, and soon my opinions had reached the highest levels of governance.

By now, Bismarck had died and my father's health was ailing; what did I say about the good life! But I was determined to keep my place, my family had earned it, I had earned it and so I applied for a position in many national institutions. Back then, women did not have the same rights as men, we are still trailing behind in that department, however; feminist groups were springing up all over the place and I ensured I was at the head of the women's rights movements.

Things began to look up for us mere women as Germany mellowed before the first great war. I also softened a little towards men and I fell in love and I even agreed to be married—though I kept my maiden name of course. Siegfried was a tall and proud man, he was a great warrior, alas that was his downfall and he never returned from those terrible fields in France where so many perished. But he left me with a son, who is now following in his brave father's footsteps. My son is powerful and fierce; wherever he goes, the name of Leshnik spreads fear and trepidation. That way, half the battle is won already. He will definitely find me in this place, he will fall on these guards and Nazis like a demon from Hell, and they will not know what has hit them, there is a reckoning to be had and a great debt to be paid.

Where was I? When the Nazi Party came about, at first, things improved further for women. As a member of the party, a woman could achieve great heights. This is where I played my master stroke. You see, everything revolved around the Nazi Party, that was where the power was and so I made sure that I secured a prominent position in it—I became a senior deputy and it was just in time.

You see, our great leader, Adolf Hitler is the type of person that cannot make up his mind, and, after a change of heart, once again, German women were reduced to lowly positions in society—our place was beside our men, housewives—pah! But I had already wedged my foot in the door, I had secured my place and I was going to keep it.

I applied to become a secretary to some idiot of a bureaucrat who worked for the lowest level of governance. The man was fat and ugly, he was without a brain and utter useless—I detested him. However, his lack of ideas and total ineffectiveness could not be hidden and he was shown the door. Without a replacement, I stepped up one rung of the ladder. Now I had the chance to show my worth, after all, I could not have been worse than my predecessor.

I was not expected to climb any higher, but you know what they say, never say never and I broke all the rules and as it happens, the higher I climbed, the people who dare challenge my authority grew less in number. Before long, as my reputation spread, I was working alongside ministers who were ruling the country, then as Hitler gained more power, these ministers were replaced with generals, and although, I was not granted an official rank, it was not required. You see, I had gained my place amongst the strongest men in my country, I was respected and I was listened to—I had influence.

Have you heard enough about my past life? I think that's enough, it's making ME nauseous let alone you. Let's talk about what's happening now shall we? If you remember, you left me lying on the ground. That miserable captain had slapped me with all his might across my face, how it stung—smarted! But it was not enough to keep a Leshnik down; we are as tough as granite and as vicious as fire. Swearing revenge I picked myself up and sized-up my enemies, absorbing their faces so I would never forget them—all of them. I had never been so angry in my whole life; I needed to scream, either at someone or simply into the air. But I could not scream, my dignity was intact and I would not lose that to the actions of that little man, and my intelligence had also warned me to be quiet—I needed to take stock of this situation, what was going on here, what had we got ourselves into? I did not yet know. What I did know was that it would take cunning and intelligence and a little stealth to get out of it.

To the left of me I watched as Otto, Gunter and a few of the others were marched away. To my right I could just make out Mona, her head up, searching for the others, in need of answers. What a good girl I thought as she walked away in the other direction, I could only presume she had the little children with her, but I could not be sure. That hurt—the not knowing. I had failed in my duty—some noble protector!

Right now I needed to protect myself. I would not fail in this task. I needed to make a quick decision, which way should I choose. Hard work, surely, was waiting for Otto's team and who knows what was awaiting Mona—I had my suspicions. I absorbed the shameful scene unfurling in front of me, it was chaos. Then I noticed something that no one else had noticed—Me! Everyone ignored me, the prisoners and the guards alike; it was some sort of miracle, I had been forgotten. So my decision was made, I would neither follow Otto nor Mona, I would go my own way.

My way would be that of a mad old woman. After all, I wasn't all that far off. The children had always called me a witch, I knew this already, before Mona's revelations. Come to think of it, when I remember my grandmother, I believe there may be some truth in it! So I would become a mad old witch. My plan was to confuse the guards, from what I already knew of them, they were stupid, and most of them were superstitious; poor farmers mostly from backward countries. A mad old witch who goaded them and insulted them would also intimidate them, she would challenge their beliefs, she would test their metal— if she was convincing that is.

I set about my task with vigour, with relish. My task was to live and Frau Leshnik had no intentions of dying just yet. Lifting my face into the air I released an ear-piercing scream which I turned into a maniacal laugh, a witch's cackle. A few guards smirked and I met their gaze—my first challenge. Their faces remained blank and I smiled. "You will all die when my son gets here." I yelled at them. "Just you wait until Herr Leshnik arrives. You will hang from the nearest tree—every last one of you."

The guards laughed at me and I felt a great feeling of relief spread through my body. Excellent—my plan was working. I walked away, pleased with my efforts, a good start anyway. But what about my next move, would it all go so well, I could but wait and see. I told myself, don't forget who you are, you are a great woman; you are dealing with imbeciles. I wandered aimlessly for a while, my head spinning, fighting with my heart, trying to fathom out how this place functioned, desperately trying to work it all out—this whole mess.

It was obviously a concentration camp, I knew all about them and was ashamed to say that I had approved of these places; in fact, many years earlier, as a prominent political leader in the Nazi Party I had actively encouraged them. In my defence I had never, in my wildest dreams or worst nightmares, believed that these places could be so brutal. A judge would say that ignorance is no excuse. I should have visited these places, before, just to see for myself, but I felt it was below my rank; and now I find myself horrified by what I see on my very first day here.

This camp was full of Jews: It was a death camp. All the others, the Gypsies, the Communists were long gone; dealt with by this efficient machine—this monster. There were thousands of prisoners here, more came in every day, from all over Europe, and more were disposed of. They were everywhere, busying themselves with this menial task and that, never stopping; their heads fixed on the ground, never looking up. Scattered around were guards, either solitary or in groups. Some had dogs, most had clubs or canes; ALL had guns. There were more guards in towers, these were armed with machine guns to ensure the Jews did not reach the fences, and there were so many of those, tall wire fences, topped with barbs.

In places, I could see the guards tormenting the prisoners or handing out punishment, probably for the most minor offence, and worse, others were paying the ultimate price, execution—in open air where everyone else could see—an act aimed at spreading fear and ensuring subservience. These weren't the only dead bodies lying around; other Jews had collapsed, from exhaustion or disease, dying on the spot, like animals, awaiting the garbage collectors!

I was left unmolested. My new identity, the mad old witch, was working a treat, or should I say, 'trick or treat'! What, you don't find that funny? Well, excuse me, but that's the only joke I have.

Anyhow, eventually I found myself among rows of huts. They were the ugliest of buildings, made of wood and in a state of disrepair, with broken windows, rusted hinges on doors and huge holes in the roof. There were no gutters or drainpipes and dark green slime was covering the walls where water had dripped off the roofs, forming puddles of water on the ground. At least, here some plants grew even though they were only weeds. Each hut had been repaired many times and a whole army of Jews were busy fixing the damage as I looked on.

"Do you want to get shot old woman?" a skeleton of a Jew asked me. "The guards will see you soon."

The Jew was high up a ladder, removing debris from the roof. I watched as he threw a rotting old branch to the ground. "I am a mad old witch." I shouted my reply so that all could here. "The guards beware or my son will kill them."

The Jew checked me out for a second and then continued repairing his roof. "You will die soon," I heard him mutter.

His words caused me to question my plans. There was no better one coming to mind, and besides, I was committed. "I will not be alone when I meet my maker my good man." I answered.

"I am not a man," the Jew replied. "I was once a woman…now I am nothing, less than a slave. You are correct mad old witch. We will surely die together." She smiled. "Do you have a hut?"

"I have just arrived," I said as the Jew descended her ladder.

"I can see that. How come you still keep your own clothes?"

"I am a mad old witch. I do what I please."

The Jew offered another faint smile. "My name is Justina," she said and lifted her ladders onto her shoulder. How she did not break I'll never know. "Come inside, I will find you a bunk."

"You are a kind woman offering charity to a mad old witch." I said whilst retrieving the branch from the ground. It was indeed rotting, it was twisted and weak, but I had my cane back. I found this comforting—a good omen.

"All are welcome in this hut. Even witches. The place will keep you dry at least. Whilst you live that is."

"I intend to live for many years to come. I can promise you that."

"You know what old witch. You are standing there unmolested when you should be dead by now. I do not doubt your words…Come inside, you are most welcome."

I was humbled and embarrassed by the kindness of the Jew who was, without hesitation inviting a stranger into her…home! Never had I felt the need to cry so much. The sins of my entire life hit me like an arrow to my heart, an arrow tipped with the deadliest poison—Aryan pride. I entered the hut in pieces.

Inside, the hut was full of skeletons much like Justina, I could barely tell them apart. All with shaved heads, all skin and bone, all very ill. This was a hut full of the damned. Like me, they should all be dead by now. "Why are they here?" I asked, my voice revealing a compassion that I had long forgotten.

"They are of no importance." Justina smiled, "Well, at the moment at least. Much like you I suppose, no one sees them. They are not registering on anyone's radar. No one cares about them. Why bother, every last one of them is doomed to die…soon. The guards are leaving them to it, hardly worth a bullet—any of them. There are thousands of us in this camp, and there are many more camps just like this one. We number millions. As many as the trees in the forest, and we will all be cut down."

"Cut down."

"Killed! Slaughtered! It was just a figure of speech. We are all starving to death."

With eyes open wide an idea hit me as if I had just awoken from a dream. I smashed my new cane down hard onto the floorboards and the sound it made seemed to echo throughout the hut. "Then I have found my calling," I declared. "I now know why I live. I have clearly found my new vocation. I will tend them. I will water them and feed them. They are MY trees. This is MY forest. They will become my children. I will do my best to protect them."

"I don't know what it is about you, mad old witch," Justina said, "but yet again I don't doubt you. I'm sure you will complete your good deed before you die. But first you must rest. It will be difficult, but please, make yourself comfortable."

Justina was right. I did not sleep well at all on the first night in the hut. Though comfort is a word that does not apply in these huts, this was not the problem. The problem was in my head. All I could think about were my eleven children, especially Mona, and what had happened to us. In particular, the part I had played to lead us here, the mess I had got us into. What a stupid and mean old woman I had become. Indeed it had all been my fault—I had so much to answer for.

Then there were these poor people in the hut with me, all of them mere hours from death. I had to do something for them. I had made a promise, both to them and to myself. I would help them; I would get them what they needed most— food. It would take all my wits and intelligence, but I still had those things in buckets. I simply could not fail. It was more than just a good deed, somehow I felt responsible for the nightmare that these poor, poor people were going through. I was an Aryan, part of the Master Race, and I stared in wonder at the hell that we had created.

So where to find food? I could go to the kitchens. Perhaps beg or steal. But that is only robbing Peter to pay Paul. Food was obviously scarce, for everyone. I would not take from other prisoners; there was no chance of that. Where then? Where to get the precious sustenance for my fellow hut mates? How to feed my trees? There were two options open to me—the guards and the kapos, neither would prove easy targets to the common man—but I was not common, and I was not a man.

There were hundreds of kapos here. They were all prisoners of course, but they had accepted the responsibility to supervise the other prisoners at their work. They were hated by the others for it, seen as selfish traitors who only had their own interests at heart, a price they were willing to pay. They were better fed and received preferential treatment with slightly better living conditions. But when all was said and done, the kapos were simply trying to survive.

In charge and occupying most of the prominent positions were the SS. They belonged to the Death's Head Unit who had been running camps like this for years. I had already decided to avoid these men having worked alongside them before; they were most unreliable and unpredictable.

Below the Death's Head Unit were many other guards drafted in from many foreign lands. Some of these were criminals, others had been prisoners themselves and some were simply evil men who had found their place here. They should have been fighting in the wars but preferred this place, this safe sanctuary away from the fighting—cowards the lot of them. It was our fault they were here, the true Aryans that is. We had encouraged them and invited them to join us. These criminals, cowards and rogues were my intended target, and if that failed, I would target the kapos.

I left the hut and very soon I found my first victim. I approached him mumbling curses and spitting on the ground. The guard was alone and watched me approach, his face amused and sarcastic. "Get out of here," he ordered in broken German.

I entered mad witch mode. "You stinking Slav. My son Herr Leshnik will hang you."

The guard mused; astonishment crossing his face for a mere moment. I had upset him, that was clear to see, but he just laughed. "What name do you mumble?"

"I said Leshnik. It is a name you should not forget in a hurry. For it will bring your death."

"I have heard similar names. They also have brought death. But I do not believe you old…old hag. Go away or be shot." He nonchalantly took a cigarette from his pack and searched his pockets for a lighter. His pockets were empty; my luck was in.

I offered my own cigarette lighter and the surprised guard allowed me to approach. "Where did you get that?" he said as he studied me with interest. "And where are your stripes."

I shrugged and he took away my lighter. "Give me food and the lighter belongs to you."

"Are you mad? The cigarette lighter is mine now. I said go away."

"You ask if I am mad. Why yes of course, that is plain to see. I am also a witch. You do not believe in witches I suspect? I am very powerful and I will put a curse on you if you are not careful. How do you think I keep my own clothes?" I was struggling for ideas. What to do next? Yet my plan was working, at least I thought so. But yet again, this man was no ordinary guard, he was a clever fellow, and quite cunning. I was not entirely convinced that I was fooling him at all. I pointed my stick at him, not too forcefully, enough to amuse him. "This is a magic staff. Beware of it and beware of my son—Herr Leshnik." The guard simply smirked.

I pressed on. "How do you think I possess a cigarette lighter? I will tell you, because the commandant is afraid of me. He is afraid of my power…and so should you be." I needed to be more daring and take my game to the next level and so I pointed my stick again, my new cane, a rotting branch that I had named staff, and I threatened. "If you don't return my cigarette lighter, I will use my powers to summon my son. He doesn't like Slavs. You are a Slav aren't you?"

He laughed again. Then unexpectedly offered more. "I come from a place called Moldavia. Do you know it?"

"Of course I do. I am not stupid. Just because I am here does not mean I am uneducated. Do not mistake me for a Jew. My son is fighting in that direction."

The guard's eyes widened, I did not miss it, I would have to be blind to miss it—did he know my son? "This son of yours—you named him Herr Leshnik? Fighting is he—the Russians?" He asked, his face now inquisitive and disturbed.

"Who else is there to fight in the east?" I said.

"There are no other armies, but there are many others over there who are seen as enemies—to the Nazis."

His words had put me on edge. This particular guard was showing a level of intelligence that I had not expected. He was definitely putting my wits to the test. I saw then that he was testing me, but what was he getting at? I needed more from him. "The Nazis have many enemies I suspect. I'm sure they have their reasons for naming them enemy."

"Nazis don't need reasons—only hate. I know of a place. A very fine place it was, until the Nazis came. The leader was a demon. I am sure of it. They declared everyone there to be enemies, without apparent reason…You can guess the rest."

"I'm sorry to hear your news. This fine place was obviously dear to you."

"Very."

"Yet you are here. You have joined the Nazis. You have become one of them—have you not?"

He smiled and changed the subject. "I know your game old woman. You are a very clever old woman. You are very cunning." I simply waited in silence. "As it happens I do believe in witches. I believe in many things; tree spirits, hobgoblins and demons. The great Leshy for instance has visited my village many times throughout history. I believe he is still at large and very busy. So you see in that respect you are wrong. I have lived with witches before…and their kin, their sons who have the power to exact terrible revenge on those that anger them. But powerful witches and their sons can be destroyed old woman. So beware. If you continue to name yourself witch, you are no safer than the Jews in this place. You are actually in more danger." The guard held my gaze and without blinking he continued to talk. "Your secret is safe with me. A mad old witch will keep the superstitious fools away—yes. But I am no fool." He smiled again, his eyes shining. I met his gaze and I could see he was working something out in his head. "I will tell you a secret. It is only fair as I am aware of yours. You are no witch, and I am no Nazi…and guarding mad witches is not my true purpose here."

"Are you a spy? Why give me this information. I could have you shot."

My warning was met with raucous laughter. "You have no voice here. First and foremost you are a Jew. Secondly, you are mad—a mad old witch."

"Then what is your purpose here?"

"I am looking for someone—something. I am waiting. This is the best place to start my search. This is an evil place…and the man I seek, the thing I seek is also evil—it will come here—eventually. I now know this for sure."

"And then what." I asked though I was no longer interested. I had wasted too much time with this man, who I was beginning to think was the true mad one here. I changed the topic of our discussion as subtly as possible. "The lighter is cursed; the commandant knows this all too well to his discomfort. He does not doubt that I am a witch. I may release him from the curse one day, when I am feeling benevolent."

"You lie to me. Now go away. You are boring me."

"Why do you not ask the commandant if you believe that I am a liar?" It was my turn to smile, "Give me something." I demanded. "Or be cursed."

The guard smiled. But there was a hint of uncertainty in his face. I held my hand out, daring him to refuse. Unable to face me, he began to search his pockets. "Here," he said and offered a solitary toffee wrapped in tissue. "This is all I have. Come back tomorrow, I will have food for you."

"You are a good man. I lift my curse and my son, Herr Leshnik will not hang you. What is your name my boy." I asked this as I made my retreat. My nerve was beginning to fail me by now.

"Good," he said. "I am relieved he will not hang me. My name is Ardit. What do I call you old hag—Frau Leshy is it?"

"That is near enough, but old witch is more accurate. Mad old witch."

"Mad old witch," he repeated, then offered something I did not understand. "Perhaps Baba Yaga is more precise. I will watch out for you, and your son. Now be off."

I walked away and within seconds Ardit called out, "Old witch." I stopped dead, expecting to die. I turned slowly; Ardit smiled. "Here!" he said and tossed back my cigarette lighter. "Keep it safe, I may need to borrow it again. But no curses, you promise."

This is how it started. Word about the mad old witch whose son, Herr Leshnik, would hang them all, quickly spread between the guards. I believe Ardit was responsible for spreading the rumours. We met regularly; he picked my brains as much as I his. I became a source of entertainment for the guards and I caused a little unease. The more they saw of me the more they believed I was a witch who would curse them—fools, all of them, except Ardit. To discourage the curse, they offered food on a daily basis in return for a light of their cigarette from my cursed lighter.

All the food was given to the poor souls hiding in my hut. It did not save them but at least it eased their misery. These people became my new wards, and I became Delma again, the noble protector. One by one they died but there was always someone else to take their place, my work would never stop.

Now you have heard what I have to say. I hope it was to your satisfaction, it makes no difference to me. By the way, I was very interested to hear what Mona Lange had said about me. I'm not altogether pleased with what I heard but I suppose I deserve it. She was right about most of it. I am a mad old witch. But what her mother said was wrong, partly in any case; Mona may be a better person than me, but her parents are not, never have been and never will be, no matter what they care to think. This tale is testimony to that.

Chapter 14
Mona Unbroken

The hairbrush was painted gold, but underneath, it was made of the finest wood. I had no idea what the bristles were made of, but they were soft and wonderful to touch and separated the tangles in my hair with ease. Ola applied long, even, strokes to my blonde wavy hair until it shone like silk. I drifted into the clouds, and as usual, Ola and my bedroom were gone; replaced by a forest this time, a huge sprawling forest. It was green and so peaceful. As if by magic I was taken deep inside, where the green leaves were replaced by golden leaf litter.

It was dark but I was not afraid. There was someone here with me. Whether man or woman I could not tell, all I knew was they were powerful and magical—mystical! Not only was this person protecting me, she, for now I saw the shadow of an old woman, was protecting the whole forest. I was calm in her presence, so calm it felt like I was floating, I had nothing to fear. I began to rise, high into the clouds once again and my protector had gone.

So had the calm, it had been replaced by commotion! There were people here, poorly dressed farmers perhaps, their wives in scarves and mittens. Children cried and dogs barked. Now, the blurred image of a man dominated the view, all black, surrounded by white light. As he came into focus the sharp edges of his lapelled shoulders and commander's cap told me I was looking at a powerful man. In his hand, he held a note—it was important information. Waving the message in the air, he ordered in a voice that could not be ignored. "Find my Mother."

I woke up shivering; another day in Hell had begun!

My day began hard and only got harder, minute by gruelling minute. Klaus, the girls, Ola and her gang and the entire laundry were hard at work. There seemed to be less of us today, especially at the shed entrance, where initial sorting and emptying of suitcases occurred, which obviously caused the whole process to slow down. Though it meant the washer women had less to do and more time to do it in, this would simply not do.

The morning parade was to blame of course. It had been long and painful; it had claimed many lives including many shed slaves, as we sometimes called ourselves. As a consequence, production was down and a mountain of suitcases had begun to pile up. The sergeant who managed the shed would not be happy again. Recently he'd been growing more annoyed. We had suspicions that things weren't going too well for him and he had fallen out of favour with the camp commandant. As Nazis go, he wasn't at all bad, and we considered ourselves lucky, despite his odd temper tantrum when things weren't going as planned, he was never cruel, like the others; he never hurt us.

As you know, we had named him 'Captain Crooked' due to his constant pilfering. Anything of value that was small enough to fit into his tunic pocket was quickly snatched up; I swear he owned the largest treasure chest in the world by now. Ola was less trusting, she believed that he was controlling his anger, she believed he, like all Nazis, had evil hidden deep inside just waiting to pop out.

It was weird, thinking about him. I had been doing this for a few days. Not just him, but the entire sorting process. It simply wasn't efficient. Production had slowed and we were behind, great piles of garments and other personal items were testament to that. We needed more workers—more slaves; or things were going to go downhill fast, then we would see how angry the sergeant could get.

Someone needed to say something, to tell him, the sergeant, where things were going wrong. Though none of us liked working in the shed, it was better than any other duty the camp had to offer. Laundry and shed slaves were considered spoilt compared to all other camp workers, despite the job being incredibly dull and tedious, and dangerous come to think of it—I couldn't remember the last time my arms were free of sores. We couldn't deny it though, none of us, we had the safest positions in the camp.

The sergeant was obviously not skilled in business affairs. At least, he had no idea how to manage the sorting process. Neither could he control the guards. I suspect if he had been posted at the front, the stupid man would have been killed on his first day. Maybe I should step up and show him the errors of his ways, but something held me back—the damned will to survive! Ironically, this was beginning to falter with every day that went by in this prison.

My head spun with all the crazy and mixed thoughts that whizzed around in there. Half of which convincing me I no longer cared what happened to me—to us, whilst the other half kept worrying about the shed, and the washer women and how we—no, how I, was going to save the place. I was concentrating on the wrong things and as I scalded my legs for the thousandth time I suddenly decided enough was enough—I simply couldn't go on like this. My strength, my determination to live, my resistance had abandoned me; it had to have, otherwise I wouldn't have done what I did next.

So, pushing Klaus and all my loved ones aside, I decided to act, I had made up my mind, I was committed, and I did not know why. What I did next should not have been done lightly. It should not have been done at all. I wasn't doing it lightly I suppose, in fact I had given quite a lot of thought to what I was about to do, though I still did not feel prepared. Nevertheless, a madness had taken over and I closed my eyes. At that very moment, I felt like someone stepping off a cliff. I had never felt braver. I was proud of myself. I had risen to another level and finally set my plans in motion—I would either sort out the shed or end my suffering here and now.

I lowered my buckets to the ground. Images of Klausy, Magda and the others visited my mind. I instantly regretted my actions; I was having second thoughts. Should I stop, could I turn back or was it too late? I could sense someone watching me—It WAS too late. Soon the guards would fall upon me and I would feel…I would feel their fists and boots or, if I was lucky, I would hear a gunshot and all would be over for me. I was indeed being brave, brave and stupid. I dared to glance in the direction of the guards, they were always in the same place, casually chatting to each other, laughing and smoking; funny really, they reminded me of Mama at the school gate, yet they couldn't be any more different. I sort of half smiled, the lazy guards were ignoring me, what a relief—had I got away with it. Even Ardit, who always watched us like a hawk, had taken his eye off the game. I was flooded with what can only be called terror. I wanted to stop, I had changed my mind, this must stop, regardless of who had seen me; I must save myself. I quickly retrieved my buckets and turned to glance at the person who was looking at me.

It was Ola. I had never felt such relief, though I was still in big trouble. Ola was so angry her eyes could have turned me to stone. Now I really was in trouble, I would get such an earful from my best friend; something along the lines of 'Do you want to die' and 'After all I do for you' and 'You are so ungrateful, how could you do this thing' and so on until my ears hurt. Then I would say how sorry

I was and she would hug me, all the while little Leni and Magda would be smiling and shrugging their shoulders at us and I would be overcome with guilt.

Ola was right, of course, she was always right. We must not give up! And a simple thing like putting my buckets down was indeed giving up, an invitation to die as sure as facing a firing squad; you do not get a second chance in this place.

We were beginning to resemble skeletons by now; there was no weight on us at all. We could not deny it was becoming increasingly difficult to look healthy which was the only thing that assured our existence. Look the part and act the part, at all times—that was the good advice we lived by, it was our mantra—we must never forget it.

This is why we had lasted so long. Simply by keeping our heads down and working hard, regardless of the pain and the hunger and the illness and weakness. Many other girls, much healthier than us had come and gone whilst we carried on. But though I had escaped death today, our problem remained, we hadn't had any new girls join our teams for quite a while and the sorting shed was in need of help. The heaps of clothes were getting higher and many buttons were left un-salvaged, destroyed with the rags. Other areas were struggling too. Everywhere you looked there were masses of bags and shoes and suitcases, all awaiting sorting. The guards were of little help. They just stood idly by, smoking and laughing, without a care, day after day. It seemed only I was concerned. Did they not realise that if things didn't improve, the Nazis would move us all out and replace us—they could do this in an instant if inclined to.

Today was different, a little, how do you say—respite I guess. Captain Crooked had turned up and with a crack of his whip had knocked the guards into shape for a change. I almost laughed at them. The sergeant had not visited for some time and his sudden appearance had left little time to cover up the mess he had returned to. Now the guards found their easy life in jeopardy, this would put them in fierce moods; another reason to do something. The sergeant must have been counting the fortune he had stashed away, or something like that, but now he was back with a vengeance and he meant business. After a quick look around, he sent Gregor running away on an errand and within the hour the shed was full of new girls.

These girls were not new arrivals to the camp and as such were in very poor condition. With so many of them inexperienced at the kind of work we did, the sorting process remained inefficient, which only added to the sergeant's bad mood. That was when I had my idea. Again, I lowered my buckets to the ground and, this time, two pairs of eyes were on me, one scowling pair, belonged to Ola of course, the other, more curious pair, belonged to the sergeant. I lifted my chin and met his gaze—head on.

Before he could yell at me, I spoke to him. "Please sir," I said, and I did not flinch, I think I was as surprised as much as the sergeant at that, and so I continued. "I have been here such a long time…"

I could see Ola in the corner of my eye, pleading with me, mouthing the word 'NO' in silence. The entire shed was watching by now, I knew they were even though they kept their eyes on their tasks. For the very first time, I ignored my best friend, it would be the first of many 'firsts' to come. This time I was committed to my actions and I had discovered my courage again. I can't tell you how good I felt at that moment—regardless of the peril I had placed myself in.

"I know how everything works in this shed…I can…I can show them…If it pleases you."

There was a moment of complete silence, a moment where my entire life flashed past my eyes. My mind was completely still, I could detect nothing; sound, movement, breathing—I was completely numb; what had I done. I simply froze, awaiting my fate.

The sergeant frowned. "I have seen you before—many times." He stared hard into my face, scrutinising me, still my fear alluded me—where was it? Where was my will to live? I should be turning to jelly from head to foot by now, but I stood and faced the man who could kill me in a second. He approached, so close I could smell his breath, he had been drinking alcohol; he smelt just like Papa after a house party. "You have been here a long time, a very long time. That is a major achievement I think. You are a survivor it seems." He smiled now and gently placed his hand under my chin, then squeezing his fingers, he moved my head from side to side, examining me. Was he wondering how long I had left! "Yes, perhaps you are the correct person for the job."

I looked into his face, deep into his blue searching eyes. He was a handsome man—a true Aryan. He smiled again, this time revealing perfectly white teeth. I did not smile back, not because my own Aryan teeth were now all brown and bad, but because I hated him with all my heart. "Okay," he said, "I have made up my mind. You are in charge. You have one day to put things right in this place. If you succeed, you shall be rewarded with food. If you fail, you will not see another day."

Oh dear! What had I got myself into? I was in charge. I was the boss! I had not expected that. I merely wished to give advice. I was happy, can you believe that. Yet if I failed I would be dead. I looked at Ola who gawped directly into my face. I knew what she was thinking, that I was a crazy girl who had sealed her doom. But her face had a perplexed look, was she angry or pleased, I would soon find out.

I pointed to her and shouted. "You—Ola. Come here." Everyone around, including the guards, stopped what they were doing and watched. Ola gave me her most disapproving look; in some ways it was worse than the Crooked Captain's. "You are my second in command," I said with a hint of uncertainty in my voice. I leaned into her and whispered so no one could hear. "Stop scrubbing Ola, you have had enough of that, and help me get this place in order." I couldn't help releasing a giggle.

Ola whispered in return. "You are a bad girl Mona. You are reckless. Why are you doing this?" Her face was stern. "You are breaking all the rules and you have put our lives in jeopardy."

"I am doing this to help you Ola. You can't do it all by yourself. We are partners now." I thought I was helping, but I suddenly felt terrible, was I pushing my friend out?

"And I love you for its Mona—you are amazing!" Mona's face changed then, from a frown to a smirk, and I knew she approved. "I knew you would be the death of me one day. If we survive this day, I am going to kill you!" I sort of half smiled. "This will make us or break us, and anyway, you may be surprised to hear, that I, just like you Mona, have had enough of this place. Many times I have thought about ending my life Mona. It seems I am not as brave as you are. Thank you my friend, my dear, dear friend, I have a reason to live again."

We wasted no time. We would start at the beginning of the process, where the suitcases and other belongings were brought into the shed. There were only four women working here, where normally there'd be twice that number. It was hard and demanding work and required an organised person to take charge. "We need girls we can rely on here Mona," Ola's advice did not need an answer. "And I know just where to find them." Within minutes, Ola's fellow washer women were removed from their scrubbing tubs, these women and girls had the cleanest and softest hands in the camp, but they were only too eager for a change in their duties. I watched as they stood and stretched their aching backs whilst drying their wrinkled and red hands on their stripes.

The initial sorting began in earnest and the piles of shoes, spectacles, hats, wigs and trinkets began to mount up further. Again we were short of hands. These were the easiest work sections in the shed and I had already decided to give the jobs to those that had suffered at more difficult tasks. Another girl, who had recently joined me as water carrier was moved to sorting shoes into pairs and more girls were brought to help her. Klausy and Magda too were set to work cleaning spectacles, and other long-lasting residents of the shed were paired with the new girls as mentors which made their tedious jobs all the easier.

So now the process was underway efficiently and effectively. I stood back and I was pleased. But we were still short of workers and the posts at the latter stages of the process remained empty. I still had a job to do. It was probably the worst job of all. Nervously, I awaited the return of the sergeant. I knew he would return soon to either praise me or kill me.

He did not disappoint and it is a good thing that we had made good progress in such a short time, for he was back within the hour, perhaps trying to catch me out. The lazy, thieving man detested the place, only staying long enough to line his pockets and to kick the guards into shape; they were always in a worse mood when he was present. I watched him approach, aware that I needed to address him bravely as before. Inside I was fighting back the butterflies that danced in my stomach and threatened to make me retch. I had experienced many uncomfortable feelings since my arrival here, but this one was new to me. I shook it off, unwilling to accept it on this occasion. I saw his face. He had a broad grin on it. I relaxed—just a little. He acknowledged the increased activity with a nod here and there and his smile increased to a laugh—how pleased he was.

I stepped forward and he noticed me, calling me closer with the slightest movement of his hand. I approached slowly, continuing to meet his gaze as I had done before, all the time knowing I should lower my head to the ground; that was the prudent way, the safest way. I struggled to control my nerves, my hands shaking; again I gained control. Though he smiled this was no guarantee that I was safe. The Nazis had proved themselves sly and devious on every occasion. I wouldn't be surprised if he suddenly produced a gun and blew my head off.

"You have done well girl. What is your name?"

I was taken aback. Never had a Nazi been interested in a Jew's name. But I wasn't a Jew was I? I could barely answer; a whisper that's all and so he asked again. "Speak up, what is your name."

"Mona...Sir," I uttered, my bottom lip quivering so. "Mona Lange."

"Lange! Mmm. That is a good name. A prominent Aryan name come to think of it. We will stick with Mona I think. Well done girl." He looked into my face—again scrutinising—what could he see? "I am pleased. You will be rewarded. Now what do you need?"

My relief was immense, both from his reaction and his question. Of course I needed something. I needed more workers. But to ask for something often meant death. But I had a feeling about this sergeant. He was a cunning fellow; I believe he knew what was best—especially for him. Though he cared little for the prisoners, he at least understood the value of them, that we were more useful to the Nazis alive and put to work. I braced myself for my question.

"I need more workers sir…" He studied me, in utter silence and I closed my eyes for a mere second to receive the expected blow. But it did not come. I was right about him; he could be cruel at times, but he was not as bad as the rest. I opened my eyes to see his wry smile. He had moved forward; we were so close—again; those deep blue eyes—shining like ice. So now I gazed at him, hiding my hatred, or so I hoped. He wasn't fooled. This man understood exactly how I felt and what I was up to. He did not care on both accounts. I would make him money. The moments felt like hours as those eyes shone with a sick amusement whilst my own begged him for an answer, so we could end this game. Still he remained silent; thinking, musing over my request.

He searched his pockets and took out a packet of cigarettes. I nearly collapsed as he offered one to me. I shook my head, literally stunned and he smiled. He lit his own and politely blew the smoke away from me, the grey cloud floated into the air. I inhaled a breath full of warm musty air. Somehow I had lost my wits; at least that is what it looked like to the other girls as, without permission I spoke again. "As you can see," I pointed to my friends busy sorting the contents of bags as if there were no tomorrow—which was often the truth. "The initial part of the sorting process is up and running, it is working really well—I think. The clothes washing is also moving well, as are the salvaging, the fire maintenance, and the drying, those areas are less skilled and the new girls can manage them well," I lied. The new girls weren't doing well at all but the sergeant could not see this as I could. I had already decided that I would keep my own job; I would continue to scald myself. "We need workers, new ones, for the packing section. They do not need to be skilled." I watched in silence as he scanned the room, his eyes now mere slits.

Then, finally he turned to me. Those blasted eyes now boring into me, searching for my soul. I could not read him. Was he annoyed or pleased—was he thinking still? This man was beginning to irritate me, was he doing this on purpose to make me feel uneasy? Just what the hell was he playing at? Testing me further—I couldn't put such a thing past him. I needed to end this torment and so I delved deep for the last remnants of courage that I possessed and though I was beginning to falter—to weaken, I somehow continued to hold his gaze. For the second time that day, everyone present was watching me; the entire place was silent, awaiting the sergeant's reply.

"You shall have them, Mona," he said. Then turning to a guard he ordered him to bring more workers, at least ten.

"But sir!" I interrupted. Now I was pushing my luck.

He remained calm. Was there actual respect in his voice, surely not, I refused to believe it. "What is it, Mona?"

I gasped. "May I choose them?"

"You! You wish to choose them. Why would you need to do that? These are not skilled workers that you need. You have already said that—have you not?"

"Pardon me, sergeant sir. I said that, yes, but I was wrong. Please pardon my error. The packers need a careful hand, perhaps there is some skill required for the task, a lesser skill—perhaps. Please allow me to explain."

"That is not necessary. Go on," he ordered. "Choose your packers. I have a feeling this place is going to get really busy soon." He turned and walked away. Then, a short distance away, he abruptly turned back to face me. "You are a sensible girl Mona. Yes, a very sensible girl. You have done well so far and I do not doubt that you will continue to do well." He smiled again; it was quite natural with no sign of malice or scorn in it. "If you do well Mona, then so do I. Go and find your lesser skilled workers." He turned to the guards. "Take her to the separating tables. A train has just arrived full of these lesser skilled workers."

A few minutes later, Ardit was accompanying me to the separating tables that we had encountered a lifetime of horrors earlier. This man gave me the creeps. We didn't like any of the guards of course, but this one in particular worried me. He worried us all, especially Ola, who hated him more than anyone around. I sped up to pull away and put a few yards distance from him but the damned guard was determined to keep close to me and as he was much fitter and stronger I had to accept my new companion, though as reluctantly as I dared to show. To be fair to the brute, he really did not pay much attention to me, to any of us, any longer that is. At first, he did though, he seemed to stare continuously in his never-ending search for something or someone familiar. But after a while he seemed to be satisfied and left us alone. I suppose that short period of time, whilst he showed interest, was enough to make us all hate him. You see, I was ignorant of his sad tale at that time. But we know better now, don't we?

We moved further from the shed and through a series of gates, at each one Ardit had to explain our intent. The horror of the separating tables came back to me in an instant. The terror I had felt then, returned and consumed my entire body. I began to tremble as I remembered the fight I had put up to keep hold of my brother. Nothing had changed here. Still, the strong and the young and the fit were directed to the right whilst the children and the decrepit limped off to the left. As we approached the line moving to the right I suddenly stopped and changed direction. Ardit pulled me back in anger but I persisted in my goal. "NO!" I screamed. "I need to choose from the line heading to the left." Those taking the path to the right did not need me. It was never my intention to go that way. I would help those walking to the left, as Ola had done an eternity ago, those unsuspecting people with no hope, those heading for the gates and…and the monster!

Ardit took hold of me and slapped his hand across my face, somehow it looked worse than it felt—was he holding back? I scowled at him in return, my mind firmly made up. I would not lose this fight, "Orders from the sergeant!" I screamed my lie and dared the guard to challenge it. His scowl was worse than mine but miraculously he didn't hold it for long, I watched in amazement as it changed to a frown. He quickly glanced around to ensure no other guards were watching. They were all busy, Ardit seemed relieved. What was he up to, had he caved in? Had I got the better of him? If so, he would be known as 'Ardit the coward' from now on—I would see to that.

I followed the line and immediately realised I had created a massive problem for myself. I could not save them all—how the hell was I supposed to choose who will live or die. At least, the first dozen people in the line were ancient and bent—they would never do, there was no way I could explain their presence in the shed to Captain Crooked.

Further along the line, children gazed at me with painful eyes that broke my heart but still I moved past them—they were too small. This was so difficult. Every person I left behind in my search broke my heart a little more.

Ardit became prickly and began urging me to choose. The pressure was immense and the line kept moving forward, I was moving with it, at this rate I could end up being forced through those terrible gates myself—the gates that terrified me above all else, the same ones that made my chest hurt as if a dagger had been thrust inside and twisted; every person in this line must be feeling that very same feeling. I had not come this close the first time around and hadn't appreciated the size—my-oh-my, the monster behind must be a big thing and growing each day. One gate had been pushed open and already, a line of children and elderly prisoners were unwittingly marching to their doom.

I stopped, to take a breath if nothing else. Then I found myself walking across the large bare field, away from the gates, the dust clouding my view, did it ever rain on this ground? Without thinking, I was taking a shortcut to join the line again where it curved; at last, I had spotted some people who may be suitable for the shed.

Time was running out though, my new work mates were walking towards me, fast approaching the huge fence with the massive sinister gates; I pushed into the line and stopped my chosen few. An old woman looked at me, her face sad and baffled. She could not come with me but I would save her granddaughter. Though her language was foreign to me, she understood my intentions and pushed the girl towards me after a hurried kiss as a final goodbye. My heart broke at that moment—for it was me now doing the parting.

There was a healthy young girl with her right arm in a sling, I could not choose her. But I took her younger sister, a girl of about ten years. How the elder sister fought me off; how I wished she could understand my intentions were good. A younger boy holding his grandpa's hand would do to fetch wood for the fire, but he was limping—he would do, his grandfather's face told me HE WOULD DO! I was too near the gates now and needed to move, Ardit was getting more anxious every minute, I could not understand why he cared. We moved back along the line, this line of sheep, they were all the same, and all heading to the slaughter. I still had some serious choosing to do, and it was so difficult. Ardit followed, herding my little flock along behind me.

The line went on and on and at the other end, the furthest away from the monster, more people were joining. I scanned the entire line and found more, less skilled workers, I was doing it—I was choosing, I was making progress. Now I had decided what I was aiming for. Avoiding the children who were too small and grandparents who were too old, they would never be accepted, I had to ignore them, not even a glance; fearful that I would offer hope, even though many now reached out to me. These people were already dead, they did not know it, but I was their only salvation, and I was blind to them. I stepped away from the line—I couldn't breathe there—I was suffocating!

I was not blind to all of them. I would choose at least ten of them—to start with. My mind made up I approached the line again. I had to be strong, I had to be brave—I had to be tough and determined—and I was.

Another boy joined my crew, aged at least nine years unless he was small for his age. His grandmother made a protest but I shushed her with a simple but stern 'NO' and a look in my eyes that would surely kill. But the old woman was not easily frightened, neither was she stupid; her mothering instincts telling her that I was here to help. Her initial anger subsided to reluctant acceptance which helped her release the boy to me and to life. I passed him over to Ardit who held a disapproving look of his own that I easily ignored and moved on to my next choice.

Two more girls were quickly plucked from the line, how many was that— only six—ONLY SIX! I needed to do better and soon I was picking them out without applying any criteria or rationale to my choices at all. I didn't care. I would save them and I would look after them in the shed—I had to; if not me, who would help them? The Crooked Captain and the lazy cowardly guards were no problem to me now. Without realising it, this had become my mission, my reason to live, I remembered how only a few hours ago I had put down my buckets and given up.

When I had chosen ten, Ardit pulled me away from the line. I brushed his hand off my arm and rushed back to the prisoners. "MORE," I snarled at the guard. His command of the German language was good, I knew he understood me, yet I spelt it out for him, another threat, "Sergeant—NAZI." I don't think he was fooled as he simply rolled his eyes at me, but at least he allowed me to continue. My count reached fifteen, mostly children under nine with a variety of disabilities, one girl only had one arm, but I kept her regardless and probably because I felt guilty for the girl with the sling I had refused earlier—how heartless I had become. A terrible thought entered my head—I must save her!

I quickly turned to run towards the gates but the strong arms of Ardit held me back. I pushed forward, struggling with all my might to release his grip, but he held fast. I scanned the line in desperation and panic, where was she? Then I saw her, she was nearing the gates, was it too late for her. Ardit would not let me go and I began to shout, "WAIT. WAIT—PLEASE." But there was no one listening to me and the line did not stop moving, for an elite Aryan maybe, but not a Jewish prisoner dressed in rags and nothing but skin and bone. I did not have the strength to push past Ardit…and I did not wish to return to the gate. I was too afraid and so, to my shame, I stopped struggling and stood still. Consumed with despair I watched as the girl with the sling, disappeared through the gates into the jaws of the monster.

The girl was gone for good, along with the chance to reunite her with her sister—I would never forgive myself for that. But her death had served a purpose—it spurred me on. Ignoring Ardit I continued to search the line, pulling out people as fast as I could, barely stopping to apply any logic at all to my choice—I would face the sergeant later. What was the worst he could do—kill us all!

By now, even the elderly were stepping out of line. But that was too much for Ardit, who pushed them back. I ignored the guard. Now out of control I continued to pull more folk out of the line, children, disabled people, boys and girls alike, making no distinction. How ironic, it was Ardit that was now making sense and with all his force, he took hold of me, his arm around my neck, and he dragged me to the ground. "NO MORE" he bawled at me. "ENOUGH."

I suddenly stopped moving, my head was a mess, I could neither understand nor hear Ardit's words—was I about to faint? My entire body was numb—had I drawn attention to myself—unwanted and dangerous. Had I made a spectacle of myself—had I killed myself!

Then his voice filtered through. A voice that irritated me, a voice I detested. Yet it was speaking sense. "Save these," it warned. "Do your job. Mona—do your job. Or you will lose them all."

I came to my senses. He was speaking the German language; he was making good sense. "Save these," he said again and I looked at the group of confused and terrified children and old people—there were thirty-five of them. It was too many. But they were mine.

"Come back again," Ardit offered and I was stunned. I could see in the guard's eyes that he approved of what I was doing, what I was trying to achieve. He had allowed me to do this; what was going on, what was his game, was this some sinister trick? But no, I didn't think so, I could read his eyes, they never lied, everything was there, in those eyes; the horror, the fear, the anger, the grief. Ardit was helping me; he was doing good and I had no idea why.

But enough was enough. Ardit knew this and so did I, the moment I had counted thirty-five; thirty-five broken children and old people was the time to stop. Any more would not be tolerated. I had done what I could, for now. I was devastated and I was tired. Perhaps I can do this again, now that Ardit was with me; for surely he had put himself at risk. I was to take ten prisoners, ten workers back to the shed, yet I had rescued thirty-five people and Ardit had allowed this to happen; there was indeed some goodness inside of him.

I touched his hand, trying to show my gratitude. He pulled away quickly, but there was a different look in his eyes, the normally mean and malicious eyes had kindness in them, a mere glint, but it was there.

And so it dawned on me what I had done. With help from the most unexpected source, the most overzealous and cowardly guard named Ardit, I had saved thirty-five souls from immediate death, from the clutches of the monster— at least for a short while.

Inside though, I have to confess, I hid a guilty feeling. It's so hard to explain. But you see, these people I had saved were not the ones that I wanted to save. I wanted my own friends back. I wanted Gretl and Heidi back; I needed Boris and Ludolf and I missed the little boys, those rascals; Gunter, Victor, and lovely little Otto, so cute. I missed him most of all. I wondered how they were faring, and I feared I would never see them again.

Chapter 15
Boris' Band

"I wonder how Mona is doing. Is she still alive? I miss her so much. She was like…like a big sister to me."

Hello everybody. My name is Otto. I am one of the eleven children sent away to a safe haven; if only my mama knew what had happened since I left her on the station. She was sad then, her tears made me cry, as you may remember. I'm so glad she doesn't know where I am now. I don't think she would ever stop crying.

As you know, most of us were split up from Mona and the little kids; Magda, Leni, and my friend Klaus. Boris is also missing; I can't believe how much I've come to miss him; he had always scared the life out of me. Anyway, he has gone and Ludolf is busy protecting us, he spends all his time telling us what to do and working out what's best for us—so far it seems to be working—we are still alive aren't we. Ludolf doesn't care if you are not kept informed though, so it is up to me to tell you about the things that have happened to us since we got here. Mona will be wondering what has happened to us and although we are unable to tell her our side of things we can tell you, Mona would like that so I'll do my best to fill in the gaps.

There were six of us in our gang, of the original eleven, and thankfully there still are; we could not bear to lose another person, we are a family now—we love each other. Of course we have been joined by many others, but Ludolf can't look after everyone, and many of the new ones don't last long. People just come and go around here without any time at all to make friends.

After separation, I looked back and was sad to see Mona walk away in the opposite direction, I wanted to cry then with all my heart. I didn't realise it before, but I really loved Mona. She was so brave and strong and…and nice; she always stuck up for me. Seeing her leave my life for good was hard, I say for good because I believe that now. I had to be strong, that is what Mona would have said to me—be strong Otto—you can do it. In any case, Mona was holding the hands of the little ones. They formed a sort of huddle, how sad they looked.

I held out my hand to Heidi and to my surprise she took it and squeezed it so hard. Never before had she touched me or even looked at me before that moment. I could feel her trembling. I thought at first that I had found a replacement for Mona, someone to look after me. I was wrong, it was Heidi who needed looking after, and I would do it, or at least help. That is what my time with Mona had given to me—courage!

That's when Ludolf slapped me on my back. At first, I thought he was hitting me, for nothing, as usual. But when I saw his face, he was showing me how pleased he was. He nodded in silence; at last I felt like he approved of me—another first.

Ludolf showed us all he was a natural leader and soon gathered the rest of us together. Then we walked on, not knowing where we were heading or what awaited us, we just followed the line. It was a terrifying time, the only comfort we had was each other and for now we were not going to let each other go—no matter what!

We were pushed towards a hut. A sort of long shed. It was old and dirty with broken windows and rotting wood nailed onto the sides. Outside it was a grey colour. Inside it was dull and dark; and I suppose mostly grey as well, this place had never seen any paint. I remember thinking, what's happened to all the colour around here? The roof was made from wooden planks and full of huge gaping holes, surely we would get wet if it rained and of course it was cold and damp; I shivered at the sight of it.

We were completely silent as we entered through the door which was jarred open; I noticed how one hinge had snapped with rust. Only small light bulbs provided enough light to create the weakest of shadows. You know something, I have always been afraid of the dark, and I hate spiders, and I'd wager there were hundreds of them in this hut. Never had I been more scared. Well actually, that is incorrect. I have been terrified ever since we were thrown into that damn train wagon. Our fear was renewed, were we going to live here? This was certainly not what we were used to. I remember how Gretl began to cry and then Heidi, soon we were all doing the same except for Ludolf who was doing his best to hold back his tears.

I did not know what to expect, but what I saw surprised me. It was full of barber's chairs, each one occupied by a silent prisoner who sat and stared into space whilst his or her hair fell to the floor. I was both relieved and horrified. Relieved that this was not our home after all, but here, we were to lose our hair. Many prisoners lined up for their turn whilst others that had long since been clipped swept up the discarded hair and placed it into sacks.

We joined the end of the line and awaited our turn in the chair. I was the first of our little bunch to lose my hair. It wasn't all that bad for me. My hair had already been quite short, it's how Mama liked it. By the time the barber had finished, I barely had any hair left though, it probably looked awful, I couldn't see of course, there were no mirrors to see, but it was alright, we all looked the same after all. I instinctively rubbed my head and watched the others who had occupied more chairs, each with their own tireless barber. Our blonde and gold locks fell to the floor and were swept, with all the rest, into piles. It was a bit of a shock to see each other like this and if we were back home at school we would have laughed our heads off. But not here, they had taken our hair without permission, this felt wrong somehow. My head felt strange, all bare and cold, but it was nothing to a boy, a tough lad like me. I felt sorry for the girls though.

The old Jewish barber was good at his job; by the time he had finished with me, he had already shaved fifty prisoners so far that day without rest. He was just finishing up with Gunter who had obediently taken my place. Gunter was gently pushed out of the chair and the next person in line occupied the chair. Without a word from his parched mouth, the barber set to work again. Next to him, five other barbers unceasingly removed hair from heads, their nimble fingers moving quickly across the ever-changing scalps beneath them.

We had quickly said goodbye to our locks. Gretl had been more reluctant than the boys to lose her hair which was beautiful and styled in the latest fashion. She had unwisely made the meekest of protests and had been rewarded with a vicious slap across the face by one of the guards. Her hair was carted off along with the rest—a great mound of it, and she was left sobbing. How I desperately wanted to comfort her.

Things only got worse after that! I remember how we were pushed into a second line. It was all lines in this place, a line for this, a queue for that. In this one, we were ordered to open our mouths wide. A very scary officer made his way down the line and peered into each of our mouths in turn. "Oh no what now?" Gretl sobbed as she rubbed her sore cheek, she had not recovered from losing her lovely golden hair and now she had to face this, she trembled so much and began to pee herself. As she sobbed I grabbed hold of her hand. I think this helped me more than it helped her. It turned out, the officer was searching for gold teeth and anyone unlucky enough to have one had it removed there and then. That was difficult to watch, I can tell you. I was almost sick with fear and afraid to say that I also wet my pants. It was then that Gretl squeezed my hand in return and together we even managed a smile—only a very little one.

Luckily, apart from a few gaps, all our teeth were in good condition without the need for gold ones and so we were marched to a second hut where we were to give up our clothes. We had to strip together, boys and girls, men and women. Poor Gretl hated this even more than the haircutting, but for some reason, no one minded her, all the Jewish prisoners seemed to show respect for each other—they were all quite dignified. Us boys also felt terribly embarrassed and exchanged our clothes as quickly as we could. Ludolf was the most embarrassed, cursing throughout. Since we had held hands, Heidi seemed to be doing better than all of us, her face more annoyed than afraid.

Soon we were all wearing striped pants and tops made out of a thin grey cloth, now I was sure there was no colour to be found anywhere in this camp. Our new uniforms were covered in stains and there was a very bad stink to them which added to Gretl's misery. She had always been so pristine in her pretty dresses and now she was reduced to wearing these dirty rags that had been used by many people before her. There was mud, dust, blood and worse things staining them, and they were covered in lice; we felt sick just touching them—nevertheless we had put them on quickly, to cover ourselves up.

At last, shaved, examined, and dressed, we were herded together, like sheep, and ordered to move; the usual butt of a rifle urged us on through yet another broken door. Outside, the rain had begun to fall in buckets, we were soon soaked and it was strange how the rain hurt our shaved heads and ran down our faces really quickly. Now in line again, we trudged barefoot through the deep muddy puddles; the cold water hurting our bare feet.

In utter silence, constantly afraid of being beaten, we marched for a long time; none of us knew where we were going. We were drenched to the bone, shivering from the cold, and terrified. By now, none of us had any tears left to cry. Instead we kept our heads down, holding hands whenever we dared. At last, we reached our destination. Orders were shouted and our march stopped.

Horror struck, we saw what awaited us, a place where many others of all ages were already busy working. The scene was ghastly! It matched the one we had witnessed when the wagon doors opened. In front of us, there was a huge field.

It was full of rocks and I should have guessed immediately that it was a quarry. The sky was black and full of rain, the whole place was as expected—a range of greys. I watched as prisoners struggled past with heavy barrows full to the brim with rocks and dust. Others shovelled, some used rakes and more pulled huge heavy rollers. All were half dead—living skeletons as grey as their surroundings!

Long rows of very thin people stooped over whilst passing large rocks to each other. Some were bent double, the weight of the rocks pulling them to the ground. None of them dared to fall those final inches. All were willing their legs to hold them up, fearing this would be the end for them. Little did we know at that time, that anyone who fell in the mud would not get back up!

"What are they doing?" Gunter asked.

"Building a road, you idiot," Ludolf replied. "It looks like we will be joining them soon enough…Look," he added, "it is heading towards those factories over there." He pointed to the dark silhouettes of factories in the distance. "There is a long way to go." Ludolf's voice trailed off as a soldier dressed in a hat and cape walked quickly towards us; rain dripped off the brim of his hat to fall on the soaking and pitiful Jewish man that ran obediently behind him, his bare feet bleeding on the rough surface.

"You little rats," the SS officer shouted. "Stand still and listen carefully. This snivelling little dog will give you your instructions." With a large cane, he pushed the little Jewish man towards us; he landed on hands and knees at our feet. Gretl instinctively bent forward to help him, but Ludolf held her back and gave her a cross look. Though annoyed with him, Gretl knew he was looking out for her. She kept silent and made herself stand straight and tall.

The officer growled his words at her as she hid behind Ludolf. "Work hard and you shall be rewarded. Disobey and you will be severely punished." With that, he turned sharply and marched away, leaving the little Jewish man crumpled in a heap on the muddy ground. Despite his earlier warning to Gretl, Ludolf now bent down and helped the little man to his feet. How we change! There was a time when Ludolf hated all Jews; after all they were our enemies!

The little Jew informed us of our duties which consisted mainly of moving heavy rocks from one place to the next and digging up huge tree stumps which was even harder work.

For the rest of the day, that first day, we worked hard. Harder than we had ever done before. Stopping only when the violent guards turned their backs on us, if they caught you resting, you were in for a beating either with a stick or a boot. It was horrendous! We worked for hours with little rest and even less food and water. How we survived that first day we'll never know; it seemed we possessed a strength we did not remember. Deep down inside, our subconscious thingy, I'm not sure what you call it, whatever it was, it had taken over; it was guiding us and keeping us alive—for now.

We had a rule—we must stay together so that we could look out for each other; it was the only way we knew how to survive. Heidi proved to be the weakest of our bunch, but Ludolf—the brains, had secured her a rake from a dying man who was subsequently carried off. Ludolf's quick thinking had relieved Heidi from the heavy lifting, which would certainly have finished her off in a day or two. Nevertheless, even she had to work hard, especially when the guards were around.

At last, we did stop. It had grown dark and the guards didn't want us to escape. Our poor hands and feet were sore and bleeding; rest coming only after another long march through a river of mud to a dirty hut. It turned out to be in a worse state than the barber's hut; dark, dingy and flea infested. The hut needed much attention, it offered very little comfort. Nevertheless, it was where we would sleep that night and every other dark and cold night afterwards. We would have never believed it then, but we would eventually call this wreck, this collection of rotting planks—our home.

Mona has probably described what it looked like inside the huts. Ours was jammed with bunk beds, rows and rows of them. The people that lived here had very few possessions other than the clothes they wore. If you were lucky, you might have a dirty woollen blanket of your own, but most of us had to share. A mattress was a thing of dreams. The beds were very basic, made out of the same old wood as everything else. Most were occupied by other prisoners; all of them in a poor state of health. These poor people, men and women, had been worked half to death, they were starving and diseased. The place would have been silent if it weren't for the odd cry of pain, the moaning, the sobbing, coughing and sneezing, and the harsh breathing sound the dying people made. Those that did speak did so in whispers. We watched helplessly as our fellow workers climbed into the empty bunks leaving no room for us.

Seeing our plight, the mean guard laughed loudly. "Leave it for an hour or so, then search the bunks," he smirked. "Throw out the dead ones, you will have a bed each and some to spare." He left, slamming the door shut behind him, his awful laugh fading in the distance.

Despite being tired and in pain, the prisoners fidgeted in their beds, unable to make themselves comfortable on the hard planks. "The evil pig is right," one of them said, a scrawny woman with dark sunken eyes. "It is time to remove the lucky ones."

"Lucky?" Victor repeated.

"Yes Victor, she said lucky ones," Ludolf enforced.

"Does she mean…"

"The dead ones, yes Victor."

"The dead ones," Victor repeated in a whisper. "Is Boris with them?"

"Boris is not dead yet; he is far too strong. He will not be beaten. Mark my words, and neither should you be." Ludolf's words were almost an order but we didn't mind, we were all pleased that we had him to lead us and to hide behind.

"None of us have given up yet Ludolf," Gretl stated flatly. She had found an empty bunk and was busy tidying it up. "Heidi, you can share with me, it is going to be cold and uncomfortable. We must all stick together."

"Our own little Hitler Youth Group," Victor said; an idea that would have once excited each and every one of us.

"No! Not Hitler, don't let the others hear you say that. Anyhow, I hate him. We are Boris' Youth group," Gretl said smiling.

"How about Boris' Band," Heidi offered with an unexpected smile.

"I like it," Victor returned her smile. "But we must keep it secret."

We all agreed.

Chapter 16
A Den of Kindness

It's all around us, everywhere we look; crisp white snow, covering the fields and roads to form a thick ice-cold blanket that stretches for miles as far as the eye can see. Not a roof top is spared; the snow sliding from the roof tiles to form huge mounds and the ice dangling from every ridge like giant icicle teeth. The pine trees, evergreen, are laden too, with every branch and twig bending under the weight of the white stuff that threatened to bring every last one of them crashing down. Everywhere, all of it, from the highest peak to the deepest gorge had drowned in it, wonderful, white, cold snow. So deep that we struggled to move, but we moved anyway—what fun!

The mountains are so beautiful! Our little house is perched on the very top surrounded with pine trees of every kind. Some, the tallest things I've ever seen. I watch as Klaus reaches the top of the slope once more, he is exhausted—will he ever tire of tobogganing? Magda and Leni are building snowmen and Gretl and Heidi have run inside to escape the tirade of snowballs launched by Ludolf and Gunter. From a short distance, Frau Leshnik is watching as always, leaning on her stick and missing nothing with those eagle eyes of hers. She looks different today, there is a sort of green tinge to her complexion, she seems to blend into the forest somehow. She is eating food—a delicious chicken leg. She calls out to me, something about toffees, or medicine, it's very confusing.

Boris is holding my hand! Is his face red from the cold or is he bashful? I know he has been taunted by the others, behind his back of course. None of them, not even Ludolf dare risk annoying him and his notorious right hook. Boris has become a well-respected fighter. We thrust our feet through the snow. The chill is beginning to bite, but we don't care, we are all so happy in our snowy mountain paradise!

But wait—what's that noise, that loud bang. I have heard it before, sometimes in the distance and sometimes much nearer—it is very near today. Someone is hurt, someone is screaming; screaming always follows that noise. Artur, our guard, is weeping and his nasty brother is screaming at him. Other men are screaming also and dogs are yapping and everything goes dark. The Frau's voice is heard above the din, repeating over and over I'm looking at a dead man—I'm looking at a dead man—I'm looking at a dead man!

There is a witch and…and a knight, he is all in black. They are angry, the forest is in danger, the trees are in peril; I watch as the trees miraculously turn to people, they each have a yellow star. Then barbed wire crosses over the skies and falls upon us, pinning us to the ground. We are in such pain and then the bang returns, again and again—the gunshots. This time Victor just lies there, unmoving! What's wrong with Victor, is he hurt, and something else is wrong—where is Otto, I am aware he is missing. I scream—Where's Otto? Then, as always, I wake up shivering.

This dream continues to affect me in this way; it makes me colder than the real weather somehow, and there is always a chill in the air these days. I'm left disturbed. But I am alive to face another day, when so many others will not make it through the night—how bad must that final dream be? Or perhaps it is a nice dream, perhaps they die during the snowball fight and not the gunfight. Nice things do still happen. They have to, don't they? Yes that is what our last dream is, a nice experience, a good thing to end this awful life we all live. When I say we, I mean us prisoners, you know that right—of course you do.

I realise it is not yet morning. I have woken in the middle of the night again; it often happens to all of us. It's useless trying to sleep now. I can't help wondering about the others you see, those we have lost. They visit me at night like ghosts. I just can't get them out of my head, they're my friends. Where IS Otto? What has become of poor Victor, how I do hope he has not been shot, and Ludolf and Gunter; I miss Heidi and Gretl so much, and where is Boris and Frau Leshnik? I need them all so much right now. Even the Fraulein! Especially the Frau! If there is a god up there, please send her back to me.

I sit upright and feel the aches and pains run through my weary body. It hurts more every day. The first thing to hit me is the stench of the hut, will I ever get used to it. The place is filthy; I could never have imagined it. It has never been cleaned I am certain of that. Human waste now lies on top of more human waste. It coats everything, including us. I spend my day fetching hot water to wash clothes, but not my own clothes, not the filthy rags that cover my own body, the same rags I have worn constantly since our first day here, the same rags that have never been washed or mended, the rags that are only fit for burning.

How long have we been here now; I can't even guess. I overheard a woman in the shed say it was June, which means we have only been here for a couple of months! She must be mistaken. It seems much longer, like a lifetime. I've lost all track of time. The days just come and go so fast, they are all the same; they drift into one long day broken only by the nights that bring the same nightmares and very little rest.

Regardless how long we have been here, it has always been non-stop hard work! All of us are exhausted; the water carriers, the cloth washers, the button pickers, the road builders and most of all, the body collectors. It's more than being tired, more than fatigue, we are simply losing the will to live—we are fading of course, despite all our efforts to survive. Yet we must live, we must survive. Somewhere hidden deep inside, and I mean inside of us that remain, are fighting spirits that crop up to torment us with reasoning and rationale. Just when we have had enough, these fighting spirits keep coming back; they speak to us, spurring us on with relentless annoying encouragement and persuasion. We want them to go away, we pray for it, all we want to do is carry on fading away until there is nothing left—no pain, no hurting. But you know what, and this sounds like I am contradicting myself, none of us really want our prayers answered, not in that respect; these voices keep us alive—we must not stop listening. Though none of us really want to carry on like this either, the spirits always win, at least for one more day…until the last one.

That final day must come of course. It comes to everyone. Only in this place it arrives a little sooner than expected. The fighting spirit cannot last forever and each day many people just give up, thoroughly defeated. To put an end to the suffering here is easy—really. All you have to do is put down your tools and refuse to work. The end will come without a doubt, it will be quick, I'm not sure if it will be painless; a loud bang and a scream and then all suffering is over.

As I scan the hut my eyes adjust to the din and there they are; the skeletons, all around me, in every stage of death. If only we had a little more food. Food; good edible food, has always been scarce here. So much so that what there is has to be fought over; and I could kill for that chicken leg that torments me in my dreams. How hungry we are. It must be worse for the smaller children who rely heavily on us grown-ups, for that is what I am now; at least it's what I feel like.

I must provide for the little ones; they are my responsibility. Ola and a few others help me, the pickings are slim of course, but we consider ourselves lucky.

Hunger is one of the biggest killers here, after the monster behind the gates that is. Disease probably comes in third, especially tummy bugs, many thousands have died from diarrhoea; it is the dirty water you see, and even the common cold is a death sentence to people who are little more than skin and bone. We have no chance against the weakest of illnesses—no chance at all!

We die in the night and we die in the day, both are hard to bear. Days are a constant physical effort, but nights—well, in the night you have time to think, to wonder what will kill you first, just like I am doing right now. Will it be hunger; the endless list of diseases waiting to grab hold of me; or the vile behaviour of the Nazis? Or will I finally lose my fighting spirit and just give up; will I put down my tools and wait for the loud bang. Will someone scream for me? I think so, I hope so, and soon I will find out, you see I have decided that this is the way I will die, I will not simply succumb to the fading. I've thought about it many times and I have even tried it, but as you know I was not fully committed. But as each day wears you down further, the decision to give up comes easier—just a little. But before I die, I would like at least one good night, settled and warm, where my dream does not end in a gunshot and a scream, and I will know, this is my last day.

Does that sound like me? I wouldn't say so. How could I even think of leaving Klausy and the others—surely not! But I have changed. We all have. Seeing so much death, each and every day, turns you into a different person. The dead bodies that first horrified us are now ignored, looked upon with, I think you say, indifference; they are part of daily life here. You see, we have little time to worry about the dead, maybe a silent prayer for them, that's all we can offer before we turn our efforts to surviving another day—that damned fighting spirit!

Don't let me digress.

Little Leni, as usual, lay next to me. She had started doing this since we arrived. Someone needed to settle her before she would sleep, and the job fell to me. So now we share a bunk and my brave little brother has made way for the little girl. How hard it must be for Leni. When even the adults cannot understand what is going on, think how bad it must be for her and for all the little ones who had somehow escaped the monster. When I first started comforting her in this way, she was heavy and she made me uncomfortable in the night; but now I can barely feel she is there at all, I often fret that I will hurt her in my sleep, crush her little bones. She has begun to fade; it is happening fast.

Though she is worn out she too is awake, every time her weary eyes close she coughs or sniffs or clears her throat which I know is hurting her so. Her little button nose is all red and her skin is burning up. Yet she shivers, like she is in deep snow—she has a dreaded fever!

Tonight, she has clung to me so tight, her weak arms wrapped around my neck. She was whimpering something that I could barely hear. "Shush, shush. Save your breath," I whispered and gently brushed her sweating head in a vain attempt to comfort her. She desperately needs medicine, but where from? Without realising, I voiced my thoughts out loud. "Oh, I need medicine. If only there was some, something to help my little Leni."

"Your daughter needs medicine you say, there is some if you know where to look."

"Who said that?" In alarm I searched the hut, adjusting my eyes to the darkness.

"Here, over here," the faceless voice replied.

I looked harder and saw a woman. Old, I think, older than myself anyway. She lay on her bunk and waved a thin arm at me. "She is not my daughter, we are friends."

"You look older than your years. But don't we all these days. I feel a hundred years old and I probably look it, but I am only thirty years old; I think it is my birthday next week."

I nodded in the dark, I don't know why. I suppose it was a little rude to agree with her. "Happy birthday," I said and the woman laughed.

"Thank you," she replied. "Not for the happy birthday, but for making me laugh, I'd forgotten how to do it."

"You said there was medicine. Where can I get it?"

"Three huts down. You will find an old woman, even older than my hundred years; she must be a thousand years old." She laughed again. "They say she is mad; the guards call her the Mad Old Witch. They tease her and she insults them, she spits at them and curses them and threatens them with a branch of a tree. How she gets away with it, no one knows; but she does. Perhaps she is a witch after all. The guards even reward her for her insults. They give her food and other things, and the witch gives it away. She helps people—well her own people at least. She says they are her trees and she must protect the trees. I think she is a joke to the guards you see, as we all are. They don't take her seriously, knowing she will be dead soon enough."

"I need to find her."

"Yes—but you will need something to trade of course."

My head dropped in despair. "I have nothing." I said sadly as I glanced at Leni who moaned and wriggled. Tears began to run from my eyes.

"Here," the woman's voice said louder. I craned my neck to find her standing over us, she held out her hand offering me something. "Take this, get medicine for your little friend." She urged me to take her offering. "This is valuable," she added. "So make sure you get plenty of medicine; don't let the mad old witch cheat you."

I took the object from her hand and looked at it closely. I was amazed. It was a sweet, a toffee! Was this the woman from my dream—how could this be! "Where did you get this," I asked. "Is there anymore?"

She laughed again. "Don't ask how I got it; you are too young to know; I am not so ugly to some. I used to be very beautiful you know; I had all the young men chasing after me." She smiled, perhaps remembering her former life. "And no, there isn't any more…so make it count."

I was overcome. This sudden kind act had floored me. All around us were people fighting for their lives and here was a woman who was thinking of others, yet she too was in deadly peril. I shook my head in wonderment. Now it was my turn to be kind, to be thoughtful. "I can't take it. It is too much to give. How can I repay you?"

Her answer was simple and quick. She was so sincere, and so decisive. Where had this woman come from? Why hadn't we met before? Then it hit me, she was another angel—just like Ola. I smiled. "Just talking to you is payment," she offered. "It has been a long time since I met someone as kind as you…I haven't had this much fun in ages."

"Mona, my name is Mona."

"A beautiful name, you are worthy of it. My name is Vanda. Take the sweet, you deserve it. And thank you."

"For what?"

"For giving me the opportunity to do something good," she sighed, "before I die!"

"You are not dying Vanda…Not yet"

"Thank you again…look around you Mona, we are all dying here. All of our days are numbered." Vanda offered a sad smile. "Now leave her with me. Go now and be careful. If the guards see you, they will shoot you dead."

I gazed at the woman, still amazed at this sudden and unexpected kindness. "Why are you doing this?"

In the dark, I could see she was smiling. Despite the malnourished state that we all suffered from, her eyes sparkled and her cheeks glowed, the most surprising thing, she had kept her teeth in immaculate condition, a row of pearls, a hint of her former beauty. "I suppose it is to make peace with God," she said. "I have not been a good person. Also you make me laugh. Now go," she urged, "before I take my sweetie back."

I gently placed Leni down on Vanda's knee. The little girl was so unwell, so pathetic. But I had no time to comfort her further, and so, without hesitation, I left her and opened the door, only a slit so that I could quickly peek outside. It was as expected, wet and quiet. I wasn't nervous. I had slipped out many times before in search of food to steal; I had become quite successful at it, a result of all the sneaking around my garden with Klausy I guess.

It was deadly quiet outside, just the odd cough and sneeze now and then. Though there were some lights in the distance, between the huts it remained dark. Without thought I tiptoed outside, suddenly turning into a commando or a burglar. I was quiet. I was quick. It was me against the guards and I had the advantage, because, you see, they were all stupid, and as Jewish prisoners were too terrified to make trouble, the guards had become complacent and lazy and so were easily avoided. I moved down the dark alleyways with ease, always sticking close to the hut walls, my heart beating too fast and my mind racing faster. What if the old witch wasn't there—she might be dead! If she was there, how would I know her and worst of all, what if she refused to help? The discussion took place in my head; it would not be resolved before I reached the third hut down.

I opened the door quickly, almost falling inside. I knew what to expect, all the huts were exactly alike and packed with the usual rows of people, in varying states of sleep and death. I was not disappointed. This hut was much like our own; I don't know why, but it seemed to smell much worse. No one noticed my presence, I did not stand out in here, just another unfortunate prisoner; a thin skeleton, a meagre portion destined to be fed to the monster behind the fence.

I adjusted my eyes. Hundreds of people lay in fretful sleep, ravaged by illness and tortured by the cold. Coughing, crying, and moaning dominated here. Where did I start my search for the thousand-year-old mad witch? It was an impossible task, just like searching for a needle in a haystack. But anyway, I started to hunt around for her, up and down the rows of filthy bunks, craning my neck to see those above and stooping to examine those on the lower levels. I was the only one moving, yet I disturbed no one, no one cared about the stranger lurking at the end of their bed, no one saw me as a threat, no one here feared death. I searched a long time with no luck of course; we all looked frightfully alike in daylight, let alone here, in the dark.

I began to panic! What if I was too late; the witch could be dead already, it was more than likely. I would have to wake someone up. What a shame to disturb them, but I really had no choice.

I gently shook the nearest person; I couldn't tell if it was a man or a woman. I could feel bony ribs through their clothing, I expected that. But this person felt harder somehow, he or she did not stir. I should have experienced something then, some emotion, but there was nothing there; I was empty! Without feeling, without sympathy for this dead person—what had I become?

I was about to pluck up courage to nudge someone else when I heard a voice coming out of the darkness, it sounded familiar somehow, comforting in a very strange way. "What do you want? Why are you disturbing my family? You do not belong here."

Startled, I replied. "Please, please miss," I said to the darkness. I could locate where the voice was coming from, but I couldn't see who was talking. "I need medicine and a friend told me I could get it here. I have something to trade—I am looking for an old…"

"…Mad woman?" she finished my sentence and then cackled. "A witch…perhaps?"

"I seem to be making people laugh a lot these days, though this is not a laughing matter."

"I do not laugh lightly," the woman answered more seriously now. "What do you have to trade with?" The familiar voice demanded in the darkness.

"I need to find the old woman first; she has the medicine. Do you know where I can find her?"

"Yes I do, but first tell me what you have. Let me see."

"How can I trust you? You may take what I have for yourself."

"You can't trust me. But I suspect you have a friend. Someone who is ill and is depending on your success or they are likely to die. As I see it, you have no choice. Now show me what you have, you have little time to lose."

I sighed deeply. This woman was very clever; the crafty ones were always the worst to deal with. "Okay then, show yourself at least."

A few seconds passed before an old bent shape appeared at the end of the row of bunk beds. She limped towards me, held upright by some sort of stick or cane, a mere shadow in the darkness—a wraith. At an arms-length away, she stopped and held out her bony hand. I reluctantly offered the sweet. She examined it closely and when she realised what she held; I heard her gasp. "My oh my! Just a little thing it is, little and insignificant. Yet in this place at least, more precious than gold." She glanced up and though I could not make out her face I felt there was something familiar about her, something in her manner. "Your friend is lucky to have you," she said. "Not many would do as you are doing. But of course you are not like any other, you never were. You always had the ability to surprise me…Mona Lange!"

"What! How do you know me?" I stared hard through the darkness at the witch. "Wait…is that you…Frau Leshnik!" A second of silent suspense followed, a glimmer of expectancy before she answered, but it seemed that time had stopped. Her answer was yet a bigger surprise as she grasped me hard, pulling me to her, hugging me with strength she should not have.

Her breath stank like the latrines, her clothes even worse, but yet I experienced a comfort that I could scarcely remember. This embrace seemed to me then, more precious than any I had received from my mama in happier times. I could not stop tears from running down my cheeks. I hugged the old woman hard in return, threatening to break her bones. We could not let go, the moment was too good, and it seemed to last forever.

Then at last, Frau Leshnik pushed me away from her. "Yes, yes it is me. How could you forget me? Mona you are a silly girl. Did you think me dead; if so you never really knew me," she declared. "I would have liked our little conversation, our little wrangle to have continued," she said. "You know how I like to irritate my opponent; it amuses me. But I can see this is a serious matter—time is short. Come, come, quickly, take me to the children. I know you have them; you have saved them—you clever girl. I must see them; I have missed them so…and one of them is in need." She thrust the sweet back into my hands and pushed me towards the door. I had found a witch, but she was not wicked, she never had been.

Outside the huts, I carefully manoeuvred from one hiding place to another. But Frau Leshnik, having miraculously lost her limp, seemed full of energy; she simply marched on in full view of the guards, uncaring and unconcerned. As we approached my hut a guard turned the corner and walked straight into her. I froze. Surely we were dead. But no, a second surprise from the old woman. "Oh, Ivan, it's you," she said, pushing the startled man away with her stick. "Out of my way you buffoon before I have you disembowelled and fed to the pigs."

The guard chuckled. "To your bed, old witch, before the cold kills you."

"You will die before me, I promise."

"Yes, yes, I know, when your son gets here," he replied as he wandered off in the other direction. I gawped at the Frau in amazement. She frowned and shook her head. "What's wrong with you Mona? He is just a stupid guard. Ivan is the first on my list; soon he will get what's coming to him—mark my words."

Moments later we had reached our hut, I burst through the door, Frau Leshnik following close behind and then I suddenly stopped. I was overcome with a foreboding, a feeling deep down in my bones—something was wrong. This was not the usual kind of fear that engulfed all of us on a daily basis, this was different; it seemed to seep into me, chilling my nerves. Frau Leshnik stood close behind me, she could feel something was wrong too; everyone in the camp felt this feeling sooner or later. I wanted to scream out, but I couldn't make a sound. I approached Vanda. The kind lady held Leni tightly and lovingly, just like a mother would. She looked at me sadly. We were too late—little Leni was dead!

I offered her the toffee back. "Keep it," Vanda said and closed my hand around it.

"It seems this is a den of kindness. At least, you were in good hands, little one," Frau Leshnik said as she knelt beside Leni's body stroking her head gently.

I knew Leni was going to die, of course, it was a miracle she had lasted this long; it had only been a matter of time. Indeed how had any of us lasted so long when we had seen so many others arrive only to fade away in front of our eyes? I thought I'd be consumed by grief when the time came, but I wasn't. As I have already said, I'd encountered death every day for months on end and it had changed me, hardened me. All I wanted to do was cry out loud. I wanted the tears to flow like rain and I wanted to fall to my knees, shaking with grief—but it would not come to me. Instead, inside I was now filled with the strangest feeling, a feeling of calm. Leni's ordeal was over, she was at peace now. I almost envied her. I examined her face, it was so thin, but beautiful—she was sleeping, she was…she was in Heaven.

Ironically, it was Frau Leshnik that shed the tears. She was distraught; how she cried and cried, sobbing all through the night, clutching Leni's body tightly to her; as though Leni's death had released some inner pressure, some inner pain that she had allowed to grow inside her. Pent-up emotions spilled out of her, destroying the years of hiding behind the hard façade she had created; the tough unfaltering and unloving Nazi we had all known and hated—the wicked witch! Now the genuine Leshnik emerged, from the broken shell. The Delma, and she had enough compassion for both of us: how we had all changed.

Chapter 17
Without Leni

We have had bad days and we have had terrible days, but so far, the day Leni left us was the worst day of all. That was a fortnight ago, I had decided to keep count of the days since her death and I now know for sure we were in July, which means we had been here nearly three months or perhaps a little more. I know because an American Jew told me so. The poor woman had come to Europe to find lost members of her family. She arrived here on the fourth of July, a special day for the Americans—Independence Day. How she was allowed to visit is a mystery, she said she worked for some foreign agency but that's all she could say, and that was too much. Three days later she had lost her passport and her independence—how ironic. She is a brave woman, but also a little stupid, I think.

When Leni died, I entered a very sad period, I was in danger of giving up again and needed to focus on the positive things. Frau Leshnik had come back to us, and that was certainly a good thing, though I wasn't sure how long she would stay around. This last week had brought another surprise, the sunshine had arrived! Yes the sun had finally shown its face but working indoors meant we didn't see much of it; only in small amounts, but it was there, and that helped to boost our ailing spirits a little. Leni would have enjoyed the sunshine; it always made her smile and her lovely cheeks would glow—bless her!

Today though, a fine rain had started to fall which cleared the mist away and managed to drench us through to our aching bones as we lined up for the morning inspection. The captain's evil voice faded into the background as my mind drifted away. Was I fainting: was I going to die at last? Thoughts of Leni came to me then, how I missed her already, and yet, I didn't expect to. The poor girl had been fading for some time; I think we were all aware of it—even Klaus. I was wrong when I said I couldn't feel grief. It had descended onto me late, but it was there nonetheless, and it hurt. I hadn't realised I was still capable of feelings, and longings, that were once so natural, but there they were—yet another surprise.

The rain blew into my face and the sky turned black again and the clouds made ghastly shapes, as if demons were watching from above. My thoughts turned to angels. Where are they—the angels, where is God? I looked into the sky and spoke to…probably no one, yet I hoped HE was listening. "Everything is greyer than usual, if that is possible," I said, and then asked. "Where has the sun gone? It hasn't been around very long. Bring it back. Can't we at least have some blue sky and warmth for a change?" He did not answer and the dark remained.

Dark days bring shadows. They are all around, moving about quickly, darting here and there and catching my eye; they are in charge today—little demons creating mischief. I should feel afraid, but I simply don't care anymore.

The shadows make me feel even sadder, another surprise—being sad has no limits. Mixed with the sadness, there is a hint of hope. Am I making sense to you? I think of the Frau again. She is a survivor, she brings hope, and…and I also have Ola, don't forget wonderful Ola. How can we be afraid when we have these two to protect us? The Frau returned out of the blue, I reckon this was the angels doing. I know there are angels at work around here somewhere; they too like to play games you know. I am still convinced Ola is one of them, perhaps the Frau too, but they refuse to confess. The Frau is certainly no witch, not to us. She will make us strong again. She will give us courage.

Leni crossed my mind again, though I had grown to love her, like a…like a daughter, she has gone now and, of course, I'm sad, but I also feel relief. That's right, I feel relief. Leni has gone to a far better place you see. I know Heaven exists, as does God. I expect that surprises you after all we have seen and suffered. But I will not give up on God—he has to be there, he must be there, there has to be somewhere better for us to go when we leave here! When the blue skies return for good, I will know for sure he is there, in Heaven, waiting for us. He has Leni with him right now, she was responsible for the short burst of sunshine and blue skies we have had already, she will be asking for more, I just know it.

Yes, it's true. Leni has gone to Heaven and with her is my responsibility for her. Does that sound bad? Does that make me a bad person? You may think so. You may think that Mona is a bad person. But…but you have never lived in a death camp—have you? Leni's suffering is over and I ask you—what kind of mama wants her daughter to suffer? She is now with God who can care for her much better than I can.

Things are different here you see. Things are different in Hell. I still have a brother to care for, I also have Magda and there are a few others that are relying on me now. I have a burden that no girl of my age should bear, but I do my best—I have to focus and remain vigilant—I must not fail in my duties. Of course I can share my responsibilities with Ola and Frau Leshnik, we are one big family after all. A big family, but a changing family, all too easily members of our family are leaving us, but we welcome others in to take their place. Frau Leshnik has an entire hut full of people who depend on her, she calls them her trees. I have no idea why; there's something strange going on, deep, inside her head perhaps. You know I have always thought of her as mad, horrible and mad, but now I think of her as mad and…nice! We need her and we need her trees, there is strength in numbers—the only good thing I learned at Hitler Youth.

The daily whistle releases me from my thoughts and the assembled prisoners of Hell move in different directions. Some to the forest to cut wood for fuel and building yet more fences, it is hard work but they appear healthier than most; I think the forest offers shelter and perhaps food. Others have marched off to the factories where they make weapons and other things for this blasted war. Though it's dry inside those huge, corrugated buildings, there must be something in the air that is not good for a long healthy life, as these workers tend to die from conditions that affect the lungs. I've seen many cough up blood—that's not nice to see. The worst off, though, work in the quarry. I can't think of how hard it must be moving rocks around all day. I sometimes see these poor things coming home late at night, their backs bent and their heads down, exhaustion is the killer there.

It is fair to say that a large part of today's assembly will die. If the conditions don't kill us, then the blood-thirsty Nazis, waiting for the slightest excuse, will kill us. They are hunters you see, nothing but sadistic predators that like nothing better than the sight of suffering and blood. They apply reason to their actions, picking out the weak and the sick, ridding themselves of the useless, the ones that have become a burden!

Our party of all girls, except Klaus, yet again run over towards the sorting shed. There is a new load of clothes to wash and press. It is bigger than ever; it seems the murder process has picked up speed. The night has been busy; three trains have unloaded their cargo and gone away to reload, leaving the damned and wretched souls who will feed the monster or work for him till they die. For Klaus, as always, there is a huge pile of wood to move, there have been gangs collecting this through the night, we hear the sound of their chopping, carried on the wind, all the way from the forest; there is no one protecting those trees, they need Frau Leshnik!

I watched my brave boy struggling with logs and sticks full of thorns. It reminded me of better times, when he would wrestle with similar branches in our garden to make dens so that he could launch an attack on me, how much fun we had, even now it makes me giggle—they will all think I've gone mad if I start laughing for nothing.

The little ones are busy too. Magda has been joined by those I picked out of the line. I do not know their names and I'm afraid to ask in case we grow close. They have thousands of buttons to remove from the rags that cannot be salvaged and they work so hard when all they long for is to play. Surprisingly, there are a lot of rags today, more than usual and far more than the good quality clothes. Most of the trains are bringing very poor people from other prisons. People who have already known suffering before they arrived here; and the trains are arriving more often than usual. At least, the separating has stopped, the monster behind the fence is unable to cope and though there is still a line of prisoners heading that way, most of the new arrivals are assigned to huts for a short while until the hungry beast catches up. This means we have more time to rescue some of them by allocating work at the shed. I don't think I remember the laundry and the shed being staffed so well, but there is always room for more.

For me, it is back to the fire and heavy buckets of boiling water. I have two helpers, both girls younger than me. Yet I am sad when I see them, for I know it won't be long before we start to reduce in number again and I will have to request more shed mates from the sergeant. Ardit will accompany me again, in-fact he is pressing me to return, but I'm not sure if I could face the line going to the gates—not so soon after Leni…perhaps later! I am making life or death decisions you know, my delay to return to the gates has meant that someone I could have saved has died, it's a pity for them, but it is lucky for the ones arriving on the next train. Some will win and others will lose!

Meanwhile we make do with what we have for now. I will scald myself again today which brings on the most horrendous pain, my wrists and calves are covered in scars, badges to remind me of my suffering until my last day. Yet every time I gaze into the bath of boiling water, I think of Mama adding hot water to my bath at home. I used to lie there soaking for ages, submerged in soap suds up to my chin. Then when I had finished, Klausy would be dunked in kicking and screaming, he hated the bath and always moaned about having to go in after me—he is such a funny boy.

When they have received enough hot water, the new washer women immediately start scrubbing and many other gangs set about mending and sorting. I should shuffle them all around again, to relieve the monotony, they will like that.

Salvaging the clothes is a good thing really, they are badly needed. We have all seen the bombers fly over recently, heading towards the big cities and we have all heard the bombs go off in the distance. There will be lots of German people in need of these clothes; like us, they are struggling to survive. I have no problem with helping them, with providing them with clean clothes, if only the clothes had not been stolen from those even worse off, those who have been murdered.

We work for about two hours before we are allowed a very short rest. A whistle signals the time to stand and stretch our aching limbs. A young girl brings us water; there will be no food for a long time yet. It's funny when you don't expect any food your body no longer seems to feel hungry. Each day we all waste away a little further, soon there will be nothing left. My own striped rags are far too big for me now and Klaus and Magda's keep falling off their scrawny little limbs, they were far too big to begin with and now the pair have to roll the arms and legs up further to keep them up. It's strange not to see Leni there, in her usual place. She was a good girl, always keeping herself busy, working away in silence and never complaining. Just fading away, right in front of my eyes whilst I watched—helpless!

Ola's gang now sorts the suitcases. I noticed she has some new members to replace a few of the faces I had grown to like. There is no point asking where they are, it will simply add to the sadness around this place. There are new faces everywhere. I have refused to get to know them well and so have to ignore them when we meet. They probably think I am a horrid girl. But it is too dangerous to get close. It can place you in jeopardy. We must not forget there is danger around every corner, today was one of those days, a reminder of how we all walk on a knife edge. This is what happened.

I remember I delivered a bucket of water to one of the new girls and as I turned to leave, she caught my eye. Her sudden movements and the nervous look on her face told me she was up to something; instantly, I began to panic. In fear of the guards catching her and implicating the rest of us, I turned away quickly so I couldn't work out what was going on. I turned to God again and prayed; "Please don't get us all into trouble."

I reached the fire too quickly which put me in danger of attracting the guards, though they appeared to be ignoring us, you could never tell if one of them was watching, or what mood they were in. I slowed my pace a little. My breathing was too quick, I was panting and I was trembling a little, they would surely notice something is up! Fighting for control of my wits I dipped my bucket into the boiling water. My hands were shaking and the inevitable scald quickly followed, but I held my breath and with full buckets, I turned slowly to make the dreaded return journey with my next delivery of fresh water.

As I approached the girl a second time I could see it; a quick movement, almost a sleight of hand. The girl had passed something to her friend—she was smuggling. It was well known that hidden deep in the lining of clothing there is often treasure to be found: money, gems, family heirlooms, or simple keepsakes that the prisoners have endeavoured to conceal from the Nazis; something to keep for harder times perhaps, something to ease the suffering—how little did they know.

Normally, the clothing is thoroughly checked before it reaches us. Yet every now and then something turns up in the wash. We all know what we must do of course—declare any items found immediately to the SS officers. For anyone caught contradicting this rule, it is certain death, not just for them, but for the whole work party. The foolish girl didn't know it, but she was risking not only her life but all our lives. I had to warn Ola!

Although I was in charge of the sorting process and these girls, I simply could not think straight. I was not coping with my first crisis; Ola was the girl for that. She was definitely the best at getting us out of trouble and so I approached her. The guards are used to the pair of us talking, they think we are making plans for the shed, but most of the time we talk nonsense as there is really very little to organise in this place. On this occasion, Ola knows something is wrong.

Was it my imagination or were the guards watching us more closely. I dared not tell Ola of the problem immediately in case we were overheard. One particular mean guard, Dima is the name I have heard him answer to, has become the sergeant's favourite, even the other guards are wary of him—especially Ardit, who, like Gregor actually helps us these days, whenever he can; a little food here, a blind eye when we need a short break—nothing too much of course, we must not take advantage. That is what this new girl was doing right now, taking advantage and placing us all in jeopardy.

Dima is creepy! He is constantly finding ways to ingratiate himself with the Crooked Captain. It is only a matter of time before something catches his eye, some misplaced movement, some secret look. I stole a glance in his direction and saw he was staring directly towards the new girl; he would certainly notice something—soon. How infuriating, that damned man! I dared not speak my mind, so how to tell my friend who must be warned of the danger we were all facing. My nerves were on fire. I was sweating, I was shaking all over, I felt like I would either faint or vomit—both were as bad. What could I do?

It's funny how in the worst of times when you expect your wits to desert you, something from deep inside, deep inside your brain takes over and the solution is there, plain as day for you to see. Have you experienced times like that? For me, this was one of those times. The answer to my quandary, thankfully, came sudden and unexpectedly.

"Sorry Ola," I announced a little louder than usual. Though work talk was permitted in the shed, my words attracted interest from the guards almost immediately, including Dima who, instantly, directed his attention from the new girl to me. "This water is not for you," I added and stepped over to the new girl and indicated my intension to pour the water from my bucket into her wash basin. Surprise appeared on her face, she didn't need more water, but as she glared directly into my face I returned a look that could have killed. My disapproval was a clear warning that she could not ignore. As I cleared my throat I also whispered, "Be careful, this is hot water!" The new girl thanked me for the water and set about scrubbing a shirt with vigour. But it was too late, Dima's suspicions were aroused and he began to approach.

Now there was no time for caution. Ola who had been watching closely had read the situation perfectly and did only what Ola could pull off, she caused a commotion. Without warning she brushed into me, entangling herself with my empty bucket before declaring, "Mona, that was stupid," she screamed into the air and began rubbing her pants as if hot water had soaked through them. "You scalded me, you silly girl," she said and stepped backwards directly into the path of Dima. Dima looked both surprised and angry and was about to slap Ola. But the girl was too quick and bent down to rub the fake scalds on her legs. "Forgive me sir," she cried. "Have pity. I did not mean to make a commotion." Dima pushed Ola to the side and turned his attention once again to the new girl.

We had not been lazy. The moment Ola screamed I had pushed my empty water bucket in front of the new girl who was disappointedly slow to understand my meaning and so I had to risk everything, even my life. "In the bucket," I ordered, "Now!" The witless girl quickly retrieved the object from her friend and dropped it into my bucket. It made a clang that surely sealed our fate but I was committed to sorting this mess and walked away as quickly as I could. Dima began to shout at the new girls who cowered in terror. Meanwhile I had took the object, a broach of precious metal, from my bucket, and without hesitating I deposited it at the feet of another girl who had worked in the sorting shed much longer and who I knew, could be relied upon.

Immediately, this more experienced girl announced the finding. "Call the sergeant," she said and held the object into the air. "I have found something."

To Dima's dismay, it was Ardit who reached the girl first. He took possession of the object and smiled, personally I think this was because he had beaten Dima to it. Ardit glimpsed at me for a second and I could see he was aware of our cover up but his persistent smile told me we were safe. On the other hand, Dima was fuming. Was it desire to own the brooch that shone in his eyes? I decided not. He had simply lost the opportunity to please the sergeant, who would certainly pocket this meaningless thing. Dima glared at Ardit, who merely smiled back— What was he up to?

Ardit remained a mystery. I felt I knew this man better than anyone, I had been watching him for some time now. He wasn't like the other guards, he had secrets of his own and one day I would find out what haunted him. Ardit had also become unlikely friends with Frau Leshnik. They both took every opportunity to get to know each other better; Ardit particularly interested in the Frau's son who was fighting in the east. I would often caution the Frau but she was not concerned. She always managed to come away from their meeting with an item of much needed food, calling the guard a superstitious fool who still believed in monsters. I was not convinced. Ardit was up to something and it involved the Frau, or maybe, her son.

I have digressed again, haven't I? Captain Crooked appeared and the brooch was safely deposited in his pocket, probably never to be seen again. Ardit retreated, but not until he had shot me a warning look, a knowing look. There was something there that surprised me. He was telling me off—next time Dima may get his way and we would be dead. Did Ardit actually care for us? In the early days, we had unfairly misjudged him, that was for sure; he was our friend and trying to help us in some way. But the question of what he was up to was to fascinate and torment me for a long time. From that day on, I decided that I would go out of my way to get to know Ardit better. Ola would not be happy at all.

Later that night I was celebrated as a hero. The new girls were given a good old telling off and best of all Ola's gang received a small box of potatoes as a reward for good work. I had proved something to myself. I had been scared, and I had been brave—I had felt alive again.

Chapter 18
Friends forever

"Hi. I'm Gretl Neumann and this is my friend Heidi Wolf."

"Hi."

We would like to tell you what we have been getting up to whilst you have been listening to Mona and the others. Is Mona okay? If only we could hear for ourselves what is happening to her and our other friends, little Leni and Magda. Klausy is also missing, is he still alive do you think. Have you heard anything of Boris, how we need him so. We actually know Frau Leshnik is still around. We have heard the tales of an old witch; it has to be that old cow.

We expect you already know about the nice train journey, don't you, I'll bet Mona has told a wonderful tale of mountains and rainbows. So I will skip that part and go straight to the second train. Now the journey on this train, inside that filthy wagon, was absolutely horrendous to say the least. When our papas find out what happened on that platform, those soldiers will be in big trouble, I can tell you that for nothing.

We were cramped up in such a small place with all those other people; how it hurt us every time the train jolted…and the smell—it was stifling. But Heidi and I would gladly climb back inside that wagon if we could get out of this place and make the return journey. When the wagon door opened, I actually thought I had arrived in Hell, can you imagine how scary that was for us? I still shudder when I think about it. The skies had turned black and the rain poured down and we were greeted by those beastly men and their ferocious dogs with huge teeth and constant barking and biting. We fell out of the wagon, didn't we Heidi? Then almost immediately, we lost poor Boris. Heaven knows what has happened to him.

I'm sure you know about the shaving of hair—I can't bear to think about it, it was horrendous to see all my lovely hair, that I had cared for, that Mama had cared for; it just fell to the floor and was swept away. The funny thing is, now our hair is growing back, it is all knotted and nitty, I think we were better off without it. I would actually be glad to be rid of it again. After the hair shave, we were changed into these vile rags which stunk so much then, you would die if you got a whiff of them now. But we all stink as bad as each other; we begin not to notice it. I remember one of the guards laughing, "You'll get used to it," he said, and of course we all did.

After we were dressed so nicely, we all went on a picnic! "Didn't we Heidi?" Oh no, sorry, it wasn't a picnic, it was a long and painful march through the mud and the cold rain.

"Stop teasing Gretl. Get on with it. I need to sleep. Anyway, you forgot the tattooing."

"Oh yes, I forgot about that—that part really hurt. We were all tattooed as well; some stupid identity number on our forearms, I've often wondered what purpose it serves—perhaps it's a way of telling us apart, since we all look the same! Are you happy now Heidi?"

"If you are telling the story, then get it right."

"You get grumpier each day! Anyway, if Heidi has finished interrupting, we next went on a march."

"You've said that already."

"Oh shut up! Anyhow, that first march was really hard and all the others since, have been harder. Have you ever tried walking fast in thick, sloppy mud? You slide all over the place, I can tell you, and when you fall behind, the guards beat you to ensure you keep moving. The blasted mud just seemed to get deeper and when it wasn't muddy, the air was full of dust, it's either one or the other—never nice. Along with everything else we owned; they had taken our shoes which made things worse than ever—our poor feet!"

"I say they! I mean our enemies, the guards, but actually, they are our own soldiers. That's right, isn't it, Heidi, they are German soldiers? If not, they are soldiers fighting on the German side, that's for sure. This whole camp is run by Germans you know, Aryans I believe; we all found this so hard to believe at first."

"For days, we thought there must be a reason for this camp and how we were being treated. We thought it was some kind of test, an endurance test or something, but it never seems to end. And no one has given us the time to explain that this is all some terrible mistake. No one, not a soul seems to care."

"Anyway, back to my story. Our first march took us through woods and over a little stream that chilled our feet to the bone and then through more muddy fields until we finally stopped at a sort of building site. We were given tools and put to work on a road; a road! Can you believe it! Young children working on a road, actually building a road! I still can't believe it."

"Get on with it will you? We will be back there soon enough."

"Oh yes we will." Of course we will. Each day is exactly like the last. We have to carry rocks and gravel in wheelbarrows that are full to the top, they are so heavy that sometimes it takes two of us to push them, which is a very difficult thing to do you know, especially in mud. It is getting a little easier now, the days are slightly warmer and the mud is drying again, we'll have dust to contend with next.

The bigger rocks are laid down first to form the base for the road. You see, I am at least learning something.

"Yes. When you get out of here, you will make a great road builder."

"Shut up, will you!" Anyway, next, finer rocks, which are actually the bigger rocks that have been broken down to gravel and dust, are laid on top of the big ones; that is what we do, Heidi and me, we spread the fine dust with rakes, we call ourselves rakers. The whole thing is then flattened by teams of men and boys pulling heavy rollers. It is such hard work. This is what Victor and Ludolf do. Gunter and Otto help fetch the big rocks—how they struggle. Victor is not looking well lately; we are all worried for him.

As I've said…Every day is the same with very little rest and even less food and water. People actually die on this road and they are just carted off to God knows where and immediately replaced by other people who have recently arrived on other crowded trains just like we had. It seems so long ago; I have lost track of time. Each day brings more trains, and each train brings more people and they are all from different countries, all speaking with different languages and accents, yet all of them Jews. The poor Jews—there are so many of them!

Heidi was struggling at first. "Weren't you Heidi?" I didn't think she would last long; I can tell you. "Until Ludolf found you a rake—remember? You know, I think that rake saved your life."

"Shush Gretl."

Good old Ludolf, he's such a nice boy. He's in charge of our group—Boris' Band, what would we do without him? I'm sure we'd be dead by now, every last one of us. "We all agree, Heidi and me, Gunter, Victor and Otto; that Ludolf is our leader and our protector. He will get us out of here, I just know it!"

We found out today what the road is for. It goes to a factory that makes parts for fighter planes and tanks; which is why there is an urgency to get it finished. Our armies need these weapons to keep the Russians away. At first, we wondered if it was good to work there in the factory, but after seeing the workers leave each day and we see their injuries where some horrid guard has beaten them, we are pleased to remain where we are thank you—better the devil you know, my mama used to say. Our guards are bored stiff with their responsibilities. I suppose it's as hard for them as it is for us, having nothing else to do except watch us all day.

"You are talking nonsense—get on with it."

"You get grumpier by the minute—you know."

I think the guards have even grown tired of beating us for nothing, and only do it when ordered to—that's a blessing in itself. They also talk too much and often give us news of life outside the camp. There is nothing for us Germans to worry about it seems, the war is going well for us. Perhaps soon we will beat our enemies and the war will come to an end, then we can all go home and it will all be alright; we can forget this place—forever.

"I think you have gone mad Gretl. How can we ever forget this hellish place?"

The days are so…so long and by the end we could all lie down and die. We long to return to the huts to sleep but at nighttime we are no better off. Our hut is disgusting; full of human waste! It smells foul, not just vomit and poo but there is always sickness and always death. How would you like to wake up and find the person in a bed near you has died in the night? It happens all the time to us. Then, if they have them, we steal their shoes! I know that's not so nice but not many prisoners have them and we so desperately need to protect our feet from the rocks or we will get infected by some awful bug.

There are all sorts of illnesses and diseases here. Eventually something will take hold of all of us and…and put us out of our misery—the lucky ones! That's what we call them you know. We have very few blankets and the ones we can get hold of have usually belonged to the lucky ones and so are covered in disease and stains and they smell so horrid. But we have to do our best with what we have. Each night our group snuggle together, it is the only warmth and comfort we have and has perhaps kept us all going for so long. If you are alone in this place, you have very little chance of surviving long…you have no chance!

Each night though, we manage to get some sleep, which is more than most. "Are you kidding?"

Sometimes, if we are lucky enough, we sleep so deep that we actually dream. Dreams have become important to us, they give us something to talk about, we have been known to discuss our dreams for hours, they seem to give us comfort somehow, something to enjoy during our awful day.

My dreams are always nice and have become the best part of my life. I often dream of home and my warm house where we eat the best foods like salmon and beef steak and tomato soup, and we laugh ever so much…and we talk! We talk all the time, especially at the dinner table. We discuss all kinds of things, all nice things. We tell jokes and we laugh a lot. Here, we eat our breakfast in silence. It is usually some sort of disgusting soup and a piece of bread. It is tasteless, but at least it is warm—if you get in the front of the queue that is. Breakfast doesn't take long and we don't have to line up for morning parade—the job we do weeds out the weaklings and the sick—no need for a doctor to decide. The Nazis also, can't wait to get us back to work and we can't wait to hear about each other's dreams.

No sooner have we started our hard labours do we begin telling of our adventures and the nice things we have experienced in our sleep. It was just Heidi and me at first, now though, all the boys have joined in and on some days, even strangers take part. It seems to keep us going.

I sometimes dream about going to balls in huge ballrooms and dancing with handsome boys. I don't know where this dream comes from as I have never even been to a ball. I wear sparkling dresses and wonderful slippers and sometimes, even a tiara—how I do hope this dream comes true someday. Heidi dreams of her family a lot, and her friends which is a lovely dream; the boys tend to dream of football, they are always scoring the goal that matters, the one that wins the game or they are great war heroes and other such things. Heidi and me—

"I! It's Heidi and I—What would your mama say Gretl?"

Heidi and me don't really like the dreams the boys have, but we listen and smile at them anyway. Today Otto's dream was different. He had dreamed of home and was spending the day with his mama and papa. They had a picnic; it was such a nice dream. Last night Ludolf had been a great high-ranking officer. We all listened intently as he told how he had rounded up all the guards and camp officers and then tortured them in a terrible fashion before having them shot; not a nice dream at all, but yet I pictured it with glee and wished it would come true, even before my own did.

Victor always seems to have the best dreams. We keep his until last as he never fails to cheer us up. The dream he had last night has become my favourite of all. He dreamed he was at a ball with me. I thought he was going to say we were dancing together, but no. He was also wearing a sparkling dress and fancy slippers and he was dancing with Frau Leshnik who was madly in love with him. They danced and spun in circles before the old woman suddenly turned into a sort of wood elf before vanishing into a cloud of dust. How funny. How we laughed. Well at least until the guards screamed at us. My sides were hurting, I hadn't laughed for so long you see. Of course, we all knew that Victor was making it all up and was only doing it to cheer us up a little. But it worked, as always. He does the same each day, without fail. Good old Victor, he has shown a hidden talent, turning his nightmares into fairy tales.

One day, a short while ago, I had found Victor crying. He was all alone in the corner of the hut. He took a lot of comforting before he told me what his dreams were really about. Each night he dreamed of Mona and Boris, little Leni and Klaus, he had also dreamed of Otto and all of his dreams were bad. In his dreams, there were blazing fires and boiling water, there was fist fighting and boys hiding under piles of clothes and sometimes Frau Leshnik turned up, casting spells like an evil witch and threatening to set her son onto people. Her son was a demon in disguise, and there were people chopping trees with great axes, and the trees came to life and thrashed back with huge spiky branches, their roots took hold of Victor and dragged him underground. Victor's dreams weren't nice at all; they were the worst nightmares ever, which made his funny stories all the more special. I remember giving him a gentle kiss on his spotty forehead. How he smiled.

I explained that they were only dreams and they would never come true. "How could they Victor," I said. "Surely Frau Leshnik must be dead by now and Otto, well Otto was safe with us, under Ludolf's protection and a member of Boris' band." He wasn't entirely convinced so I told him, "Don't forget, there are no trees around here, the forest is far off, at the other side of camp. Surely then, Mona and the others would be safe. Yes, these were only dreams Victor." My words reassured him. How ironic, we were living the nightmare.

So, as another day breaks, the cycle will begin again. We wake up cold, as usual. We will eat our soup; it will warm us up. We will then pick up our tools and march to our place on the road, which is nearly complete—what then! We will tell each other our dreams and Victor will lie to us again and make us laugh. We will work until we ache and we will see some of our fellow workers die—as usual. The rain will fall down hard to drench us and make mud, the sun may burn our faces and turn the mud to dust, the wind will thrash us—as usual. This will continue of course, until at last it all comes to an end…and surely it must end. Soon our papas will rescue us—I'm certain of it.

Chapter 19
The Brave Boy

Hello, my name is Mona. I am fifteen years old; actually I am nearer sixteen, only a month away, in September, the eleventh to be exact. September is normally a nice month, but after that the weather will turn horrid again and the sun will disappear and we will be back with all the grey! Oh dear, I don't think I could manage a winter here.

So—nearly sixteen, but I look older; yes…much, much older. I am very tall for my age, but now I walk with a bent and aching back, always facing the ground. I dare not look up, in fear of what I will see. I would tell you my surname, but I am ashamed of it.

I will continue with my story…my horror story. You've already heard some sad parts. Unfortunately, it only gets worse from here. Just to recap; this horror story began when my brother Klaus and I, along with nine other children, set out on a rainy and very miserable day on a journey aboard a secret train, leaving our much-loved mamas behind. At that time, it was the most miserable day of our lives.

I am a German—a true Aryan, whatever that means; it has brought us nothing but misery. Papa called me his Aryan princess; my younger brother, Klaus, his Aryan prince. This was in better times. Happier times; times when we believed we were great. What fools we were then and how ignorant we were! Now, nearly four months later, our lives have changed beyond recognition. We are now called rats, vermin and cockroaches and I can't, for the life of me, understand why?

My father is called Ulrich. He is a powerful army officer—a colonel. My mama's name is Maria; she is very beautiful and is such a lovely person. How she doted on my brother and me, and how she agreed with everything Papa told her. It's not enough to say she was wrong to agree with him, if only she knew just how wrong. Would she agree with him if she saw this place, this hell hole where we are living; or should I say, barely existing! And why doesn't Papa use his power to rescue us before it is too late, before we are all carted off beyond the gates, where an ever-hungry monster awaits to gobble us all up!

I have many questions that require answers, most of them start with why. I have a why question for every person in this camp—this death camp! I have a why question for every person who has been in this camp before me, and who will come after me, and there will be so many more. And guess what, there are many, many camps like this—WHY?

Yes, there was a time when we were very happy. We were the lucky ones, bound to rule the world! How our fortunes have changed. At one time, we all had straight blonde hair, Mama used to put ringlets in mine. If only she could see my dirty lice-riddled scalp all covered in scabs, some of which refuse to heal and constantly leak fluid. Thank heavens we haven't a mirror, I daren't look at what's going on up there. You know, I don't even think I am able to grow hair anymore.

Mama wears her hair up in a bun, at least she used to, I haven't seen her for such a long while. We all have big blue eyes—true Aryan, our mama used to say they shone and sparkled so. Not so now, only dull and lifeless eyes with barely a sparkle in them and only enough shine for one more day if we can manage it.

Let me tell you of another day. It is much like the rest, gloomy and dark. Yet this day was, how should I say—extraordinary. There were two very different incidents on this day, both significant events that caused havoc with my emotions.

Now you know we have had some sad days, some worse days and more horrid days than we can remember. We have witnessed more cruelty than you could possibly imagine—terrible, terrible cruel things. How can ordinary people be so cruel? I ask myself this constantly. Yes, it is fair to say we have had some very bad days indeed. This day promised to be one of the worst, but actually turned out to be one of the better, more memorable days…and for a good reason.

Despite the bad days, we, by that I mean, our little family, have actually been lucky I guess. In our little laundry, we are sheltered you see, from the daily terror of this place. Only when we are too weak to work will we have to face the true horrors here. Hundreds, thousands, hundreds of thousands of people arrive on a daily basis just as we did by train. But they do not remain here for long. What happens to them…they go directly to the monster! I call it a monster, but I now know the truth of course. It is a chamber. A chamber that smells of death, a place where we are thrust into and…gassed!

The monster exists though. It is a real thing. But it is hidden. It is deep inside the guards and officers that are stationed here; it is hidden deep inside our leaders and the people who created this place and it is hidden deeper inside everyone who calls themselves Aryan. But mostly; inside of my very own papa, a man I once loved, the man I called Papa—he was the one who let the monster out!

I have not seen these chambers, not yet, and I dread the day I do see them. I have only seen the black smoke that belches from the monster's nostrils to constantly fill the sky and destroy the beautiful clouds. I have seen the ash, which is spread on the fields, and of course, the monstrous gates that haunt me every time my eyes close.

Another day comes, another miserable day in Hell. Let me tell you of it. Let me take you there so you can experience it.

"Come, Magda, Klaus, Mona. We must not be late for the roll call, if we are missing, they will presume us dead and someone else will get our delightful jobs." Again, Ola, our Jewish saviour, breaks us from our gloomy reverie. She remains our only hope of survival, keeping constant vigil over us to ensure we make it through each day. The girl has such determination to survive, she will never be beaten. Not only does Ola deal with the guards ensuring we are left alone, she even manages to acquire extra rations of food at times. She also insists we are in the right place at the right time so we don't attract unwanted attention from the guards. And she makes us appear healthy so that we pass the daily inspections which declare us fit to work. She has many tips and uses every trick in the book to do this. There is no proof behind her methods of course, merely things she's invented in her own crazy head. Like saving our energy by doing as little as possible when we are not working, this helps us stand up tall in front of the medics and we must ensure we breathe deeply without coughing, how she insists we keep our mouths healthy to prevent gum and tooth loss, a sure sign of ill health that guarantees a first-class ticket to the chambers.

Ola is a born survivor, she is a wonder to us, there is no one else like her in the world, I'm sure of it. Though she has lost her entire family, her determination to live through this nightmare is unwavering. I wish I was more like her. Oh, I have just thought what I said, our Jewish saviour—she is our very own Jesus Christ. This thought makes me smile, something I haven't done for a very long time. I know I will live today.

My other saviour is here also; I have two—how lucky I am. Frau Leshnik is back with a strange sort of comfort only she can offer. She is a naughty woman, taking risks where none of us would dare. Every day she keeps up her pretence of being a mad old witch. Funny really because that is what all of us thought she was all along.

She is walking a very thin line, thinner than all of us, but yet she manages to stay upright—alive. Apparently she has left again; no one knows when she left or where she went to. I should be upset at this loss, but I know she will return somehow despite the odds being against her. I am beginning to get used to the surprising ways of Frau Leshnik who should have been long dead. How she survived her meeting with the officer when we first arrived at the separation table is beyond my understanding. But yet here she is, living a very strange life and doing better than most.

I have to admit I am a little worried about her. You see she is spending more and more of her time with the guards, especially Ardit. We all suspect that Ardit is up to something and though we can guess, we don't know for sure what it is. Right now, there is no way of warning the Frau; she will not listen in any case, the two are like two peas in a pod these days. I confronted her you know. I asked her what they were up to. All she said was they were helping each other out and she would say no more. Then she produced a small piece of paper and a pencil, again, something that is unknown around here, and she began to write a letter. Though she told me, in the old Frau voice, to keep my nose out of her business, I followed her and watched her slip the letter to Ardit—that was not right!

So here we were again, awaiting our fate. As we had done many times, we lined up quietly and stared at the ground awaiting the selection officer's decision to save our lives for another day or to feed us to the monster. But today was different, yet another surprise. Instead of waiting for the dreaded tap of death on the shoulder, a new captain, even nastier than the usual one bawled at us to look forward.

In front of us was a truck load of bodies, piled up and dirty, skeletal arms hanging limp over the sides, dead eyes staring into space, expecting sympathy, but receiving none—we have none to spare. This spectacle did not affect us in the least. But then the captain yelled at us again, demanding our attention, we dare not disappoint. "Listen carefully," he screamed, and every last one of us gave him our full attention. We listened in utter terror as he informed us why the bodies were in the truck. How the unfortunates had attempted to escape.

"Fools," I whispered to myself, "no one can get out."

Then another surprise, as a line of men and boys were marched into view, single file, with their heads down they lined up in the parade ground. Another shout and they were turned towards us and forced to lift up their heads—to look at us. There were at least a hundred of them, their ages from around fourteen to about fifty. I know this to be true as there were very few still alive who did not fit into this age range I can tell you. Each man clearly afraid, some of them visibly shaking and others, so scared that they had wet themselves; a few began to cry and more than one vomited.

"Listen very carefully," the captain repeated and glared at us, his eyes wandering down the line, connecting with every one of us, daring us to turn away, or close our eyes. Then, when he was satisfied he had our full attention, the reason for this diabolical spectacle was declared. "Because these men," he said indicating the dead bodies with his cane, "have tried to escape."

I observed the bodies and felt nothing. Then I glanced at the line of men, and felt nothing…and that's when I saw him, standing out in the crowd like a sore thumb—Otto! He was in the middle of the line, not shaking or vomiting like the rest, but staring defiantly, directly at the captain. I mouthed his name but no sound came. I kept my eye on him. I had no need to look for the others, for Ludolf and Gunter, Victor and Boris, for I knew if they were in the line, they too would also be staring straight ahead, strong and proud.

Then I noticed something else, the biggest machine gun I had ever seen. Mounted on two wheels it took three soldiers to get it into position. When ready, the captain's voice filtered back into my head as I caught his last words. "FIRE!"

It was all so quick. The petrified audience flinched and screamed as the machine released a hail of noise and bullets that shot across the parade ground to smash the line of men to pieces. Most of us covered our eyes, turned away or crouched to the ground in an attempt to escape the horrific spectacle; all the while the captain growled orders to keep watching, and I did as he asked. I watched, transfixed, as every last man was flicked into the air like a rag doll to fall in a twisted and bloody lump on the ground. Within an instant, their suffering was over.

The gun stopped and complete silence returned. Maybe it was my imagination but Otto seemed to be the last to fall. I am sure our eyes met before he died. I called his name and I am sure he heard, I am convinced that he turned towards my voice, that the poor boy saw me, that he recognised me and I hope it gave him some comfort. Of course I was overcome with grief, yet I smiled. He was brave and I was proud of him. He was another one that I no longer had to worry about anymore, my burden relieved yet again. But you know something, seeing Otto alive made me suspect the others were alive too…and that made me feel alive!

Immediately after this horror, the first of the day, we were dismissed to continue our duties. The fire had been started and lots of water was boiling in a huge metal bathtub suspended over it. I entered my zombie mode, not thinking about what I was doing I half retreated into my own thoughts, into a nicer world I had created in my head. A place where I could be a young happy girl again, only leaving this world to check up on Klaus and the others and to stop myself from being scalded by the boiling water.

Even my happy place was different though. All I could see was Otto's face, staring at me. His expression was calm, he had known what was going to happen to him and he had accepted his fate. I smiled at this thought. Poor Otto: bravest of us all.

I did not tell the others I had seen him. I started filling the buckets as usual and delivered the scalding water to the waiting washer girls who were so eager to start work in fear of upsetting the guards. They immediately plunged dirty garments into their tubs disregarding the temperature of the water. It was better to suffer a little pain now than be singled out as a malingerer by the guards who were now all fired up after the recent slaughter. We had all witnessed our ailing friends carted off in a vicious manner and we had learned how the Nazis liked to use examples as punishment.

To work was to survive. Working people blended together and became invisible despite disabilities, illness and weakness. If you were seen to be failing in your duty, you were immediately taken away to the monster—to the chamber.

Magda was approaching nine years old, she understood this rule well and to my relief, she ensured Klaus, who had a tendency to daydream, also understood it. Her constant nudges, shoves, slaps and jibes kept Klaus alert. Although this was painful for a big sister to watch, at the end of the day I made sure I thanked Magda for her vigilance and encouraged her to keep it up.

As far as I knew, only two of our original eleven had died. Though it was unlikely, I forced myself to believe the others were still around somewhere. As for our little sub-group, we continued to live, though all our strength was failing by the day—we had all begun to fade—just a little. Unless we obtained more food, which was one thing we could not do much about, someone else would die soon.

This day had been much like all the others before it—it brought death, and it was not yet finished. Something else occurred! This thing scared me more than anything that had happened so far, let me tell you whilst it is fresh in my mind, are you ready?

I was approaching the fire with my empty buckets. At the other side of the fire sat some girls, including Magda who seemed so lonely, sitting there without Leni, they were busy removing buttons from a new pile of clothing. Klaus had just delivered some wood for the fire so I knew he was safe also. This was my time to check up on them. I was always relieved to see them busy about their tasks.

Occasionally Klaus would give a quick wave which always sent shivers down my spine as he was breaking a major rule by attracting attention to us both. However, I have to admit it made me happy. On this occasion though, he broke another rule—he left his post!

I continued to approach the fire and was horrified at what I saw. Klaus had got down on his hands and knees; he was rummaging in a pile of rags. I felt the urge to shout at him, but fortunately for both of us, I was dumbstruck. I watched as he almost disappeared into the pile of rags, to my surprise I was urging him to conceal himself completely. I looked at Magda and received a further shock; instead of stopping Klaus in his mischief she was actually encouraging him. I watched as she discreetly glanced at the guards, then back at him, urging him on—she was acting as…as lookout! What were they up to?

Oh heavens! I had reached the fire. As slowly as I could, I began to fill my buckets from the tub of boiling water. I could not concentrate on what I was doing, distracted by Klaus, my eyes were fixed on the two imps. Right then I thought if the Nazis didn't kill them, I certainly would. Then I accidentally submerged my fingers into the boiling water, only for an instant, but I felt the scalding heat. The sudden pain caused me to drop a bucket into the great tub and it sank to the bottom. I could not reach it, not without removing the skin from my arms—I was in deep trouble.

Instinctively, I attempted to stifle my pain, but I had succeeded in attracting the attention of one of the guards. I dare not turn around. I could not tell which guard it was. How I hoped it wasn't Dima, he didn't like me, I was sure of that. Magda was also staring at me, an expression of horror on her face.

I could not allow myself to panic. I had two things to do. First, with my eyes and head movements only, I had to urge Magda to alert Klaus. She had always been a bright girl and understood my meaning completely. Then I had to retrieve my bucket before the guard reached me. As you know, our guards were docile, but they could also be mean at times. We didn't know them all and today most of them were unfamiliar to us, including the one that had eyes on me. Who knows what he would do, probably force my entire arm into the water to retrieve my bucket. The skin of my arm would certainly peel away and I would die of the pain. I glanced around quickly for something to use, something with a hook maybe. There was nothing.

In my panic, I began to scout around further, others became aware of my plight, fear spread through the entire laundry like some horrid disease. This could spell trouble for all of us if the guards were in a bad mood. I turned quickly, pleading for help. Then I turned around again and I felt the strong hands of a guard grab my shoulders.

Terror struck my heart as I stood motionless, my head to the ground for a second before a rough hand grabbed my chin, forcing my head up. I saw the amused eyes of Gregor. Relief consumed me and I did a terrible thing, I fainted to the ground. Soon after, two other guards were on the scene, Gregor would not be able to help me now.

Ola kept calm. Taking two buckets off another water carrier, she approached quickly. One of the guards was already pushing me with his foot. I came to my senses but made no effort to move. I had turned to stone, consumed with fear. I was going to die; surely he would kill me there and then, or I would be taken away; this had to be my last day. My mind was made up, I would be just like Otto, I would be brave. After all, this was the day I had been preparing for and I was ready to face. As it turns out, I wasn't ready at all—I was simply petrified.

"Aah, Gregor." I heard Ola's sweet voice, but I could not see her as she forced the guards apart. And there stood the brave young girl, amid three grey clad guards that towered over her. "Your good looks are causing the girls to faint," she added. Her wits were on fire, I was awe inspired. How could she come up with such a statement at such a time—her courage was astounding!

All three guards laughed as Ola raised me to my feet. "Now please, handsome gentlemen, allow us to continue our work; the clothes need washing and the sergeant will not be happy with any diversions."

The mention of the sergeant was a masterstroke. He was a German SS officer and these guards were from some East European country, they were not true Aryan. They fully understood that the sergeant could and would punish them also, and so they turned away, half feeling humoured and half annoyed by Ola's rationale. Gregor proved ever faithful to Ola at least, he placed his rifle into the water and hooked out the submerged bucket filled with water.

"Thank you, Gregor," Ola smiled. "You are so strong." Gregor shook his head, smiled in return and walked away. "That was close, Mona," she began to scold me but I wasn't listening. I was watching Klaus, he had returned to collecting firewood, and Magda was busy with her buttons, everything was back to normal. I gave them all fearsome scowls for the rest of the day. My scalded fingers hurt like hell and they were responsible for it. How could they be so naughty, how could they flaunt the rules, what had possessed them?

The rest of the day was hard for me, you don't realise how much you need your fingers until you hurt them and of course when you hurt them once, they continue to hurt you for a long time afterwards. At last, the day ended and we returned to the hut. Though I was suffering I couldn't wait to get my hands on Klaus. As I approached my brother, he, Magda and Ola had smiles on their faces. Frau Leshnik was also present—where the hell had she been? I was so angry with her as well, but she would wait. "Klausy!" I said in the angriest voice I could conjure. "Klausy come here."

My little brother's face was flushed red as he slowly walked towards me, his hands behind his back. He wasn't afraid, in fact he was smiling, that infuriated me further—just what was he up to? Then, from behind his back, my little brother brought out a dead squirrel.

"Surprise, Mona!" he cried; his eyes lit up with pride. For a second, I was stunned, trying to work out what was going on. All the while, Klaus stood and beamed. My mouth opened, but I could not speak.

"I caught it Mona, and killed it…all by myself. It bit me twice and that hurt. But I got it—for you."

"Fresh meat," Ola helped. "Klaus spotted it and caught it; how brave he is."

"And I have potatoes," Frau Leshnik said revealing three small potatoes. "We will make some soup. It will be a celebration meal." I gave her a quizzical look. "To celebrate the exploits of a very brave boy," she said as she pulled Klausy's ear. Klaus laughed and the Frau lowered her voice and added, "or two very brave boys, though one of them will not be joining us." She gave me a knowing look and smiled. I returned her smile, though I did not commit to it, as images of Otto filled my mind.

I grabbed hold of my little brave brother and hugged him tightly. "Don't you ever do that again," I said before kissing his face many, many times as he tried hard to wriggle away. Magda laughed at his embarrassment, then flung her arms around my little brother's neck and kissed him some more. Ola and Frau Leshnik joined in as Klausy tried to wriggle free.

How we laughed. We would live a little longer—at least.

Chapter 20
The Party Invitation

From that day on, I felt much more positive about our situation. What else could I do? Hope was all we had left and though there was little of it, it kept cropping up in the most unexpected places. It was the second of August by my Leni calendar, though I couldn't be sure. Yet another month had passed us. It had been a hot month, which was good for drying the clean clothes, but now the mud had turned to dust which definitely wasn't so good for any garment hanging on the washing line.

Klaus had proven himself to be brave and cunning and as I clipped his head every morning to warn him to behave, I also made sure he knew that he would make a good soldier after all. He seemed to walk taller somehow, and I felt that I didn't have to worry about him so much; a sort of relief, though I could not completely relax.

Magda didn't need to bully him as much either. They had developed a mutual respect and kept an eye out for each other, it was safe to say they had become great friends. Klaus had even dared to talk to the guards, something I never imagined my timid little brother would do. They seemed to have grown fond of him and on rare occasions offered him food; an apple core, a sweet, maybe some vegetable peelings, not much of value, but it offered us a rare taste of things we once knew all too well. On one occasion, Klaus returned proudly holding a piece of chocolate. We were amazed, even though it did seem a little old. He offered a portion of it to me, but I declined his kind offer, knowing that he really wanted to give Magda a taste. It was a pleasure to see the smiles on their faces. I remember I had tears in my eyes, I think I had begun having feelings again.

Frau Leshnik was proving to be a great help. She continued to be favoured by the guards, though we couldn't understand why. She would hurl insults at them at every opportunity, threatening them with a violent torturous death at the hands of her son. We would cringe whenever she did this of course and ducked out of the way; angry guards will lash out at anyone nearby. But the guards never became angry with the old woman, they just put up with her behaviour, time after time; instead of shooting her head clean off as expected, the soldiers would laugh with her and even offered her cigarettes. They seemed to respect her courage and pride, whilst we, however, thought that she was very lucky and more than a little mad.

Nevertheless, she managed to get through each day, alive and healthy, and always surprised us at the end of the day with a piece of fruit, or an odd vegetable or even a sizeable piece of bread, which she would gladly share. The old woman stayed with us at our hut and continued to help the very ill people that seemed to find their way to her old hut—her trees failed to thrive, which was very sad for her. She always left the place angry and threatening some form of retribution which was upsetting, and so was her growing relationship with Ardit which worried me, more so after she had given him her letter.

How she had changed. I admired her so, maybe I even loved her! In fact, I think by then, I loved them all and I believe they shared the feeling, though no one actually said the words. Ola, Magda, Klaus and Frau Leshnik; we had become a little family. We had gained great respect and love for each other and we would look after each other and care for each other, no matter what horrors we faced.

And so it continued. Day after day, week after week, we set out to do the laundry and Frau Leshnik would be on her secret errands. Each day was much like the last; constant work, tedious repetition and unimaginable fear of putting a foot out of place and attracting unwanted attention. The only reward was to return to the hut at night alive. Every now and then, there would be a change to our day. Klaus' squirrel day was one I would never forget. Another different day etched in my mind was the day my duties changed!

A cold chill runs down my spine as I recollect the events of this particular day. As usual I reported to my post, picked up my buckets and lined up with a few other water carriers at the boiling tub. The water had not quite boiled so we were allowed a few moments break before our back-breaking work began. We used this time to eat a few dried biscuits which had been provided for breakfast in place of the usual thin soup or sometimes porridge. Then all hell broke loose!

Well, to be honest, all hell had not broken loose, it was already here. It was all around us, in the faces of the guards, the diseases in our huts and the smell of death in every nook and cranny. I know it sounds crazy, but that was a hell we had somehow grown used to. Stranger than that, it was a hell that had given us a purpose—that purpose—to live. To be alive at the end of the day in spite of everything the evil Nazis could throw at us.

However, to us prisoners, the sight of two SS officers, other than our regular sergeant, was like all the demons of Hell ascending upon us anew. I was reminded of father and Uncle Heinrich and I wondered at how pleased I used to be to see such proud and powerful men in those smart uniforms. The same uniforms that now made every person around freeze with terror.

The evil pair started scouting around our little laundry; it soon became clear what they wanted. Marching directly up to various groups of prisoners, the officers started shouting orders. "Stand up tall, show me your teeth, show me your arms," all this whilst they prodded and poked with their canes.

They made their way over to the little ones. Powerless to intervene, I froze to the spot. Ola stared at me and subtly shook her head, a warning to keep quiet. Relief washed over me as the officers ignored the little ones and turned towards us. They started examining the laundry girls as they passed them, checking them, their teeth and their bones, prodding them and handling them as if they were cattle at an auction. Slowly they moved from one girl to the next and as these vile men approached I began to feel nauseous. At any moment, I would be sick and then, a second after that, they would shoot me for the innocent act.

Soon one of them, the more senior was squeezing Ola's jaw as he inspected her face; the poor girl was shaking like a leaf in the wind as her face was forced to look up at his. Despite his age, he was tall and strong. He had piercing blue eyes beneath wire spectacles that rested upon a large sharp nose. His mouth, framed by a well-trimmed beard, seemed to be stuck in a sarcastic smile and his entire face was crossed with deep lines, almost scars—he was scary. "This one— yes," the officer announced. "A little skinny, but attractive for a Jewess," he added before moving on to his next victim—me!

"Not much of a specimen but one of the better ones I've seen." He said to no one in particular. Then suddenly his hands were on my cheeks as he calmly stared at my face, he added, "You have blue eyes, almost Aryan, you will come too. How many is that—six? Yes, okay." He turned to his companion, a stocky little fellow with a chubby, clean-shaven face. "I am not entirely happy with them. But they will have to do. Are you sure there isn't a train expected to arrive until the visit is over." Again, no answer was expected. "Pity, fresh Jews would have served our purpose better. We will make them more presentable, cover their scalps perhaps."

With his last words ringing in my ears, the six of us, unfortunates, were herded together and marched out of the laundry. Of the six, Ola and I were probably the poorest specimens. The other four had only recently joined us in the shed, drafted in by the sergeant who had followed my example and unexpectedly decided to supplement our ranks. Daina and her younger sister Amelia, Zofia and Julia were all Jews with huge brown eyes and pretty faces. I had not allowed myself to know any more of them. They looked terrified and I pitied them. There was little comfort I could give except to offer a reassuring smile as Ola encouraged them to hold hands.

I had barely enough time to glance at Klaus and whisper goodbye as we left the shed. I was numb inside—dead! Klaus and Magda remained motionless; visibly trembling, tears running down their cheeks, but in utter silence. I knew the same question was racing through their minds—would we ever see each other again?

I walked out, barely able to breathe. Yet again convinced I was going to my death: the time had finally come to meet the monster!

We were pushed against a fence where a third officer further inspected our health, a doctor this time. Again, we six prisoners somehow passed the test—what was going on? Finally, a very senior officer approached and as the other three saluted and stepped aside, he began speaking to us quite civilly, our daily surprise! Though we had encountered nice Nazis before—I can tell you, they are all false! This one was tall. Around his mid-forties and as proud as any officer I had seen, he was confident, as they all were, and of course, he was handsome. Like the others he had blue eyes, but there was something in them that I did not like, I could not meet them as he spoke, they were malevolent. Yes, that is the word for them—this man was the nearest thing to the monster that I had met. We stood there in absolute silence, trying not to tremble, willing ourselves not to fall. Questions raced through our minds; why all the checks, what had we done? No one dared ask, there would be no answers. Once again, we were resigned to our fate.

How wrong we were, yet another surprise as the senior officer explained what was about to happen and it appeared we were very privileged indeed. A very important party of officials was due to visit the camp and there was to be a demonstration of how well the prisoners were treated. This sort of thing happened on occasion and usually newly arrived prisoners were chosen for the task in line for us, however, the trains had slowed recently and the quality of new prisoners arriving was deemed poor. We six were considered to be in reasonable condition, considering it was wartime. And so we would be proudly paraded in front of this party and we would demonstrate our health up close, by serving the food and waiting on the tables.

When we realised what we were to expect, one of the girls fainted—with relief! She fell heavily to the ground as the officers looked on in disgust. My own heart pounded like crazy, and we were all in a state of shock. The SS officers shook their heads as they stomped off. I couldn't help thinking with sadness and disappointment how they reminded me of my papa.

My heart finally stopped racing. I couldn't wait. Hope had sprung swiftly into our lives yet again. Surely this was an opportunity to acquire food, proper food, nice food; the colourful tasty stuff that melted in your mouth! I began to remember every party I had ever attended, there was always far too much food, and plenty of it was left, wasted, when the party was over, destined for the rubbish bin. This is what I had set my mind on acquiring and I hope the other girls were thinking likewise.

But first we needed cleaning up, and so we were marched off, through areas of the camp I had never seen before, and before long we arrived at a brick structure. On sight, I could tell instantly what it was—a gas chamber! Ola looked at me and as our eyes met, we guessed what each other was thinking, it could only be the worst. What the hell was going on here? First they were tantalising us with the promise of food and now they were about to gas us to death.

Though none of us spoke, all six were thinking the same alarming thoughts. The gas chambers were now common knowledge to the long termers in the camp, not a day went by now without them being mentioned in casual conversation. I had tried so hard to hide their existence from the young ones, but secretly, I think they too had heard of these abysmal buildings.

Between you and me I had decided not to believe in their existence. Something so despicable would take years of planning. Surely not, who could be so wicked to engineer such a thing. Yet I had heard they were situated behind the gates of no return, somewhere in the monster's lair. I still refused to believe. But here we were, standing in front of a building that resembled the shower block at our little school in our idyllic village, and my companions were convinced we would be gassed here. But we had not passed through the horrific gates; we had not been near them. Either we had bypassed them somehow, taken another route, or these buildings were simply nothing more than shower blocks. If I was wrong, if the gas chambers did exist, then the monster was near, and yet, for some crazy reason, I was feeling relieved! My only disappointment was that I would die without tasting the nice food.

Hope is a funny thing. It leaves as quickly as it arrives and now my heart began to pound in my chest. One girl in the party, Daina, began to wet herself. This was not an uncommon sight, but then to our surprise, she lost control of her emotions altogether which was not like her. First she began to tremble and then she sobbed. Ola gently placed her hand on the poor girl's shoulder in an effort to calm her but to no avail, and we watched in horror as Daina progressed to screaming at the top of her voice whilst thrashing her arms about, before finally doing what should never be done—Daina ran away!

She was instantly caught in the clutches of a huge guard who started to beat her around the face. The rest of us stood still, immune to the brutal sight. But a sergeant of the guards put an end to the beatings and, surprisingly, reprimanded the vicious fellow. I questioned these actions, if we were going to die in the chambers, why would this sergeant protect us? And why would the senior officer spend time explaining our duties? This made no sense at all!

It mattered not, we were about to find out. An order was barked and the entire group marched towards the shower block. The door was flung open and we were pushed inside, I had guarded myself against the smell of death, but it did not linger here. Instead, there was a damp smell and was that a hint of soap in the air. Seconds passed before I realised how clean the place was, all tiled in white, with rows of shower heads hanging from water pipes. There were benches and hooks to hang clothes. Underneath a bench, I noticed a lost sock and here and there, hung damp towels. I was instantly transformed back to my village school, to a day when Gretl had persuaded me to creep into the boys' changing rooms— just to have a look—that's all. It was just like this! I smiled at the girls; this was actually a shower block—the best surprise yet.

All six of us now had huge smiles on our faces as we undressed. How pleased we were to rid ourselves of those dirty striped threadbare rags, the guards laughing and leering throughout. But we didn't care. Instead we stood under the showers and listened to a squeaky tap being turned and waited in anticipation for the wonderful water to fall onto our bodies. Would it be hot or cold, probably freezing which made us a little anxious and excited. I brushed the awful thoughts from my mind. No more would I think of gas and death, soon we would be all clean and dressed in nice clothes and handling wonderful foodstuffs which we could take back to our little family.

Water fell from above—from the Heavens! It was clear, it was refreshing, it was cold—it was like magic! I turned my face to the shower head and let the water flood over me, soaking as much of it up as possible. Mixing with the water—tears—happy tears, tears of relief. The water was wet! Of course it was wet. What a silly thing to say, but when you haven't washed for months—wet is good, wet is wonderful, wet is the most fantastic feeling. Not rain wet, not damp, not harbouring illness, this was just the opposite—I never wanted it to end.

Soap was thrown into the shower, a whole bar each. It smelled of carbolic and it soon removed the stench of dirty bodies, I almost felt my wounds and scabs healing at the touch of it. But then I realised the others were crying too, their trembling bodies the only sign as the tears washed away in an instant. Then the water stopped and the disappointment was huge. But a final surprise. Clean towels! Again the tears flooded our cheeks as the soft material caressed our bodies, mine smelt like Mama! Next we were shown to six piles of crisp new clothes. Black dresses with white lace trim—we were to be maids. I could feel my head spinning and I almost fainted myself. Surprises turn up everywhere in this place and hope had returned yet again; we were not to die today and I was sure I would return to my brother and my little family would be reunited.

Wearing proper clothes brought back a long-lost comfort. I advise you to never take anything for granted as the most basic daily chore is a blessing in disguise. This was like a dream to us, a comfort we had long forgotten. Then, transformed into serving girls with our little waitress hats covering our short, but clean hair, we were lined up and marched out of this marvellous place of comforts.

Five minutes later we arrived at the big house where the camp commandant lived. It reminded me of home, except that the grass had been cut short and neat. The house was grey, as everything was around here and huge red flags bearing the swastika hung from each window. More flags hung from a huge marquee that had been erected in the middle of the lawn. Very elegant people mingled with smartly dressed Nazis; the party had already begun.

We had never been so nervous—all six of us. We were to be displayed in front of important people, we would be observed, scrutinised and judged. We had not prepared—what if we failed? What if we did something wrong? Our lives depended on our performance; I was sure of that. We would have to behave! I remember taking deep breaths to control my nerves.

They led us over to a tall, thin man with a well-trimmed moustache; he had a mean face, tanned from recent sunshine that August had brought us. He scowled at us as we approached and from a distance I caught the whiff of garlic. He mumbled a curse, in Italian I think, and then started handing trays of food our way.

"Aperitifs, aperitifs—hand them out—to the guests—you go—now."

He thrust a silver plate of the most fantastic and bizarre looking food I had ever seen into my hands. The bite-sized pieces made my mouth water and as the delicious smell rose into my nostrils, I licked my lips and felt faint again. The other girls were laden with similar foods and I could sense the delight they were experiencing as the wonderful aromas tainted the air.

"Go—go—go!" the horrible Italian ordered, and instantly we all turned and reluctantly walked towards the marquee. My legs had turned to jelly, surely I would fall and if I did, it would be the end of Mona. But I would not spoil this day. I would return to my brother with delights he could not imagine in his wildest dreams. His face would be the greatest surprise of all.

We approached the marquee and two uninterested doormen pulled open the tent flaps as a third announced the food. It was warm inside, the air still—stifling. The guests stopped talking and stared silently towards us, the whole place was unbelievably quiet. I couldn't help thinking how bizarre this was. We were visibly shaking as we entered, they weren't interested in the food; their attention was focused on us. We were completely lost, none of us knowing what to do or how to act. Though we weren't in any immediate danger, this experience seemed to be as terrifying as any other I had so far suffered.

Here in front of me stood dozens of immaculately dressed people, obviously enjoying a night of socialising as if they had not a care in the world, let alone being in the middle of a world war. It was ludicrous. They were oblivious to the thousands of people suffering the worst kind of nightmare imaginable, just a skip away from here at the other side of a simple fence…and to add further insult, we six starving prisoners, were to hand out this incredible food, most of which would go to waste, whilst our loved ones starved to death, less than a stone's throw away. I suddenly realised; it hit me like a thunderbolt. The hosts of this incredible party were the true Aryans, a class of which I had once belonged—no more, thank God!

The other girls were scared and confused. Someone had to take the lead, to show the way. It had to be me. I was the closest to these people. I had been one of them. I approached the nearest person to me, a slender woman in a blue silk dress, she smelt of roses and her face was immaculate and covered in make-up. Her hair was brown and shiny and curly…and long. I offered my plate and allowed myself a quick glance at her face. She took the time to examine me from head to toe before politely thanking me. Job done, not so bad after all—I moved on.

The girls followed my lead and we mingled with the crowd, as we strolled through, every last one of them scrutinised us. Our shaking began to ease a little, but our minds were racing. What was it all about, what was going on here? These people were polite and courteous, including the SS officers. At first, we were very uncomfortable, ensuring we did not put a foot out of place, our heads held down at all times, how difficult it was. But as the night went on, we relaxed a little and began to make eye contact with each other. I noticed Amelia smile at Zofia as they passed each other by. We dare not speak and we definitely did not look at any of the faces directly, doing so would definitely land us in trouble. We had begun to enjoy ourselves—just a little, and now and then as we returned to the horrid Italian to refill our plates we made minimal contact, a brush of a hand, a discrete wink, this may sound like nothing to you, but to us, it was the world.

I approached a serious looking gentleman who was locked in conversation with a senior SS officer. He wore small round spectacles behind which smaller beady eyes challenged the officer without fear or hesitation. "You see," I heard the officer say. "The prisoners are in good condition considering there is a major war on. A little thin of course, but we have had minor problems with supplies and illness lately; why our brave troops on the Eastern Front are faring worse." The serious man wasn't easily persuaded and asked many interesting questions as I hovered within earshot of his conversation.

Though I gazed at the ground I was aware he was staring at me, scrutinising me for whatever reason. I became intrigued by him; he excited me though I couldn't say why. Something began to nag me, a sort of madness. I had experienced this before, when I had taken charge of the laundry and confronted the sergeant with my ideas to improve production and again with Ardit the time I pulled the workers from the lines heading towards the monster. I was having those ideas again and I was afraid. There was something I needed to do, that I couldn't resist. It was something I wouldn't ignore; this was the perfect opportunity—I must not miss it!

I had a theory about this party and now I was convinced. The SS had to prove something to the visitors and they were achieving their goal by lying. This was all an elaborate illusion and a way of covering up what was really going on. Who were these visitors, these officials, and what power did they have? It occurred to me that they were not experiencing true life in the camp, this was all wrong. At last, I had the chance to do something, I had been waiting for this moment ever since I arrived here—my time to act. I was going to spoil the party!

Crazy feelings: panic, unease, excitement, all raced through my body. I needed to control myself. Spotting Ola in the corner of my eye, I wandered over to her. She caught my eye and didn't like what she saw. Leading me over to the side of the marquee, out of earshot of the guests, she dared to whisper, "I know that face, what are you up to, you haven't stolen any food have you?"

"No but…" My attempt to answer was interrupted by a waiter who had noticed us lurking out of the way. With a nod of his head, he made it clear that we should get on with our work. So Ola and I reluctantly split up, my friend giving me a very stern look as we moved apart, a warning to behave, desperately urging me to stop! But I had made up my mind. I would not lose this opportunity, regardless of the consequences.

So now, I continued to wander around the huge tent, handing out the little parcels of food as I went along. This time I was not wandering aimlessly, I knew exactly who I was heading for. The SS were insincere in their thanks, but the visitors were friendlier and always smiled. I listened to the conversations as I moved around, I was spying again—I was good at this.

The conversations were mostly about war; or Adolf Hitler; which cities had been bombed; how we were doing on the Eastern Front; how we were doing on the Western Front. All the usual enemies of the true Aryan race were discussed; I was so reminded of my father's conversations, especially that day in our garden at home, when Klaus and I spied on him and Uncle Heinrich.

At last, I found what I was looking for. The serious man was still disagreeing with the SS officer who was not only pig-headed, but his chubby red face resembled a pig more than anyone else I had ever laid eyes on. It became clear that this charade was not enough for the visitor; he wanted to see the camp. Yes— that is exactly what he must do! I stood and gaped at him, directly into his face, how my heart beat furiously in my chest, I was more than trembling; my tray shook like an earthquake. The man, the official, was drawn to me and peered hard into my eyes; there was a hint of a smile as he asked how he could help me. There was no turning back now; I was fully committed. I was struck dumb, stuck to the spot and shaking like a leaf in the wind. "Yes," he prompted me politely as the SS officer turned and glared, his pig face a twisted hate filled scowl. I could feel his anger burn into me. I had stepped over the line; I was surely done for.

"Can I help you?" The man ignored the officer and stepped towards me.

I could not speak; we had been severely warned that to do so would mean instant death. But I had been in the camp long enough to know that I was dead already and the visitor, his face reassuring, smiling, encouraging me to speak had now clasped me by my arms; I nearly dropped my tray. The marquee fell silent; a pin could have been heard to drop, as my mama used to say. The tension mounted as my face flushed red and my nerves buckled. But they held out; and…and I spoke. There was no sound! How could this happen, I was failing, and you know what? I was almost relieved. But then I became aware of my voice, a whisper at first, nothing more. "We are dying!"

"I beg your pardon." He leaned closer.

"Guards, guards," the SS officer bawled. "How dare you speak out of turn—get out."

I had moments only; I used the time well. Summoning up all my courage I spoke out again, this time loud and clear, for all present to hear. "We are dying of starvation." Instantly, two guards had lifted me off the ground and in seconds I was manhandled towards the door. The plate of sandwiches I carried clanged to the floor and the entire party watched in disbelief; half of them concerned, and the other half, the bad half, extremely angry.

"They kill us daily—thousands of us."

"Get them out of here, now." Pig face roared and I realised with great regret that I had condemned my five companions with me, I had doomed us all. I glimpsed at Ola, our eyes met, did she hate me? No never, not my friend Ola, her face smiled with pride—I was glad, I was encouraged. Knowing I would soon be dead there was nothing more to lose and so I now bellowed at the top of my voice. "They are killing us—the chambers—the gas chambers—there is a monster! They kill us, those hidden monsters!"

Outside the marquee and out of sight, searing pain rampaged through my skull as a heavy rifle was smashed into it.

Within minutes, all six of us were carried beyond the fence into the main camp and flung harshly onto the ground. I saw them then, the girls I had killed, as if I had pulled the trigger myself. Daina, Zofia, Amelia and Julia were on their knees, silent and in shock. Ola glanced at me and I saw pride still—only pride. "It had to come Mona, this day. It comes for us all. It is not your doing." The guards took their rifles from their shoulders expecting to shoot us on the spot. We covered our eyes and Daina released a whimper; another girl sighed; any moment now it would all be over.

But no! A voice interrupted proceeding. It was new, it was familiar! "Do not use guns tonight." The voice was calm, and it held authority greater than all others present, even greater than the camp commandant. And I recognised it; this was the second time a familiar voice had saved me, yet this one would be anything but an angel. I looked up into the face of the new arrival. "Uncle Heinrich. You're here…at last!"

The highest commander of the SS approached slowly and glanced down at me, a puzzled expression on his face. He was uncertain, but something was niggling him—what was it? He approached and knelt beside me. Though my life depended on it, I could not speak again. Did I need to, hadn't I done enough? The great commander examined my face and watched as blood trickled from a huge hole in my scalp, running into my eyes and coating most of my left cheek. He placed his right hand on my shoulder and I dared to touch it with my left. I could feel his eyes searching my face, taking in every detail, trying to make sense of it. I met his gaze, those eyes, always kind to me, now blank—confused! I could almost feel it, the struggle raging in his head, the torment. I willed him to make the connection. Recognise me! You must know me!

Then I saw it, at last. He had made his decision. "No it can't be? Mona is a fine young lady; she always makes me happy." He uttered the words to himself, but as I scanned his eyes, I realised he did not believe what his own head was telling him—the doubt remained. He pushed my hand away and at that moment, I felt that there was no longer a place in this world for Mona Lange! Uncle backed off.

I remained stunned for a fraction of a second, then, overcome with urgency I managed to plead, "You always say that…Uncle!"

His back turned, Uncle Heinrich stopped in his tracks, turned his head slightly and said, "Impossible!" I watched him step away, a sinking feeling in my heart as he returned quickly to the party, taking with him my only chance of survival.

Chapter 21
Giving Up

It was Christmas! Though it meant nothing to the Jews, neither did it mean anything to us. Klaus thankfully roused me from my nightmares; he had been doing this a lot lately. I was slipping—fading, in both body and mind. Usually I am the first to wake up. Always ensuring I am positive and smiling; my effort to keep my darling brother going in this dreadful place. In the same way, Ola offered her constant encouragement and support. I had always been pleased to see her with her face full of smiles despite the horrors of the day she was about to face. But today was different, I was not pleased to see my best friend, neither had I a hug for Klausy. I knew why—I had given up! When the second most important man in the entire country refuses to acknowledge your existence, what hope was there?

Six months had been ticked off on my Leni calendar. I barely thought about the little girl these days and it had been four months since Uncle had refused to acknowledge my existence. Yet again the day was wet and grim and far colder than usual. When we arrived at the laundry, I fell into a kind of despair I suppose. My head was spinning, my eyes teary. As I stared at the piles of everyday things that kept growing higher and higher, every item once treasured but brutally snatched away from a dead person, I could have easily thrown myself into the tub of boiling water. At last, that stubborn fighting spirit we were always talking about; had begun to desert me.

But life is a funny thing. No matter how hard it gets, there is always a little feeling inside, urging you to keep going. This feeling, this lifesaving feeling, had given up on so many before me. But so far, by sheer determination, I had somehow managed to keep a firm grasp on it. Was this the day I finally let go? I needed to—please! I allowed the fading process to take hold of me, yet as fast as I felt myself receding into some unknown darkness, warning sounds inside my head were telling me to apply the brakes, regardless of how hard I tried to shake them off, I obeyed once more…and continued to live.

Memories returned and soon I began to make sense of things again. Uncle Heinrich, I still call him that, only God knows why, had neglected to order our deaths, as we most certainly had expected. In fact, we had been totally forgotten, left in our maid clothing even. We were completely baffled by all this and my quick-thinking friend soon had us changed back into our stripy rags before discarding the maid clothes amongst the garments in the laundry. You wouldn't believe this, but it actually felt good to be back in stinking stripes—normal again!

Ola thought they were afraid to kill us, just in case the serious looking man wanted to meet us again. So I survived another day, much to Klaus' pleasure, and then I survived another week and then a month. That's if you could call it survival—more of barely existing, but we were getting used to it. We weren't dead yet, though at times we weren't even sure of this. Our physical condition continued to deteriorate on the meagre rations we received. The weather deteriorated faster and our mental health fared even worse; too much horror will do that to a person.

It was an unremarkable time for us. Whilst thousands upon thousands of miserable people arrived and disappeared, we continued, unmolested, unharmed—lucky! But of course, it was not to last. A chill took to the air, bringing frost and a speedy death for many. The ground froze solid and those employed outside found their hard labour even harder. The wood cutters responsible for feeding the fires were forbidden rest—there had never been as many bodies to dispose of.

It's strange how fortunes turn, isn't it. For now, as the long-term prisoners began to perish in droves, newly arrivals were in demand to fill their places, to pick up their tools and work the vacant stations, and so the line to the right grew longer and the line to the left, the one leading to the monster slowed—just a little!

We carried on regardless. Our sergeant, our Crooked Captain, sent me time and again to rescue more shed workers from the monster. I found them lurking in dark huts, unless a train had just arrived then I would look to see if the separating had started up again, which it did from time to time; the ones in immediate danger of death were my top priority every time.

There was another monster to face these days of course. The cold had become our greatest fear now. The guards and kapos took a back seat as the icy nights brought coughs and sneezes. The Frau remained strong somehow, though her trees were falling fast and her efforts to save them failed on a grand scale. How she cursed. How she swore vengeance for those that she had cared for. Klaus and Magda also carried on, stronger than most, this partnership was working a treat. They had even started helping other young ones. Our family was growing again, though I was aware that the next one to leave would be me.

Everyday brought dangers and horrible things happened as we were made to watch. Most are not worthy of discussion, and were soon forgotten, but there were two very significant events that I must tell you about. They both caught us completely by surprise. The first brought a little hope to us all…the second finished me off!

Frau Leshnik returned to the hut. She had been laughing with the guards, telling them, as usual, how they were going to die in a variety of painful ways. She rushed inside, quickly slamming the door and blocking the draught holes with dirty rags. Then she urgently gathered us all around her; that is everyone in the hut that could spare the energy or cared to hear. She had a secret to tell; she was very excited and just couldn't wait to share. It seems one of the guards, newly arrived from the East, had recognised her. Well, not really, it was Ardit who had introduced them and told the new guard about her son—Herr Leshy.

"Leshnik. You fool." The Frau had corrected and instantly the new fellow became very excited. The new guard had just been released from her son's squad and was very pleased he had. Herr Leshnik had been his captain and was not a million miles away from here. The guard, a Romanian I believe, spoke of his time with Frau Leshnik's son who had a fierce reputation. However, there was one thing he loved—his mother, and he had been searching for her since her disappearance last spring.

Herr Leshnik had interrogated the two guards who had been assigned to guard his mother on the train. They had suffered terribly but had revealed nothing—poor Artur! Ever since, all Herr Leshnik's men were aware to keep an eye out or an ear open for any sight or word of the old woman. The reward would be handsome for any intelligence leading to the discovery of Delma Leshnik. It was simply not like his mother to miss a letter; something must have happened to her. The guard's final orders were to keep a look out, to ask questions and to find his mother.

Herr Leshnik had received a letter, but he was unsure of the authenticity, it resembled his mother's handwriting, but it could be a trap! After all, Herr Leshnik had many enemies. A second letter would be dispatched immediately informing Herr Leshnik of his mother's presence at the camp. Meanwhile it was agreed that from now on the two guards would protect Frau Leshnik at all costs. They would provide plenty of food and other rarities such as soap and clean warm clothes. Already she was wearing new stripes which she instantly swapped with Ola stating she would have clean ones for all of us by the end of the week.

Anyway, yet again I'm digressing; I'm always doing that.

The Frau was happier than I had seen her in a long time. She had never doubted she had power and now she could prove it and there would be a reckoning for sure. How crazy the world is? How easily our fortunes turn? I had grown to love the old woman that I once hated and now I was pleased that the original old hag was resurfacing—just a little. What a crazy thing the human mind is, capable of so much goodness, yet so much terror? The Frau could wield them both ever so easily; I began to pity the guards and captains that had upset her in this place.

Frau Leshnik's son was to lead a very unlikely rescue party. As soon as either he or at least a letter written in his handwriting arrived, we were certain to be released and Frau Leshnik would have her revenge on them all. The wicked witch would certainly surface, and death would come to all her enemies.

"We are all saved, children, my son will save us all." Frau Leshnik danced around like the mad woman the guards thought she was, I was beginning to think the same thing. But her happiness, a strange thing in this hell, was surprisingly contagious. Klaus and Magda joined in first, and soon we were all very happy for the first time in a very long time. All except Ola of course—she was a Jew. There was no hope for Jews, not here!

I stopped smiling and approached my very best friend, who sat down on her lice ridden bunk bed, head in hands, sobbing.

"You will not lose us Ola. I will not leave you."

"Nor will I," Klaus said.

"Me too," Magda added as we all gathered around our great friend.

"What is wrong, Heidi," I heard Frau Leshnik say and remember thinking how the old woman had really gone mad. Though we all looked alike, close friends could tell each other apart, and Heidi was missing, she was not part of our little family. How had Frau Leshnik mixed up the names? "Perhaps Gretl is more appropriate then." She smiled. "Come Mona, catch up! You were never this dumb…though I had my suspicions."

226

A flash of anger consumed me which I failed to hide. This made the Frau laugh out loud. "Ah Yes Mona—you dumb-ass, I knew you were still in there," she added before turning to Ola. "Okay, you may not pass for Heidi, but with your thin bones and small frame you most certainly can pass for Gretl. The same age, fifteen I believe, sixteen by now maybe."

"What are you talking about Delma?" I asked in annoyance and was astonished at the Frau's expression.

"So you know my first name? Not all that stupid then. Have you caught on yet?"

And at that very moment, I did catch on. It dawned on me what the crafty old woman was up to. "Of course! Why, you sneaky old bat," I exclaimed. "If we are to be rescued, then Ola is coming with us. After all, we owe her so much. Gretl has disappeared along with all the others, long since. Otto is the only one we have been able to account for and although we could search for them when the Frau's son arrives, it is unlikely we will find them all alive. Ola will take one of their places."

Frau Leshnik smiled, "I knew you would work it out soon enough, Mona, you always were such a clever dick." We all laughed out loud again; this time Ola included. But Frau Leshnik was not done, she had one more surprise. "Why stop at Ola, I was charged with eleven children in all and at least eleven children will be saved. I say at least, you see my son, who by the way, is an idiot like all the rest, does not know the number of people that set off on our secret train all those many moons ago." She paused, the entire hut listening to her every word. "All the children and young girls and boys that remain in this stinking cesspit we call home will leave with me. They are mine now. I am a mad old witch and they are my trees. I have lost too many, I will not lose anymore. They will live—I guarantee it."

Frau Leshnik's words were met with both cheers and sobs and still she continued to amaze us. Suddenly, she pushed open one of the rickety windows and ignoring the chill that raced inside she announced to the guards within earshot, "The war is ending. You are all in grave danger. My son is coming to kill you. I warned you he would come. But you imbeciles did not listen, and now it's too late for you. I will personally see to your executions." I tried in vain to shut her up, but she simply wasn't bothered. "My son is on his way here," she continued her threats. "Mark my words, he will help us, and he will kill you." Then, turning back to her amazed audience, she simply declared, "They are so stupid." Without warning, she clasped her arms around me, with that strength she still should not possess. "And you young lady, are going to feel my cane for calling me an old bat!"

Klaus and Magda giggled so! Once I realised she was only joking I joined in too; it was a happy night and one in which I had a good dream, the first one for a very long time.

From his post outside, Ardit lit a cigarette and smiled. "I thank you, old mad witch of the woods. You have called your son to you, but I will be awaiting his arrival also…Indeed, there will be a reckoning!"

I promised you two significant events didn't I. The next morning, I awoke before Klaus just as it should be. But he didn't wake at all. Klaus was dead!

Chapter 22
The Boxer

Hello, my name is Boris. Of course there is no need to tell you who I am, you already know most of it. I was separated from the others soon after leaving the train—you know this? The guards beat me bad—bloody cowards. I almost died in the dirt. But I did not shame myself and managed to throw a few punches of my own. More than one guard received more than he bargained for that day I can tell you, more than one of them left with a bloody nose or a black eye. You see, fighting is nothing new to me. I love boxing. I did it all the time at school; it is my favourite sport. I excelled at it. I still do. Papa says that one day I will be a champion.

As I lay there in the dirt, I really thought my number was up, you know. I could barely see; my eyes were swollen and full of blood…and tears I suppose. I simply lie there, still and waiting for the next punch or kick. I had received so many, that I had stopped feeling them. A final one would surely finish me. Instead of a kick though, I was given a hand, a friendly hand. An old man, a Rabbi, rescued me.

He was the fellow from the wagon, the old man who sparred so well with Frau Leshnik. He had his wits about him and ordered some Jews, family members or friends of his to help me to my feet. They forced me to walk, to join the line. We headed towards the men separating us into the line that meant work and life or the line that would bring death. It didn't take a genius to work out which line I would be heading for in my poor state. Mona and her little brother had gone that way. My heart was broken!

Surely I would be directed to my death, after all, I could barely stand and my face was battered bloody. I still couldn't see anything, my eyes had almost closed shut by now and I had ringing in my ears. Personally I thought I had suffered severe damage internally to my lungs and every time I coughed I produced too much blood for my liking, though that could have come from my damaged mouth. It was the last time I saw half a dozen of my teeth I can tell you and my legs were completely useless, I had no idea why. I was more than aware that I was totally reliant on the old Rabbi and his friends.

It turns out the Rabbi was a very persuasive man. As I was being dragged to my death the old man had managed to convince the captain of the guards that I was a champion boxer and that, in this place, I could make him a lot of money. "I can prove it," he had said, "look at the state of those three guards over there, battered and bruised, at this young man's hands…Three of them at once no less."

The captain wasn't completely convinced. He mocked me and pulled at my face and examined my mouth before, amazingly, declaring me a healthy specimen that could actually pass for a true Aryan, what with my blue eyes and blonde hair—just like his. A second check of my muscles; first in the arms and chest and then my calves, finally convinced him I was a fighter and then a quick glimpse at my knuckles and the job was done. I was in—the man was an idiot.

But it's no matter. Thanks to the old Rabbi I had been given a chance to live and I would not mess up again, be assured I always learn from my mistakes. To add to my luck, I would be doing something that I actually enjoyed, which is more than can be said for every other person in this place including the guards. So, I was nursed back to health and fed better than all the other prisoners; it was agreed that I needed to maintain my strength, so that I could train and fight. And fight I did. Not for the captain, but for my life.

The captain was a crook, I suppose. He was very ordinary looking, you know, Aryan all over. I avoided eye contact when I could, I didn't like his face; he had an ugly mouth, as though he had been punched too many times, his lips always seemed wet and he had a funny smell to his breath—sort of fusty! You can guess what nickname I gave him.

Each day, he would order healthy men to be taken from the newly arrived trains. They were hidden away and brought to a make-shift boxing ring at the back of the huts. Here I would fight them. I had the advantage over these fellows, you see, I was well aware of the stakes! These men had not yet seen the horrors that awaited them around every corner like I had, they had not yet realised what it would cost them to lose. Each fight was attended by a mixed bunch of guards and Nazi officers. Lots of money was won and lost. Luckily for me, more money was won and 'Captain Bad Breath' was kept very happy.

Every day I fought at least once. It depended on my injuries. If a fight was easy for me to win, I would fight again and sometimes a third time. If I had difficulties and was beaten, I would be rested. As the months past I realised it was sometimes better to be beaten than to fight time and time again, and on a few occasions, I would throw the match. Even that was difficult, because my bewildered opponents would not hit me if I made it easy for them, I sometimes had to encourage them by goading and insulting them, and at times, I have even begged them to hit me.

A knockout was the best result, either for my opponent or me, it ended the fight quickly which was always a relief and I could go back to my bunk. I didn't work; I needed to save my energy for the next fight. I couldn't tell you what happened to those that I beat, I hope they were put to work and not murdered.

My lucky streak continued for quite a while, though I couldn't tell you how many days I fought without a break because most of the time I returned to my hut in a bloody daze. I no longer had to throw the fights, I was growing weaker, soon enough, Bad Breath would replace me. Then finally, after taking a vicious beating, the second of the day, I found myself lying on my bunk, well not really, it wasn't my usual bed, I had simply wandered into the first empty hut I came to, they were all the same, anyhow, my point is, I was begging to die. It was early afternoon and the place had been cleared of the dead. Though I was the only person in the hut, the stench was unbearable. I was in pain, my face was all swollen and covered in cuts, my eyes were black, and my body was a mass of bruises and I couldn't find an inch of me that didn't ache.

I had fought a huge man, from the Ukraine or somewhere that way. He was a monster and he beat me to a pulp quite easily. I thought Bad Breath had found a new champion, but it turns out that the big man had been unable to control his rage and had actually punched Bad Breath in his fat lips. You see I was correct; these people did not know what waited around the corner. No doubt, the big man was put to death instantly. All the better for me—I suppose.

So I climbed onto a discarded top bunk. I was more concealed here. I settled and tried to sleep but of course sleep would not come and so I simply gazed at the ceiling, wide awake and unable to get the rest I so sorely needed. That's when I noticed the graffiti carved into the ceiling planks and rafters. Some of it was newly carved, some looked old. Most of it was simple, just names mainly, there were many names—all those that had used this bed before me, all long gone no doubt. They'd left messages to loved ones which were extremely sad and I believe the word is poignant. One such read, 'Mika, I will always love you Sachia x'. Others left instructions—who to avoid, who to trust, some were prayers and yet more simply listed family names. In places, there were rows of simple scratches where someone had started counting days, six vertical and one horizontal scratch striking through them, indicating a week had passed. There were a dozen sets of these marks scattered here and there, none had reached more than a year.

I studied them in silence. It gave me peace, an unexpected calm I hadn't experienced since arriving in this cesspit. I think it was because it made me realise that I wasn't alone. Then, as I searched I saw something that amazed me. Another message, it was no more than a faint scratch and it had been crossed with later and much deeper marks. But I saw it, and after being alone for so long, it filled me with a warm feeling that I had forgotten. I felt joy—it read 'Boris' Band'.

At first, I was delighted but my pleasant thoughts soon turned to worries that wouldn't leave me. I began to think of my friends, where had they gone? I had neither seen nor heard from them and I was surprised how much I missed them. This was the first time I had really thought about them, did this make me a bad person? I had seen the death cart earlier in the week and lying on top of it was the skinny body of a boy that resembled Otto. Poor Otto, I do hope the dead boy was not Otto, what had become of him? Mona and Klaus were gone, surely if any of us could survive here it would have been Mona, but it wasn't so. There was always something about her that I liked, I should say loved; I miss her most of all. Another one I am lost without is my best friend Ludolf. He will be looking after the others. Good old Ludolf. He was a better leader than me—he at least kept his head when I had lost mine, I am such an idiot. Yes, my best friend will look after the others; Gunter and Victor and the girls, some of them are so little, I don't know how could they possibly survive this place? They must surely be dead!

As I stared at the ceiling my thoughts began to focus. Boris' Band, whoever they were had helped me come to an important decision—I had had enough! I could not take it anymore. I would not fight for those evil pigs; I would not provide their entertainment anymore. Anyhow, it was an impossible task to fight without rest on a daily basis; it could only end in my death. So my mind made up, I climbed down from the bunk and left the hut as fast as my aching limbs could take me and without hesitation I entered the outside world, my only possessions the filthy rags I wore. I had absolutely no idea what I would do next.

Outside it was getting dark and a chill had descended, yet there was activity everywhere; groups of people being marched about, returning from a hard day's labour; others busy at their duties still; some being beaten and others receiving worse treatment. I realised what I was staring at—chaos and tragedy, a horror show unfolding right in front of my sore eyes—how I wished then that I couldn't see at all.

Everywhere, people were busy doing this and that, lining up here, being shot over there. A group of prisoners rushed towards me, terrified expressions on their faces, they were not heading towards a hut and as there was no way of finding out where they were going or why, I had to decide—quickly. They may have been heading to their own death but nevertheless, I stepped out and joined them as they passed by, simply allowing their group to swallow me up.

Now, at last, I was one of them; a simple, every day, ordinary prisoner; no more was I a valuable and privileged fighter. With this new-found identity, I had no idea what the days had in store for me, I was overwhelmed with uncertainty—this may have been my very last day! I thought about turning back, but that was no longer an option. I was now part of this bewildered work party who had suddenly acquired a new member and there was no leaving this group as we headed towards the gates, the main camp gates, heavy wooden things entwined in barbed wire and guarded by vicious dogs, and before we knew it, we were outside.

We had left the camp, to do what? That was anyone's guess. I worried, I fretted so; my heart pounded and though I was running as fast as I could, my legs trembled with the effort; I thought I was the fit one, yet the skeletons running alongside of me kept leaving me behind. The ground was rocky and full of potholes, surely I would fall! But to fall in this place is to die and so I held on, my spirit not wholly broken. Not wholly, but I was not convinced that death did not wait for me at the end of this run.

We ran for miles. It was completely dark now and a fine snow had begun to fall. The running kept us warm or we would have frozen this night. Finally, and thankfully we reached our destination where more prisoners waited. What was this, this meeting in the dark woods! I needed to see for myself and so I pushed to the front of the assembled prisoners. The relief that followed hurt more than the fear that racked my bones. Tears began to fill my eyes as shovels, picks and axes were roughly handed out. There was no machine gun waiting for us as I suspected and so, at last I was allowed to start some good honest work.

In front of me lay a huge pile of trees and earth—it was a mudslide and it had blocked the road. This was a clean-up operation—no more—we were not to die here. But how to survive when this job was done? That was a problem for tomorrow and you know what, I did not know if I even wanted to!

Beyond the fallen trees there was a line of cars waiting. Vicious men were shouting orders, there were important officers here. Where had they come from, what misery would they bring down on us? One man in particular stood out, some high-ranking officer, I was too far away to see clearly but he was totally in control, continually barking orders in a voice that did not accept no for an answer, failure was not an option here. This man demanded respect, all feared him; this dark shadow, a silhouette in the moonlight—a demon! Other officers and guards scrambled around like headless chickens eager to please him—he was not easily pleased.

I kept my head down and busied myself with the task at hand. It was not an easy task, and many prisoners suffered at the hands of this commander who threatened to kill us all. I had never felt so afraid. We worked throughout the night, never stopping to rest. Those that were caught slacking were marched into the woods and a gunshot pronounced their end. I had already prayed to God and prepared myself for death.

My strength was failing; I could not go on much longer. Things became urgent as the sun came up, only half of the road was cleared by then, and someone else would surely die at the hands of the demon who was never satisfied. As my strength finally gave up I heard screaming. "Out of the way—now!" and instantly, the line of cars rushed past me as soon as a gap was made big enough to allow them through; the evil commander was gone. Stunned and relieved, the remaining prisoners stopped and dared to take a breath. The guards who now found themselves in charge grouped together and lit cigarettes, then, amazingly, one of them beckoned us to put down our tools.

I had been lucky again and was able to return to camp a few hours later when the road had been cleared and made safe. We were marched to a hut and told to rest, from now on we were on road clearing duties; there had been a dangerous amount of rainfall lately and landslides were common in these parts. We had a few hours only, before we would be back patrolling the nearby roads.

The hut was like my other, a thoroughly disgusting hole. The smell was awful—stifling, there was little room to spare and the air was full of coughing. But I was no longer alone, I had a team, I had a family—I smiled. This was the perfect spot for me, providing the perfect hideout. All I had to do was conceal my battered face for a few days and I would disappear, become no one, along with all the rest.

Chapter 23
The Champion

Hello. It's me again, Gretl. How are you? We are not doing so well I'm afraid. Otto is gone, we lost him ages ago and poor old Victor is ill. He's been ill before, who hasn't, but I'm afraid to say that we are quite worried for him this time. If we were at home with plenty of food and a nice warm bed, maybe with some sort of cough linctus and a glass of hot milk, that would do the trick and his illness would not be so serious. But here, in this pathetic place, any illness is serious and fatal.

We have hidden him away, under dirty blankets all alone, my wonderful Victor, without anyone to comfort him. Right now all he needs is his mama and a nice cosy bed. We are all so weak you see, exhausted. It was Ludolf's idea to hide him. We argued at first because if Victor is caught hiding he will be instantly shot, but right as always, Ludolf said another day of labour would finish Victor off anyway.

There is a hut where they leave those that are dying alone. There is a mad old woman there who looks after them; they say she is a witch. I wanted to take Victor there, but Ludolf disagreed and Heidi is afraid of witches. I begged them to let us at least try but the answer was definitely not. We do not need anyone else, remember the rules, we look after each other—we are Boris' Band. Victor has, at least, managed to have a day of rest—how I hope he is alright, I can't help but think of the worst. I'll be with him soon and I will put my arms around him and maybe, even, kiss him. How we have missed his jokes today, our dream stories weren't half as funny without Vic.

So here we are, returning to our hut at the end of a very hard day. The road is nearly finished and the Nazis have an urgency to complete it quick. There have been lots of cars arriving lately with important looking people in them; smartly dressed men in black suits and women in posh hats and fur coats—I remember those days! More soldiers have arrived also, whole convoys of them—word is they are from the east. Ludolf swore he saw Frau Leshnik's son, he said he's here to rescue the Frau and kill everyone. I told him to stop telling fibs. He's never met or even seen the Frau's son has he? But Ludolf insists he has met him at his papa's office. I still don't believe him…though I wish it was true. I would like to see these kapos and guards lined up and shot. Heidi says that's not a nice thing to wish for. She says I have changed, but I can't help it, I hate the guards and I detest the Nazis.

Anyway, as I was saying, the road is nearly complete. The Nazis have stepped it up a little and as a consequence we have all felt the cane today, or the boot, or the whip. Everyone is battered and bruised. I'm not sure if the commandant will be happy with our progress, he expected the road to be finished and quite frankly I'm surprised we've been allowed to stop at all tonight—I think the Nazis have realised they are flogging a dead horse so to speak. Either way will be bad for us; unfinished, we will receive further beatings no doubt; and finished, we will be marched to the gas chambers.

You see, lots of new prisoners arrived today, they were all fit and strong which has not been the case recently. So now the Nazis can replace some of the less healthy, and I reckon that includes all Boris' Band. Yes it's true, I think we are coming to the end of our stay here…and I am ready.

Today, as we returned to the huts we could hear a commotion of some sorts. It would be some poor person either being beaten up for no apparent reason or even worse, they were being put to death—murdered! By now we were used to such goings on and normally we would simply look away and ignore the awful sight—it only added to our nightmares at any rate. Today though, or should I say tonight, as it was dark already, I found myself drawn to the noise.

As expected there was a group of guards huddled around someone, kicking them no doubt, but as we drew near, our own guards became excited and rushed over to watch the spectacle. Instantly, without any supervisors to tell us what to do, our party stopped dead and stared. I craned my neck to see and immediately wished I hadn't.

The guards had formed a circle and in the middle were two men fist fighting. There was a Nazi officer present, probably a captain, who screamed at the fighters incessantly. The fighters were prisoners of course, I think they had just arrived. This had to be true as both were in possession of their own clothes and hair. They were bare-chested, their shirts and coats discarded in the mud, though both had braces holding up their pants and they had managed to keep their boots which were now caked in mud.

One man was much taller than the other. He was huge and had big muscles in his chest and arms. He was obviously the strongest by far; this was not a fair contest. The big man's only disadvantage, that I could see, was his long brown fringe that should have been swept back over his head, but of course, whilst fighting it just kept getting into his eyes. The smaller man had ginger hair. He had no chance and was taking the beating of his life, his face all bloody and his back was covered in mud where he had been floored already. But it wasn't all bad for him; he was fast and kept dodging the other man's jabs. He was also clever and every time the big man's fringe obscured his view, the little man would quickly lunge and land a good punch on his opponent's nose.

The guards were so excited, urging on the fighters with their taunting and shouting. I watched as the captain of the guards, an obvious Aryan, took money from them and wrote the sums in a little book. Many bets were placed on the big man to win but at this stage, with the little fellow's quick wit, somehow, the fight remained even.

But it wasn't to last. Eventually the big man landed a punch square in the little man's face. He fell like a stone, flat on his back in the mud. A huge cheer rang out from the guards who had won their bets and the poor loser was hauled away. The guards demanded their winnings but the captain refused to pay them. He wanted the chance to win his money back and announced a second bout. The guards protested but the captain ignored them, already he was looking for another fighter. It did not take him long to spot us, our group of exhausted workers stood helpless and waiting his pleasure. The captain rushed towards us and started manhandling the men, examining roughly, lifting chins, inspecting arm muscles and estimating height and weight—perhaps he would find his champion fighter here. I seriously doubted that.

All the men, bar none, had frozen to the spot, every last one of them utterly terrified, all praying that he would pass over them. I remember praying to myself, take one of the new men—leave my boys. I extended that sentiment not only to Boris's Band but to others I had worked with for many months. I had grown to know them all and to love them, we were a team. Sharing bad experiences, even with total strangers, has that effect. Surely this captain, this evil monster, would do better with the healthier new arrivals.

I had a really bad feeling; this man was also in some sort of panic you see. He was losing his money and he only had a very short time to win it back before the other guards took their money and moved on. Yet he could not find what he wanted amongst our ragged clan of mud and dust-covered slaves as he urgently moved from one man to the next. Finally, and in despair, he gave up on his search. A sigh spread through our line and as the captain strode away he glanced at the fighting ring and that was too much for him—he was not a loser! So suddenly he stepped back and pulled a man from our line at random. Inside I wept for Stan who must have been forty years old but looked sixty, and could barely walk yet alone fight, this would be his last day…his last hour.

Again, bets were placed and the fighting began. The big man remained the biggest and although he was tiring fast, Stan was soon dispatched with very little effort. The poor man was dragged away through the mud; I would never see him again. The captain was furious, having lost money yet again. The guards though, were desperate to leave, especially whilst they were winning, but none dared cross the captain who was revealing a vile temper and knack for cruelty. He would not release them until things had evened up. So, he approached our group again. This time he pulled out the first boy he came across…it was Gunter!

Gunter trembled as he was pushed into the ring of guards. Then, noticing the big fighter, the poor boy fell to his knees, his face pleading, his pants wet. The fighter gave an obvious look of pity and glared at the thugs egging him on. There were no choices here, the big man knew exactly what he had to do and in a language I couldn't understand, he offered his apologies just before the captain ordered battle to commence. I could not bear to watch. Ludolf was struggling also and lunged forward, but I quickly pulled him back, the brave boy was falling on his feet, he could offer no help to Gunter. How I wished for Boris, I literally prayed for him then. Beside me Ludolf began to shake in anger and despair, tears fell freely down his cheeks to mix with the rain now drenching us all.

The big fighter threw his first punch and you wouldn't believe it…he missed. The guards cursed and the captain cheered his new champion, Gunter, as if he had actually tried to dodge the punch. But Gunter had stood still expecting to absorb the blow whilst the big man stared in disbelief at his scrawny opponent. Unable to comprehend the boy's inaction the fighter shook his head and prepared to throw another punch—the final punch. All the time the guards screamed at him to end it quickly, whilst the captain bawled at Gunter to hit back, all of them, oblivious to this mismatched game. A second more and Gunter would be carried away to join Stan. I closed my eyes. But then…

"Stop!"

The voice was loud and clear and cut through the cold rainy night air. Every person there, even those who previously dared not look up from the ground, turned to gawp. A figure stepped out of the shadows. He was tall. He was strong. He was proud. I knew him instantly—He was Boris. Our very own Boris had come to rescue his very own band and my prayers had been answered.

The captain's face first scowled with anger, his own fists clenched and he stamped his foot in a puddle of mud now forming at his feet. I watched amazed as his awful mouth slowly turned upwards into a smile. "Where have you been hiding my friend? My champion, you have been missed. I am losing my money, my fortune. I am becoming a penniless man; and that will never do. Ha hah! You know what is good for you—yes? You have returned to me. Perhaps you are hungry? For food, yes of course. But also, for victory."

The captain turned to the guards and pushed his way into the circle. He ordered Gunter to be dragged away as great protests rose from the guards who had already laid down money on the fight that had just begun. But the captain dismissed their protests immediately doubling the stakes to appease them, then beckoning to Boris I heard him say, "Win and all will be forgiven. Lose and…"

There was no need for him to finish. Boris had already removed his striped shirt and entered the ring. The fight began.

Boris was quick, as the first man had been. He was also clever, and most importantly, he had experience; which taught him what to expect and he was well aware of what was at stake for him. Boris had been watching the big man closely, for a long time he had hidden in the shadows, studying his opponent until finally, he had worked out a strategy to defeat him—that was Hitler Youth camp for you, there you learned how to prepare and plan. Boris had chosen his moment carefully, awaiting the perfect time to step back into the ring, what better time than to save his friend Gunter, who was the only motivation Boris needed, the best of reasons to fight.

The big man was slow and fatigue was making him clumsy. But he wasn't stupid, he was aware of his limitations. He was keen to get the fight over, just maybe it would be the last tonight, this captain could not control these guards forever, and so he rushed in with all the force he could muster and punched with all his might. A left cross and a right jab followed by another left cross. If they had made contact, Boris would have been knocked out in an instant. Every guard willed their champion on, how they bawled and screamed their encouragement; surely this was another win for them.

But Boris was quicker, and he was prepared. Boris ducked and danced in the mud as quick as anything, his feet steady when they should have slipped. So the big man's blows came to nothing, sapping his strength; he began to tire.

Boris smiled. This is what he'd planned all along. He had allowed the big man to spend his energy. Now it was his turn. At last, he pushed forward and instead of attacking his opponent's head, he landed two blows to the man's belly. He bent double, and Boris, who had now stepped back, attacked again, this time with an uppercut to the face.

Boris had found strength: he was fresh and determined, his feet had dug into the mud, he had assumed total control and he meant to keep it—it was almost a miracle to see him in action. The big man was now on the back foot, both winded and stunned, throwing his fists blindly, hitting nothing but the rain. The guards were miserable—crest-fallen. It seemed they had lost all their winnings whilst the captain was ecstatic. Again Boris attacked, more fiercely this time, he was so impressive and a joy to watch. He danced and he dodged with energy no man in this camp should possess; he had the devil in him and he was out to prove something—who knows what? Surely the fight was his.

"Yahhhhh!" The captain screamed. "Kill him."

Boris attacked again and again, every punch hitting the mark, every punch counting. All the time, the big man strived to guard his face but there was no stopping Boris now, he was in a trance.

The guards fell silent as they watched their winnings dissipate into the rain. Only two sounds could be heard now, that of fists hitting home and the excited yelling of the captain. Boris didn't like either sound, his trance was broken and his vicious blows slowed and subsided. The captain noticed the sudden change and urged his champion on, but inside, Boris was seething—how he hated the captain. He slowed further, offering the big man a chance to catch his breath. Instantly the guards yelled and screamed encouragement at their man. He had been offered an unexpected opportunity; it was clear for all to see. But the big man needed time to clear his eyes, to recover his breath.

The captain shrieked, urgently demanding action before it was too late. But Boris loathed this man, who was the cause of so much misery, it was payback time. Instead of renewing the fight, Boris slowed even further, so much he almost stopped fighting, then after more screams, now tainted with anger, Boris stopped completely, simply staring blankly at the angry captain, his hatred for the man shining from his clear blue eyes, cutting through the pouring rain. The guards remained silent, watching with interest, whilst the captain renewed his cursing, frantically urging Boris to end the fight, but to no avail. Boris had made a decision; he would not be budged. Instead of throwing another punch, Boris now turned to face his opponent, offering his unguarded face, inviting him on. Yet again, the big man was confused—what was going on. Was this some sort of trap?

Boris had clearly given up, there was no more fight in him, and was that a smile on the boy's face. It was true, Boris was pondering over something, but what? I was so proud of him and I was terrified for him and I was so happy for him, all at once, though I could not figure out why I felt all these strange and mixed things…What are you doing Boris?

The captain screamed and screamed, I have never seen anyone so annoyed or frustrated; I thought he might burst! The ugly man had begun to push and kick Boris, much to the guard's delight, who had found courage to start demanding their winnings. At last, having finally come to his senses, the big man had worked out what was going on, Boris had thrown the fight and was actually inviting him to take him out. But he was a good man, a decent man, he would not hit Boris. But he would hit someone! And so with all his might, the big man punched one of the guards squarely in the face—it knocked him out cold—felled like a mighty tree.

Incensed, the captain reached for his gun, but the other guards were quicker and had attacked both the big man and Boris; a huge ball of fighting men fell into the mud, arms punching and legs kicking everywhere. The captain ordered them to part and I closed my eyes and awaited the gunshots. They didn't come. Instead, another voice screamed out.

"Stop!"

I opened my eyes to find a new set of soldiers running towards us. All had rifles and they were pointing them…at the gambling guards. "There will be no more killing."

"Who orders this?" the captain hissed.

A soldier ran up to him and with the butt of his rifle, knocked the captain to the ground. Oh I can't tell you how pleased I was. "Do not question orders you dog. If you value your life, you will obey."

The captain was lifted out of the mud, he was clearly furious. He reached for his gun and was instantly knocked down into the mud for a second time. Another captain, a new arrival gave him a vicious kick for good measure. "Take this man away," he ordered. "Take them all away. Put them in chains."

The captain and the guards were beaten some more before being dragged away in the same manner as Stan. We had no idea what was happening. We had never seen the like. My heart was pounding. Not with the usual feeling of dread, but with excitement—I had forgotten what this felt like, can you believe it. Soon afterwards, we were all herded back to our huts. Gunter followed close behind, with Boris leaning on his shoulder—how they smiled.

Chapter 24
The Black Knight

Without thinking, I cradled my little brother in my arms. He was so light; there was no weight to his skinny body at all. He had been fading away and I hadn't noticed. It was Leni all over again! Some big sister I turned out to be. Inside I was broken to pieces, to tiny pieces, each one sharp and every last one hurting. I stared and stared at my brother's face, unable to let go, my tears would not come, I barely breathed. I could not take my eyes from Klaus' face, I felt like I needed to absorb his features, commit them to my memory, to soak him in. I needed him with me you see, I had not realised how much I relied on him, my little brother who had depended on me so much, had become my rock. I hadn't really noticed before, but having the chance to examine him this closely, I thought I could see my beloved brother's skull beneath his skin. A fine young Aryan!

I needed him till the very end and it wasn't the end. Funny thing is, instead of wanting the end to come, more than anything, I wanted to live—how awkward! I had this feeling that there was something I was supposed to do. My story was not over yet. This tale does not end with Klaus.

How brave he had been in the end; he had not complained of any illness. Despite all my care and attention, I'd had no idea how ill he'd been. Later I found out from Magda that he had been feeling unwell, but he didn't want to worry me, and so the two friends had kept things quiet. Magda cried and cried; how she had grown to love him. Turns out he wasn't a fine young Aryan at all, he never had been and my little brother would not thank me for those words. In the end, he had become a wonderful Jew, a little rat, and a slave that had learned how to survive—and I loved him all the more for it.

I carried his pathetic body outside and held him whilst the cart arrived; like clockwork, it never failed to turn up. It had grown really cold outside and had begun to snow. Klaus had loved the snow so much. I could imagine his little face lighting up as soon as he saw it. He would be so excited and eager to build a snowman. But it wasn't settling today, the ground was too wet from the sheets of rain that had fallen in the night, which meant I had to step into a puddle as big as a lake to reach the cart.

The two men pulling the cart splashed through it ankle deep and then stopped in front of me. The guards were clinging to the hut walls to avoid the wet, they did not harass me, recognising that I was working, clearing out the dead. A kindly man tried to take Klaus from me but I shrugged him off, I needed to do this—only me. Then I kissed my brother for one last time before laying him down next to the other unfortunates, this was his funeral, there would be nothing more. I mourned him for a few moments only before other bodies were brought out of the hut and piled on top of him. My brother disappeared from view and immediately, the now heavily laden cart was turned towards the furnaces.

I did not question his death. It was a miracle he had survived for so long, that we had all survived—we had all been so incredibly lucky really. There were still no tears for Klaus; I remained empty inside, without feelings at all and I doubted I would ever feel again. I took one comfort; that my baby brother had died in his sleep, sleep that had followed a short period of laughter. He had escaped the cruelty of the camp and he had avoided both the gas chambers and the hungry monsters. He was the luckiest boy. Well done, my little brother. Well done, little soldier, little Jew. I am so proud of you.

The cart had now gone but I realised I was still standing there, doing nothing but staring, blankly into space. But it wasn't that I was doing nothing—I was actually waiting, awaiting the shot; the shot that never failed to destroy a prisoner who was not working. The shot that I was meant to face—it still did not come! I was lucky again. This time the luck was not wanted, and again I had the feeling that there remained something for me to do. I was definitely ready to die today and I was totally without fear. It seemed my ordeal would continue for yet another exhausting day. But I made a promise to myself. This WOULD be my last day in this world, I would complete what I had to complete and then, I would prepare for the next.

I focused again. It seemed different in the camp today. There was chaos of course, but the usual urgency was missing, replaced with a new sort of fear; a different kind of unease had descended. Everywhere, all around, people ran like crazy ants, all busy about their business, guards and prisoners alike. As I watched I realised they were cleaning up, reorganising—excessively! The guards were more nervous than the prisoners, something important was definitely going on—that's for certain. I shrugged; I didn't care! Instead, I just wandered around, consciously inviting the gunshot…come on, I'm ready, where are you.

Incredibly, I was ignored by all, even though I had decided not to go to the sorting shed today. I needed to find my true purpose, that one thing that waited for me—only me. Then, at last, I could rest. I strayed between the huts, across empty yards and fields, at one time I actually clung to the wire fencing, just standing there, almost daydreaming. I couldn't believe my luck, or bad luck! How I wished they would just shoot me and end it all, to be murdered like the millions that had been murdered before me. I was inviting it, praying for it, but no, it alluded me: it was all very strange. Perhaps I would be reunited with Klaus, but for that there had to be a heaven, and for that there had to be a God…I had my doubts.

I found myself back amongst the huts and turned a corner, maybe my bullet was waiting for me here. No—no bullet and no true purpose—what was I thinking! Then it struck me, there weren't any bullets at all today. I hadn't heard one shot so far, despite all this commotion, usually someone would be dead by now. There was no bullet for me—but something worse turned up, something worse than a bullet—what could that possibly be? I will tell you. I turned another corner and there he stood, larger than life—The monster at last—Papa!

He stood there directly in my path; tall, smart, pristine almost, not a drop of mud had splashed his uniform, even the snow seemed to avoid him. There it was at last—my purpose, today was the day I faced the monster! It had finally come out of its lair, revealing itself to me, and of course, I was the only one that recognised the evil thing. It stood there, growling in the rain, directly in front of me. I had waited so long for this moment and at last it had come. I saw it and knew it for what it was, but it did not know me.

He was surrounded by important men, all senior officers. He simply said the words and instantly, these minions rushed about, shouting orders and whipping prisoners into lines—an inspection. These things only meant trouble for us and this was a big inspection, bigger than normal. The monster was at his game.

The longest lines of prisoners formed in record time. I had no time to count but guessed at least twenty lines and there must have been a hundred people in each line. The snow which had begun to fall heavier settled on their bare heads and every last one of them shivered as they faced the ground. Though the day had turned cold, it was terror that caused the shivers; I had experienced it myself many times. It was quiet in the lines; they all breathed hard, their breath filling the air, resembling smoke from rows of chimneys. Keeping as still as possible, they hid in the crowd, amongst their friends and family—safety in numbers, willing themselves to sink into the mud and out of sight. I knew this to be true; I had stood amongst them more times than I cared to count. Hiding in plain sight so to speak. But we were fooling ourselves, all were seen here, all had been noted, no one escaped the monster when he was abroad.

Yet here I stood, I had stopped dead in my tracks, frozen stiff, standing apart from the crowd. I could not be missed, yet I remained untouched and unmolested. A thought crossed my mind—was I dead, had I been shot already and…and not yet realised it. It was not dread that held me in place as I stood and watched, but hate. My eyes were on him—and him alone. I had a monster to tame but it had hold of me, it held me tight like a rabbit in the spotlight, amazed and mesmerised.

I couldn't believe what I was seeing. My very own papa was the man behind this camp, he was the true monster and he had been let loose, he had shown himself at last! Now I saw him roar, I saw his might, I saw the fear he spread, and I recognised it, I had seen it with Samuel, our gentle house servant, how could I have been so blind. Now I saw my papa for what he really was and…I was stunned. He strutted about, throwing away orders like they were nothing of value, yet each one had the power to end life, and every word spread dismay through the entire assembly.

I realised a strange thing then. Not that I harboured hate for my once adored papa, it was more surprising than that…I was going to kill him…this was the one thing I had waited for. This is why I had survived against the odds. This is why I had not met my bullet.

When to do it? How to do it? Not yet! It wasn't the right time; it seemed this day had not revealed all its surprises just yet.

A prisoner stepped out of the front line; surely, he would die at the hands of my monstrous papa. He was badly beaten and he was as thin as a rail, yet there was strength in him, both physically and mentally, there for all to see; the way he held his head aloft was enough to confirm this. His head was shaved and full of scabs and his face a mass of bruises. His nose was a bizarre shape and his eyes all puffed up. Despite his wounds, I could see the prisoner was a young man. There was something familiar about him, he was determined, he was brave. I smiled; My Boris had returned!

Boris was alive and he was angry. He'd stepped out of line and as he moved I saw the others around him, trying to hold him back. I saw Gretl and Heidi and next to them, standing taller than the rest was Ludolf and another tall boy—taller than I remembered—Gunter! I gasped as time stood still, my heart skipping a beat. Floods of tears burst from me bringing the relief I craved. I needed them to see me, but I could not move—I was stunned. Silence seemed to rule, the snow cushioning all sound except the panting of breath. All eyes looked up from the ground and fell on the boy in an instant.

My brave and foolish Boris had learned nothing. Ignoring the eyes, the warning eyes, he slowly made his way towards the officers. They did nothing! Perhaps Boris had surprised them; he had a knack of doing that. He had obviously found HIS purpose also. Perhaps they were stunned by the…the audacity I believe is the word I am looking for. No one expected a prisoner to dare to move without permission—not in this place, not in a million years. I watched in awe. I had most certainly been noticed by now and still I was left untouched. Even the resident Nazis daren't move—what was going on here. Why…just why had the monster been released?

Boris had singled out an officer. This was his goal, this was his task; a tall man with neat blonde hair showing beneath his snow-covered cap, his immaculate SS uniform protected by a cape, now dripping with melting snow. This man, yet another monster, like all the others had a proud face, yet there was something remarkable in his eyes, something you don't expect from a Nazi— sadness. Boris had now reached him and stared silently into this face. I waited for him to slap Boris to the ground. Time stood still, the world now silent and motionless, even the breathing had ceased. There was a moment of uncertainty, of confusion and then, finally…recognition. It was a miracle—they exist, along with angels; Boris was allowed to speak. "Papa," he uttered with a broken voice. "It's me, your son—Boris."

His reply came from behind—a shriek breaking the tension. My heart broke along with it and every soul present jumped in alarm. At last, it came, the violence—where had it been? The expected blow, vicious and sadistic, directed to the back of poor Boris' head. Boris the brave, Boris the foolish, my Boris, had felt this pain many times. This was once too many, he was floored. The assaulting guard began to kick him viciously. Snow flew in many directions as heavy boots connected with the boy's ribs—intent on killing the Jew that had dared to step out of line, the boy that lay at his papa's feet; at his papa's mercy.

Now I have said before that this place is full of surprises, but this day was riddled with them. The guard was halted in his tracks—by Boris' papa.

"STOP you imbecile!" he snarled and brought an iron-tipped cane down on the guard's head. It was the guards turn to fall, stunned and confused. The whole yard stood deadly silent, no one dared move, not even the papa I had come to hate. The SS officer, enraged, stepped forward and hit the guard again and again. His anger burst from him as screams from both victim and attacker captivated the field of onlookers. Blow after blow struck home until finally, the guard fell silent and the officer's rage subsided.

Clearly filled with regret, Boris's papa stood and inhaled deeply. Then, releasing a sigh, he slowly fell to his knees in the deep snow, his arms open to embrace the boy, hurting on the ground.

In agony, Boris moved towards his papa. As they met, the blood-stained officer clutched Boris' face and leaned closer and then closer still; looking hard at this bruised and beaten boy now sprawled helpless in front of him, scrutinising every inch, trying desperately to recognise his son, yet all along hoping he was wrong. Surely this was not Boris, how could he be here—in this nightmare! I watched as the puzzle fell into place, first the recognition, followed quickly by confirmation and finally—remorse. "How can this be?" he whispered. "How can this be," he repeated again and then again. He raised his voice and roared. "HOW CAN THIS BE?" His eyes fixed hard on his superior officer, accusing him, accusing the monster responsible for it all—my papa!

Papa shrugged. He remained remarkably calm and simply added. "You are mistaken; I tell you the children are far away—safe!"

"But we haven't heard from them, have you heard from them? None of us have heard from any of them. And we have reliable intelligence that Leshnik's mother is here."

"That is nonsense, I tell you the children are safe—ALL of them."

Boris opened his eyes, penetratingly blue; his father saw him. "My son—this is surely my son. Oh, my God, what have we done to you?" He was on his knees in the dirty snow, clutching his son with all his might, he kissed him and his tears fell onto the boy who was now sobbing with all his heart.

In disgust, my father grimaced. "You are mistaken," he screamed in fury. "This cannot be your son, he is safe, he is with my children; they are all SAFE I tell you…If this is your son, then…"

"NO!" This was a second officer, with a powerful voice, a voice of authority; a voice that was practiced in spreading fear. He sat upon a great horse, black as coal against the pure white snow. Every head turned, including the prisoners, at least two thousand pairs of eyes peeked at this demon from Hell. Darker than his mount, this giant held his head high and proud, at least nine feet above all others; his face a dark malevolent shadow high up in the descending snow, his eyes, glinting, seeking, demanding answers. To those that looked upon him, he was a huge black knight. To me he was nothing but another monster.

Papa stopped to acknowledge this other officer. He looked him up and down and then scowled. "What the hell are you doing here? Have we beaten the Russians? Have you deserted your post to follow wild rumours? Your mother is far away, doing her duty, like all good Aryans should. You will be punished for this Herr Leshnik. I will see to it personally."

The officer ignored my papa and pointed to the bravest of boys. "This IS Herr Smidt's son—Boris; I have it on good authority."

But Papa remained unconvinced, refusing to believe the officer. Stubbornly he bellowed. "How are you so sure?"

"I have my intelligence," Herr Leshnik said flatly. "I have ways of finding what I need to know. You know this; you can't deny it. There are systems in place to find the truth, to know what is going on. I know many things. My own mother is here…somewhere!"

"Who told you these things? They are liars."

The officer was not perturbed. "My intelligence is sound and I know my mother's handwriting anywhere." He held up a letter and turned so all could hear. And in his terrifyingly commanding voice he called out, "WHERE IS MY MOTHER?" Silence prevailed for a fraction of a second before Herr Leshnik confidently asked his question again. He turned to the guards, who, both perplexed and in awe of this important officer, stood silent much like the prisoners, not daring to move. Herr Leshnik ignored them and asked his question a third time, only this time he read from his letter, "I am imprisoned in some camp. Conditions here are hard and I do not know how much longer I will survive. Some of the children are here also. I am known as the mad old witch who has a son that will kill them all." He stopped reading, there was absolute silence. "I am that son, and I am missing a mother—find my mother—NOW." A short uncomfortable pause followed; this did not discourage the demon on horseback. He expected results.

I suddenly became aware of a man to my left. I felt him rather than saw him. I dare not turn my head; I needed to stay till the end. "Shall we tell him where his mama the mad witch of the woods is? What do you say Mona."

I turned then, slowly, and looked into the guard's eyes. Ardit smiled. Though this was beyond comprehension I returned the smile. "I do not care for him. However, the Frau deserves better. She has summoned him here."

"Yes," Ardit said. "She should be reunited with him. The evil pair should be together...before they die!"

Had I heard right? "What...?"

"Before, I kill them!" He smiled again. "You don't understand Mona. They need to pay for their deeds. Justice is owed...and I intend to see it done...We all have a purpose. I know what mine is Mona and I think you are aware of yours."

"What?" I was lost for words, totally confused. I had always been aware that Ardit was a strange one, that he was up to something. Even then, at that very moment, he had me totally perplexed.

"We are here to kill monsters are we not Mona? There are plenty around here, enough for both of us—Yes?"

I did not doubt him, Ardit had proved himself cunning...and determined. "Please," I whispered. "Not the Frau." But Ardit had gone; vanished as quick and silently as he had come.

Meanwhile Frau Leshnik's son was not disappointed, "No need to search...my son." The old woman emerged, straight and proud from the ranks of prisoners, like a witch emerging from a forest, her rotting tree branch, normally used as a walking stick barely touching the ground as she pushed through the snow. She gazed directly into her son's face and said bluntly, "You took your time, you swine."

The demon officer dismounted and the horse was led away by a monster hunter named Ardit. "I will take care of him for you Herr Leshy," he said with a smile. "It is good to meet you again."

"My name is Leshnik you fool and we have never met before."

"This man is Ardit. We are indebted to him my son," the Frau said, as she stepped up to the SS officer that everyone feared and began brushing snow off his immaculate overcoat. There was no long-awaited hug, no show of affection, just a simple exchange of smiles.

"I will find the rats that did this to you, Mother," is all he said.

"You will not have to look far," she replied and strode over to yet another officer, a captain with a whiny voice. I was astonished; it was the man from the station, the fool that had thrown us into the wagon on a day that seemed like an eternity of suffering ago. The Frau looked him square in the face. For an instant, the old evil Leshnik returned and I liked it. He smiled nervously, and there were those awful gums and uneven teeth. The Frau returned the smile and then with her twisted cane, she tapped him on the shoulder, calmly saying, "Once I made you a promise—you ARE a dead man!" She repeated the very words she had uttered on that fateful day; her face malicious, her promise triumphantly delivered.

The face of the whiny captain turned white. Horror struck; he swallowed the spit accumulating in the back of his throat. "Impossible!" was all he could utter before two SS guards grabbed him from behind and started dragging him away, screaming in protest, his feet leaving muddy marks in the snow.

"Will someone tell me what is going on here?" I heard my father's evil voice echoing around the camp. He did not like how things were piecing together. He was growing nervous. I could always tell when Papa was nervous.

I stepped forward. "Perhaps I can answer," I said. My time had come at last.

Chapter 25
Killing a Monster

Tears washed down my face. My chest heaved. Afraid I would fall apart there and then I clutched my arms around my top half, holding it all together. My bottom lip trembled and I bit into it. I tasted the blood, it was bitter. I was bitter!

Papa gasped; his bottom lip mirrored mine. But he was both confused and angry. He was angry at Herr Leshnik and at Boris and his papa; angry at not really knowing where the children had ended up; he had lost us after all, and not just us, he had lost his men, their support, their respect, he had lost everything; including control of the whole situation unfolding around him. His legs heavy, he was unable to step forward or backwards, but it wasn't the cold that prevented his movement, it was his rage. The monster was trapped with nowhere to go. It was his move. Everyone watched, even the prisoners, especially the prisoners, who stood motionless in their lines. In an instant, I saw them all, Ola and Magda with the Shed workers, Zofia and Amelia, the Frau and her son stood like grotesque statues, Ardit lurked in the background, a sinister smile on his face, Gregor was there looking very sad; Gretel, Heidi, Gunter and Ludolf, eager to show themselves and end their suffering, and there were others I recognised, the men who pushed the cart—the death cart, and...and many more. They all watched—another crazy day in this nightmare of a camp.

Papa glanced at me for an instant of complete silence, blood now flooding his cheeks. Guards moved towards me, but they were quickly stopped by a sharp word from Boris' papa who had forbidden any more beatings until the camp was thoroughly searched, or he would be answered to.

My papa's confusion shone through, his eyes blinked and he shook his head in his indecision. Our eyes met and I could sense he'd been stunned—had he recognised me. He dared not deny me, not with lost loved ones turning up like bad pennies. In an instant, his anger left him to be replaced with a look of wonder, of disbelief, he seemed to deflate in front of my eyes.

"And how can you help," he muttered in a voice that was barely a whisper. He could not hide from me now, the moment he spoke to me, the very second he'd acknowledged me, I knew I had him. A sudden relief flooded over me. It was all over now, one way or another. I had won!

Papa sighed deeply, this was not the confident man I had known and loved. I could hear the tremor in his voice and I despised him for it. I had been watching him in all his splendour for most of my life. How I had admired him so, how I had listened to his every word, and how I had believed these words. In my eyes, he had been a hero! How wrong I had been.

This man I called Papa now stood still in the freezing snow, he was soaked and he was cold, water dripped off the peak of his cap—he was miserable, oh so miserable—I was pleased. "Who are you? I have had enough surprises for one day," he demanded with renewed agitation. "I am running out of patience… rapidly."

This man was no hero, but a devil. He was an evil man, a misguided man; a fool. It was my turn to be angry. I found strength inside, if you asked me now where it came from, I could not tell you. I was invincible! "You know me," I said calmly. "You know me better than anyone else here, better than anyone else in the whole world…Or at least you did."

"You are mistaken." Papa answered, though he was uncertain, I saw it in his face. Despite his own eyes, he was denying me, or trying to at least. In truth, he was denying that he was wrong, he had never been wrong before and this was no exception. He glared at Boris, who was now standing tall, his papa's arm tightly around his shoulders, ensuring he did not lose him again. I could see the doubt creep into my papa's eyes, the fight raging inside his mind now threatening to consume him.

"If that is so, why am I not dead yet?" I asked. "Surely a great commander of the SS would not give his precious time to a lowly Jew like me—PAPA!"

"No!"

"Yes."

"You are NOT MY MONA."

I said nothing. The entire place had fallen silent. No one moved. Even the snow had stopped.

"My Mona is safe. She is far away from here…You are not her." A simple gesture with his hand was all he could do to dismiss my existence. But I stood firm in my resolve to confront him, to die in front of him. My silence unsettled him, intimidating him somehow, I felt his discomfort. "NO!" he screamed, "definitely not…you are not her; you cannot be her; I will not accept it." Despite his declaration, he stepped closer; unable to help himself, racked with doubt. He could not or would not believe his own eyes. Yet he would not turn away, he was not fully convinced.

"I am Mona. You are my papa—Ulrich…You are an important officer in the Third Reich. My mama is Maria, she is beautiful, she has blonde hair and blue eyes, she always agrees with you Papa, with your views, with your notions—your silly notions. My brother is…"

"…Klaus."

"Little Klausy."

The bullet had finally been fired. It hit Papa directly in the heart—he was overcome. I watched as an expression of horror slowly appeared on his face; he had acknowledged me at last. He had broken, utterly and completely. I watched, almost with pity as he bit hard on his bottom lip and not knowing what to do with his hands, he rubbed them down his cheeks to nestle his chin in them before crushing his face, pulling at it like a baby; just to do something, anything to try to make sense of the information he was receiving from his eyes and ears that he dared not believe.

"Mona—is it you?" he whispered, "My princess!" There was no going back now. "You are her…My Mona, my Aryan princess—how? How can this be?" He suddenly lunged for me, I stepped back quickly, my reaction offending him, hurting him. I did not care. I could not allow those hands, those claws to touch me—ever!

He stopped still, breathing hard; his breath the only sound to be heard on this very strange day. "Do not touch me." I replied calmly. I pointed at him, accusing him. "You were once my papa and I loved you with all my heart and soul. But…"

"…But what Mona? It is me, Papa. This has all been a mistake. But it's okay now. Mona—we will make it better. I will put it all right…soon you will forget this place."

Yet another surprise! This time I surprised myself—I laughed when I should have been enraged. "Put it all right Papa, make it all better. How will you do that?" He took another step closer and I stepped backwards, keeping my distance.

I could not bear to be this close to the man I now hated the most in the entire world. "How will you put it right? Can your tear down these fences? Can you resurrect the dead, the millions of dead; can you soothe the suffering Papa; can you turn back time?" My face was blank, though I wanted to show my hatred, my disgust. "How can I forget Papa…How can I forget the daily suffering, the stench of death, the bad things Papa, oh the bad things, the constant fear—Papa! How can I forget Otto, and little Leni and…and Klaus…How can I forget them Papa?"

He began to plead, lowering himself to his knees, regardless of the snow and mud. All emotion came from him, I myself had none to offer—I was incapable of feeling any. "I am no longer your daughter," I announced plainly and clearly for all to hear. "I am no longer Mona; I am no longer Aryan. I am something different…I am something better!"

Papa began to tremble, to visibly shake. I could tell inside he was in turmoil, but still, I had no pity for him. There was no feeling at all inside the empty shell that was Mona, the Nazis had seen to that. The proud and magnificent Aryan had been replaced by the lowly slave, by the humble Jew.

"How have you come to this, what happened? Tell me Mona, I must know." His voice was hoarse, breaking under the weight of his emotions: anger, despair, self-pity. He suddenly lunged, making a grab for me. But I was too quick for him, stepping further away. Guards instinctively moved closer, but they were uncertain, and Papa waved them away.

"You already have the answer Papa. It is the work of the Master Race—you know them Papa. Look at yourself. Your silly notions, your lies, your Aryan ideals…Look what you have done to us. To me…and Klaus, to all the other children," I waved my arms around, "and to all these others. See the misery…Papa, see the suffering. This is your doing…You are a bad man Papa, a very bad man. How you have messed up. You have become a monster Papa. I was afraid of it you know, the scary monster that lived behind the gates, yet all this time I have lived beside it, shared a home with it…almost become IT."

"No. Mona, please. Please, Mona." He reached for me again, this time catching my arms. Still kneeling, Papa held me in front of him. Tears now streamed freely down his cheeks. His face even redder, as if he would burst, he blubbered like a baby, not caring what anyone thought; all the pride he had carried for years now vanished into thin air. "Klausy!" he dared to utter.

My face was like a stone, I had set out to kill my papa. But I am Mona, I am no killer. But neither did I love him. I gave him nothing; I owed him nothing, no forgiveness, no consolation, no hope. He would feel as we had, for all these months. "He is with the others…Papa," I said flatly. "Klaus is with the enemies, the enemies of the great Aryan race. You know them: the old women, the old men, the disabled, the weak…The children Papa, you know them, they are the ones that are of no use, and then there are the people who don't agree with you—don't forget them Papa." I waved my arms around in the air. "Look around Papa, you will see Klaus. He is all around you; in the air, on the ground we walk on. Look down, Papa, you are walking on little Klausy's bones, he is dust in the air and mud on the ground. He is with millions of others, falling with the snow, the poor innocent people that were sent to the monster. That monster is you—PAPA!"

He shook his head. Was the horror of this camp finally reaching him—perhaps not, he had been denying it for many years. "What do you mean Mona? I do not understand, explain to me, please—Klausy?"

"He is dead Papa. Your only son, my little brother—he is dead!"

The bullet finally reached his heart. I swear my papa died there and then. "WHY?"

"Why, you ask? Why is Klausy dead? Why is Leni dead? Why is my friend Ola's family dead? You knew them Papa, you used to buy your suits from them; they were our friends Papa. And why are millions of others dead Papa? I have been asking why, I ask why for all of them. For each one of the poor souls that has entered this camp—there must be millions of them Papa; and there are other camps out there, you know this to be true. How many are dead Papa? Millions Papa, you know this—Millions!"

"Please Mona. Please don't be so cruel. You were never cruel Mona, my darling Mona. Please have pity."

"How dare you Papa. How dare you ask for such a thing…There is no pity in this place. There never has been and never will there be, especially for men such as you." I looked around and spoke to them all. "All of you listen to me; you officers and you guards. There is a place reserved in Hell for you. Do not ask for pity."

"Forgive me, Mona."

"I can't do that."

"Please."

"Impossible."

A loud scream, a release of pain, he clutched me tightly by the arms, thrusting his face into my chest. I could feel his grief, his sorrow, his outrage, his strength threatening to break my weakened bones. I clenched my fists and held my ground. I lowered my voice so that only he could here. "You were wrong, Papa, all this time you were wrong. I knew you were wrong, deep down, I did not believe you. Why? Papa—WHY?"

"Because…"

Anger took over. I screamed at him; I could no longer hold back. "I was right all along!" Tears of rage fell from my eyes as I began to pound him, harder and harder, on the top of his head.

Soldiers surged towards us but Boris' papa ran forward also and knocked one of them over. "NO!" he ordered. "You do not touch the girl."

They had no need to worry. Soon enough the little strength I possessed subsided and my anger faded into, into resentment and I stopped beating my papa. The power had left him too; he fell to the ground, face down in the mud, facing HIS nightmare. Without a word, I pulled myself free from his grip— appalled, and finally I confirmed it, I had nothing but hate for him. I could see he was hurting—but it was not enough!

I backed off and then turned and walked away, back the way I had come; leaving my footprints in the crisp unbroken snow, I did not look back. Behind me, Papa's voice pleaded for me to return, louder and louder he called. I half expected him to order the guards to stop me, but no order came. I was no longer a prisoner, no one dared touch me—I was the daughter of an eminent Nazi. I suddenly felt free, a freedom I never expected in this place, a freedom I had never experienced in my whole life. I had him to thank for that I suppose, for opening my eyes, for changing my life.

My mind was made up. I had left one monster behind and I was heading for another—it was time we met, today would be my last day.

I turned a corner, not really thinking where I was going. There were more people here, all standing still. I was about to lose myself in the crowd when a second voice called out.

"Wait, Mona."

"What now?" I stepped back a pace and watched as Boris pulled himself free from his papa. I saw the concern in his papa's eyes, the confusion—the alarm. Boris ran to me, his long legs striding over the snow, he too had found strength in all this. His own papa pleaded for him to return. But it was too late. Though we did not relish what was before us, we utterly detested what was left behind. We had made our decision. There was no going back now. Together, hand in hand, we paused for a moment and as our blue eyes met, I noticed a sparkle in his. Where had that come from? "I love you Mona," he said simply.

"I know that Boris," I replied. "I love you too, I always have."

It was difficult to smile but we somehow managed it. It was nice! Then we moved on and soon we were lost.

A crowded chamber, much like a shower block, a hiss of gas, a hidden monster at last revealed. And now I'm here and guess what, I am happy!

My brother Klaus is with me and my best friends Gretl and Ola are somewhere around. A boy I love, you know him—Boris is holding my hand, I don't think he will ever let go. And little Leni is here, she is swinging from the arms of Otto and Victor. The others have not joined us yet. Maybe they will get lucky but for now their story continues. I hope they keep you informed.

There are others with us—millions of them. Not just prisoners from the camp, but soldiers and civilians of many nations—there are so many. There are surprises here too. There are unexpected guests joining us. Ardit is here. He had some unfinished business that had unsettled him, but now he has been reunited with his wife and child. I am told that Herr Leshnik is here too, though I haven't seen him. They say he is waiting for his mama. But Frau Leshnik refuses to travel here, not just yet.

It is time for us to say goodbye. I hope our sorrowful tale has enlightened you, just a little.

A word of caution—please don't believe everything you hear. Do not allow others to influence you. You have the ability to make up your own mind.

Chapter 26
The Silly Notions of the Master Race

My name is Maria; Maria Lange. I have something to say. I know you want to hear it.

I must talk to someone; I need to understand. I am so confused you see. What has happened to us; to my wonderful little family—to my happy life! Can anyone tell me where it all went wrong?

"Are you Maria Lange?"

"I've just said so, haven't I. Were you not listening?" I did not like this little man. This judge! I did not like any of them. Who were they to judge me—to judge us! They didn't understand—how could they. Had they experienced the feelings that the people of Germany had felt these years past? Had they lived through the excitement we had been caught up in; the expectations of what we were to achieve, the knowledge that we would be great? Had they heard our great leader, Herr Hitler, deliver his speeches; how marvellous he was as he stood up there on the podium, with thousands of us hanging on to his every word, to his ideas, his promises. We would be great. We would be the magnificent German race, a race full of Aryans; invincible rulers of the world.

"Not to me you didn't. I ask again. Are you Maria Lange?"

He was talking again. Demanding my attention, wanting answers from me. Answers I did not have. Yet I had to appease him somehow, if only to make the silly little man go away. He demanded answers and yet so did I. It was so unfair. My need was greater than his, but yet here we were, him asking questions that I could not answer, when all the time I was searching for answers of my own. It's a strange world—so unfair. I knew who had my answers and HIS also. I needed my husband Ulrich to speak. What had happened to my brave husband—another unanswered question!

THOSE HIDDEN MONSTERS

Trevor Ripley

HISTORY/ Holocaust

 PB £10.99   9781035824519

 EB £3.50   9781035824526

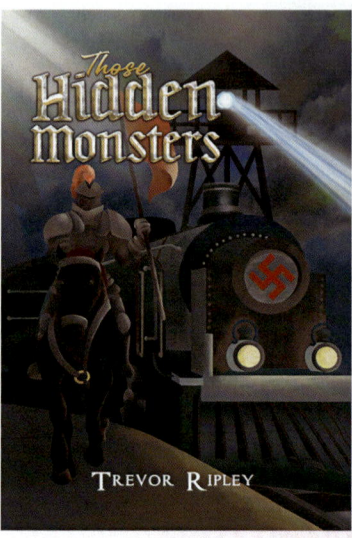

Mona seems to have it all: youth, beauty, intelligence, and a privileged place in Germany's elite Aryan society. At fifteen, she lives a life where power and wealth seem to affirm her family's deeply ingrained beliefs. But as she uncovers the disturbing truths lurking behind the façade of her 'perfect' world, everything she has been taught begins to unravel.

Those Hidden Monsters is a haunting journey through the dark corners of human nature, exploring themes of fear, flawed ideology, friendship turned betrayal, and the transformative power of love and loss. Although a work of fiction, the novel provides an emotionally charged window into the harrowing years of Nazi Germany and the Holocaust, as seen through the shattered innocence of its young characters.

While they start as fervent supporters of Hitler's regime, a series of betrayals eventually opens their eyes to its horrifying collapse. Masterfully crafted by author Trevor Ripley, the story delves into the complex emotional landscapes of its characters, revealing how evil can flourish in the most ordinary of homes, and how courage can emerge from the most unexpected places. A compelling tale of bravery and tragedy, *Those Hidden Monsters* forces us to confront the darkest and most hidden aspects of human history.

Please send me ...... copy/ies of

Those Hidden Monsters

Trevor Ripley

Please add the following postage per book:
United Kingdom £3.00 / Europe £7.50 /
Rest of World £12.00

Delivery and Payment Details

Format	Price	Qty	Total
Paperback ☐			
Subtotal			
Postage			
Total			

Full name: ....

Street Address ....

City:.. County:...

Postcode: .... Country: ....

Phone number (inc. area code): .... Email: ....

I enclose a cheque for £................. payable to Austin Macauley Publishers LTD.

Please send to: Austin Macauley Publishers Ltd®, 1 Canada Square, Canary Wharf, London, E14 5AA

Tel: +44 (0)20 7038 8212, +44 (0)20 3515 0352
orders@austinmacauley.com
www.austinmacauley.com

AUSTIN MACAULEY PUBLISHERS™

LONDON · CAMBRIDGE · NEW YORK · SHARJAH

"There is more than you, present here today SIR, that needs to hear my story, my side of things."

"I'm sure there is Madam. But you will address the court and the court only. Is that understood?" I scowled at him as he rearranged his spectacles before reading from papers spread in front of him on his desk. It was a huge desk, far too big for this little man, with his greasy black hair and his stupid moustache which he now stroked with his fingers and thumb. He was definitely not Aryan; I could vouch for that at least.

"You are Maria Lange; the wife of Colonel Ulrich Lange; prominent leader of the Death's Head Units, and commandant of many death camps."

"Yes."

"You were aware of your husband's responsibilities and duties."

"Yes…Of course."

"I see…Mmm. Your husband has been a member of the Nazi Party for many years—yes. Indeed he was one of the very first members of said party, is that correct?"

"Yes, Ulrich was proud to sign up in the early days of the Party."

"Oh yes. Not only did he sign up early, Frau Lange, he was in fact one of the founding members, is that not the case. Why he was well embedded in the Nazi Party even before Adolf Hitler took charge."

"Yes. I believe so." What was the point in all this? Why were they insistent on bringing up the past? All this information was already known, I couldn't see the point in having me, a mere housewife, confirm what was already known.

"And one of his closest associates was Heinrich Himmler?"

"Yes. Heinrich was a close friend. He was family to us. Why my children saw him as their uncle." My heart pined—what of my beloved children? My little Klausy, and my beautiful Mona. She would be sixteen by now or would she be seventeen! Oh how my head is muddled—how I have missed them. Will someone please tell me where they are?

"You were, therefore, aware of the roles that both these men…these eminent leaders played in the incarceration of those thought to be political opponents of the Nazi Party…"

"…Of course…"

"And of the murder, I correct myself, the annihilation of European Jews?"

"That's not true. That's a lie."

"There are six million corpses to prove this is true."

261

"No!" How could this be? What was he talking about, six million, where had this stupid fellow plucked that number from. Yes, of course there were deaths, we were at war. But only those that deserved it—surely. The dangerous ones, the enemies, those that threatened to destroy all we were working towards, our ideas, our future; our dreams.

"I put it to you that you were aware of these atrocities. Atrocities orchestrated by Himmler and other prominent officers of the Nazi Party including your husband—Ulrich Lange."

"Yes…I mean no. You see, I'm all muddled up, my head is spinning. They were only doing their duty, especially Ulrich! He had no choice in the matter. It was Himmler's fault; it was all his idea. He made Ulrich do it. He was his superior you know. Ulrich could not refuse—he was following orders—that's all…Ulrich believed Heinrich, he hung on every word and I on his. My husband is a good man, a loving husband and a wonderful father…But…"

"Father yes…Mmm. What about your children Frau Lange, what happened to them?"

"That's enough!"

"Be quiet Herr Lange, you will be called to the bench in due time."

"Please…Sir. My wife is innocent of any crime. Maria is a good woman; kind and thoughtful—a loving mother and a devoted wife—you could not find better. Please…allow me to take the stand. Relieve my wife of this misery that she does not deserve."

"Misery she does not deserve…how pertinent; that is something we must all reflect on. Frau Lange, you are excused. Take the stand Herr Lange."

"Thank you gentlemen, thank you Sirs. I would like to start with a confession."

"Regarding death camp atrocities—go ahead."

"Regarding the children…The eleven that were lost. It was my fault. It was ALL, my fault!"

"We will discuss the Camp—"

"All in good time Sir…I must discuss the children first. You see they were lost…"

"…We are aware of the events that—"

"No! They were lost long before the evacuation. They were lost, we were all lost…In our heads we were lost, in our thoughts and ideas we were lost, in our actions. You see; we were the best, or so, we thought. We were superior beings—the Master Race; we were to rule the world!"

"Or so you thought. We are aware of the silly notions running through the minds of the German population. What is your point Herr Lange?"

"Silly notions yes, I have heard that phrase said before; how come I didn't see it when many others did…I digress, I have always done that. My point, yes, my point is this; that we believed it all. We believed all the notions, the silly notions, we believed in our plans, how could we fail? We had these ideas put to us you see; they were very convincing. He was very convincing—he was magnificent. We would be masters of the whole world and everyone else, without exception, would look up to us. Those notions blinded us, every last one of us… Well: all except one of us… My Mona. When I saw her that day, she explained it all to me—the errors of our ways. My Mona, out of the entire German race, was the only one to fully understand—she was such a bright girl. Instead of masters, we had become monsters"

"Wait."

"Please Frau Lange, keep quiet."

"You saw her!"

"Forgive me Maria. I saw her…Yes, it was in the camp. The rumours are true…Our little Mona, our beautiful little girl; our princess…and she was no longer a little girl. Why, she was a woman grown, older than her years, and wiser still. I didn't see it then, but she was proud and she had power. She had greater power than I or Himmler or even Hitler had ever achieved."

"How can this be? What are you talking about? You never said. Are you sure…?"

"…Yes, I am sure, most definitely. It was her Maria. But she was different somehow. All grown up! She was beyond her years. She had always been intelligent and strong, and there, in the camp, she was the strongest person I had ever seen. She stood out, shining—like an angel!"

"Go on," I urged my husband. I desperately needed to hear everything, every last detail. If anything was left out, it would surely kill me not to know.

"She spoke to me, and her words were powerful. She talked of silly notions and how we had ruined everything. Look around she had said, look at the misery and suffering. This I did…and I instantly saw the mess we had made of things. It was all lies Maria—EVERYTHING."

"And Klaus…Little Klausy. What of him?"

"He was gone…"

"What…"

"I'm so sorry my darling. Can you ever forgive me…We should have listened to Leshnik. His intelligence was correct. He had been right all along. We could have acted sooner. But…"

"…You didn't believe it Ulrich. How could something like this happen to the likes of us? Our people: our Master Race. The ones in total control—surely not?"

"But it happened. We made it happen. The things we did, the things we believed, our ideas…our silly notions…Mona said as much. She said there was a place in Hell for me…She said I was a monster…but worst of all…she said she no longer loved me."

My husband broke down then, no more than a crumpled heap of self-pity. Mona was not the only one to fall out of love with him. In that instant, I am afraid to say, I did too. Our marriage was over, our bonds broken—forever!

"Silly notions!" The Judge shook his head in disgust and said, "These will be the notions that brought your country to its knees; that destroyed a continent and nearly ended the world as we know it."

"…and devastated a family," I added, and stared at my husband, accusing him. He had barely composed himself but at least he had managed to stand again on his own two feet.

"Please Maria."

I had nothing to offer this man anymore, having given him so much. He had been my world and I had given him total devotion. Never had I questioned him, his beliefs and his actions. I had committed my life to him…and the lives of my children—he had let us all down.

"Frau Lange, I must ask you to remain silent or you will be made to leave this courtroom." I did not care anymore and I did not need to hear anymore. I had my answers, though I learned nothing that deep in my heart, I didn't already know. My children were gone!

"Continue, Herr Lange."

"There is no more to say. What else is there to say?"

"Tell me about the final solution. I refer to the final solution to the Jewish question…The Holocaust!"

Ulrich fell silent. I watched as he rubbed his hands through his hair. Sweat appeared on his brow and the colour drained from his face. He did not speak for quite some time.

"Herr Lange." The Judge's words seemed to bring my husband back to reality, this awful reality that he had created.

"It is time for silence. I will not say any more."

"Then it is time for this court to pass sentence."

It was 1946. The place was a courtroom in Nuremberg. Here, justice was served on the leading men who had planned and carried out the massacre of millions of Jews, Gypsies, and political prisoners from many nations including Germany. Papa was there and at last he did something that I could be proud of. He admitted his mistakes. You may not be able to forgive him, but he was my papa…and I had loved him.

But this is the end of my story. I told you it was a sad tale. It was not a fairytale, nor an adventure; it was surely a horror story. Though you couldn't always see them, there were many monsters to face: some hidden behind gates, always hungry and constantly fed; others hidden deeper, inside people, entangled with their souls and messing with their minds; with all our minds. I have toned this story down a little, so as not to scare you too much. It was a little gloomy, I have to admit, but after all, we were in a concentration camp—a vile place.

Remember—when people have secrets and silly notions, when people think they are superior to others and when people want to rule the world, other people get hurt, many more die, and those hidden monsters are revealed.

Be nice and don't forget to open your doors and your hearts. Mona Lange x

The End…?